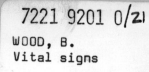

D0892282

## MISTRESSES OF LIFE AND DEATH

Beyond the curtained windows of the apartment
an ocean wind had risen and was now rattling
the panes as if trying to get in. It was a moist,
salty wind, a living wind, carrying Poseidon's
kiss from the rolling sea. It made a person turn
inward and think, take a look at what was
happening, what was about to happen – Ruth
and Mickey and Sondra, strangers just days ago,
but bound together now and setting out on an
exciting, frightening, unknown course.

These next four years were going to teach them
to be mistresses of life and death; it was no small
thing to contemplate.

Ruth cleared her throat, lifted her cup, and said,
'Here's to us then. Here's to three future doctors.'

# Vital Signs

## BARBARA WOOD

SPHERE BOOKS LIMITED
London and Sydney

First published in Great Britain by
Piatkus Books 1985 by arrangement with Sphere Books Ltd
Copyright © 1985 by Barbara Wood
Published by Sphere Books Ltd 1986
30–32 Gray's Inn Road, London WC1X 8JL

Set in Plantin

Printed and bound in Great Britain by
Cox & Wyman Ltd, Reading

This is a special book
dedicated to two special people:
Kate Medina, my editor, and
Harvey Klinger, my agent.

My deepest gratitude goes to three ladies who very very kindly shared their lives and experience with me: Dr Barbara Kadell-Wootton, Dr Marjorie Fine, and Dr Janet Salomonson.

I also wish to thank Dr Norman Rubaum for answering panicked questions and patiently reading the manuscript; and Dr Muriel H. Svec for helping me over a major hurdle.

For Kenya, a special *ahsante sana* to Allen Gicheru in Nairobi, and to Tim and Rainie Samuels for their generous hospitality at River Lodge in Samburu, Kenya.

# PART ONE
## *1968 – 1969*

# Chapter One

They filed into the auditorium like tightrope walkers, cautiously picking their way along the rows of seats as if there were pitfalls below. Five women and eighty-five men saying shy hellos and smiling nervously at one another. For many, this was one of the most terrifying mornings of their lives – the morning for which they had been preparing for years. It was here at last; many could not believe it.

The five women didn't know one another. They were strangers on this first morning of medical school, but they sat together nonetheless, up on the top tier of the amphitheatre, and in the corner, unconsciously grouping against the overwhelming majority of male students. They chatted quietly before the commencement of the Welcome and Orientation Program, taking the first tentative steps towards acquaintance.

The freshmen medical students were the cream of their colleges, chosen out of three thousand applicants to attend this elite campus on the Palos Verdes cliffs overlooking the Pacific, and with the exception of one Negro, two Mexicans, and the five women up in the corner, the 1968 entering freshman class of Castillo Medical College looked as if it had all tumbled off the same assembly line: young, white, middle- to upper-class males. The atmosphere was charged; the collective fear and apprehension of the ninety new students was almost palpable in the air.

There was much fluttering of paper along the rows as everyone flipped through the printed sheets that had been handed out at the doors. A history of the school – Castillo had once been the vast hacienda of an old Californian *hidalgo;* a welcome letter introducing the different departments and their staffs; a list of school rules and standards (short hair and no beards for the men, ties and jackets; no slacks for the

3

women, no sandals, hemlines to the knees). Finally the auditorium lights dimmed and a spotlight yawned upon an unoccupied lectern. When the audience of ninety quieted and focused its attention on the stage, a solitary figure emerged from the shadows and took his place in the light. By the photograph on the Administrative Staff sheet they all recognised the man as Dean Hoskins.

He stood for a moment with hands resting on the lectern, his eyes slowly moving over the tiers rising up before him, as if memorising each eager new face, taking the measure of each, and when it seemed he would never speak, when the moment began to stretch unnaturally and the barest breeze of a stir started to ripple along the rows, Dean Hoskins bent to the microphone and said softly, slowly, 'I swear...' A faint echo rang high up in the theatre's domed ceiling after each syllable, '...by Apollo the Physician...by Aesculapius... by Hygeia...by Panacea...' He drew in a long breath and his voice rose dramatically, '...and by all the gods and goddesses, making them my witnesses, that I will carry out, according to my ability and judgement... *this oath and this indenture.*'

The audience of ninety stared back at him intently. The dean's voice rolled solemnly, the words skilfully paced; he spoke with the intonations and inflections of a master orator, his voice provocative, seductive, creating the illusion in each member of his rapt audience that he spoke solely to him or her and to no one else.

'To hold my teacher in this art equal to my own parents... to make him partner in my livelihood.' Dean Hoskins paused, closed his eyes, and drew out each phrase to stamp each meaning home. 'I will use... treatment to help the sick... according to my ability and judgement, but never with a view... to wrongdoing...'

He was a magician. The atmosphere in the amphitheatre became electrified with the energies of ninety determined doctors-to-be; whatever uncertainties and fears and phantoms had plagued their young souls when they first entered the auditorium, Dean Hoskins dispelled them all with the sacred oath. 'I will keep pure and holy both my life and my art... Into whatever houses I enter I will enter to help the sick... and I will abstain from all wrongdoing and harm, and especially from abusing the bodies of man or woman, bond or free...'

He had them, they were his, these unformed ninety who were entering the college as clay but who would depart in four years as moulded steel. Dean Hoskins was showing them the future, and he was showing them that it was *theirs*. 'And whatsoever I shall see or hear... in the course of my profession...' another pause, and then his voice started to grow louder and stronger with each word, '... I will never divulge, holding such things to be holy secrets. If I carry out this oath and break it not, may I gain for ever reputation among all men for my life and for my art!'

They shivered. They sat with held breath. He was right, they *were* special, chosen; tomorrow belonged to them.

Dean Hoskins leaned away from the microphone, straightened up, and said in a loud, booming voice, 'Ladies and gentlemen, welcome to Castillo Medical College!'

# Chapter Two

Sondra Mallone didn't really need help with her bags but it was a nice way to get acquainted with a new neighbour. He had come upon her unloading her things from her cherry-red Mustang out in the dorm parking lot and he'd insisted on carrying all four suitcases himself. His name was Shawn, he was a freshman like Sondra, and he was of the mistaken opinion that she was too delicate to be able to handle all this luggage by herself.

Most men made that error about Sondra. Her looks were deceptive. No one could guess the power stored in her long slender arms, a strength built up over the years of swimming under the Arizona sun. In fact, Sondra Mallone was a whole package of deceptions. With her dark exotic looks she didn't look at all like a Mallone. But that was because she wasn't really a Mallone.

The day she had come upon the hidden adoption papers, when she was twelve years old, Sondra had suddenly understood something about herself. She suddenly knew the meaning of a certain mystifying grey area deep inside herself, a vague feeling she'd always had that she was incomplete, like an amputee experiencing phantom pain. Those papers had told her that she was in fact not complete; that another part of her had yet to be found, out in the world.

As they climbed the stairs to the second floor of Tesoro Hall, Shawn couldn't stop talking. He also couldn't keep his eyes off Sondra. No one had told him he would be living in a co-ed dorm. Back where he came from such a thing was unheard of, so now, when he'd just had the pleasant surprise of learning that the dorm was co-ed, he'd also been delighted to discover that one of the residents was a beautiful young woman like the kind he dreamed of.

She didn't say much to him, but smiled a lot, etching deep

dimples into her cheeks. He asked her where she was from and couldn't believe it was only Phoenix, Arizona, not with that olive complexion and those almond eyes. Sondra thought him very pleasant, someone she could cultivate as a friend. But it wouldn't go beyond that. Sondra would see to it that it didn't.

'Are you sexually very active?' one of the examiners had asked her last fall. It was during her application review, the in-person interview that made the final determination as to whether or not the applicant would be admitted into the school. Sondra knew it was a question never asked of the male students. It was only a woman who could pose problems if she was promiscuous. Like getting pregnant and dropping out and wasting the school's time and money.

Sondra had been able to answer truthfully, 'No.'

But when they had asked, 'Do you practise birth control?' she had had to give it some thought. She didn't use birth control, had no need to. But because they needed to be reassured that she was a woman in control of her uterus and therefore her life, Sondra had answered, 'Yes,' which was the truth after all: celibacy was the best form of birth control.

'What did you think of the Welcome Program this morning?' Shawn asked when they reached the second floor.

Sondra dipped into her quilted Chanel bag and pulled out her room key. She was supposed to have moved into the dorm yesterday but she'd got off to a late start on her drive to Los Angeles – a surprise party thrown by friends – and had arrived only this morning, just in time for the Welcome assembly. 'I was a little amazed to learn the school has a dress code,' she said as she unlocked the door and stood back for Shawn to go through with her bags. 'I haven't had to worry about a dress code since high school.'

He placed the three large cases on the floor and the small cosmetic case on the bed. The luggage was all white and matching with Sondra's initials in gold.

'Oh,' she said, and walked past him to the window over the desk. It was exactly what she had hoped for: just out there, the thin blue strip of ocean glimpsed between palm trees and Monterey pines.

Having lived all her twenty-two years in landlocked

7

Arizona, Sondra Mallone had applied to medical schools that were within sight of water. Large water: an ocean, or a river winding out of sight, so she could be constantly reminded that on the other side there lay another land, a new land, a land full of strangers with their own customs and ways, a land which beckoned, which had tugged at Sondra Mallone ever since she could remember. And someday soon, when she was through with all this schooling and had that medical degree in her hand, she was going to go out there, into the world . . .

'Why do you want to become a doctor?' the examiners had asked her last fall.

Sondra had known they were going to ask that. Her counsellor at the University of Arizona had prepared her for the interview, had briefed her on answers the examiners wanted to hear. 'Don't tell them you want to be a doctor because you want to help people,' the counsellor had advised. 'They hate hearing that. For one thing, it sounds phony. For another, it's unoriginal. And finally, they know darned well that only a handful go to medical school for purely altruistic reasons. They like an honest answer, straight from the cerebral cortex or from the pocket book. Tell them you want job security, tell them you have a scientific interest in eradicating disease. Just don't tell them you want to help people.'

Sondra had replied quietly and firmly, 'Because I want to help people,' and the six examiners had seen that she meant it. A lot of Sondra's strength was in her eyes: they were large and slightly slanted above high cheekbones – two drops of amber that gazed boldly and steadily and seemed hardly ever to blink.

Her reasons went deeper, but there was no need for her to go into that. Sondra's desire to help the people who had given birth to her – whoever they were – was of no interest to these six. It was enough that she felt it, that it fuelled her, instilled in her an abiding sureness in herself and her purpose in life. Sondra didn't know who her parents were or why they had given her up, but it was all too apparent in her dusky complexion and silky black hair worn straight down her back, her long limbs and strong shoulders, where half her ancestry lay. And once she'd found the adoption papers and

8

had learned the truth about herself, that she was not in fact the daughter of a wealthy Phoenix businessman but the child of some unknown tragedy, once all this had become clear to Sondra, she had heard the distant call. 'I don't want to work in a country club hospital,' she had told her mother and father. 'I owe it to *them* to go where I'm needed.'

'You're lucky you've got a car,' Shawn said behind her.

She turned and smiled at him. He was leaning against the doorframe with his hands in his jeans pockets.

'I had heard that LA was spread out,' he said, 'but I wasn't prepared for this. I've been here four days and I still can't figure out how people get around!'

Sondra's smile deepened. 'You're welcome to borrow my car any time you need it.'

Shawn stared at her. 'Thanks.'

Ruth Shapiro, in white Levi's and black turtleneck sweater, was running down the flagstone path that led to the Administration Building. There weren't enough hours in this first day of school to get everything taken care of, and she just knew she was going to find a long line at the Cashier's Office.

Being short-legged and tending to plumpness, she had to really pump along the path, and the urgency of it, the need to make it on time, reminded her of another race, one she'd run long ago.

She was ten years old then, a chubby, brown-haired little girl puffing around the muddy track that circled the Seattle grammar school, her clumsy body fuelled by the desperate need to win, for Daddy; she had to get that prize, she would take it home to him like an offering, to show him that he was wrong, that she *could* succeed in something. So her ten-year-old's heart had pounded and pulsed and her stubby legs had carried her around and around, through the drizzle and past the few spectators who had bothered to show up. Then the finish line had drawn near and Ruth had come in – not first, not second, but third, but that didn't matter because there was a *prize* for being third, a big, beautiful box of expensive watercolour paints which Ruth hugged all the way home under her raincoat and which, when her father had come home from the hospital, she had shyly laid in his lap like a Jovian sacrifice. And for the first time, for the very first time in her whole life, Ruth's father was proud of her.

No mean achievement that, winning the admiration and approval of the man who'd held a ten-year grudge against her for having been born a girl. Dr Mike Shapiro had put the watercolour box on the family mantel where the awards and photographs of her three brothers perpetually stood, and had made a point in the following days of showing the prize to visitors and saying, 'Would you believe it? Our fat little Ruthie won this in a race!'

Ruth has basked for six giddy days in father-pride, believing that everything was going to be all right from now on, no more criticisms, no more disappointed looks. And then came the afternoon he'd casually asked her over lunch, 'By the way, Ruthie, how many children were in the race?'

That was the horrible day the short-lived bubble had burst once and for all, never to be recaptured, because when she'd squeaked out, 'Three,' her father had laughed harder and louder than anyone had seen him do before or since and it joined the arsenal of family jokes, to be told again and again over the years, Dr Shapiro's laugh undiminished by time.

'Ow!' she cried out now, hopping on one foot and dropping to the grass. A pebble had worked its way into her sandal and had delivered a painful jab to her heel.

He'd come to the airport yesterday; that had been a big shock. Ruth had thought it would be just her and her mother, a kiss and a hug and goodbye for a year, but her father had surprised her by driving the car and leading her to believe, for a few anxious moments, that this might be the long awaited reconciliation. But once again she'd fooled herself. He had checked her bags, escorted her to the departure gate, then had paused long enough to shake her hand and say, 'I give you till Christmas, Ruthie. You'll see by then I was right.'

Christmas. A mere four months away. Fifteen weeks in which to see if Dr Mike Shapiro's dire prediction was going to come true. 'Medical school!' he had said last year. '*You* want to go to medical school? Ho, Ruthie, what a dreamer you are! Play it safe, stick to what you're capable of doing.

People who reach too high have a long way to fall and you know how failure affects you. You never were a good loser, Ruthie. You think medical school is a breeze? No, don't listen to me, I'm only a doctor, what do I know? Go ahead and try it. Just keep in mind that it's not an easy row to hoe.'

It wasn't fair. He never talked that way to Joshua or Max, he never tried to discourage them. Even little Judith, the youngest, was being encouraged by her father to reach for the stars. *Why only me? Why can't you love me?*

By the time Ruth was again on her feet and scooping up all the junk that had tumbled out of her leather shoulder bag and on to the grass the belltower had started to chime the noon hour. Ruth cursed under her breath. The Cashier's Office was closed from twelve to two.

Mickey Long stepped through the glass doors of Manzanitas Hall and into the balmy September noon. She paused to look around, then studied the school map again to orientate herself.

Manzanitas Hall was the fifth building she had searched since leaving the amphitheatre this morning, and so far her search was proving futile. This was not a large campus, there weren't many more buildings to go through. And if the suspicion growing inside her proved true, Mickey Long was going to be very upset. For this reason, as she struck off down one of the flagstone paths and headed for Encinitas Hall, the long, low Spanish-style building where all recreation and social functions took place, her panic started to mount.

Hurrying past the belltower it came to Mickey's mind that this was a strange campus: not at all what she was used to. Where were the card tables and posters inviting people to join SNCC and CORE? Where were the leaflets, the quad orators, the agitators? Where was Vietnam and Black Power and Free Speech? It was as if she'd stepped through a time portal into the past, into the sleepy fifties when college students were *students* and professors were still called sir. Castillo was a beautiful campus, neat and elegant and technicoloured with carefully kept flower beds and emerald lawns and flagstone paths and Spanish tile fountains and hacienda-style buildings of white stucco, Moorish arches, and red-tiled roofs. An old school with an old atmosphere; a moneyed school that fairly reeked of conservatism.

That was exactly what worried Mickey Long now: the campus was *too* quiet.

Such a difference from the one she'd just graduated from, the University of California at Santa Barbara where the kids had burned down the Bank of America. How on earth was she going to lose herself in this sleepy place? Where was her protection, the crowds, the cyclists, the couples stretched out on the grass making out? Where were the guitar players, the panhandlers, the discussion groups sitting under trees? In short, where was the camouflage that was going to enable her to blend and dissolve and become invisible? This was a shock. When Mickey had applied to come to Castillo, she had had no idea it would be so peaceful, so neat and orderly. She was going to stand out; people were going to *see* her!

*Have I done the right thing coming here?*

At last she found what she had been searching for. A ladies' room. Mickey scrambled to the sink like a desert wanderer to an oasis.

For Mickey Long the first few days in a new place were always torture. Until her new companions got used to her face she had to endure the surprised looks, then the frank curiosity, then the flicker of pity, and finally the embarrassment at having been caught staring and the unsuccessful attempt to pretend they hadn't noticed. Because of this Mickey Long always dressed 'down,' trying to hide behind 'invisible' greys and tans, wall colours, so as not to be seen. Crowds were her best defence.

She now lifted the curtain of silky blonde hair off one side of her face, uncapped a bottle of C-over and performed the ritual. When she was done and the hair was combed back over her cheeks, Mickey Long added a light layer of Revlon Laguna Peach to her lips. She liked makeup and wished she could wear it the way other girls did, bright and daring to draw notice to themselves. But the *last* thing Mickey Long wanted to do was draw notice to her face.

She emerged from Encinitas Hall and again checked her map of the campus. Surely there must be more than one ladies' room in the whole school! Deciding to skip lunch in the dining commons in order to seek out and plot all the ladies' rooms on her map, Mickey struck off in the direction of the ocean, where Rodriguez Hall stood perched on the sheer cliffs of Palos Verdes.

Sondra was still standing in the open doorway of her room and laughing with Shawn when she saw one of the other women students coming down the hall. She wore a dress the colour of a field mouse and hugged a big straw handbag to her chest shield-like; the bit of face that showed between falls of grapefruit-coloured hair was blushing crimson.

'Hi,' said Sondra as the woman drew near. Then she saw that the blush was curiously one-sided. 'I'm Sondra Mallone.' She held out her hand.

'Hello,' said Mickey, offering a tentative hand into Sondra's strong grasp. 'I'm Mickey Long.'

'And this is Shawn, a neighbour down the hall.'

Shawn studied Mickey for a brief, quizzical moment, then turned away, slightly embarrassed.

Tossing her long black hair off her shoulders with a graceful sweep of her hands, Sondra said, 'I guess I'm the last one to move in. Shawn here was kind enough to help me with my bags. I'm afraid I threw in the kitchen sink when I packed!'

Mickey stood uncertainly in the hallway, every so often bringing her hand up to her cheek to be sure the birthmark was covered. The awkward moment was filled with the sounds of muffled voices coming from behind closed doors down the hall; then Sondra said, 'Well! I guess we have to get ready for the tea, don't we, Mickey?'

Mickey nodded with relief and quickly turned away towards her own door. As soon as she was inside, Shawn murmured, 'Poor kid. I thought those things were curable these days.'

As Shawn moved on to the subject of school and the various rumours he had heard about Castillo, Sondra didn't listen. She was thinking about Mickey Long, what an odd girl she was, so shy to be thinking of becoming a doctor; and how could she stand all that hair in her face? Presently, Sondra laid a slender hand on Shawn's arm and said,

'There's a tea we women have to attend in a little while. Hosted by Dean Hoskins' wife. I should be getting ready.'

He gave her a look that said, *Ready for what, you look great to me*, then he straightened up from the door-frame and pulled his hands out of his pockets. 'There's going to be a party in the dining commons after dinner. Will you be going?'

Sondra laughed and shook her head. 'I practically drove all night from Phoenix. I'll have my light out by eight!'

He didn't make a move to leave. He gazed down at her for a minute, a familiar message plainly seen in his blue eyes, then Shawn said quietly, 'If there's anything I can do for you, anything you need, I'm in 203.'

She watched him head back down the hall, a nice, clean-cut young man who spoke with the faintest trace of a mountain accent, then Sondra looked over at Mickey's door. After a quick deliberation, she went to it and knocked.

The door inched open and a pair of timid green eyes looked out.

'It's only me,' said Sondra brightly. 'I was just wondering how you're going to dress for Mrs Hoskins' tea. I haven't the faintest idea what to wear.'

Opening the door all the way, Mickey gave Sondra a sceptical look, then said, 'You must be kidding. You can go just as you are.'

Sondra looked down at herself. She was still wearing what she had put on for the Welcome Program: a sleeveless mini-dress of cream voile with tiny white polka dots, and dressy white T-strap pumps. It was a popular style but one that few women could wear gracefully; with her slim legs and deep tan, however, Sondra made such simplicity look stunning.

'I don't have anything very dressy,' Mickey said, her hand fluttering up to the edge of her hair.

Sondra knew what Mickey was trying to do, she was trying to keep the birthmark covered, loading all that awful pancake makeup on her face and combing her cornsilk hair over one cheek like Veronica Lake. But it wasn't working. In fact, Sondra thought, Mickey's efforts to hide the enormous port-wine stain on her cheek only drew people's attention to it. And then Sondra thought that with her baby-fine hair the colour of pale lemons, and her green eyes Mickey Long could positively *emerge* in various shades of blue instead of the drab brown A-line dress she was wearing.

'Let's see what you've got,' Sondra said.

Mickey had only one suitcase and it was very old and battered. Inside, neat piles of beige and brown sweaters and skirts were flattened on top of plain dresses, all with Sears and J. C. Penney labels. Everything was outdated and had a limp, faded look.

'I have an idea,' said Sondra suddenly. 'You can borrow something of mine.'

'Oh, I don't think –'

'Sure, come on.' Taking Mickey's wrist, Sondra drew her out of her room and into her own where she immediately hefted one of the big suitcases onto her bed and opened it.

Mickey's eyes widened at the cornucopia of blouses and skirts, of silks and cottons and knits in every colour and pattern imaginable. Sondra pulled them out with little care, tossing things aside, strewing them over the bed, holding this one and then that one up to Mickey and studying the effect with a critical eye.

'I'd really rather not,' said Mickey.

Sondra shook out a Mary Quant knee-length jumper checkered blue and black with white sleeves and held it up under Mickey's chin.

'It won't fit,' Mickey protested. 'None of this will. I'm taller than you.'

Sondra considered this, then nodded and dropped the jumper onto the bed. 'Well, clothes aren't everything, are they? I'm positively spoiled by clothes. Isn't all this junk disgusting?' She made a useless attempt to get it all back into the case, then she gave up, shaking her head. 'Sometimes it embarrasses me, all my stuff.' She fell silent and her face grew serious. 'I've always had everything I ever wanted,' she said quietly. 'I've never gone without . . .'

An explosion of masculine laughter down the hall made both of them look at the open door. 'I didn't know the dorm was going to be co-ed,' said Mickey with a trace of distress.

'*I* didn't know the rooms were going to be this small. Where on earth am I going to put all my things?' Sondra pictured her home back in Phoenix, the large split-level 'rancho' where she had a huge bedroom, her own bathroom, and a dressing room almost the size of this dorm room. This was her first time living away from home. During her four years of college, Sondra had stayed in her parents' house because she had never been part of the active social scene, had never felt the need to have a place of her own for entertaining friends or men. Sondra's life had but one purpose to it and that was why she was here at Castillo. All the rest – socialising, dating – was secondary.

From out in the hallway, beyond their sight, Mickey and Sondra heard a crash and then a muttered, 'Damn!' Looking out they saw a young woman in white Levi's and black turtleneck sweater stooping over a heap of books on the floor. She ran her hands through her short dark brown hair and said with a laugh, 'Clumsy I was born and clumsy I will always be!'

As Mickey and Sondra helped her pick up books and purse, all three introduced themselves and shared derisive comments about the First Day of School.

'I feel like a little kid,' said Ruth Shapiro as she finally got her door unlocked and the three stepped into her room. 'My life seems to be one continual cycle of always starting school. Every four years, regular as clockwork!'

'They tell us this is the end of it,' said Sondra, laughing, and noticing that, like herself and Mickey, Ruth had not yet settled into her room. The North Face duffle bag was still zipped up and only a plastic toiletries bag stood open on the bare desk.

Ruth threw down her purse and ran her fingers through her short hair again. A large medallion on a chain between her ample breasts, the astrological sign of libra, caught the westering sun coming through the window. 'I feel as though I'm going to be a student all my life!'

'You have your books already?' said Sondra, reading the spines as she set them down. 'Where did you find the time?'

'I *made* the time. I intend to start cracking them tonight. Have a seat, let's get acquainted.' Ruth kicked off her sandals and massaged her foot where the pebble had stabbed it. 'I guess I'm going to have to get some real shoes if I want to stay within the dress code. And call my mother to send me down some skirts!'

Sondra settled onto the edge of the bed. 'I'm going to have to lower all my hemlines.'

'So,' said Ruth, reaching for her purse. 'Are you both from California?'

'I'm from Phoenix,' said Sondra.

They both looked at Mickey, who was still standing. 'I'm from around here,' she said at last, like a murder suspect confessing all. 'The Valley.'

'I've heard of the Valley,' said Sondra, trying to help Mickey through what was obviously a difficult process: making new friends.

'Did you leave anyone behind?' asked Ruth, studying Mickey's cheek without trying the least bit to be discreet.

'Leave anyone behind?'

'A boyfriend.'

Mickey could have laughed. Men didn't fall over themselves trying to date women like her. But that was all right. Mickey had resigned herself to that fact long ago. 'No, just my mother.'

'Where does she live?' asked Sondra.

'In Chatsworth. She's in a nursing home at the far end of the Valley.'

'How about your father?'

Mickey looked at the scarlet and lavender bougainvillea framing Ruth's window. 'My father died when I was a baby. I never knew him.' Which was a lie. Mickey's father had really run off with another woman, deserting one-year-old Mickey and her mother.

'I can sympathise,' said Sondra. 'I never knew my real father either. Or my real mother. I'm adopted.'

'You know,' said Ruth, pulling a pack of cigarettes out of her purse. 'When I saw you at the assembly this morning I thought you were Polynesian. Now you look more Mediterranean.'

Sondra laughed and smoothed her dress over her thighs. 'You'd be surprised what people come up with! One person actually insisted I was Indian. The Bombay kind.'

'You don't know who your parents were at all?'

17

'No, but I have a suspicion of what they looked like. There was a girl in high school who resembled me. People sometimes mistook us for sisters. But we weren't. She was from Chicago. But her mother was black and her father was white.'

'Oh. I see.'

'It's all right. I've accepted it. My mother had a hard time when I was growing up. My adoptive mother, that is. You see, when they adopted me I was only a baby and I looked as if I could grow up to resemble my father, who has dark hair. But then I started turning out differently. Over the years I looked less and less like my parents and it started to bother my mother a lot. She belongs to all sorts of clubs, moves in the best circles. I know that for a while I caused her a lot of anxiety. Especially when Daddy decided to go into politics. And then, lucky for me, Civil Rights came along and suddenly not only did it become acceptable but *fashionable* to help Negroes. She was finally able to stop trying to explain me away with some story about Italian being far back in her ancestry!'

Ruth and Mickey stared at Sondra, unable to accept her looks as any kind of handicap. For Ruth, who had always had to battle her weight, and for Mickey, whose face locked many doors to her, Sondra Mallone's exotic beauty and effortless grace could only be envied, not something to be 'explained away.'

'Are you an only child?' asked Ruth.

Sondra nodded solemnly. 'It was all my mother wanted. I used to dream of brothers and sisters.'

Ruth lit a cigarette, wafted the smoke from her face, and said, 'I have three brothers and a sister. I used to dream of being an only child!'

Mickey said softly, 'It must be nice to have brothers and sisters,' and settled finally on the floor with her back against the closet door.

Ruth studied the lighted end of her cigarette, her chocolate-brown eyes turning hard. Brothers and sisters were fine if there was enough father-love to go around.

'Knock, knock.'

All three turned to see a young woman standing in the

doorway. She carried a bottle of Sangria and four glasses. 'Hi, I'm Dr Selma Stone, fourth-year. I'm your personal welcoming committee to Castillo College.' She looked very East Coast, in tweed skirt and silk blouse and string of pearls; like the school itself Selma Stone looked like a throw-back to a more conservative age. She pulled out the chair from Ruth's desk and sat down, crossing one knee over the other.

'Did you say you're a fourth-year?' asked Ruth as she accepted a glass of the red wine. 'Then how come you're *Doctor* Stone?'

Selma laughed. 'Oh, in the third year you start your clerkship in the hospital – that's St Catherine's just across the highway – and they insist you introduce yourself to the patients as *doctor*. That way the patients don't know you're just a med student, and it puts them at ease. I've been doing it for a year so it's become a habit. No, I won't be a real doctor for another nine months.'

Ruth looked down at the ruby surface of her wine and thought about this dishonesty with patients, and the privilege of using a title one hadn't yet earned.

'I volunteered to welcome you personally to the school before the ladies' tea this afternoon. It's a tradition here, ever since they started admitting female students. I was the only woman in my class three years ago and was I scared! I really appreciated the senior woman who came and talked to me.'

Sondra's amber eyes took a long look at Selma Stone. What must that have been like, to be the only woman in a class of ninety?

'You'll have questions,' said Selma. 'Everyone always does.' Her grey eyes swept over the three faces, assessing each in turn: the one with the short brunette hair was going to have no trouble here at Castillo, her eyes had a relentless, survival quality to them. And the beauty, with her exotic looks, was either going to have a lot of trouble with the men or be at a great advantage, depending on how secure she was within herself. But the third one, the blonde hiding behind her hair – there was a hunted look there that disturbed Selma Stone. She doubted that *that* one would make it.

Just then the girl spoke up. 'I have a question. Where are all the ladies' rooms?'

'You can count them all on one finger. There is only one women's room in the school. It's in Encinitas Hall.'

'Only *one*? Why?'

'Logistics. Castillo has never exceeded an eight per cent ratio of women to men in a class. In fact, when women were first admitted back in the forties, the quota was limited to two women per class. And since there was no female staff, and there still isn't, it wasn't feasible for the school to tear up every building to install new plumbing.'

'Then how . . .' began Mickey.

'You learn to do without tea or coffee in the morning, and when you're near your period you wear something all the time because you won't have time to slip out of class and run across campus to Encinitas Hall.'

Mickey felt a familiar dryness contract her throat. To be so far away from a bathroom!

'How are women students treated here?' asked Sondra.

'I understand that years ago there was a lot of resentment about allowing women to be granted a degree from Castillo. It was believed we would diminish the diploma's prestige. You'll still find some resistance among the older staff. And with certain men you'll find yourselves being constantly tested. There are a few staff men who still get a kick out of finding a woman student's breaking point. Be sure to guard your tears. If you cry, you'll have your female anatomy flung in your face.'

As she raised her glass to her lips, Ruth Shapiro mentally shrugged off the doom-words of this Cassandra. Nothing and no one was going to get in the way of her reaching that finish line.

'But you'll do all right,' Selma Stone hastened to assure them. 'Just remember to maintain a professional attitude. And always keep in mind that Castillo is nothing like the open, liberal campuses I'm sure you've just come from. This school is rigid, with all the conservatism of a men's club. We are intruders.'

'And the students?' asked Sondra. 'How do they feel about us?'

'For the most part they accept us as equals, but you will still encounter a few who will feel threatened by you. They

20

will want to put you down, remind you who's boss, or they'll be curious about you, trying to figure you out. I think a few of them are even afraid of us. But if you are guarded in your relationships with them and concentrate on the central reason you're here – to study medicine – you'll have no problems.'

There was a long table covered with damask and name cards by each plate and a corsage for each woman. They began with white wine by the enormous stone fireplace at one end of the huge recreation room, getting acquainted and learning more of the rules at Castillo. Mrs Hoskins, the dean's wife, was a pleasant woman who wore white gloves and referred to the women as 'girls,' assuring them they were going to do their future husbands proud.

Sondra and Ruth and Mickey walked back to the dorm through the perfumed twilight in silence, listening to the distant breakers crash on the beach below Castillo's cliffs. To their left, the dark and formidable faces of Mariposa, Manzanitas, and Rodriguez Halls stood against the palm trees and lavender sky like ominous harbingers of what the next four years held. But to their right, across the Pacific Coast Highway, rose the golden monolith of St Catherine's-By-the-Sea, the hospital where they were going to train, shining like a beacon at the end of a dark future. The three picked their way over the hundred-year-old flagstones with apprehension.

When they arrived at the entrance of Tesoro Hall and stood bathed in the glow of light and rock music and male laughter, Ruth said, 'How on earth are we supposed to study with all *that* going on! You know, I've been thinking. How do you two feel about this dorm?'

'What do you mean?' Sondra asked.

'We're paying an awful lot of money to be here. And listen to how noisy it is. I was wondering what you two would say to the three of us going in together on an apartment.'

'An apartment?'

'Off campus. I've noticed some vacancy signs around. I'll bet that, split three ways, the rent wouldn't come to anything compared to what Castillo is charging us to stay here – with no privacy and no peace and quiet for studying.' Ruth frowned in the direction the music and laughter were coming from. 'Another thing, they charge us for maid and laundry service. We could certainly keep our own apartment clean and do our own washing. And then there's the food. What did you think of the lunch we had in the dorm today?'

They both tried to recall it. It had been something brown.

'I'm a pretty good cook,' Ruth said, 'plus I don't eat three meals a day. They charge us for breakfast, lunch, and dinner whether we eat them or not. Think of the money we would save.' She paused again. 'And most important of all, there's the privacy. No guys running past our doors.'

At this Mickey's eyes lit up. All alone, away from the men. 'It sounds like a good idea.'

Sondra was thinking of the tiny dorm room and the overly helpful young men like Shawn, pleasant and well-meaning but intrusive. 'I could do with more living space,' she said. 'But I don't want to be far from the ocean.'

It was agreed that Ruth would look around. School didn't actually start for two more days, on Thursday, which left them time to look for an apartment, move into it, and wrangle with the cashier's red tape to get their dorm money back. They sealed the agreement with handshakes.

# Chapter Three

Summer in Southern California is at its most intense in September, and on Wednesday afternoon when the three met again, the heat was merciless, with not even the relief of an ocean breeze. They set off down Avenida Oriente in Sondra's Mustang.

When they mounted the stairs a few minutes later to the second-floor apartments Ruth pulled a spiral pad out of her purse and handed it to Sondra. 'Here are the figures. The landlady wanted a cleaning deposit but I convinced her we'll keep it clean. It's a hundred and fifteen a month and she said utilities will come to under ten dollars. I estimated another hundred and fifty per month for groceries, so that all breaks down to just under a hundred apiece per month. Since it's eight hundred dollars apiece to live in the dorm for a semester, that will give us a grand savings of three hundred dollars each!'

Fishing the key out of her Levi's pocket, Ruth opened the front door and said, 'Here it is! Shangri-la!'

The apartment was small but nicely furnished and had wall-to-wall carpeting. The off-white walls were bare, as were the tabletops and bookshelves, but all three women, as they stepped inside, saw at once how it would soon look: Sondra imagined the pillows and posters, Ruth mentally spread around plants and pictures. And Mickey Long saw the privacy of it, an enclave away from the world.

'What do you think?' Ruth asked.

'Oh, I like it!' said Sondra. 'I brought some beautiful posters with me from Phoenix. Everywhere we turn we'll be able to look at castles and rivers and sunsets. Burnt-orange pillows will bring that sofa to life.' She walked to the centre of the living room and looked around with a smile. 'Maybe even an oriental rug.'

'Whoa,' said Ruth with a laugh, holding up a hand. 'I can't afford things like that. I'm paying my own way through this school. Every penny will have to count.'

'Oh, that's all right,' said Sondra brightly. 'I have money. *I'll* be the interior decorator.'

Ruth watched Mickey cautiously approach the hallway as though something lurked there, then she rested her hands on her ample hips and said, 'Well, what do you think, Mickey?'

Mickey felt a tremor of excitement. Oh yes, it would do nicely. It could be made cosy and personal, and it was so very private. Plus, now she could be certain of making ends meet. Between the scholarship and student loan and money saved from summer jobs, Mickey would be able to keep herself in school and continue to support her mother in the nursing home where she was so happy.

'We'll draw straws for the bedrooms,' Ruth said, turning towards the kitchen where there was a broom. But Mickey stopped her, volunteering to take the one bedroom without windows. Glass and mirrors were the banes of her existence.

They drove back to the dorm through the September heat, loaded their things into the Mustang, and returned to the apartment with a fiery sun setting in their eyes. Sondra opened all the windows to admit the afternoon breeze, which was wonderfully crisp and salty, while Ruth produced the few items she had bought at Safeway that morning: a pot for heating water and cooking food, instant coffee, cheese, crackers, toilet paper, and a box of fifteen-hour votive candles. Placing one each of the latter in all the rooms, she said, 'The landlady assures me the power will be turned on tomorrow. This weekend we can look for some kitchen and bathroom stuff.'

Sondra took her time setting up her room, even though the red-gold sun had dipped behind the Pacific and long shadows were stealing the last light. The Janice Nakamura poster of jungle cats went right over her bed where she would see it first thing upon waking; the leather desk set that was a graduation present was arranged neatly on the desk beneath the window; a photograph of her parents at the Grand Canyon was settled next to it; dresses hung in the right side of the closet, skirts and blouses in the left, shoes lined up like little soldiers on the floor. She smoothed the blankets, lent by the landlady until she could buy her own, fluffed the pillow, and stood back to survey her work.

The first step, thought Sondra with intense satisfaction. The first step of the final journey...

Before joining Ruth and Mickey, Sondra took a moment to stand at her window and look out. As Ruth had warned, no view of the ocean, but it was out there all the same, just through those palm trees and over apartment rooftops. Sondra's ocean. She could feel its rhythm, inhale its restless breath; if she closed her eyes and listened hard enough she could hear the surf, the pulse that promised so much – that promised the big, beckoning world beyond. Sondra would one day find herself out there, she had no doubt of it, it was one of those immutable truths that go beyond doubt. There were wrongs to be righted, something owed to the blood from which she sprang. And there was an identity to be forged, her place in the world, a returning no matter how remote, to the dark race who were her distant kin. Sondra Mallone felt she stood on the edge of a great, summoning sea and it excited her now in the same way Dean Hoskins' recitation of the Hippocratic Oath had on Tuesday morning – the promise of the fulfilment of a quest.

In the kitchen, Ruth was spreading cheese on crackers. She worked by candlelight and she worked alone. Mickey was still in the bathroom.

Ruth was amazed that her hands were so steady; inside she trembled. She was here at last, taking the big bold step. *Despite my father*, she thought. *I won't fail. If it kills me, I'm going to make it to the end, and I'm going to come in First.*

Her father, one of the best-known and busiest general practitioners in the state of Washington, had been disappointed twenty-three years ago when, in defiance of his wishes and plans, his wife gave birth to a girl. A hasty eleven-months later produced Joshua and all was forgiven. Then Max had come along, and finally David. When the last child was born, the last and therefore the most cherished child, it was a girl. As if there hadn't been a first daughter at all, as if he'd been saving it all up just for this, Mike Shapiro became sentimental over little Judith and turned her into the princess that, by rights, Ruth felt she should have been.

But in another way Ruth didn't blame him. She'd been a chubby, clumsy, disappointing child, the one who always knocked over the milk or walked around with cake crumbs on her chin. Today, as an adult, she was competing with her brothers: Joshua was at West Point and his picture dominated the family fireplace; Max was at Northwestern in pre-med preparing to step into his father's practice as a partner; David was showing great promise of developing a keen legal mind. 'You'll never do it, Ruthie,' her father had declared when she'd filled out the medical school applications. 'Why can't you just accept what you are? Find a nice boy. Get married. Have children.' But that was just the thing: Ruth had never failed at anything, not really. At times in her childhood and adolescence Ruth might have sunk to the unpardonable level of *average*, but never to failure. She just wasn't a gifted child. It wasn't her fault that the only race she'd ever won a place in was a race that no one else had shown up for because of rain and that no matter how far behind she'd come in, the prize would have been hers anyway. Still, one good thing had come out of that debacle years ago: Ruth Shapiro had tasted for a brief time the savour of a father's admiration. And having once tasted it she hungered for more.

*This time,* she thought as she spread the crackers out on a paper plate, *I won't come in third. I'll come in first. First out of ninety.*

Mickey was a long time in the bathroom, not because she was applying makeup or combing her long blonde hair over her cheek, but because she was staring at the face of the woman in the mirror. A face that mocked her.

When she was born the stain had been pinprick size, a fairy's kiss her mother had told her. But then it had slowly started to spread until now the port-wine birthmark extended from her ear to her nostril, from her jaw up to her hairline. Some of the kids in grammar school had been cruel. They'd say, 'Hey, Mickey, you've got jam on your face,' or they'd pronounce her skin poisonous and say that no one was to go near her. They used to dare one another to run up and touch her cheek; Stanley Furmanski declared that his father had told him port-wine stains get bigger and bigger until they burst and your brains spilled out. And then the teachers would lecture the class on being kind to unfortunate people and Mickey would want to die. She'd run home crying and her mother would always be there, to hug away the pain.

In junior high school it was no better. Girls made friends with her only so they could ask her personal questions about her face; well-meaning teachers humiliated her with kindness; and boys dated her on dares from their friends, winning five dollars if they kissed that cheek. In all those years her mother tried doctor after doctor. Most of them pronounced the stain too vascular and sent her away; a few experimented with scalpels and liquid hydrogen and dry ice, leaving her face uglier and more scarred than before.

Finally, the worst scars were not on Mickey's face. She had raced through high school, and squeezed four years of college into three, making her, at twenty, the youngest in Castillo's freshman class. By now Mickey Long was unalterably convinced of her inferiority and that her role in life was to dedicate herself to work.

She had thought it odd at first that the six interviewers last fall hadn't asked her why she wanted to become a doctor; she had thought they would ask that question of everyone. But then, maybe they'd taken one look at her and figured it out. They were doctors, they weren't dumb. Anyone in the profession would guess the number of doctors' offices Mickey had been to in eighteen years, starting at the age of two when the port-wine stain was no bigger than a dime. So many cold hands on her face, so many gravely shaken heads; she'd been too many times on the wrong side of the needle and blade, had too often heard the verdict 'no hope.' It must be plain to anyone who looked at her that somewhere along the way Mickey had decided to dedicate herself to the cause of helping people like herself, to discover a way to eradicate this humiliating affliction – even if it was too late for herself.

A knock on the door startled her. She opened it to find Sondra on the other side of it, her smiling face illuminated by the candle in her hands.

'Sorry I took so long,' Mickey said. 'I promise I won't be hogging the bathroom all the time.'

'That's all right. I was just knocking to let you know the banquet is ready.'

Ruth had set the cheese and crackers out and was pouring Coke into Dixie cups. 'I'm going to have to go easy on this stuff,' she said as her roommates settled around the table in the circle of flickering candlelight. 'I have to watch my weight every minute. When I was little, every time I was caught drinking a Coke or eating candy, my father deducted a nickel from my allowance. When I was in the seventh grade he offered me ten dollars if I lost ten pounds.'

'We'll go shopping this weekend,' Sondra said, picking up a cracker and devouring it. 'We'll get some Diet-Rites and Frescas. What do you say we take turns cooking, alternating weeks maybe?'

They both looked at Mickey for concurrence, but she was silent. 'You know, Mickey,' said Ruth, picking crumbs off her T-shirt, 'you're going to have to learn to be more outgoing if you're going to be a doctor. How do you expect to communicate with your patients?'

Mickey coughed slightly and bowed her head. 'I'm not going to be that kind of doctor. I'm going into research.'

Ruth nodded, suddenly understanding. Personality and looks don't matter in a lab, just brains and dedication.

'What about you, Ruth?' asked Sondra. 'What kind of medicine are you going into?'

'General practice. Only now they're calling it family practice. I'm going to have an office up in Seattle. And you?'

'I'm going out into the world,' Sondra said. 'I've had this feeling inside me all my life – I can't describe it. For as far back as I can remember, I've always needed to see what's on the other side of the hill.' Her amber eyes reflected the flame's glow. Her silky black hair drifted over her shoulders and tumbled down her chest. 'I don't know why my real mother gave me up. I don't know if she died giving birth to me, or if she just couldn't keep me. The thought of it haunts me sometimes. I was born in 1946 when interracial relationships were frowned on. I wonder what happened. Did she meet my father, fall in love, and then was ostracised by her family? Did they stay together or was she abandoned? Was my mother black, or was my father? I'd like to go to

Africa after I do my internship. I'd like to get in touch with the other half of me.'

Beyond the curtained windows an ocean wind had risen and was now rattling the panes as if trying to get in. It was a moist, salty wind, a living wind, carrying Poseidon's kiss from the rolling sea. It made a person turn inward and think, take a look at what was happening, what was about to happen – Ruth and Mickey and Sondra, strangers just days ago, but bound together now and setting out on an exciting, frightening, unknown course. These next four years were going to teach them to be mistresses of life and death; it was no small thing to contemplate.

Ruth cleared her throat, lifted her cup, and said, 'Here's to us then. Here's to three future doctors.'

# Chapter Four

Carved into the stone lintel over the double doors of Mariposa Hall were the words: MORTUI VIVOS DOCENT. The freshmen had passed under it many times in the past six weeks but only today, the first day of cadaver dissection, did they fully appreciate the significance of those words: the dead teach the living.

Ruth took her usual place on the top tier of the amphitheatre and, because she was early, pulled Guyton's *Human Physiology* out of her canvas tote, and opened it to 'Genetic Control of Cell Function.' In these six weeks since the first day of school, since Dean Hoskins' inspiring recitation of the oath, Ruth had settled down into a determined grind of study; every extra minute was snatched for cramming. On this October morning, as her classmates gradually filled the seats and fingered the dissection kits in their laps, Ruth Shapiro tried to memorise the RNA codons for the twenty common amino acids found in protein molecules.

'Hello.'

Ruth looked up. A pretty young redheaded woman was taking the seat next to her. This was Adrienne, a classmate, who was married to a fourth-year student.

'I'm nervous,' Adrienne said to Ruth. 'No matter how my husband has tried to prepare me for this dissection business, I'm still dreading it. I've never even seen a dead body before!'

'It'll be all right,' said Ruth with her usual pragmatism. 'Once you accept that it has to be done.'

'Listen, let me warn you.' Adrienne leaned close and lowered her voice. 'My husband says one of the anatomy instructors is really down on women, hates having them in his class. If one of us gets Moreno, that woman is going to suffer.'

'How so?'

'He does it every year. You go into the dissecting lab after this lecture and it never fails that one of his tables is missing its cadaver. And it's always the table where a woman is assigned. Moreno makes a big show of picking someone, seemingly at random, to go down into the basement and bring one up. But he *always* chooses a woman.'

Ruth stared at her in disbelief. 'Oh, I hardly think –'

'It's true. My husband said that the first day of his anatomy class a woman was sent down to the basement and she didn't come back.'

'What happened to her?'

'When she saw the pool they keep the dead bodies in, she broke down. She ran back to the dorm crying.'

'Did she ever come back?'

'Oh yes. She's a fourth-year student now. You've met her. Selma Stone.'

Ruth turned away, mulling over this new information and saying to herself, *Let Moreno try it on me.* Then she spotted a clipboard being passed along the rows, with each student writing on it. 'What's that?' she asked.

'It's sort of a sign-up sheet.'

'I thought they never took roll here.'

'They don't. This isn't for attendance, it's for dissection assignments.'

When the clipboard reached her, Ruth puzzled over it. There were all the class signatures on it, with a number scribbled after each; at the top were instructions to write your name and your height, nothing more. Ruth signed her name and added: 5' 4".

The clipboard got to Mickey after Adrienne; she had just rushed in under the wire and taken the last seat in the row – almost late again because of her detour to the Encinitas Hall women's room. She signed quickly and wrote 5' 10". The last in the amphitheatre to get the sheet was Sondra, who was chatting with the young man next to her. She barely paid attention and so signed her name and her weight of 110 lbs.

Dr Morphy came out onto the stage, whipped out a jointed

31

pointer and, without any preamble whatsoever, commenced his anatomy lecture. After an hour of rapid diagrams on the blackboard and a quick run-through of general terms such as 'anterior' and 'posterior' he sent the class to the labs.

As they were funnelled down a long, cold hall and shown where the lab coats were, everyone was strangely quiet, apprehensive. The women, except for Mickey, had trouble finding lab coats to fit and ended up rolling up the sleeves; into the voluminous pockets went notebooks and dissecting kits.

A lab assistant, holding the clipboard that had circulated earlier, rapidly shouted out names and table numbers. As people moved to their assigned places, the mystery of the sign-up sheet was dispelled: quite simply, the dissecting tables were set at different heights and students were assigned to work at a table compatible with one's height. As a consequence, Mickey was alone with three men; Sondra and Ruth and the other two women were all together at another table.

Unfortunately, the women all wound up in Mr Moreno's lab.

Moreno was short and pompous as he marched into the lab. As the students shifted uncomfortably by their tables, the covered cadavers on them, Moreno intoned dramatically: 'In the fourteenth century, students of the School of Salernum were required, before dissection, to celebrate mass for the salvation of the cadaver's soul. While we do not go to that extreme here at Castillo, we do insist upon respect for our cadavers. There will be no, I repeat, gentlemen, NO misuse of your cadavers. No sneaking in here in the middle of the night and filling them with jelly beans, no sausages up the vaginas, no missing penises. I've taught anatomy for twenty years and *I have seen it all*. There is *no* infantile medical school prank I have not seen. None of them is new or cute or funny. Any desecration, gentlemen, I repeat, ANY DESECRATION of a cadaver results in immediate dismissal from this school!'

Moreno lowered his pointer and looked condescendingly at the bright, terrified faces, fully knowing that the pranks were going to occur anyway – they always did.

'Now then,' he proceeded a little less stentoriously. 'You will find an information sheet attached to each cadaver. It gives vital statistics and cause of death. For the most part, these are poverty cases, people with no families, no one to pay burial expenses. To put your minds at ease, gentlemen, the school will give their remains proper burial at the end of this course.'

He wound his way among the tables, among the green-sheeted mounds that lay in grotesquely distinct outline. 'There is a dissecting syllabus at each table, and disposable gloves.' He paused at the last table and frowned. The room was deathly still, mostly because the students were trying not to breathe in the heady, sickish fumes of formalin. 'Well,' Moreno said in mild surprise. 'Your cadaver wasn't brought up. One of you is going to have to go down to the basement and get it.'

He turned and marched back to the lab bench where the clipboard lay. Arching his eyebrows in exaggerated off-handedness, he said, 'Let me see, who's assigned to table twelve? Ah, here we are. I'll choose a name at random. Mallone, where are you?'

Sondra raised her hand.

'Okay, Mallone. Go down and get a cadaver. Take that elevator there and go all the way down to the basement. Tell the attendant that he shorted us one body, and bring it back up with you.'

The elevator creaked, the subterranean corridor was filled with unbreathable smells. The overhead light bulbs were bare and dim, and shadows seemed to menace from all sides. Sondra felt her heart thump with each step she took. Several closed and unlabelled doors went by before she began to wonder if she was lost, and when one of the shadows did in fact move and step out, Sondra nearly screamed.

'Howdy,' said an elderly man in overalls and plaid shirt. 'Been 'specting you.'

Sondra gulped down her fright. 'You have?'

'First day of dissection, right? You got Moreno, right? This way, follow me, missy.' He limped through an open doorway and led Sondra into a large, tank-like room that was so thick with formalin fumes that tears immediately sprang to Sondra's eyes. 'I'll pick ya out a nice one,' the old attendant said, reaching for a long pole that looked for all the world like the old vaudeville hooks used to yank bad acts off the stage. 'Nice ones ain't so scary.'

And then she saw through her blur of tears. The big pool sunk into the concrete floor, a pool that might have been in any gymnasium or health club except that it was filled with preserving fluid instead of water and the bodies, brown and mummified, didn't swim but bobbed gently. She watched him throw out his hook, draw a cadaver to the side of the pool, and start to haul it up.

The face was covered, wrapped completely around in white gauze, and the hands were tied together over the chest as if in prayer. Sondra saw that this was the body of a young woman.

'Doin' you a favour, missy, givin' you a nice one like this. Don't often get 'em so young. This one's a Jane Doe. County Hospital's got a deal with the school. Not only does this save the county the cost of burying her, the school gives 'em money for the body besides.' He rolled the cadaver onto a collapsed stretcher. 'Does this every year, Moreno. Got a mean streak in him. All them other cadavers upstairs, all old and grizzled, won't get much outa them. Now you, missy, 'cause Moreno done this to ya, well –' He pulled up the stretcher and locked the legs. 'Well, I'm giving ya the best one we got. You and your partners'll be the envy of – Here, here!' His hand shot out, catching her arm. 'You gonna faint?'

Sondra brought a hand up to her damp forehead. 'No.'

'I'll go up for ya. I'll take the body up in the elevator and you kin take the stairs.'

'Did you say . . . did you say that he does this every year?' Sondra asked in a whisper.

'Only to a woman student. He don't like women to be in his medical school. So he likes to make 'em squirm.'

'I see.' She wanted to take a deep breath but couldn't; she felt close to passing out. 'I'll manage it, thank you.'

'Here, missy, I don't mind takin' it up for ya.'

'No, I'll be all right. Do I go back the same way I came down? Would you please cover it . . . *her?* Thank you.'

By the time the elevator reached the third floor and the doors started to open, Sondra was leaning against the wall, a roar thundering in her ears. Twice during the ride she had thought she was going to faint, but she had held on, strengthened by anger. When the doors whooshed open, she saw twenty faces staring at her in a deadly silent room.

Mr Moreno came up to her and regarded her with a flat stare. 'I'm impressed you managed it by yourself, Mallone, considering you don't even know your height from your weight!'

She had died of haemorrhage from a self-inflicted wound to the uterus. She was approximately seventeen years old, unidentified, unclaimed.

Jane Doe.

There was little that Sondra had got out of the afternoon dissection lab; her amber eyes had glazed over, her inner thoughts had churned in turmoil. *Unidentified and unclaimed.*

As Sondra walked back to the apartment in the gravid afternoon air, she was oblivious to the heavy grey clouds collecting to her left over the ocean. *Seventeen years old. Unclaimed.*

What was the girl's story? Why had she done it? What circumstances had led the poor girl to take such a drastic step?

'Don't get personally involved with your cadavers,' Moreno had advised. 'Some students develop an attachment and then they get emotional about the dissection. That's why your cadavers' faces are concealed. You are working on a *body*. Don't forget that.'

But Sondra couldn't. When she got to the apartment she found a depressed Mickey sitting at the kitchen table, one side of her face pasty white and the other hot pink. Ruth, whose turn it was to cook dinner, was silently opening cans of chili.

'What a day!' Sondra said, throwing down her purse. 'I sure wasn't prepared for that!'

'Moreno's a jerk,' Ruth muttered.

Sondra looked over the items scattered on the kitchen

countertop – chili con carne, slices of white bread – and said, 'You know what? I think it would be a good idea to go out to dinner tonight.'

Mickey looked up, her eyes brightening, then fearful. 'Gilhooley's?' She had been to Gilhooley's only once before; it was the local hangout where the med students drank beer and listened to the jukebox and vented tensions and frustrations. It was a boisterous, noisy, crowded place and it had made Mickey feel even more self-conscious. But tonight, it seemed suddenly appealing – just to get out, to do something different.

'I don't know,' said Ruth slowly. There was that Table of Osmolar Substances to memorise and fifty pages of Farnsworth to read by next Monday.

'My treat,' said Sondra, snatching up her purse. 'Come on, it's time we three had a break!'

# Chapter Five

There was a small shopping centre just down the Pacific Coast Highway, right across from St Catherine's Hospital, and it offered every service a medical community could want; the Magic Lantern, which showed movies with subtitles, a Thrifty Drug, a twenty-four-hour laundromat, a Dunker's Donuts, a Safeway, a small bookstore, a uniform shop, and Gilhooley's.

As soon as they came inside the doorway, their sweaters jewelled with the first raindrops, Sondra, Ruth, and Mickey were glad they'd come. The music was loud and did a good job of forcing thoughts out of one's head; the tables were occupied by talking, laughing men and women; there was warmth and lights and motion. And, suddenly, there was Steve.

'Oh hi!' Ruth cried happily, brightening at once. She had met Steve Schonfeld at a mixer at Encinitas Hall two weeks ago and had gone with him last weekend to see *Wild Strawberries*. Steve was a fourth-year medical student, tall and good-looking.

'He's waving to us to join him,' Ruth said.

'Let's not,' said Mickey, looking down at the floor and away from the three men with Steve, all sitting around a table in white hospital jackets, which meant they were on call.

'Mickey's right,' said Sondra. 'Let's find a table of our own and invite *him* to join *us*.'

It wasn't easy, finding an empty table in Gilhooley's. But Ruth spotted one and she pushed forward through the drinkers standing near the bar. She set her purse down on the ranch-style table surrounded by five captain's chairs, and pushed dirty dishes and crumpled napkins to the edge of the table. By the time Sondra and Mickey were also seated, Steve Schonfeld was there, grinning down at them.

'Hey, Ruth, what are you doing away from the books?'

It was already a joke between them. In the two weeks of their acquaintance Ruth had turned down four invitations, each time pleading studies. Even their two hours in the Magic Lantern trying to make sense of Bergman hadn't been free of a mimeographed sheet of enzymatic equations which Ruth had glanced down at every now and then.

After introductions Steve sat down and explained as he did so, 'I'm on call. Can't promise to grace you with my sunshine for long.' He folded his arms on the table and said, 'So, what's the occasion? Somebody's birthday?'

Ruth made a wry face. 'First day of dissection.'

'Ah, that explains the crowd. Gilhooley's is *never* this busy on a Wednesday night. I wondered what had happened. I remember *my* first dead body. I was depressed for weeks!'

Ruth felt a pang of envy. With stethoscopes in their pockets and name plates on their white lapels, Steve and his fellow fourth-years were already working in the hospital with patients. This was modern medical education: two years of pure sciences under professors who were mostly doctors of philosophy, not of medicine; and then in the third year students had their *first* contact with disease and medicine. Ruth was impatient, anxious to get started with real medicine, to do what her father did.

One of Steve's friends hurried by and said with a scowl, 'Gotta go. Two IVs to restart.'

Steve shook his head and laughed. 'That'll be the seventh time this week he's been called to restart IVs. Pretty soon he'll learn, he'll figure it out. *I* did, real quick.'

'What are you talking about?' asked Sondra, who was looking for a waitress.

'St Catherine's is a teaching hospital, so they leave as much scut work as possible to give the medical students practice. Starting IVs is one such chore. As a result, the nurses on the floors don't keep an eye on the IV levels and so they are constantly running out. When an IV runs out it has to be started all over again. It came to me one night last spring when I was called out of bed *four separate times in one night* to restart IVs. I pointed to the bottle over the bed and said to the patient, "See that fluid? See this tubing? You be sure not to let it run dry because then you'll get air in your vein and you'll die."'

'No!' cried Sondra.

'It hasn't failed me yet, in a thousand IVs. As soon as the fluid is low the patient rings for the nurse and she slips on a new bottle. That was six months ago and I haven't had to restart an IV since.'

'But that would keep the patient awake all night,' said Sondra.

'Better him than me.' When Steve saw the familiar look on Sondra's face, the disapproval of the idealistic medical student, he leaned forward and said, 'Listen. When you start taking calls you're going to realise that sleep is more precious to you than diamonds. If you're up all night restarting IVs, then you're going to be of no use on the floors the next day when the *real* work is done.'

Sondra gave him a dubious look. When *she* was a fourth-year she wasn't going to sink so low.

'The waitresses seem to be ignoring us,' said Ruth, trying to signal to one.

'No they're not. Mr Gilhooley just wasn't expecting such a crowd. He doesn't have full staff on tonight. You'd think after running this tavern next to the school for over twenty years that he'd make a note of the annual first day of dissection and be prepared.'

'I'm desperately thirsty,' said Ruth.

'I'll be glad to get you ladies something from the bar. What'll it be?'

'Any diet soda for me,' said Ruth.

'And I'd like a white wine,' added Sondra.

They turned to Mickey, who was staring off into the distance.

Before they could jolt her out of her mental preoccupation, another of Steve's classmates came up to the table and barked, 'We both got called this time. Big accident was just brought into the ER. Let's go!'

'Sorry, ladies,' said Steve, jumping up and pushing his chair under the table. 'Another time, maybe? Ruth, you'll be at the Halloween mixer this Saturday?'

'Sure,' she said with a smile. 'I'll see you there.'

A busboy, red-faced and sweating, came by and did a hasty job of clearing the dishes and running a wet rag over the tabletop, but still no waitress was in evidence. 'I'll get the drinks,' Sondra said, rising. 'You keep an eye out for a waitress. Mickey? A Coke for you?'

'Hm? Oh yes. Please. A Coke.'

One end of the long bar wasn't as crowded as the other end, where one loud young man was entertaining a knot of friends with hospital stories. Mr Gilhooley himself, a robust, ruddy-faced man with a booming laugh, was down at that end of the bar, leaning on an elbow and listening. Sondra stepped up and looked around. A young man in jeans and Oxford shirt was rummaging through jars of olives and cocktail onions behind the bar.

Glancing back at her friends, Sondra saw that they had finally got menus and were looking at them.

'Excuse me,' Sondra said to the man behind the bar.

He looked up, smiled and went back to searching through the jars.

Sondra cleared her throat and said louder, 'I would like some service, please.' That was the trouble with places like this, if you didn't like the service or the food there was nowhere else to go. They had you.

The man looked up again, blinked at her, then straightened all the way up and said, 'Sure, what would you like?'

'One Coke, one diet cola, and a glass of white wine, please.'

'May I see your ID, please?'

Sondra looked at him. She'd never been asked before. 'I'm over twenty-one.'

'Sorry,' he said. 'Rules are rules.'

Shrugging, she set her purse between two wet spots on the bar's surface, and fumbled around inside for her wallet. Finding it, she flipped it open and held it out for him to see.

He studied it, looking from the small photo to her face, then back to the small photo; he was taking longer than necessary. 'It's legal,' said Sondra.

'Are you really only five foot five?' he asked.

Sondra stared at him. He was nice-looking, not too tall, and when he smiled dimples appeared in his cheeks. 'This is

40

an Arizona licence,' he said. 'Not valid in California.'

'What!'

'Okay, okay,' he said, laughing. 'I'll do it for you just this once. But only because I could never say no to a pretty face. One Coke, one diet cola, and one Chablis coming up.'

Sondra watched him as he pulled out glasses and filled them. Sliding the three glasses towards her, he said, 'That'll be a buck fifty.' She pulled a single bill and three quarters out of her purse, saying, 'Keep the change.'

'Thank *you*,' he said, flipping the extra quarter in the air and pocketing it.

Sondra saw right away that she was going to have trouble with the three glasses; they could not be carried in a triangle because of the wineglass. While she was trying to decide whether to make two trips or call one of her friends over, Mr Gilhooley came down to her end of the bar. He was wiping his hands on a towel and saying something that, against the background of 'Monday Monday,' sounded like, 'Lookin' for somethin', Doc?'

'I need a lemon wedge, Gil. Where do you keep your lemon wedges?'

Gilhooley made a grunting sound, produced a small empty bowl, and, muttering something about somebody not being on their toes, headed towards a door that obviously led to the kitchen.

Sondra was still standing there, her hands cupped around the three glasses on the bar, her lips slightly parted. Now the man smiled at her, a little sheepishly, and said, 'Sorry about that.'

'You're not a bartender.'

'No, I'm not.'

'And I gave you a quarter!'

'Believe me, I can use it. You know what they say about residents not having two coins to rub together. Now all I need is another quarter –'

'You're a doctor?'

'Rick Parsons.' He thrust a hand across the bar. 'And I know you're Sondra Mallone, five foot five.'

When Gilhooley came back with a bowl full of lemon wedges and set it down on the bar, Rick Parsons paid no heed, no longer interested in lemons. 'So,' he said. 'Are you a nurse?'

'I'm a medical student. First year.'

Dr Parsons leaned against the bar, growing more interested by the minute. 'No kidding.'

From their table, Ruth was observing Sondra in what appeared to be a friendly conversation with a good-looking stranger. She watched them a moment – the man's obvious interest in Sondra, and Sondra's fluid ease with him, as though she'd known him for years. In their six weeks as roommates, Ruth had expected Sondra to be very popular and a heavy dater; but things had turned out quite the opposite. Sondra was popular, yes, she received male attention wherever she went. But she showed no interest in going further; she was able to keep her distance and avoid involvements. Ruth marvelled at such a skill, to attract men and yet turn them away without any hard feelings. How did she do it? But more important – why? Well, Ruth decided, returning to her menu, maybe the answer is right *there*. Attracting men was too easy for Sondra, there was no challenge in it.

Laying aside her menu, Ruth turned to Mickey. 'You feeling okay?'

'Hm? Oh yes, I'm okay. I just can't stop thinking about that dissection.'

'Yes, me too. When I was a kid my father was always telling us his old medical school stories. Some were pretty horrible.' Ruth lined up the fork, knife, and spoon on her napkin in three perfect parallel lines. 'My father graduated first in his class, out of over a hundred students.'

Mickey nodded vaguely but seemed to withdraw from the conversation, and so Ruth settled back to look over the crowd.

Many of them had familiar faces. Most of the young men were from the medical school and they had discarded the suits and ties mandatory on campus and wore jeans, T-shirts, army fatigues, and stylish bellbottoms. Quite a few were with women, most of whom were in nursing uniforms, but there was also the usual element of med school groupies – girls from nearby El Segundo and Santa Monica in Heidi dresses

42

and combat boots looking for a free meal and a doctor boyfriend. It was a lively, animated crowd with continuous eruptions here and there of laughter. But now that Ruth could sit back and study the crowd objectively, she saw that, for many, the gaiety was but a veneer. A cover-up for the contagion of fear that had gripped the Castillo freshman class.

Each table's flickering candle illuminated nervous faces, shifting eyes, haunted looks. Beer was gulped too fast, cigarettes were smoked in chains; laughter was a dash too shrill, speech was staccato. The signs were there, as readable as billboards: the med school terror was setting in.

Ruth was as familiar with it as with her own anxious heartbeat. It seemed that no matter how much she studied, devouring three-by-five cards during a quick break, memorising, reading, diagramming, taking down every word of a lecture, she still felt she wasn't doing enough. While her roommates managed to find some time for other pursuits – Mickey visited her mother in the nursing home on weekends and Sondra seemed to spend long solitary hours on the beach – Ruth didn't think she could afford such a luxury. But then, her roommates weren't as driven as she was. Mickey had once even declared that she would be happy to graduate in the top third of the class. What kind of ambition was that? Why run the race if not for first place?

The competition was staggering. The eighty-seven freshmen (three had already dropped out) were the cream of their four-year colleges, the best of the best, and each and every one of them ran the race with the same determination as Ruth: after all, there was family honour at stake, or the debt to parents who had cashed in life insurance to send a son through medical school, or there was family tradition – sons following fathers into medicine – or there was a whole clan of hopeful people back home waiting for the new doctor in the family.

You could cut the tension with a scalpel. Dean Hoskins, after his soaring opening with the oath, had brought them all back to earth: 'Work hard and you'll make it. Those who think they can breeze through won't make it. Of course, we'd love to have a hundred per cent success rate, but the law of

43

averages is a stern law. Not all of you sitting here today will get that diploma.'

Right away everyone had started sneaking looks at everyone else in the amphitheatre to see if there was a mark, a pentagram on the forehead of the doomed, to know ahead of time if one should stay and fight or step gracefully down now. But it hadn't daunted Ruth Shapiro. On the contrary, the darker the omens the stiffer her resolve.

And thinking about it now, suddenly aware that she was sitting comfortably back with her arms folded, Ruth abruptly sat up, reached down into her purse, and pulled out a stack of three-by-five cards. Pulling off the rubber band and rolling it onto her wrist, she read the first card to herself: 'Name the specific attributes of the B Lymphocyte system.'

Back at the bar Dr Rick Parsons was saying, 'Why Africa?' and Sondra was looking in the big mirror behind him at the reflection of her two roommates. Mickey appeared to be in a trance while Ruth was going over her cards. Sondra knew she should get back to them; the ice was melting in their drinks. 'Would you care to join me and my friends, Dr Parsons?'

'It's Rick, please, and sure, I'd love to join you. Just a second, let me get my jacket.'

Sondra watched him thread his way back through the tables to the corner where a group sat in smoke and candlelight, three men and a woman, all in white jackets. She watched him explain something to them, they all looked her way, then they nodded and waved him off. He came back with a suede jacket hooked on one finger and slung over his shoulder, and it made him, Sondra couldn't help thinking, look very sexy.

'It's quite a shock, isn't it?' Rick Parsons asked a few minutes later, after he and Sondra had brought the drinks to the table and introductions had been made. 'To discover that one hour of med school is the equivalent of a week in college. And it's a blow to the ego.'

Ruth smiled politely and looked at the next card: 'Describe *Extrinsic* Mechanism for Initiating Clotting.' While Dr Parsons went on about his own freshman terror of years ago, Ruth mentally recited, *Release of tissue factor and tissue phospholipids* . . .

'All these guys in here,' Rick was saying, waving an arm that glinted a gold Rolex at the wrist, 'were the tops in their graduating class back in college. They come here cocky and confident and smug, and then *wham*, the Rude Awakening.'

Sondra laughed. 'By the second week I felt like the white queen in Alice in Wonderland, the one who had to run just to keep in place!'

'It's true,' said Rick, watching Ruth grind into her cards. 'You've discovered by now that one missed lecture can never be made up. You lose an hour in med school and it's lost for good.'

Ruth flipped to the next card: 'Describe *Instrinsic* Mechanism for Initiating Clotting,' and she closed her eyes and thought, *Activation of Factor XII and release of platelet phospholipids by blood trauma...*

'Is your friend like this all the time?' Rick asked Sondra. 'It *is* all right to relax once in a while.'

'Ruth never lets up. She's Superwoman.'

Parsons turned a casual eye to Mickey, thinking that her green eyes were pretty, if only she'd brush the hair away from them. When Mickey felt his scrutiny of her face she shifted self-consciously in her chair. Clearly it hadn't been a good idea to come here after all. The company was too close, she didn't fit. She wanted to be left alone, alone with her thoughts and her worries. The anatomy dissection had touched a raw spot in Mickey, a tender, vulnerable spot, and now she was bathed in pain.

The cadaver on her table had been an elderly woman, not too old, early sixties, and, externally, physically fine. But she had died of 'complications arising from initial pneumococcal pneumonia' – in this case, an extrapulmonary focus of the pneumococcal infection in the endocardium. What had begun as a simple upper respiratory infection had resulted in death.

At this moment, Mickey's mother had pneumonia.

Mrs Long had moved to the nursing home last year when a fall had required her right hip to be pinned. Although the fracture had healed and Mrs Long had been able to get around on a walker – being one of the active, spritely residents of the home – an unexpected and violent onset of pneumonia four weeks ago had laid her to bed and melted eighteen pounds off her frail body. Mickey had gone to see her last Sunday, taking flowers and magazines, and was shocked to see how wasted and debilitated her normally spry mother had become.

And the nursing home bill had shot up. Now her mother was getting acute nursing care, medications, oxygen, lab tests, and frequent doctor visits. There was no insurance to cover what Medicaid did not, so the nearest relative, Mickey, had to find a way to pay the bills. If not, then Mrs Long would have to be transferred to a county facility, away from her friends and the sunny garden of the private home that she had come to love. Mickey couldn't have that. She'd make the sacrifices somehow, to keep her mother happy. After all the years Mrs Long had worked to support herself and her child, often working two shifts to pay the doctor bills that her daughter's blemished face had generated, how could Mickey abandon her now?

Well, a job was out – the school forbade students to work during the school year, and besides, there wasn't time. Maybe she wasn't as fanatical about studying as Ruth was, but Mickey was still putting in over thirty hours a week on the books. How was she going to come up with the extra money?

'Neurosurgery,' Rick Parsons was saying in answer to Sondra's question. 'I'm the senior resident. This is my final year.'

'Why neurosurgery?' she asked, bringing the wineglass to her lips.

Ruth glanced up from 'the antithrombin action of fibrin' to watch for a moment the interplay going on across the table. Rick Parsons was showing obvious interest in Sondra and she was treating him with her usual off-putting ease. Ruth thought about Steve Schonfeld and what an exciting man he was to be with. After the Ingmar Bergman film he had kissed her long and passionately, and Ruth had started worrying right there and then how she was going to find time for a romance in her demanding schedule. But she would find the time because Ruth, unlike Sondra, very much wanted involvement with a man.

'You never did explain why Africa,' Rick Parsons said, slowly stirring his drink. He was sitting sideways in his chair, one elbow on the table, the other arm draped over the back of the chair. His knees were just touching Sondra's.

They talked for a long time, pausing only to order hamburgers and more wine, with Sondra telling of her hope to go to Africa and Parsons illuminating for her the cloistered world of the operating room. 'You've never observed surgery?' he asked. 'I guarantee that with one taste of surgery you'll forget Africa. I tell you what. I'm doing a craniotomy in the morning. Play hooky and come and watch. Fourth floor, ask for Miss Timmons, she'll get you in.'

While Mickey scribbled figures on her napkin – estimating savings from eating fewer meals and earnings from selling blood – and while Ruth moved on in her cards to the role of Vitamin D in controlling the plasma calcium concentration, Sondra Mallone agreed to meet Rick Parsons the following morning in St Catherine's surgical suite.

# Chapter Six

'I don't get it,' said the nurse, shaking her head. 'These clothes make everyone else look frumpy and dowdy. On you they look like Rudi Gernreich originals. It's disgusting.'

Two snaps were missing in the back of Sondra's dress so Miss Timmons had to tape the gap closed with a wide swath of adhesive. Since it was impossible to find a surgery dress in perfect condition, nearly every nurse in the OR suite walked around in a state of repair; and since the stacks of dresses in the locker room were haphazardly filled by the hospital's laundry service, a nurse rarely found the right size. But Sondra's had turned out to be one of those infrequent good fits, the green wasn't too laundered out, but a nice vivid hue, and no pockets dangled. Even the awful paper bonnet looked good on her, attractively setting off her dusky colour, high cheekbones, and almond eyes.

Miss Timmons laughed again and muttered, 'Watch out for the wolves.'

It felt strange to be in the surgical suite for the first time. It had to come eventually, Sondra knew, but she hadn't expected to take this big step so soon – not until her third year when all hospital clerkships began; yet here she was, only six weeks into medical school, fresh from four years at the University of Arizona with no medical or hospital background whatsoever, invading this inner sanctum.

The place had a curious bathroom effect, covered in tile, chilly, full of echoes, and everything made of shiny chrome, glass, clear plastic. The lighting was brighter-than-sun, cold-white and harsh. A sealed, hermetic environment, it had no windows to remind one of time of day or weather or the rest of the world. There was a maze of small green-tiled rooms, all reverberating with talk, the sound of running water, the clink of bottles. A soapy, antiseptic smell filled the air; vents discharged a recirculated atmosphere that felt cool and dry on the bare skin. And it was busy, so busy that one's first exposure to it was intimidating, almost frightening.

Miss Timmons drew Sondra out of the mainstream, pulled a flowered Johnson & Johnson paper mask out of a box, and showed Sondra how to tie it on. 'Pinch the nose like this. That's right. People who wear glasses have a fogging problem.'

Once her mask was up Sondra realised why most of the nurses in the OR suite were wearing a lot of eye makeup. The eyes were the only part of the face that showed!

'There are just a few rules we should go over,' Miss Timmons said. On this hectic morning, the noise and bustle in St Catherine's surgical suite was almost overwhelming, but the head nurse, at the request of Dr Parsons, was taking time to orient this new medical student. 'Don't touch anything. Don't even move. I'll place you somewhere in the room and you are to stay there, rooted to the spot like a tree. If you have to move, ask the circulating nurse first – she'll be the one who isn't sterile. It's going to be crowded in there since it's a brain case.'

'Will I scrub?'

'Scrub? Bless you, honey, you'll be eight feet away from the table! No, we don't let the uninitiated get near the sterile field. Sorry, no gown, no gloves.'

The head nurse hurried off, leaving Sondra to stand by the scrub sinks. She watched stretchers come by with recumbent patients on them and go away empty, red anaesthesia machines being trundled out of one room and into the next; she heard orders being shouted on the coolly circulating air. Someone ran by with a panicked expression, two men in greens lounged against a wall with their arms folded, and nurses with green gowns flapping hurried by with trays of steaming instruments.

A man in greens, with mask up and hair concealed, came to the sinks where Sondra was standing, popped open a surgical scrub sponge, then slowly looked Sondra up and down as he wet his arms. 'Hi,' he said, his eyes smiling. 'You new here?'

'I'm just visting.'

His eyebrows went up.

'I'm a medical student,' Sondra said, and she saw the interest immediately die in his eyes.

She stepped out of the way when two more men in greens came up to the sinks, their faces hidden behind masks. They popped open sponges and ran water over their hands and arms as they talked about central venous pressure lines. When one of them spotted Sondra, he leaned away from the sink and said, 'Hel-lo there! Where have I been all your life?'

Sondra laughed softly behind her mask.

The second surgeon turned to look at her, stared a moment, then said, 'You have to forgive my friend, he's a jerk. You're one of the new nurses, aren't you?'

Before Sondra could answer, the first surgeon said, 'Don't talk to him, he's brain-damaged. Been sniffing the Ethrane.'

The second one threw down his sponge, came up close to her, and said with mischief in his eyes. 'Listen, life's too short for all this. What's your phone number and what time do you get off work?'

A nurse came up just then and said, 'Dr Billings, the lab just called. They say there's no blood for your patient.'

'What!' Reaching for a paper towel, he marched away from the sinks, with the nurse close on his heels. The other surgeon, still scrubbing, continued to stare at Sondra.

After a few minutes he said, 'So how come you're the only one around here not running around like a chicken with its head cut off? Is this your orientation or something?'

'I don't work here. I'm only a visitor.'

'Ah.' He lathered up his second arm. 'That explains it. Timmons never lets one of her nurses stand around. So who are you here to observe?'

'Dr Parsons.'

'Oh, right. I saw it on the schedule. Craniotomy. Ever seen a brain operation before?'

'No.'

'I tell you what. If you make it through to the end I'll buy you dinner. What do you say?'

He had nice brown eyes; Sondra could see, with thick black lashes. But that was *all* she could see. Like everyone else, his hair was completely covered, face hidden, and in the baggy pyjama-like greens it was hard to judge his build. Or even his age.

50

'I don't think so,' she said with a smile.

'Don't think what? That you'll make it through the craniotomy?'

'Oh, I *know* I'll make it through that.'

He dropped his sponge into a bucket, then rinsed each arm, from fingertip to elbow, careful to make sure the water ran off at the elbows. As he moved away from the sinks with his hands held up, he said, 'Forget Parsons' case. I'm doing something really interesting. Ever see a bunionectomy before?'

Sondra laughed again and was relieved to see Rick walk up. 'Sanford, you old rake,' Parsons said, clapping the other surgeon on the back. 'You sure know how to sweet-talk the ladies, don't you?'

'Who is she, Rick? A nurse in your office?'

'Sondra Mallone, meet Sanford Jones, orthopaedic surgeon. Sanford, this is Sondra. A *medical student.*'

Dr Jones blinked at her, pinked slightly on the forehead, then hurried away to his room. Rick folded his arms and leaned against the sink. 'Some of these guys move in on the nurses, whom they think for some reason are fair game. But women doctors stop them cold.' He paused. 'I see you made it.'

'There aren't many things that would lure me away from Physiology this morning, not with midterms next week. But this was too important to miss!'

'Who do you have for Physiology? Art Rhinelander? Well, if I recall correctly, just concentrate on DNA and nucleotides and you've got it made.' As he reached up for a mask and tied the lower strings around his neck, Sondra couldn't help making the observation that Rick Parsons looked awfully good in those tacky green 'pyjamas.' And when the mask went on, she noticed for the first time how attractive his grey eyes were. Once the mask was snugly in place, he reached up and pulled the top strings down so that the mask hung from his neck onto his chest. 'Timmons is a stickler for maskup in the suite, but I insist on making certain exceptions.'

He pulled a surgical glove out of the pocket of his scrub shirt, stretched it this way and that a few times, then, to Sondra's surprise, brought the glove up to his lips and started to blow into it. 'Let me tell you about this case,' he said between puffs. 'Our patient's symptoms started slowly: ataxia on the left side – that is, gradual loss of motor coordination; nystagmus, which is constant involuntary movement of the eyeball; headaches and vomiting due to increased intracranial pressure; head tilted to one side. Skull X-rays show a spread of the cranial sutures, ventriculograms demonstrate hydrocephalus, and angiograms reveal an avascular mass in the cerebellar hemisphere. Diagnosis: cystic brain tumour.'

When the glove was completely inflated, looking like a honeydew melon with a cockscomb on top, Rick tied the cuff in a knot, took a felt-tip pen out of his pocket, and proceeded to draw a clown's face on it. 'We're going to open the patient's skull and see what the mass is. Still want to watch?'

'Yes.'

'Good. Now pull down your mask, I want to introduce you to our patient.'

Sondra received a shock. Around the corner from the scrub sinks, lying on a stretcher miles too big for his little body, was a child no more than six or seven years old. He looked pale and sleepy-eyed, and his head was snuggled in a big surgical bonnet that had ridden up to expose his freshly shaven scalp.

'Hi, Tommy,' said Rick, coming up alongside the stretcher and laying a hand on the boy's arm. 'I'm Dr Parsons, remember me?'

Two big blue eyes stared up at him for a long moment, then the boy slowly said, 'Yes, I remember.'

Turning to Sondra, Rick said very quietly, 'The slow cerebration is due to increased intracranial pressure. He also had diplopia and blurred vision.' To the boy he said, 'Tommy, I brought you a present,' and when Rick produced the glove-clown from behind his back, although Tommy was slow to respond, the delight eventually lit up his face.

Feeling her eyes sting with tears, Sondra turned away. 'Come on,' said Rick, gently taking her by the arm. 'I'm going to have to abandon you for a while. Put your mask up now or Timmons will throw us both out. I only take it down for kids, so they can see my face and recognise me and not be so scared.'

'Rick, what are his –'

'Chances?' Dr Parsons led Sondra into the operating room and positioned her in a corner, away from the equipment and sterile tables. 'We won't know till we get there. If it's a tumour, his chances aren't so good. If it's a cyst, they're better. And if we can find the wall nodule of the cyst and get it out, then his chances are excellent. If you want to say a prayer, we'd appreciate it.'

It wouldn't be until years later that Sondra would be able to look back and make sense of the scene. It was a pastiche of chrome and green, of too many people and too much equipment, of unnatural noises and long cords and bottles that filled and emptied steadily; arctic lights and instruments going up shiny clean and coming down rusty with blood; orders snapped and vital signs called out and all sorts of counts taken and measurements read off and long pauses during which Rick and his assistant worked over the landscape of hills and valleys, all mauve and wet, that was Tommy's brain. They had made a midline incision, that is, Tommy was sitting up facing away from them with head bowed; they worked at the base of the skull, opening up the first cervical vertebra and the foramen magnum. Both surgeons wore headlights, like miners' lamps. After suctioning out a yellowish, viscous fluid, Rick turned to the circulating nurse and said, 'Call pathology, please. We're ready to hand off specimens.' And then to the room at large, for the benefit of the two nurses, the anaesthetist, and Sondra, Rick said, 'The mass is seventy per cent cystic. We are going to biopsy the cyst wall and then search for the mural nodule that is secreting this material.'

After Dr Williams, the pathologist, took the specimens back to the lab where he would examine them microscopically, the operating team settled into a wait, Rick bracing himself with one hand against the table and leaning on one leg, his assistant retiring to a stool, and even the scrub nurse stepping away and taking a seat with her hands folded into a sterile towel. Rick turned to Sondra, his mask damp beneath the eyes, the front of his gown smeared with blood, and beckoned to her. 'You can step closer than that. There, that's fine. Now bend close, I want you to see this.'

53

With an instrument called a Penfiled Four, Rick delicately pointed to Tommy's ivory cerebellum, down through the soft and buttery tissue held apart by a ribbon retractor. 'The cyst is in the cerebellar hemisphere and not in the brain stem. Notice how the inferior part of the cerebellum dimples when I touch it. You can see the distended aqueduct and that the fourth ventricle is occluded, causing the hydrocephalus. I've inserted a catheter into the ventricle to decompress and then I needled the cyst to get the fluid out and decompress along the folia. I am suspecting cystic astrocytoma, which is very common among the brain disorders children can get. If I'm right and if we can get all the nodule out, then Tommy's chances are excellent.'

When Dr Williams came back a few minutes later, returning the tissue specimens to the circulating nurse, who then dropped them into jars of formalin, he said, 'Looks like juvenile astrocytoma, Rick. The cystic wall is definitely gliotic.'

The team reassembled and spent the next hour excising the nodule from the cyst wall, delicately, gingerly, taking care to get it all out to prevent recurrence, then Rick stood away from the table to allow the circulating nurse to wipe off his perspiring forehead. To Sondra he said, 'I'm going to start closing him up now. And first I'll tunnel a catheter under the scalp to the cisterna magna so that the cerebro-spinal fluid is shunted.' He turned to his scrub nurse. 'Lots of irrigation now, please. Bipolar forceps.'

The pace eased up, became relaxed; as the anaesthetist turned on the radio to KJOI – 'If you're coming to San Francisco, be sure to wear a flower in your hair . . .' The skull was wired closed, the scalp stitched back together, and an enormous white bandage was wound round and round Tommy's head. Then the nurses took over, washing Tommy with clean sponges and towels and transferring him to the gurney, while the two surgeons peeled off their paper gowns revealing, to Sondra's surprise, scrub suits soaked right through with sweat.

Rick picked up the patient's chart, murmured something about talking to the boy's parents, then walked to the door where he turned, pulled down his mask, and said to Sondra,

'Give me twenty minutes and I'll buy you a cup of coffee.'

It was a strange feeling; Sondra couldn't quite figure it out, why she felt this way. Sitting at the bright orange table in the garish orange and yellow hospital cafeteria, she sipped her coffee and looked around. It wasn't crowded at this afternoon hour – a few visitors, change-of-shift nurses, candy-stripers giggling in a corner – and for that Sondra was thankful. She had a splitting headache.

She looked over at Rick, who hadn't yet changed out of his greens. He waved an arm as he talked into the phone – did he look angry? From where she sat Sondra couldn't tell. They'd only just got to the table with their coffee when he'd been paged over the address system.

She looked away from him and concentrated on her coffee. What *was* this odd feeling nagging at her?

The surgery had taken five hours and, on their way down in the elevator, Rick had told Sondra that Tommy had excellent chances of getting well. 'Children have such remarkable recuperative powers.'

'Will the cyst come back?' she had asked.

'I don't think so. I think we got all of the mural nodule that was producing the fluid. His pressure is back to normal so he should have a return of coordination in a couple of weeks.'

'Will he undergo radiation?'

'Not for juvenile astrocytoma. Tommy's very lucky.'

Yes, Tommy was very lucky. It had been a difficult case, a scary case, but one with a happy ending. So why had it left Sondra feeling so... peculiar?

Looking up at the huge clock on the wall, she suddenly became conscious of precious time trickling past her. Anatomy lab had ended half an hour ago. Both Ruth and Mickey would be at the apartment now, Mickey starting dinner, Ruth bent over her books. *That's what I should be doing,* Sondra chided herself. *Midterms next week!*

She looked over at Rick Parsons again. There was no denying it, he was a very attractive man. And Sondra was drawn to him. Was that the unidentifiable feeling that plagued her now, filling her with a vague sense of unease? Was it the fear of a relationship coming into her life at this stage and complicating things? Without a doubt medical school demanded every moment of one's time; it required the full attention of every brain cell for total dedication and determination. Look at JoAnne, the fourth unmarried woman in the class. She had met someone during the first week of school, fallen in love, and dropped out to get married and live in Maine. But then, on the other side of the coin, there was Ruth. Sondra knew that Ruth had had several boyfriends in the past – a steady in high school, and then a series of 'encounters,' as she called them, in college – and now she was dating Steve Schonfeld, the fourth-year student they had run into at Gilhooley's last night. Ruth had been out with him only twice and said she was interested in going to bed with him, but at the same time she was miraculously managing to avoid the complications that invariably accompanied a new romantic interest.

Sondra envied Ruth's detachment. She knew she herself could never be like that. Sondra either loved intensely or not at all, with no comfortable middle ground where everything was in balance. Unlike Ruth, Sondra could not get physically involved with a man and yet stay emotionally unattached. It was for that reason that Sondra had never really had a boyfriend, that dates had never culminated in anything, that she preferred men friends rather than lovers: her need to be totally and unconditionally free to pursue her career. It was no crime to be a virgin at twenty-two (although a few of her friends back in Phoenix had other opinions); there would be time enough, once she was established as a doctor, to find the right man and allow herself to get involved.

So why, sitting now in the cool cafeteria of St Catherine's-By-the-Sea and waiting for the senior resident in neurosurgery to come back to her table, was Sondra feeling strangely out of place with herself, as though things were not quite right?

'Sorry about that,' said Rick, returning to his chair and dropping into it with a sigh. 'Emergency call from my stockbroker!'

Sondra tried to return his smile. Her headache was starting to lift, but the queer feeling that had followed her out of the operating room persisted.

Rick didn't say anything for a few moments, instead he absently stirred his coffee, seemingly deep in thought. Finally he looked up and said, 'It knocked you out, didn't it?'

She blinked. 'I beg your pardon?'

'Surgery, it's knocked you out. I can tell. You have that look.'

Sondra scrutinized his face and she began to understand something – something about herself that he, a virtual stranger, had been able to sum up in a few words, but which had eluded Sondra herself.

*Surgery knocked you out.* Of course. *That* was it. The nameless ill-ease that had been gnawing at her since she changed back into her street clothes. It had nothing to do with love or Rick Parsons at all, or with her fears about relationships and commitments; it went deeper than that. It was a kind of primal awe, an ancestral fear, a wondering that had, until now, been latent within Sondra Mallone, a deep current running under her soul that before she'd only been vaguely aware of but which now, triggered by Rick Parson's words, flooded her with illumination. All of a sudden, for the first time, she understood *what it was all about.*

'It happened to me that way, too,' Rick said quietly. 'But I wasn't in medical school at the time, I was in high school, and my dad, who's a surgeon, had me come to watch him operate one day. It was a simple gall bladder operation, but it struck me just the same. It turned on the lights, so to speak.'

Sondra felt a strange lightness lift her up, her headache was gone; she felt insanely like shouting, 'Yes! Yes!' Instead she folded her arms and leaned forward on the table. 'Do you know,' she said earnestly, 'that until now I'd honestly thought I was the most dedicated medical student on the face of the earth? I really thought I had heard the Call. And I had, in a way. But it was nothing like *this*.' She unfolded her arms and spread out her hands. 'Like you said, it's knocked me out.'

'First time in surgery usually has one of two effects on a person. Either you're completely turned off – and that happens a lot, believe me – or you get fired up and dedicated, right on the spot. That's why I invited you to come and watch. Nothing converts like firsthand experience.'

Sondra clasped her hands tightly on the tabletop. Rick was right, so right. That was exactly what had happened – her first time had awakened in Sondra the staggering comprehension of *life and death*. To take a boy like Tommy, who seemed doomed, with no hope, and restore him to his life and his family ... *That* was what all the green and chrome chaos had been about this morning, the running and the shouting and the apparent disregard for human dignity – all that had boiled down in the end to just one thing: *preserving life*.

'That's where you really see it, you know,' Rick continued, reading her thoughts. 'In surgery. Oh, you see some dramatic things in the ER, and of course giving life is what OB is all about. But surgery is for me where the *real* lifesaving is done. Diseased bodies, broken bodies, even the ugly bodies the plastic surgeons bring in; we fix them up and send them out new and whole. It's the number-one high, Sondra. That's what you should aim for, too.'

She shook her head no. Rick may have been right in naming the feeling that had shadowed her from surgery – yes, it *was* awesome to see life and death literally at work – but he was off the mark in seeing it as her future calling. Her experience in the operating room today hadn't injected Sondra with the ambition to become a surgeon; surgery all by itself didn't interest her. What it *had* done, however, was reinforce the dream of going out into the world and taking her skills where they were desperately needed. Tommy was lucky, he had St Catherine's and Dr Parsons. But what about all those other people, the millions of suffering others who had no modern medical centres and no trained physicians to help them? What about the people like her real mother and father – the poor, the desperate, the ones without hope?

Sondra may have heard the medical call years ago, but it had been nothing like the trumpet that now summoned her. And it filled her with a feeling she had never really felt before, not since she was twelve and had discovered the truth about herself. Her day with Rick Parsons had given her at last a sure sense of place, of belonging, of direction.

Now she knew, now she was certain.

# Chapter Seven

The very last thing Mickey wanted to do tonight was go to a party.

'It'll do you good,' said Sondra as she watched Mickey apply a fresh layer of C-over to her cheek. 'You live like a cloistered nun, Mickey. Ruth and I are your only friends.'

'You're all I need.'

'You know what I mean.'

Yes, Mickey knew what she meant. She meant *socialising*, mingling with other people, exchanging ideas. It was easy for Sondra, with her outgoing personality and exotic looks; and Ruth, so down to earth and sure of herself, was having no trouble getting along with people, dating Steve Schonfeld. Mickey's two roommates hadn't the faintest idea what it was like to go through life with the mark of the thirteenth witch on their faces. The thought of this New Year's Eve party positively immobilised her: everyone was going to be there, close company and prying eyes.

But Sondra was absolutely set on her going and Mickey felt deeply obligated to Sondra.

Four weeks ago, right after midterms, Mickey had fainted in the kitchen. Only Sondra had been home, Ruth was out with Steve. It had just been a faint, nothing serious, but it had frightened them both; and then when Sondra had learned the reason for the fainting spell – that Mickey had been selling her blood to the hospital, and skipping lunches to save money – she had demanded to know why Mickey thought so little of her roommates that she hadn't come to them for help. Of *course* they would help her meet the costs of her mother's nursing home; Sondra could well afford it and Ruth, when she heard about it, volunteered to pay more of the expenses.

It had been a beautiful gesture, and Mickey had started

feeling better right away. She stopped selling the blood, began to eat proper meals, and went to the nursing home with her mother's favourite flowers. But the incident had done more than that – Sondra and Ruth had rescued her from despair. It had made Mickey realise that, for the very first time in her life, she had someone other than her mother and herself to count on – she had made real friends.

So now, when Sondra seemed so insistent on her going to the New Year's Eve party, Mickey was reluctant to let her down.

'Is Ruth going, too?' she asked as she leaned close to the mirror to make sure none of the stain showed.

Sondra put her hands on her hips and shook her head. These two! One afraid of life, the other married to books. Here it was, New Year's Eve, and what was Ruth Shapiro doing? Studying! And not only studying, but studying for a class she wasn't even *in* yet!

'I've been working on her all day. I'll wear her down, you'll see.' It was important to Sondra that her two friends go to the party; she wanted them to have fun.

Sondra was looking forward to the party because she knew Rick Parsons was going to be there. Since the day of the brain operation they had shared exactly one spur of the moment dinner and an interrupted lunch. The dinner had been the same day as Tommy's surgery when, on impulse, Rick had taken Sondra out for an Italian dinner, during which they had gone back and forth on the issue that had brought them together: Rick's determination to lure Sondra away from Africa and into neurosurgery. He hadn't won on that round, and had tried again a couple of weeks later over a pickup lunch in the hospital that had been cut short by an emergency. He was a very compelling man, hard to resist, and Sondra was actually beginning to have second thoughts about Africa when there really was, as he was insisting, so much to be done here at home.

Rick Parsons was compelling in other ways, too. For the first time in her life, Sondra saw a man with whom she could very easily fall in love. And she was wondering, as she started to get ready for the party, if she was going to let herself fall tonight.

In her room, sitting on her bed with her back propped against the wall, Ruth listened to the sounds of her roommates getting ready for New Year's Eve. Sondra didn't know it, but Ruth was torn: she wanted to go, and then again she didn't.

Sondra might make fun of it but Ruth saw nothing strange in studying for a class that hadn't even started yet. After all, that was how Ruth had been able to get such high scores on her midterms a few weeks ago – by studying when everyone else was goofing off. Twelfth in the class, that's where Ruth Shapiro stood right now. Out of a class of eighty-four, she ranked twelfth, while her roommates ranked nineteen and twenty-six. They were in the top third and that satisfied them. Not Ruth. In fact, while the other students had been over at Gilhooley's celebrating their grades or drowning their sorrows, Ruth had been back at the apartment cracking the books again.

She had almost called home with the good news, but she'd stopped in the middle of dialling. She could just hear him: 'What? Twelfth place? How many are in your class, Ruthie, twelve?' It wouldn't be enough for him, she knew that. Mike Shapiro was impressed only with absolutes, with perfection, like her brother Joshua at West Point and Max at Northwestern. Stiff competition but Ruth knew she could meet it.

Sondra knocked on her door, then walked in without waiting for an invitation. 'Come on, Ruth, SAPs doesn't even start for another month!'

That was Sondra's name for it, SAPs. Actually, the name of the course was Student As Physician and it was an experimental programme just initiated at Castillo. The vast majority of medical schools across the country started their students out with two years of sciences, only letting them set their first tentative toe into the hospital – the real swim of medicine – in their third year. By that time it was usually too late for those who discovered they didn't like the hospital environment to drop out. The administration of Castillo had come up with a new idea and this freshman class was going to be the guinea pigs: as first-year students, still in their sciences, they were going to go through a six-week

61

orientation programme over at St Catherine's. They would be outfitted with white jackets and stethoscopes, they would make rounds with real doctors and see real patients. They weren't going to *do* anything, they would just observe, but it would be enough to weed out at an early stage the ones not suited for medicine.

Ruth was getting ready for it now. She already had her stethoscope and was poring through her secondhand copy of *A Guide to Physical Examination*. She was concentrating on the vital signs – temperature, pulse, respiration – because they were the very foundation upon which the entire structure of modern medicine had been built.

'Ruth Shapiro,' said Sondra. 'I'm going to hold my breath and turn purple until you get dressed!'

Ruth eyed her roommate. Sondra was so excited that her skin glowed a dull bronze. Who could blame her? Rick Parsons *was* someone to fall in love with. Unlike Steve Schonfeld, who had shown his true colours...

'Won't Steve be expecting you to be there?'

Ruth hadn't told her roommates about the awful scene she had had with Steve. She preferred to bury the incident, pretend that he had never walked into her life. How could he have been so uncaring, so unsympathetic?

Ruth sat for one more thoughtful moment, then realised that the campus and apartment building were probably going to be too noisy for studying anyway. She tossed her book aside. 'All right, you win. I'll go.'

Ruth wore her best outfit – a pair of navy wool knit pants that tapered out from the hips and were full in the leg, and a white blouse with lace ruffles at the throat and wrists – just in case Steve Schonfeld was there and she could show him that their breakup didn't mean a thing to her. Mickey chose a tea-leaf-coloured dress and a bulky oatmeal sweater. Sondra slipped into a simple jersey shift of buttercup yellow and tied a matching yellow scarf in her black hair and the effect, on her, was sensational.

They decided it was simpler to walk the distance from the apartment to Encinitas Hall, and soon joined others in the biting December air, drawn like moths to the bright lights and loud music pouring from Encinitas Hall.

They had never seen it so crowded. A fire burned in the enormous flagstone fireplace, candles flickered in the wrought-iron wall sconces, and tables were loaded with food and drink. Absolutely everyone, it seemed, was there and talking at once, and in the background thumped the timely rhythm of the new musical *Hair*. The three roommates stood at the very edge of a sea of culture and counterculture: medical students in suits and ties with dates in mini-skirts and textured tights, professors in three-piece suits with wives in stylish Cossack hats; there was a strange smell in the air, not quite incense; coloured lights flashed from stereo speakers as the 'Age of Aquarius' dawned; and occasional words rose distinct above the roar: heart transplants, cyclamates, Onassis, Vietnam.

Resisting the urge to turn around and go back to the apartment, Ruth said, 'I guess I'll grab a beer,' and decided to press into the crowd. Behind her, Mickey looked for the bathroom and Sondra searched for Rick Parsons.

On her way to the table where beer and wine were being hastily handed out, Ruth ran into Adrienne, the married woman student in the freshman class, who was holding two beers and looking around. 'Have you seen my husband?' she asked Ruth. 'He's on call. I hope he didn't get called in and leave me here like this!' Her laugh had a false ring.

'Has he heard about his internship yet?' Ruth asked.

'No, but it's either going to be St Catherine's or UCLA. We're sure of that.'

'If he gets UCLA, where will you live? I mean, isn't it too far for him to drive from here?'

'Oh! Don't you know? I'm pregnant! Yeah, no kidding! What're the chances, you know? I fell into the eight per cent failure rate with a diaphragm! But we're really happy about it. I mean, our first kid.'

'How are you going to manage it, school and all?'

'Oh well, I'm going to take a leave. The kid will be born in the summer and we can't afford anyone to take care of it so I'm going to take next year off. When Jim starts his residency we'll have a bit more money and be able to afford a sitter and he'll also be able to spend some time with the kid. Then I'll come back to Castillo.'

Ruth stared at her.

'Dean Hoskins has already okayed it. I'll be back. I'll finish. It's just that Jim's career is more important right now, you know? If he put off doing his internship this year, you know, to stay home with the baby while I continued here at Castillo, well, he might not get such a good opportunity again. So we figured, let him finish first and get established and then I'll come back. You know?'

'Yes, I know. Good luck, Adrienne. We'll miss you.'

As Ruth resumed her push towards the bar, she couldn't help but think: It's down to the three of us now...

She hadn't intended for this to happen. She had hoped to get through the evening without running into him, but there was Steve, just turning around with two glasses of white wine in his hands. 'Hi, Ruth,' he said, blushing slightly.

'Hi, Steve,' she said softly. 'How are you?'

His eyes flickered right and left. 'Fine, just fine. And you?'

'Fine,' she said quietly. 'Have you heard about your internship yet?'

He looked right and left again. 'Not yet. I'm keeping my fingers crossed for Boston.' Then he laughed a little nervously.

'Hope you get it.'

'Thanks...'

It crossed Ruth's mind that now was the perfect opportunity for her to tell him what she thought, that for a medical student he certainly wasn't very sympathetic about her eagerness to find out her grade results. Because that was all their separation had been over, her running away from him to get to Encinitas Hall where the grades were posted.

That had been three weeks ago and Ruth recalled it now sharply. The night had been misty, salty, with a distant foghorn calling sadly out into the dark. She had just heard that the grades were posted and she'd been running across the campus to see what she'd got, and she'd run into Steve, who had wanted to stop and talk. She *explained*, damn it, why she was in such a hurry. Why couldn't he have understood that? For God's sake, he'd been a medical student for three and a half years, he of all people should know what it's like when grades are posted. So she'd said she'd see him later and had continued on her way to Encinitas Hall.

But when she'd called him a few days later and got a cool reception from him, and then heard him say that he didn't think they should see each other any more, she had demanded to know what had happened. And he'd said, 'I can't compete with books, Ruth. You're too ambitious for me. You need a guy who doesn't mind being a doormat.'

He was looking at her now in the same way, the way his voice had sounded on the phone, sort of sad, sort of baffled, even a little resentful. Maybe she *should* bring it up here, right now, in front of all these people, and tell him he had forgotten what it was like. She wanted to ask him how many women *he* had doormatted on his scramble to the top – Steve ranking fifth in his class. She wanted to know where he got off telling her she could never have a normal relationship with a man, not while she was so hung up on being *numero uno*, or the big cheese, or whatever juvenile cliché he had used.

Then she decided to save her energy. If he, a fourth-year medical student, couldn't sympathise with what she was going through, then he wasn't worth it. Why did every man in her life seem to think she should settle for second best?

'Well,' he said, inching away from her. 'Gotta go. Be seeing you.'

'Yes, be seeing you . . .'

When Sondra spotted Rick Parsons over by the fireplace, she said, 'Come on, Mickey, let's join Rick.'

But Mickey held back. 'No, you go. I'm going to find a place to sit down.'

As her friend headed for a safe place among the potted palms, Sondra worked her way through the throng to where Rick Parsons, looking very handsome in tweed jacket, tan trousers, and turtleneck, was standing with a small group of people. When he saw her, his face broadened in a smile and he waved her over. 'Hi, how are you?'

'I'm just fine.'

'Glad you came, I've got great news for you.'

Sondra decided on the spot that she didn't have to give it any more thought. She was definitely going to let herself fall in love this time. 'What's that?'

'Remember Tommy? The cystic astrocytoma?'

How could she forget? 'Yes.'

'We have an *almost hundred per cent* recovery!'

Sondra felt her smile widen until she was sure it filled the room.

'I don't believe you know everyone here,' he went on, gesturing to the people he stood with. The names were unfamiliar to Sondra even though they were preceded by 'Doctor'; it would be a while before she became acquainted with the medical staff of Castillo College. She smiled and said, 'Pleased to meet you,' to each and couldn't remember when she had last been so gay, so happy. Rick said last, 'And this is Patricia, my wife.'

Sondra stood blinking at the woman by his side. A very pretty woman, conservatively dressed, with a nice smile and warmth in her voice as she said, 'I'm pleased to meet you. Rick has told me how he's been trying to recruit you into neurosurgery. Are you going to capitulate?'

Sondra could only stare. His *wife*? Had there ever been mention of a wife? Her mind did a rapid run through all her conversations with Rick and realised that, while he'd given the impression of intimacy, he had never really told her about himself.

'No,' she said with a laugh that she hoped sounded convincing. 'I have no intention of letting him sway me. My mind was made up long ago to go to Africa.'

One of the others in the small circle, an elderly gentleman with leonine hair, said in a baritone, 'You'd think he got a commission off every new person he brought into the neuro service. Why, at this very moment, three of our residents are there because of Rick's friendly persuasion!'

Another person said, 'Maybe it's because misery likes company,' and the group laughed while Sondra wanted to find a quiet place where she could go and disappear. How could a woman as careful and watchful as she have allowed this to happen, allowed herself to make such a blunder? *He* didn't lead me on, *I* led me on!

'You don't have a drink, Sondra,' said Rick. 'Let me take you to the bar.'

'No thank you,' she said quickly, backing away. 'I can manage. Actually, I'm here with friends. See you later.'

When he gave her a puzzled look Sondra felt her face burn. *Rick Parsons had had no idea!* Saying, 'Nice to meet you all,' and, 'I'm glad Tommy's doing well,' she turned and pushed back into the crowd.

With a beer in one hand and a stick of celery in the other, Ruth was making a wide circuit of the room, travelling its periphery, watching, observing the ebbs and flows and eddies and tide pools of social movement. She recognised many people from her own class, a few teachers, a few upperclassmen, and some regulars of Gilhooley's who were on the staff at St Catherine's. They all seemed so giddy, so free of care, so *arrived*, as if the rat race out there in those other halls – Mariposa, Manzanitas, Balboa – didn't exist. Coming to a stop behind a potted palm, underneath a portrait of Juanita Hernandez, a fierce-eyed *hidalga* in full Spanish dress and *mantilla*, Ruth finished the celery stick and wished she had brought class notes with her.

Nearby was a knot of people paying rapt attention to a man she didn't know. He was holding forth about some medical theory and it seemed to Ruth he talked a little too loudly for the small audience and used rather ostentatious gestures.

'Excuse me,' came a quiet voice behind her. 'Is this an island of sanity?'

Ruth turned and looked into a pair of remarkable brown eyes, soft and gentle, and beneath them, a shy smile. 'Please join me,' she said, stepping a little closer to the palm to give him room. 'It does look as if the inmates are running the asylum!'

He wasn't very tall, only a few inches above Ruth, and not very striking at first glance, but a thoughtful study of his face revealed kindly, captivating features, a mouth that looked as if it was given to smiling easily, and eyes that seemed the soul of patience. 'I feel out of place,' he said with a quiet, self-effacing laugh. 'I'm not a medical person and absolutely everyone else in this crowd, it would appear, is.'

The loudmouth who was trying to dominate the whole room with his medical brilliance brought Ruth to turn, frown, and say to her companion, 'We're not all like that. He's one of the awful exceptions. Listen to him, isn't he pompous? With all that hot air it's a wonder he doesn't float up to the ceiling!'

The stranger reddened slightly and said, again with the soft laugh, 'I'm afraid he's the reason I'm here.'

'Oh no, he's a friend of yours?'

'Worse. He's my brother. That's Dr Norman Roth, and I,' he held out his hand, 'am Arnie Roth.'

Ruth stared at him for a moment, then said with a groan, 'The next sound you hear will be Ruth Shapiro crawling into a hole and pulling the hole in after herself. God, I *am* sorry.'

His smile remained open and ingenuous and the hand continued to wait. 'It's all right. Norm's got an ego and he knows it. Otherwise, he's a decent guy. Are you lost in this crowd, too?'

Ruth shook his hand and laughed a little. 'I'm afraid I'm part of this god-awful crowd.'

'Are you a nurse?'

'I'm a medical student. Freshman. You're not in medicine like your brother?'

'God no. Norman fulfilled that family obligation, thank goodness. I never could stand anything to do with medicine or sick people.'

'What do you do then?'

'I'm an accountant. Certified public. My office is in Encino, nice and clean, no blood, no death.'

'Medicine isn't all blood and death, Mr Roth. There's the other side of the coin – life.'

He nodded in an unconvinced way. Then his large brown eyes, liquid and soulful like a deer's, settled for a long moment on Ruth. 'So, you're a medical student. Is it as rough as I've heard?'

'Whatever you've heard, it's a hundred times worse.'

'I know, it's a lot of work. Are you able to get out much, socialise?'

Ruth studied his candid smile and thought, reluctantly, *You don't want to get involved with me. I can't have a normal relationship with a man.* 'I'm afraid I'm the kind of student that barely comes up for air. You see, I intend to be the best, to graduate at the top, and I'm afraid that leaves little time for anything else.'

'That's very admirable.'

Her eyes widened. 'You think so?'

'I admire people who know what they want and go after it, willing to make sacrifices.'

'A few of my friends don't see it that way.'

'Then they're not really your friends, are they?'

She slowly shook her head from side to side, finding herself relaxing by inches and all of a sudden glad, after all, that she had let Sondra drag her here. When Arnie Roth said, 'What do you say we try for some of that buffet?' and stepped aside for her to precede him, Ruth gave him her best, most encouraging smile and thought, *Steve Schonfeld, what the heck do you know . . .*

From her hiding place in the corner, Mickey observed the party. How she envied Ruth, who was right now sharing a cold-cut plate across the room with a smiling stranger, tossing back her short brunette hair and laughing. To be so at ease with your body, to be so *secure!*

Mickey was looking around for Sondra when she saw the man over by the entrance.

Staring at her.

Her heart gave a leap and she instinctively started searching for an escape. She looked at him again; he had just come in with some other people and he was definitely staring right at *her.*

Mickey felt the old familiar panic start to rise. Pushing away from the wall, she looked right and left. Then a quick glance his way again. Good heavens, he was starting to come towards her!

Mickey slid along the wall, ducked behind a giant potted palm and found, to her immense relief, the doorway that led to the rest rooms. *Haven.* In blind panic, she fell through the door, then hurried down the short hall to the ladies' room.

Once inside, she was relieved to find it deserted, and went straight to the sink to examine her face. Why had that stranger been staring at her? Hooking her blonde hair over her ear, she took the jar of C-over out of her purse and began another application. That done, she meticulously combed the hair forward, trying to make it look as if it naturally fell close to her nose, then, satisfied, turned and walked out.

He was waiting for her.

'Hello,' he said with a smile. 'I saw you come in here. I'm Chris Novack.'

Mickey stared down at the offered hand but didn't take it. The little hallway was suddenly close and threatening; the closed doorway at the end, through which came muffled sounds of the party, seemed far away.

'Are you a student here at Castillo?'

She tried not to face him fully but kept, as was her habit, her left profile to him. She studied him for a moment and saw to her further dismay that he was very handsome. Tall and slender, late forties.

'You do speak English, don't you?' he asked, widening his smile.

'Yes...'

'I saw you standing there all alone and thought you might want some company on this last night of 1968. Can I get you a drink or something to eat?'

'No,' she said quickly. 'Thanks.'

'I'm new here in Los Angeles and don't know many people.' He paused significantly. 'So... are you a student here or a nurse or...?'

'I'm a medical student.'

'Oh? What year?'

Mickey looked down at the purse handle twisted in her fingers.

'I'm sorry,' he said finally. 'I didn't mean to come on so strong. But I really wanted to meet you and thought it best to be direct.'

Now she lifted her eyes and saw a smile of genuine apology on his face. 'It's my fault,' she said at last in a small voice. 'I'm not used to someone coming up to me like that.'

'I can't believe that, a beautiful woman like you.'

Mickey looked away.

'Now, can I get you something after all?'

'Yes, I'd like a Coke. I tried to get to the bar a while ago but never made it.'

He laughed softly. 'It's a jungle out there. What's your name?'

They turned and headed down the hall together. 'Mickey.'

'Mickey! An unusual name. Is it short for anything?'

'No, I'm just Mickey.'

'What made you choose to go into medicine, Mickey?'

When they arrived at the door, Chris Novack reached for the knob and at the same time lightly took Mickey's elbow. 'It's because of my father,' she said, praying he wouldn't cross behind her and walk on her right. 'My father died of an incurable illness when I was little,' Mickey continued, telling her stock lie. To tell the truth, that a thousand trips to doctors' offices had made her decide to go into medical research, would have drawn attention to her face. 'My mother and I sat for hours with him. I guess it was then that I thought I'd like to help save lives.'

'Have you chosen a field yet?'

'Some sort of research. I like laboratories.'

They plunged into the crowd and tried to make their way to the bar. Chris Novack tightened his grip on her arm and kept her close to him. When they finally pushed through and picked up two slippery bottles, Mickey's handsome companion looked around the room with a frown. 'There isn't one inch of space in here. What do you say we try our luck outside?'

They fought their way through the crowd towards the doors with Chris holding the Cokes up over his head, and then the blessed whisper of winter night air and lacy mist touched their faces.

The patio was crowded but not as fiercely as inside and they were able to find a damp bench where they could sit. 'You might be changing your mind over the next couple of years,' Chris Novack said after taking a long draw on his Coke. 'When you start rotating through the hospital in your third year, you'll change your mind with each specialty you're exposed to. In paediatrics you'll declare you want to be a paediatrician. In pathology you'll decide you want to be a pathologist. It always happens.'

Mickey watched his profile as he spoke, his right profile because she had hesitated before sitting down and then had put herself with her left side to him; a skill she'd perfected over the years. They sat beneath the hundred-year-old Californian white oak, listening to the strains of music, the laughter and chatter. Then Chris Novack took another long draw on his Coke, weighed his next words very carefully, and finally said, 'May I talk to you about your face?'

Mickey felt the bottle slip through her fingers. There was a shattering crash and a wash of liquid over her feet.

'Oh –' said Chris, jumping up. 'God, I'm sorry!'

Mickey got shakily to her feet. 'I didn't think...' She raised a trembling hand to her cheek.

'I'm sorry,' he said again, and when Mickey turned to run, he quickly laid a hand on her arm and said, 'Wait, please, listen to me. I know it's difficult for you to talk about, but –'

'I have to go,' she choked out.

Just as Mickey started away and Chris Novack's hand tightened on her arm, the chimes in the campus belltower started ringing out over the foggy night. With a roar of yells and shouts and the honking of horns, as 1969 was welcomed in, Chris Novack turned Mickey around to face him and said loudly, 'I'm a doctor, Mickey. A surgeon. That's what I wanted to talk to you about. I think I can fix your face.'

# Chapter Eight

This was Ruth's first hour in the Labour & Delivery suite, and already she was counting the minutes till it was over. She hated it, she absolutely hated it.

It was February, and the second week of Student As Physician. The course had begun well, with excitement and tours of all the departments, an orientation of hospital structure and staff hierarchy, and finally, a real honest-to-goodness lesson in the use of stethoscopes, blood pressure cuffs, ophthalmoscopes, and reflex hammers. The freshman class had been divided into groups, each student was issued an exam kit, and they had practised on one another, learning to read diastolic and systolic, to pick out valve sounds, to evaluate the vital signs. Then the groups had separated, each off to a different department, four days in each; at the end of the six weeks there would be a practical and written exam to see what they had learned and to see if the experimental program was going to be beneficial.

Yesterday they had made rounds on the GYN ward where they had learned how a pelvic exam is done. Dr Mandell had gathered them around a bed at the end of the ward where a nice woman didn't seem to mind being asked intimate questions and stared at by twelve strangers. And when Mandell had drawn the curtain around the patient and she slid down in the bed, he announced he was going to show them how a pelvic exam was done. The woman had continued to be a good sport, helpful even.

'She isn't a real patient,' Dr Mandell had explained prior to rounds. 'She's a prostitute hired by the hospital to lie in a bed just for the morning and play the part of a GYN patient. It's the only way to teach pelvic exams. A real patient is too tense and tightens up and nothing can be learned.'

Ruth had enjoyed the GYN rounds and felt she had got a

lot out of the day; but today it was her turn to tour the Labour & Delivery suite.

Only two students at a time were permitted in L&D; they took turns, each pair coming in for three days while the rest of the Student As Physician group continued rounds on the other services. Dr Mandell had brought Ruth and Mark Wheeler in this morning, showing them where to change, and then had met them again at the nursing station.

After a brief introduction with Mrs Caputo, charge nurse in Obstetrics, a dour woman who reminded them that they were to stay out of the way and not ask questions, they went around the suite of two labour rooms, four delivery rooms, two substerile stations, and a recovery room – all cold and sterile and uncomfortably impersonal. And the noise!

Dr Mandell and his two charges were ignored. This was one of the suite's busy days. A difficult delivery was going on in one room and when Ruth glanced through the small window in the door she saw a large, green-sheeted mound on the operating table being attended by three masked men and two masked women. In the next room, a lone, hassled nurse was hastily setting up for an emergency Caesarean section. They paused in the doorway of the recovery room to see a pale, slumbering woman being watched over by a green-dressed nurse, and ended the little tour outside one of the two labour rooms.

The Labour & Delivery suite was exactly like the operating suite of the week before, which surprised Ruth a little. She had never quite thought of birth as a surgical procedure, and the noise was phenomenal. Through the thick door came the cries of the delivering mother and the encouragement of her attendants: 'Push!' and 'Don't push!' Several cardiac monitors filled the air with asynchronous bleeping. The two steam autoclaves hissed and clanged. A nearby phone rang unanswered. An argument between two unseen men was coming from a substerile room. And finally, like a dramatic exclamation point, a shriek tearing the air and causing the two jittery Saps to jump.

'That's how you can tell this is the labour room,' Dr Mandell said. 'Just follow the noise.'

Ruth accompanied Dr Mandell into the room but Mark

Wheeler hung back, his face as bleached as his Malibu-blond hair; only one of the four beds was occupied and when they came around to look at the patient, Ruth was stunned.

She was a child!

'Now then, let's have a look at her chart, shall we?'

The chart was yellow, which meant she was one of the charity patients, the ones whom all students, interns, and residents practised on. Pink charts were untouchable, Ruth knew; these were private, paying patients and had their own physicians.

Ruth offered a weak smile to the child in the bed but got none in return. Two enormous hazel eyes dominated a white, thin face; stringy blonde hair hung in damp ropes; the lips were grey; her hospital gown clung to her in sweaty places. She eyed the two strangers warily but with no curiosity: as a charity case she would by now have been seen by many people in white coats or technicians' uniforms or surgical greens, many of whom would not have bothered to introduce themselves.

Ruth forced her attention back to the chart. 'Lenore here is five centimetres dilated,' Dr Mandell was saying. 'Since a fully dilated cervix is ten, we can say she's halfway there.' He clapped the chart shut and hung it back on the foot of the bed. 'Well, no use wasting our time here. Let's get you in to see that C-section.'

As they left, Ruth looked back. The two large haunted eyes followed her.

When they were out in the hall, another cry came from the room they'd just left and Dr Mandell said with a smile, 'Well, we certainly timed that just right!'

He stopped for a moment with Mrs Caputo, who'd been chastising a red-faced nurse, and Ruth saw her shake her head and hold up one finger. When he came back, Dr Mandell said, 'I'm sorry, only one at a time in the room. Come along, Mr Wheeler. You can be first.'

Ruth watched them go into the, as yet, unoccupied delivery room, where she heard a female voice say, 'Well, okay, but he'd better not faint,' then she decided to take another look through the small window in the next door.

From where she stood, Ruth could see over the doctor's

shoulders. The birth was still in progress, and for some reason it wasn't going well.

She saw the top of a little head come to the surface and then, as if not ready, disappear back inside. With each crowning the recumbent woman cried out. Ruth heard the doctor say, 'Oh, for God's sake, give her some more epidural!'

She throught she heard the woman protest, but soon she was silent and now the crowning had stopped, too.

'Push!' shouted the obstetrician, whose hunched back was streaked with sweat. 'Come on, push!'

The woman obviously was trying but with little success. The anaesthesia had reduced her muscle control.

Finally the doctor picked up a forceps and at last the baby came out, into the sterile hands of the assistant.

Ruth moved away from the door and stared at the wall of cold, green tile opposite.

A green blur rushed past her eyes. Ruth saw a nurse fling open a cupboard, snatch out a green bundle, then run back past her and into the delivery room. As the door yawned briefly Ruth was overwhelmed by a wave of noise: heart monitor bleeps, a baby's wail, the clunk-whoosh of a respirator, the slurp of the wall suction, and 'What the hell is this!'

Ruth moved away from the door and inched along the wall. She was just thinking, *I'll get through this somehow,* when the double doors at the end suddenly burst open and two white-uniformed men literally flew in with a stretcher. At once, green attendants materialised, shooing the white ones out of the suite, snapping orders, taking orders, whipping the blanket off a very pregnant woman, cursing the absence of something from the chart, cursing the crew down in Emergency, then all wheeling her in under the order, 'Christ, come on, we've gotta get that kid outa there!'

As the door was swinging shut Ruth glimpsed an ashen Mark Wheeler pressed up against a wall, but no sign of Dr Mandell, who had returned to the rest of the SAP group, which was in Pathology, Sondra and Mickey with them, and where Ruth desperately wished she was right now.

A pathetic cry brought her attention to the open doorway

of the first labour room. Ruth went to it and looked in. The girl named Lenore, a wasted thing of no more than fourteen or fifteen, turned huge frightened eyes to Ruth. 'Help me,' she said.

Ruth went to the bedside and looked down. Being the eldest of five, she was no stranger to the company of a very pregnant woman, but she'd never been part of the birth process – always her mother got bigger and bigger until the time came and she went calmly to the hospital, returning a week later with a clean, pink baby.

This was all alien to Ruth. Lenore was half propped up against damp pillows, her skinny hands resting protectively on her swollen abdomen, a blanket over her legs. From under the flimsy hospital gown came several wires which led from the girl's abdomen to a machine parked on the other side of the bed. It bleeped ominously and belched out a strip of graph paper. One of Lenore's thin arms was taped to a stiff board and from her wrist came an IV tube, connected to a bottle over the bed. The upper half of her other arm was wrapped with a blood pressure cuff. On the night table there were two types of stethoscopes, a box of sterile rubber gloves, a surgical flashlight, an emesis basin, and a thermometer.

Ruth looked around the room, which she gathered was supposed to have been designed to be 'cheerful': pale yellow wallpaper with daisies on it, the curtains around each bed patterned with lemons and pineapples, and Scotch-taped to the back of the door, a poster of children chasing butterflies. But the hospital dominated: the glaring, brighter-than-day lighting, the shiny chrome beds and starched sheets, the polished linoleum floor, the overall institutional air about the place, and Ruth was surprised by an unexpected thought, *I'll never have my babies in a place like this.*

When she looked again at Lenore, she saw a silent plea on the unhappy face and knew the girl wanted to know who she was but was afraid to ask. *Always introduce yourself as Doctor,* Dr Mandell had said, *it will give the patient confidence.*

'Hi, I'm Dr Shapiro.'

When Lenore's face relaxed in visible relief, Ruth felt a stab of guilt. *Please don't put your trust in me; I haven't the faintest idea what's going on.*

'I'm scared, Doctor,' the girl whispered.

'Of course you are,' said Ruth, patting her shoulder. 'It's understandable. I guess this is your first?' Silly question!

'Yes.' Lenore looked down at the burden her hands covered and seemed to want to say more, but didn't know how.

Ruth asked gently, 'Are you all alone?'

Lenore raised her head. 'Yes, I am! I don't have nobody. My old man, when I told him I was pregnant, he took off and I think he's up in San Francisco now. We lived with a bunch of kids, you see, but me and Frank, we were a couple. I was his old lady. I didn't sleep around or nothing. When he left, the group broke up.'

'Where do you live now?'

'Oh, around.'

'Where's your family?'

'Back East. I hitchhiked across the country last year. It was far out. And then I met Frank and decided to settle down. Turned out to be a bummer, though.'

'I'm sorry,' murmured Ruth. 'But at least now you'll have your baby.'

'Yeah . . .'

They were interrupted by the sound of two male voices, and Ruth turned to see two green-clad men coming in, recognising one of them as the doctor who had just a while before done the forceps delivery. The front of his surgical shirt was smeared with blood.

'I tell you, I give all my girls scopolamine,' he was saying as they came towards Lenore's bed. 'They may rant and rave and carry on like maniacs during labour and delivery, but they don't remember a thing about it afterwards. They bless me for it. No pain, no memory of the birth. Okay, here's a ward case. Primipara, five centimetres. Came in through Emergency. Cases like these, you always be sure to check for VD.'

Ruth stepped away as they came up either side of the bed. The obstetrician silently read over the chart, then handed it to his assistant. After a look at the strip of graph from the foetal monitor, he pulled a pair of gloves out of the box and slid his hands into them.

When he pulled the sheet down and Lenore instinctively drew her thighs together, he said, 'It's a bit late to keep your legs closed, don't you think? Come on, honey, we haven't got all day.'

As they both examined her, the two doctors talked over her, never once looking at Lenore, and ended with: 'Eight centimetres, head's still pretty high in the pelvis. Come on, let's grab some coffee.'

When they straightened and pulled off their gloves, Lenore piped up in a sudden burst of courage: 'My baby's down low. I can feel it.'

'No it's not, honey, you have a while to wait yet.'

'Please, could you give me something for the pain?'

The first doctor patted her. 'We can't do that, dear, because it could slow down or even stop your labour. Now stop being such a baby, this is a very normal thing you're going through.'

As they turned away, Mrs Caputo came hurrying into the room. 'Dr Turner, ER just called. There's been an accident on the Coast Highway. One of the injured is a pregnant woman and she's gone into labour. There might be foetal distress. They're bringing her up now.'

'Oh, Christ. Come on, Jack, you help me on this. Caputo, call my office and tell them to cancel my reservation at Scandia.'

Ruth came back to the bedside in time to see two big tears tumble down Lenore's cheeks. Before either could say anything, the girl's face drew into a grimace and she arched her neck with a groan. Then she screamed and sank back breathless. 'It hurts so much,' she cried. 'It's killing me! I'll die!'

'You won't die,' said Ruth, taking one of Lenore's hands. 'The doctor was right, this is a normal thing.'

'Yes, but he was wrong about my baby's head. It's not high up, it's down here. I felt it fall.'

Ruth stared at her a moment. 'Are you sure?' Then instantly regretted her words. The universal medical philosophy: doctor knows better than patient, patient is ignored.

Lenore had no time to respond. Her face scrunched up

again, veins bulged at her neck and temples; then she let out a shriek and fell back panting.

Ruth looked at her in alarm. The contractions were coming awfully close together.

'Oh, God,' whimpered Lenore. 'I'm bleeding.'

'You can't be,' said Ruth as calmly as possible. She glanced over her shoulder – where *was* everybody? – then gingerly drew down the girl's blanket. Between her legs was a show of fresh, clear fluid. 'It's all right,' said Ruth in a calm she didn't feel. 'It's not blood. Your water just broke.'

'Here comes another –' Lenore tightened up in another contraction and squeezed Ruth's hand so hard Ruth almost screamed with her.

'Help me, Doctor! It's coming! Oh, God, I'm scared!'

Ruth pried Lenore's fingers off her hand. 'I'll go for someone. Don't worry, it's going to be all right.'

But it wasn't. Out in the hall, chaos had broken loose. The car accident victim was being taken into a delivery room with six people working on her, someone cutting away her bloody clothes, another trying to hold an oxygen mask to her face, a third wheeling up a cardiac 'crash' cart while a fourth dropped gel onto the defibrillator paddles. Every available person not working on the C-section in the next room was fighting for this woman's and her baby's lives; even two nonsurgical personnel were on the team. It was utter pandemonium and Ruth looked on transfixed.

Then she spotted Mrs Caputo. Running up to her, Ruth said, 'The girl in labour is starting to have her –'

But the charge nurse pushed by brusquely, her arms cradling an emergency surgical pack. 'Stay out of the way! That girl is Dr Turner's patient, he's monitoring her. If you interfere again I'll have you thrown out.'

Ruth hurried back to Lenore, not aware that she was now thinking of the girl as her own patient, and found her writhing in another contraction. The foetal heart monitor chattered in an erratic rhythm, the IV bottle clanked against its pole, Lenore's abdomen rose up and rippled, the blanket fell away.

Oh, God, thought Ruth, dry-mouthed. It's coming.

In a lightning-quick move Lenore clamped a hand around

Ruth's wrist. 'Help me,' she whispered coarsely. 'Help me *please*, Doctor.'

Ruth tried to pull away; she looked frantically towards the door. If she called out for help, it would panic Lenore. Ruth had to at least appear calm.

Lenore tightened up in another contraction and Ruth saw the stark horrifying truth: she couldn't leave the girl alone.

*Dear God, dear God, dear God,* she thought as she fumbled with the side rail of the bed. *Where's the call button? Why don't they have an emergency switch you can hit? Why doesn't someone at least look in here?*

Her very worst fears were confirmed on the next contraction. She glimpsed the top of the head.

Shaking, Ruth pulled on a pair of rubber gloves the way she'd seen Dr Turner do, then set herself firmly between Lenore's open legs. On the next crowning, Ruth thrust out her hands, ready to catch a slippery football, as she'd read it described. But the baby wasn't going along with the textbook: the head receded and Lenore relaxed.

*I'll run for someone now . . .*

But the head started crowning again and this time Ruth had a shock: something was looped over the baby's skull.

She broke out in an icy sweat and thought for a second that she was going to pass out. The obstruction could be only one thing: the umbilical cord.

'Wait,' she said to Lenore. 'Don't push next time.'

'I have to! I can't hold it!'

'No, don't push –'

Another contraction, another crowning, and Ruth's horror mounted. A purplish rope preceded the soft skull but stopped at the opening, then turned white as it was pressed upon by the head. Ruth's mind flew far ahead of itself. With each push against the cord, the baby was cutting off its blood and oxygen supply from the mother. If this kept up, it would kill itself before it was born.

Ruth was unaware that she had started to cry. What she saw through a blur or tears was only her own hands, moving on their own, instinctively, without eyes or logic, slipping into the vagina, her fingers finding the soft round head, feeling the pulsating rope, and with the next contraction,

81

holding the head off the umbilicus. But when it subsided, Ruth felt the cord fall back into place and knew it would be blocked off again the next time.

Without thinking, she sprang off the bed, ran to the foot, and started frantically cranking the handle. Gradually, Lenore started to angle backwards as the head of the bed sank and the foot rose up. Leaving her at this gentle tilt, Ruth returned to her place and watched for the next crowning. The cord wasn't as endangered this time, but it was pinched nonetheless; she slid a hand in and supported the skull.

Ruth swore that hours and days passed with the two of them like this, Lenore crying out and bearing down, Ruth with her hand inside, cradling the head up and away from the cord, and when she started to shout for help she didn't know, or how many times, but when someone did run into the room and say, 'Jesus Christ,' her tears turned into open crying so that by the time a nurse replaced her, sliding a gloved hand into where Ruth had been holding hers, Ruth broke down sobbing. She felt a strong arm go around her shoulders and guide her to a chair in the corner; there were some hurried footsteps, the sound of the bed being wheeled out of the room, and then silence.

A few minutes later, a nurse with a quizzical look on her face brought Ruth a cup of coffee and relieved her of her bloody gloves. And then a little while after that, Ruth didn't know how long, a man in greens came into the room, sweaty but without blood on his clothes, a stranger who also stared at her quizzically and introduced himself as Dr Scott.

'I'm afraid I don't know you,' he said, drawing up another chair and searching her chest for a name tag. 'Are you a nurse?'

Ruth swallowed hard. She was recovered now but still a bit shaky. 'No, I'm a medical student.'

'Oh, I see. Third year? Fourth?'

'First.'

His eyebrows shot up to the edge of his surgical cap. 'A *first*-year medical student? What are you doing in here?'

She explained about the SAP programme and that today was her first of three days in L&D.

'So, you're getting a taste of what medicine is really all

about,' he said with a nice smile. 'You're lucky. When I was in medical school I didn't set foot inside a hospital until my third year, and let me tell you, it was a shock. I fainted when I observed my first spinal tap! It's a smart idea to give students a bit of a taste early on. It gives those who haven't really the heart for medicine a chance to quit, because in the third year it's really too late to quit, and you're stuck.'

He fell silent and studied her for a moment. 'Did this experience sour you against medicine?'

'No.'

His smile broadened. 'You must have had some experience before this. Nurse's aide? Paramedic?' To her head shakes he said, 'Absolutely nothing? You mean this was your first time with a delivery?'

'I've never even seen a cat have kittens.'

He leaned back with his arms folded across his chest, his face now taking on a look that Ruth couldn't quite read. But his tone said it all. 'That's amazing. You knew just what to do. You didn't panic and run out. You stuck by her.'

'I burst out crying.'

He shrugged. 'We all do at one time or another. You've gotten yours out of the way.' He considered her for another thoughtful moment, then said, 'Are you going to go into OB?'

'General practice.'

'You might consider specialising. Where you're needed is here.'

Ruth's eyes widened. She looked around the room, at the silly wallpaper and lemons and pineapples, at the vacant spot where Lenore's bed had stood. And she thought: *Here?*

'Is Lenore all right?'

'She's fine. She had a healthy little boy. Apgar of eight, thanks to you. Would you like to see him?'

'Yes, I would.'

Dr Scott rose with Ruth, put a hand on her upper arm, and led her out of the labour room.

# Chapter Nine

'Will it hurt?'

'Only the local injections. And afterwards, when the Xylocaine wears off.'

While Dr Novack assembled his tray of instruments, Mickey turned away, not wanting to see. She settled her gaze on the window, which, being seven floors up, admitted a view of the Pacific Ocean as it rolled and churned beneath the February rain.

'Are you afraid, Mickey?'

'Yes.'

'Do you want a tranquilliser?'

'No.'

She spoke without looking at him, without seeing what his hands were doing with the terrifying instruments on the tray. Her palms were moist; she continually wiped them with a crumpled handkerchief.

Mickey had tried, in the seven days since she had agreed to let him do this, to prepare herself for this moment, but all his reassurances and all her own intellectualising seemed to dissolve in the grey rain. This was, after all, a highly experimental procedure: no guarantees.

Back on New Year's Eve, at the Encinitas Hall party, Dr Novack had held her arm and said, 'I think I can fix your face.' She could not run from him after that; she had sat back down on the bench and he had explained.

'I have a research grant with St Catherine's. I'm a plastic surgeon experimenting with different methods of eradicating haemangiomas. That's why I was staring at you so rudely. I've been looking for someone to be my write-up case. I've done quite a few now with my new method, all successfully, but they've been small blemishes. For my write-up I need a dramatic case. And here you are!'

Mickey had said nothing. She was terribly afraid, not of Chris Novack or pain, but of disappointment; she'd repeatedly asked him if it would work and he'd repeatedly said 'no guarantees.'

'Yours is a very large stain. I can't recall having ever seen one that so totally covered one side of the face. That's a sensitive area and it's a sensitive procedure. I'll do a test patch on your back first, where it won't show, to see if you're going to have any reactions.'

'What will I have to do?'

'Nothing. Just come to my office every third Saturday, it'll take an hour. I estimate six or seven sessions. You'll have to let me take pictures of you before and after, and I'll need your signed permission to use your name and your picture in my papers and lectures.'

'What if it backfires?'

'You mean, will you look worse? No.'

And just when Mickey had swallowed with a dry throat and decided to take the plunge, Dr Novack had said, 'One more thing, no makeup during the whole process. We can't risk infection.'

That had stopped Mickey. If he was going to do only a small patch at a time, then that meant the rest of the port-wine would show, and to go around without C-over on it was like walking around the campus naked. She wouldn't do it. And she told him so.

What she hadn't counted on, however, was a certain irresistible force known as roommates, a cheerleading section of two who worked at her, pushed, cajoled, threatened, and gave her no rest.

'I've been disappointed too many times,' she had cried, and Ruth and Sondra had replied almost as a chorus: 'Disappointment never killed anyone.'

They wore her resistance down, bit by bit, with their optimism and enthusiasm while Mickey tried to fight it: 'It's not *your* face! You don't know what it's like!'

It was Sondra who made the bold, deciding move: while Mickey slept she dumped out all her bottles of C-over, flushing the makeup down the drain. And they were out there now, in the hall, Ruth and Sondra, with books on their laps, waiting for Mickey to emerge from her first session with Dr Novack.

'Everything's been tried,' he was saying now as Mickey sat petrified in the chair that was like a dentist's. 'For years doctors have tried all sorts of remedies for haemangiomas, all with poor results. That scar in front of your ear is the result of an attempted skin graft. Don't worry, Mickey, I can remove that.'

He didn't have to tell her about all the methods that had been tried – the burning, the freezing, the cutting – because she'd been through them all, and for the most part they'd not only been unsuccessful but incredibly painful.

'You're very lucky, Mickey, that what you have is a capillary haemangioma. If it were the cavernous variety, I'd have to have a neurosurgeon operate first to cut off the major blood supply.'

When his fingertips touched her hair, she flinched. The first time he had done it, drawing the hair back to have a look, Mickey had thought she would die of shame. To feel air on that side of her face, to feel his eyes examining, his fingers probing, as if he explored the very most intimate, guarded part of her. She would never get used to it, never.

'I'm going to start closest to the ear, Mickey, and that way, if something does go wrong it won't show.' His voice was gentle and soothing as he worked. The hair was pinned back, then a towel draped over it. Mickey had done as told that morning, washed her face well with Phisohex. With Mickey's head resting back and her face turned to the wall, Dr Novack clipped another towel beneath her chin, then washed the right side of her face again with Phisohex. Next she heard him put something down, pick something up, and say, 'Okay, Mickey, a few pinpricks now. This is the Xylocaine.'

There was a bit of shooting pain and then her right cheek felt like it was floating up off her face, drifting over to Dr Novack's hands where he would work, detached from her.

'I've taken great care to match your skin pigment, Mickey. You have beautiful skin, women would envy you if only you would let it show. And you're very pretty, Mickey, but how's anyone to know if all they can see is your nose?'

She felt his fingers massage her cheek. 'I'm applying the pigment now.'

Then she heard the sound that made her want to bolt and run. The dreadful click of a switch and the hum of a motor. She closed her eyes and pictured what he held in his hand: an instrument that looked like a fountain pen with a tip of tiny threads that vibrated back and forth and which would drive the pigment into her skin – the tattooing needle.

When she came out an hour later, a little shaky, very pale, but smiling with infinite relief, Ruth and Sondra shot to their feet. Chris Novack had his arm around Mickey's shoulders and was saying, 'Keep the dressing on as long as you can. If anything goes wrong, call me at once. Come back Wednesday afternoon so I can have a look. Remember to keep your hair pinned back while it's healing. And good luck.'

Sondra ran up and embraced her while Ruth stood back with her hands on her hips. Eyeing the bandage and the scarlet skin that emerged from under it, she said with a grin, 'Jesus, Mickey Long, you look like the Bride of Frankenstein!'

And then it was May and finals were only days away.

A pall seemed to settle over Castillo College as the exams drew closer and closer and students withdrew into panicked study. This was the crucial point, when those who weren't going to make it were dropped, the deciding time for the rest of one's medical career. If you got through your first year, everyone said, the rest was a cinch. Mixers dwindled, then stopped; Encinitas Hall gradually emptied until Saturday afternoons and evenings found only occasional white-jacketed third- and fourth-years resting between hospital calls. All social life was put in suspension; the beach grew deserted; phones stopped ringing; mail went unanswered; and lights glowed all night through dorm and apartment windows as an air of waiting and wondering filled the quiet campus.

The three in the apartment on Avenida Oriente were just as obsessed, just as occupied, but their microcosmic atmosphere was shot with additional tension and suspense.

For Ruth, it was the time to move up another place in class. From twelfth last November, to ninth in January, to eighth the last midterms. She couldn't afford to slip back a notch and she refused to stay at eight.

For Sondra, stretching before her was a warm summer, to be spent with her parents in one of the last spells of togetherness, she was certain, they would have for a long time.

And for Mickey, the hour of her final session with Dr Novack was drawing near.

No one had stared. Oh, at first a few heads had turned in lecture class, or passing her on the quadrangle paths, vacant stares, a bit of mild curiosity – had she been in an accident? – and then the ignoring she was used to and comfortable with. Mickey had come to face her visits with unutterable excitement, usually showing up early; but still, she avoided the mirror. When she washed, combed her hair, brushed her teeth, she did it like a blind person, fearing her own reflection, not wanting the disappointment to come too soon, prolonging the 'unveiling' of herself. When Ruth and Sondra looked at her, they saw nothing tremendously dramatic: Mickey's face was swollen most of the time, black and blue, and covered with dressings. And finally, because of impending finals and the rush for high class standings, they turned off the spotlight and Mickey's ordeal was almost ignored.

It was the weekend before the gruelling Statistics final that Dr Novack asked Mickey if he could show her at the annual Plastic Surgery seminar.

He was removing the tiny nylon sutures from in front of her ear, where he had excised the old scar. There would be no tattooing today, that had ended last Saturday. 'Would you mind, Mickey? The seminar will be held in two weeks, the last weekend before school is out. It's a yearly event where papers are presented; there will be quite a membership, about sixty plastic surgeons from all over. Do you think you could do it?'

She sat as usual, with her head turned to the wall, her hands resting in her lap. 'What will I have to do?'

'Not much. I'll show my slides and give a short talk. Then I'd like you to come out and let them see you.'

'I can't,' she whispered.

The last stitch was out. Dr Novack wrapped up the little gauze bundle and dropped it in the bucket. Then he wheeled around on his rolling stool so that he could face Mickey. 'I think you can do it,' he said gently.

'No.'

'I can't force you, of course. But think what a wonderful thing it would be. Many of those doctors will be there to hear about my new technique. They'll look at you, see that it can be done, and return to their home towns to help other people that are where you once were.'

She gazed at him with hunted eyes. 'As I once *was*?'

'You haven't been looking at yourself, have you, Mickey? Here.' he picked up a hand mirror and held it before her face. Instinctively, Mickey closed her eyes. 'Go on, look. I'd say we were a smashing success.'

She opened her eyes. She stared. The right side of her face was a horrible sight: pink scar lines, redness, swelling –

But no port-wine.

'This will all settle down in time,' Dr Novack said, touching various places with his fingertips. 'In fact, in six months, if you take care like I told you and stay out of the sun, no one will ever know what this was once like.'

She stared at herself a moment longer, then turned to Chris Novack. 'All right,' she said with a tremulous smile. 'I'll do it.'


'Here she comes,' said Sondra, ducking away from the window and letting the curtain fall.

Ruth made a dash for the kitchen and Sondra joined her where both stood in the darkness, holding their breath. When they heard the key in the lock, both had to stifle the impulse to giggle. The door opened and Mickey stood in silhouette against the lavender June twilight. 'Hey,' she said into the dark apartment. 'No one home?' Then she muttered, 'Must be out...'

Sondra hit the light switch and Ruth screamed, 'Surprise!' and Mickey almost jumped to the ceiling.

With her purse and papers fluttering to the floor, she pressed her hand to her breast and gasped, 'What the –'

'Surprise, surprise,' chanted her roommates, running to her and each grabbing a wrist. 'Come on, it's a celebration.'

'What are you –' She let them pull her along to the bedrooms. 'Have the grades been posted?'

'Not yet. Come on.'

Sondra fell behind and Ruth pushed Mickey forward into her bedroom. All three stopped and formed a tableau, Sondra and Ruth grinning, Mickey staring with her mouth open. 'What *is* this?' she finally whispered.

'This is your coming-out celebration, Mickey Long.' Ruth gave her another little push on the back. 'Go on. From now on, that is the New You.'

Mickey slowly approached the items on the bed as if they might bite her: the beautiful sleeveless dress of sky blue silk, the chic sling-back pumps of the same blue, the little box holding a pair of gold stud earrings, the makeup case full of colours, the clear plastic box of steam hair rollers and dryer, a scarf with a designer name on it, a heavenly swirl of blues and greens and aquas, draped elegantly over the foot of the bed with a little tag on it that said, 'Use me to keep your hair back.'

'I don't understand...'

'These are from me and Ruth. Our coming-out present to you.'

'No, I can't accept –'

'Listen, Mickey Long,' said Ruth with her hands on her hips. 'This outfit is as much for our sakes as it is for yours. How do you think we would feel, our Mickey going to that posh dinner tomorrow night, standing up in front of all those surgeons dressed like a mud hen? We have our image to protect!'

Mickey started to cry. And then Sondra did. Ruth shook her head and reached for a brush off the dresser. 'And the first thing we're going to do,' she said, grabbing a hank of Mickey's straight blonde hair, 'is change this!'

Chris Novack had said he would pick her up at seven. The dinner was being held in St Catherine's largest conference room, not a far walk from Mickey's apartment, but he had insisted they go in his car. Sondra let him in and Ruth waved from the kitchen.

'We had the devil of a time making her go! She's in the bedroom now, trying to decide what to wear.'

He laughed and shook his head. In time, Chris Novack was certain – he'd seen it happen often enough – Mickey would get used to her new look and would allow herself to change. For some people, it just took longer.

'Hello, Dr Novack.'

He turned. The smile fell. 'Mickey?'

She came uncertainly into the living room, as if she were walking for the first time in shoes; her head was bowed because her hair was pulled tightly back and held at the nape of her neck by a stunning scarf. When she came up to him, Mickey finally raised her head and offered a frail smile. There was a touch of pink on her lips, a hint of blush on the crests of her cheeks, a kiss of green shadow over her eyes. But she wasn't just Mickey Long wearing makeup. Another change had taken place, almost as if the very bone structure underneath had somehow shifted; it was the spirit that had changed, and the flesh had been remoulded.

Dr Novack was speechless.

'Have a good time,' said Ruth, turning away and fumbling with something. 'We'll wait up for you, Mickey.'

It was their last walk along the beach. Back at the apartment, suitcases were packed, airline tickets lay in purses. Sondra and Ruth would go, Mickey would stay; a summer job as a nurse's aide at St Catherine's would enable her to keep the apartment for them.

They dug their bare feet into the warm sand, filled their lungs with the salty sea air, let the wind lift their hair and whip it around their faces. It was a perfect day with a deep blue sky, scudding white clouds, gulls crying over the crash of breakers. Ruth and Mickey and Sondra were all filled with a sense of walking over a threshold, of standing on a brink. And they were filled with a deep sense of accomplishment.

Ruth was going back to Seattle with an eighth-place standing in the class, and with Arnie Roth waiting for her here when she came back in the fall. Sondra had been accepted into a volunteer programme working in Public Health on an Indian Reservation. Mickey had her new face, shaded now by an enormous sun hat.

There was so much behind them, so much yet ahead. And September seemed so far away.

# PART TWO
*1971 – 1972*

# Chapter Ten

Mickey was running down the hall when she collided with the young man with the movie camera.

She had so many things on her mind: getting her internship in Hawaii, whether or not to attend the surgical seminar this weekend, the child in Six who'd swallowed an open safety pin. She crashed into the young man with the camera because she'd been looking at her watch: only two hours on the shift and already she was behind.

When she had passed the nurses' lounge a minute ago, Mickey had smelled the aroma of fresh coffee and had felt her stomach yawn. She had been in the Emergency Room until after midnight the night before, hadn't bothered to go home but had napped instead in an exam room, had risen at dawn, gone up to the surgical suite to shower in the nurses' locker room, and had dashed back down to the ER to start another gruelling eighteen-hour shift. She was thinking about when she'd last eaten – some pineapple upside-down cake gobbled hastily in the lounge around noon yesterday – and was wondering when she'd have time to eat again when she literally knocked the young man off his feet.

'Oh!' she said breathlessly, startled. 'I'm sorry!'

He reeled back a couple of steps, balancing a large movie camera on his shoulder. 'My fault entirely,' he said, recovering. 'I wasn't watching where I was going.'

'Are you all right?'

He laughed and swung the big camera down. 'I'll live. Hazards of the trade.'

She looked from him to a young man standing behind him who supported a large black case that hung by a strap from his shoulder. 'Can I help you with something?'

'Oh no, we're fine, thanks. Just go ahead with what you were doing.'

Mickey had been hurrying to see her next patient. It was eight o'clock on a fine October morning and the Emergency Room of St Catherine's was still fairly quiet. But soon, Mickey knew, it would be chaotic. 'Are you reporters?'

The one with the camera stared at her for a moment, then said, 'Oh, you don't know who we are. I'm sorry, I was told everyone had been briefed.' He thrust out a hand. 'Jonathan Archer. And this is Sam, my assistant.'

Puzzled, Mickey slipped her hand in his, a firm handshake, and nodded to the assistant, who smiled boyishly. 'I don't understand,' she said. 'Who are you and what are you doing here?'

'Jonathan Archer,' he said again, as if she should know the name and that would explain everything. 'We're filming a movie.'

'You're what?'

'I really thought everyone had been told.' He eyed her white jacket, the stethoscope, the medical chart in her arm. 'Are you on the staff here?'

'In a way.' Mickey wrestled with the impulse to dash away. A year in hospital clerkship had conditioned her to keep for ever on the move and to do three things at once. Fourth-year rotations barely left time to grab a cup of coffee, let alone stand and chat with a stranger. But she was curious. 'What sort of movie?'

Jonathan Archer's smile broadened. 'It's a documentary. Sam and I will be filming all over the hospital for the next few weeks, capturing events as they happen. Pure *cinema verité*.'

Mickey studied him with undisguised interest. Jonathan Archer looked like any ordinary workman who might be in the ER to repair something. His blue jeans were clean but heavily patched, his faded T-shirt, which said 'I Live In the Reel World', strained over broad shoulders and muscular chest; and his chestnut hair touched his shoulders. Mickey guessed he was a year or two shy of thirty.

In return, he regarded her with sharp blue eyes, amazed to find such a beauty hidden away in a hospital. That long neck, the platinum hair drawn severely back from her face, the high cheekbones and narrow nose – she looked like a prima ballerina, a classic beauty. 'And whom do I have the pleasure of being knocked off my feet by?'

'I'm Dr Long.'

'Oh, you're a doctor.'

'Well, no. Actually I'm a medical student. Fourth year. We're supposed to introduce ourselves to patients that way, I guess it's a habit with me now.' She smiled apologetically. 'Did I spoil something? A shot?'

'No, we aren't shooting yet. Just scouting the layout, the lighting, angles, that sort of thing.'

'Are you the cameraman?'

'I'm the producer, director, cameraman, script girl, and best boy.'

She gave a little laugh. 'I thought movies were always filmed with big lights and reflectors and folding canvas chairs and fifty people standing around.'

He returned the laugh and Mickey noticed that his eyes crinkled at the corners. Beautiful blue eyes, set in a handsome, tanned face. 'It depends on the kind of movie you're making. This is no *Ben Hur*. *Cinema verité* doesn't call for a large crew. Sam and I are it, the hospital is the set, you are the actors.'

'What's the story?'

'The hospital tells its own story.'

How strange. Three minutes ago Mickey had been in a mad rush with a million things on her mind and now here she was, discussing, of all things, *movies* with a total stranger.

'Can I buy you a cup of coffee?'

Mickey wished he hadn't asked that question, because it was exactly the one thing in the world she most wanted to do right now. But the painful reality was she had to say no. Mickey knew that no sooner would the last patient be seen than the exam rooms would all be full again. There would be lacerations to suture, plaster casts to apply, IVs to start, spinal fluid to draw, hysterical mothers to deal with, exasperated doctors to please – the list was endless. And somewhere in all of that she would have to manage lunch on the run, probably skip dinner, run to the apartment for a change of clothes, and maybe, if she was lucky, grab a quick nap on a vacant bed.

'I'm sorry, I just can't.' She started to move away. 'Good luck with your film.'

'We'll be running into each other again, Dr Long.'

Mickey hesitated, started to say something, changed her mind, and hurried away.

She collided with him a second time, taking a corner blindly and too fast, and they both laughed about the odds against *that* happening again; and Jonathan Archer asked her to lunch and again she declined. When she ran into him a third time, but not literally, Mickey was on her way to the medical records office in search of a lost chart; Jonathan and Sam had been filming in the psychiatric wing. They were able only to exchange a few words because Mickey edged away from him, apologising, declining his offer for coffee and doughnuts. The fourth time, Mickey had been so preoccupied with the logistics of moving to Hawaii in eight months, should the Great Victoria Hospital accept her, that Jonathan Archer had to grab her arm to get her attention. This time they were in the right place, the hospital cafeteria, and it was the right time, noon; he asked if he could join her for lunch, but Mickey had work-ups to do and so had to run off. Jonathan Archer was beginning to wonder if she was avoiding him, and by coincidence, Mickey was wondering the same thing.

She was nervous. As she did an assiduous scrub at the sink outside the operating room, Mickey tried to remember everything she'd learned last semester when she'd done her first real surgery rotation: thoroughly wash hands and arms first, scrub with Betadine brush while counting the strokes – twenty on the nails, ten on each finger and hand, six strokes around the wrist, six strokes on the rest of the arm past the elbow. Rinse, starting with fingertips, all the way down the arm while bringing the hand up, making sure the water runs down from fingers to elbow. Then transfer brush, add soap, and repeat on the other hand.

Like all beginners, Mickey was scrubbing too hard and consequently wincing with pain. In time she would learn just the right touch for getting out the skin bacteria without removing the skin itself. Just as she'd learned to keep her body away from the sink and to remember to put her mask up before starting the scrub. Why do surgeons in movies always scrub with their masks down? she wondered now. They'd get kicked out if they tried that in a real hospital!

Mickey looked up at the clock. If you did your scrub correctly it should take exactly ten minutes. She was concentrating hard on doing a good job because she was about to assist Dr Hill in surgery. Dr Hill who was the Chief of Surgery, and who, it was rumoured, ate medical students for breakfast.

Now came the tricky part: getting across the hall, through the closed door, dried and into sterile gown and gloves without once contaminating oneself. Last semester, one nurse (since it was the nurses and not the surgeons who taught the medical students this procedure) had sent Mickey back to the sinks three times before she was satisfied. Holding her arms up before her face so that the water dripped off her elbows, Mickey now walked backward into the room, pushing the door open with her rear end, and was thankful the scrub nurse had the towel ready because her arms were cold and stinging. Under the critical eye of the circulating nurse, Mickey dried first one hand, then the other, without touching the towel to her dress, then her arms up to her elbows, pinching the towel between thumb and forefinger and tossing it into the hamper. She slid into the gown that the scrub nurse held and then fumbled into the gloves without tearing them – not an easy thing to do – while the other nurse tied her gown in back.

The surgery hadn't started yet and already Mickey was perspiring.

'You gonna assist Hill?' barked a voice behind the anaesthesia screen.

Mickey couldn't see him. Since the patient was already asleep and prepped, the scrub nurse had laid on the sterile drapes; the anaesthetist sat hidden behind a green barrier. 'Yes I am,' she said to him.

'Good luck.'

That was the sixth good-luck she'd received that morning. Surely Dr Hill couldn't be that bad! 'He's a regular bear in the operating room,' Miss Timmons, the head nurse, had told Mickey in the locker room. 'Thinks he's God or something. Likes to see medical students slink out with their tails between their legs. And watch out, he's a knuckle-rapper.' That last Mickey had heard from several others in her class, those who had already done their obligatory rotation through surgery. If you made a mistake, Hill whacked your knuckles with an instrument.

'All right, let's go!' boomed a voice as the door swung open. A tall and imposing man in greens presented dripping arms to the scrub nurse and did a rapid drying of his hands. As he was being tied snugly into his gown he sized up his assistant with chilling eyes. 'You the fourth-year that's supposed to help me on this?'

'Yes, Doctor.'

'What's your name?'

'Dr Long.'

'Not yet it isn't. Ever helped on an appy before, Miss Long?'

'No, Doctor, but I read up on it last –'

'You stand on that side,' he said, crossing to the table in three long strides.

Swallowing hard, Mickey did as told and took her place opposite Dr Hill, resting her hands very lightly on the green sheets. Beneath them, she felt a faint warmth coming from the patient underneath, and the gentle rising and falling of assisted breathing.

'If you feel faint during the surgery, Miss Long, step away from the table. Now then, ladies, are we all set?' The two nurses nodded. 'Chuck, you awake back there?'

'All set,' came the terse reply from behind the anaesthesia screen.

Dr Hill planted himself foursquare over the small patch of bare abdomen left exposed by the sheets and gave Mickey a long, calculating look. Then he said, 'We always start with the scalpel. I presume you have heard of a scalpel, Miss Long? When signalling for the blade, you don't hold your hand out flat like you would for other instruments, you'll lose a finger if you do. The signal for the blade is made by holding your hand in the position it will be in when you are using the blade. Like this.' Dr Hill held his arm out over the sterile operative field, wrist bent, hand pronated with thumb and fingertips touching – a praying mantis hand – and the scrub nurse slipped the handle of the scalpel between his fingers.

'Ideally,' he went on, 'you should never have to ask for a single thing. Gestures ought to suffice. And if your scrub nurse is on the ball, you won't even have to use gestures because she'll have the next instrument ready before you need it. We're going to cut now, Miss Long. Have a sponge in your hand at all times. That is what is meant by assistant. You *assist* me, is that clear?'

'Yes, Doctor.' Mickey reached up to the Mayo stand, plucked a four-by-four off the stack, and dragged down three haemostats and a loaded suture with it.

Dr Hill, calmly laying the scalpel down, lifted cold grey eyes to her and said, 'That, Miss Long, is a no-no. Do you see these sponges down here that our scrub nurse has thoughtfully spread out for us? That is what she is here for, Miss Long. To help us. *We* work in this area where the wound is, *she* works at the Mayo stand. Never take anything off the Mayo stand.'

Red-faced, Mickey tried to disengage the curved suture needle from the gauze but succeeded only in making it worse. Dr Hill said nothing. His wintry eyes bore into Mickey as her hands fumbled with the gauze and suture, until finally the scrub nurse leaned over and said gently, 'Here, I'll do that.'

Mickey mumbled, 'Sorry,' and picked up one of the stretched-out gauzes.

Dr Hill picked up his scalpel and resumed. 'Now then, when the human body is cut it bleeds. That blood needs to be kept mopped up while the surgeon works. That is what God put you on this earth for, Miss Long, to do my mop-up. If I ever catch you without a sponge in your hands I will assume you have no notion of why you are in an operating room and I will ask you to leave.'

He made a nice, clean sweep, cutting through skin and fat in one slice, and immediately Mickey stuffed a gauze into the wound. When it was soaked with blood, she pulled it out and inserted another one in its place. Dr Hill said nothing. His hands didn't move. Mickey's head started to thrum as she mopped, discarded, seized a fresh sponge, mopped and discarded again. She was about to press yet another clean gauze into the wound when Dr Hill said dryly, 'I assume you intend to keep that up until the patient bleeds to death? *Blot* the blood, Miss Long, and then get the hell out of my way so I can cauterise.'

He picked up an instrument that looked like a ballpoint pen with a needle protruding out of one end and an electrical wire leading out of the other. Applying the needle to the various points of bleeding, Dr Hill left a path of char spots along the wound. It took a few minutes and Mickey quickly got the hang of it: she saw where Dr Hill was heading and blotted just in front of him, rapidly clearing off the blood so he could see the bleeding point until soon, miraculously, the sponges came away clean and the open wound was pink and dry.

'At this point, Miss Long, you will keep a haemostat in your hand at all times. If my blade should nick a big bleeder you'll need to clamp it at once. Hold your hand out flat like this.'

She did so and automatically, like iron to a magnet, a haemostat was slapped firmly into her palm. Mickey reflexively reached up with her left hand to hold the clamp while she slid her fingers into the handle rings. Like lightning, Dr Hill's hand shot out and smacked her left hand hard. Startled, Mickey snapped her head up. 'Never use two hands, Miss Long. There are no wasted movements in surgery. You hold your hand out and the nurse passes the instrument already in position of use. There will be no fumbling, and *one hand only*. Do it again.'

Swallowing down her anger, Mickey dropped the haemostat and held her hand out. Again the nurse slapped in the clamp and again, reflexively, her other hand came up. This time Dr Hill used the first haemostat to deliver the blow, a painful, stinging whack across her knuckles.

'Again,' he said.

Furious, Mickey locked eyes with him. Throwing down the clamp she held out her flat hand, felt the firm seating of the instrument, and then struggled, really struggled single-handedly, to slip her fingers into the rings. The clamp dropped out of her hand, landed on the sterile drapes, slid off, and clanged to the floor.

'Again,' said Hill, his cold, hard eyes holding hers.

Mickey lost the next one to the floor, had her knuckles

rapped a second time, but on the sixth haemostat managed to wedge her fingers clumsily into the rings. 'Bravo,' said Dr Hill thinly. 'Those are the wrong fingers.'

She wanted to fling the clamp in his smug face, she wanted to slap him, she wanted to ask him if he was born with the skill of handling surgical instruments, she wanted to tell him where he could stick his damn haemostats. Instead, Mickey held out her hand, received the clamp, quickly slipped thumb and third finger into the rings, then dropped the tip down to the wound.

After a few more minutes of sponging and cauterising, Dr Hill laid down his instruments and said, 'The charm of the McBurney incision, Miss Long, is that you don't have to cut the muscle, you just split it.' And he inserted the first two fingers of each hand into the wound, raised his elbows, and stretched the wound open.

'Now then, Miss Long, what are the clinical aspects of non-perforated appendicitis?'

She thought a moment, then said, 'Mild general abdominal pain beginning in the epigastrium, usually associated with loss of appetite and vomiting, resolving after a few hours into localised pain in the right lower quadrant. The fever is usually only slight. Muscle spasm is often seen in the lower right abdomen, an elevation of leucocyte count, and sedimentation rate can be –'

'I don't employ the sed rate in my appendicitis patients, Miss Long, as it is not usually diagnostic. Nurse, give my assistant a Goulet.'

As his fingers delved into the pelvic cavity to find the appendix, Dr Hill said, 'One must always be certain to handle this carefully in case the appendix is too friable to permit flection without rupture, in which case the base is separated from the caecum first, instead of the other way around. Babcock, please, nurse.'

Once the pinkish, wormlike bit of tissue was removed and dropped into the specimen pan, Dr Hill buried the ligated appendiceal stump with a purse-string suture, saying as he did so, 'There are various ways to do this, Miss Long. Can you tell me why I choose this method?'

'I would imagine, Doctor, that it is because in the event an abscess should form at the site of the buried stump, there is more chance it will rupture into the caecum with this closure than into the peritoneal cavity.'

'Very good, Miss Long,' he said slowly. 'You're sharper than most.' Then he turned to the anaesthesia screen and said, 'Going to close now, Chuck.'

A green-hatted head popped up. 'Vital signs are stable, Jim.'

'Oh-Chromic,' Dr Hill said to the scrub nurse, holding out his hand. 'And give Miss Long the Mayo scissors. If I wait for her to think of asking for them, we'll be celebrating the turn of the new century.'

The anaesthetist pulled the stethoscopic earpiece out of his ear and, as he watched Hill draw the abdominal layers closed, said, 'So what do you think of this movie fellah, Jim? He's got the hospital all turned upside down.'

'He doesn't bother me, as long as he doesn't get in my way.'

'Did you see his last movie?' asked the circulating nurse from her stool in the corner. 'I was crying halfway through.'

'What movie is that?' asked the scrub nurse, loading another suture.

'You haven't heard of it? It's caused an awful uproar. They say the Justice Department tried to stop its release in this country.'

'I saw it,' growled Chuck, 'and I thought it was a bunch of Commie crap.'

'What *is* it?' asked the scrub nurse again.

'It's called *Nam!* and it's a documentary on the war,' said the other nurse. 'Really graphic but also quite beautiful. They say he got right there in the middle of combat and filmed it all through the eyes of one GI. It gave me nightmares but I also found it very moving.'

'Damn it, Miss Long,' snapped Hill. 'You're cutting them too long. Nurse, cut for me, please.' He yanked the scissors out of Mickey's hand and threw them onto the Mayo stand.

'It said in the LA *Times*,' the circulating nurse went on, 'that Jonathan Archer may be young and new at movie-making, but he's definitely someone to watch.'

Mickey stood with her hands flat on the surgical drapes.

She kept her eyes on Dr Hill's rhythmic sewing, the periodic snipping of the sutures by the nurse. She swallowed with a dry throat. She tried to moderate her breathing. This was not going to happen to her a second time; this was never going to happen again . . .

# Chapter Eleven

It was a Thursday afternoon, cool and blustery outside with a grey ocean sending angry waves to pound the sand; the Emergency Room was relatively quiet.

Mickey had just spent an hour watching the senior resident withdraw a penny from a child's throat and was washing her hands at the sink when Dr Harold came up, a kindly old attending surgeon. 'I remember,' he said, folding his arms and leaning against the wall, 'I was in here one night and a kid with a coin in his throat was brought in by the paramedics. They called Dr Peebles, the ENT man, and told him what it was. He said he was in the middle of dinner and wasn't about to come in to get a penny out of a kid's throat. The intern said, "It's not a penny, sir. It's a dime." "In that case," Peebles said, "I'll be right in."'

Mickey smiled politely; she'd heard the tale many times, each with a different name, a different coin.

'Miss Long?' said the desk nurse, coming up and holding out a chart. 'There's a man in Three. Severe abdominal pain.'

'Thank you, Judy.' Mickey opened the chart and scanned it while she rubbed cream into her hands: A Mr L. B. Mayer, early sixties, nausea, pain in lower left quadrant, NO INSURANCE.

Fourth-year medical students did not make final diagnoses, did not prescribe, did not admit patients to the hospital, they only went through the motions. After Mickey, an intern would see this man, then a junior resident, possibly another resident, all asking the same questions, doing the same exam, writing all the same information down, and then at last the senior resident would step in and make the final decision. Even though Mickey was the first and lowliest step of this process, she tried to approach each case as if it were indeed her sole responsibility and as a result her exam was always thorough.

The chart revealed little. Five pages of blank lines were to be filled in by her, and it usually took an hour or two. She knocked first on the door of Three, then opened it, smiling professionally and saying, 'Good morning, Mr Mayer, I'm Dr Long and I'm going to –'

'It's afternoon already, Doctor,' said Jonathan Archer with a devilish grin, jumping off the exam table.

'What –'

He rushed behind her, closed the door, clicked it locked, then took the chart out of her hands. 'L. B. Mayer, get it? Louis B. Mayer? Please sit down, Doctor. Look what I brought.' He reached for a basket by the sink and lifted a checkered cloth. 'Bagels and cream cheese.' He pulled out a thermos. 'Jamaican coffee.'

'Mr Archer –'

'No protests, Doctor, you don't know what I went through for this.'

'Mr Archer, what are you doing?'

He fluffed out the checkered cloth and spread it out over the tissue-covered exam table. Then he started to unscrew the thermos. 'Aren't you going to sit down?'

'I want you to tell me what you think –'

He turned abruptly and faced her seriously. He said quietly, 'I finally figured out that the only way I'm going to see you is by being a patient.'

'But you're not a patient, Mr Archer.'

'I can be.'

She stared back into a pair of uncommonly blue eyes, saw the tiny crinkles at the corners, and said, 'Oh, you wouldn't.'

'Try me.'

Mickey started to feel silly. And flattered. 'I have work to do,' she said unconvincingly.

'Dr Long, all I want is to spend some time with you and get to know you. Now look, I told the nurse to send you in here when you had nothing else on. It's a quiet day. We'll have a bite to eat, talk a bit . . .'

'In here?'

'Why not? If you're needed, the nurse knows where you are. What do you say?'

She looked at the food in the basket, smelled the inviting

coffee, looked again at the winsome smile. 'I simply can't. It wouldn't be right.'

'Okay, you asked for it.' He started for the door.

'What are you going to do?'

'I can also act, Dr Long. I intend to roll around on the floor out there screaming in pain.'

'You wouldn't.'

'And then I'm going to tell them how you refused to examine me. And I'm going to shout "sue" so loud –'

Mickey started to laugh.

'– that a thousand women named Susan will come running –'

She leaned against the sink bringing her hands to her cheeks.

'– and then I'm going to expose it all in my movie and you'll be dragged through such scandal that –'

'All right.'

'– you'll be lucky if you can practise medicine in Toad Suck, Arkansas –'

'I said all right.'

'All right?'

'I'll stay.' She quickly held up a hand. 'But only because I'm starved and desperate and only for a few minutes.'

'Do you really like this?' he asked five minutes later, waving his hand around the small, pristine room, indicating the blood pressure cuff on the wall, the small instruments soaking in a pink solution, the neat boxes of sutures and dressings.

'Yes, I really like it.'

He offered her a refill of the coffee, then drained the rest in his own cup, drinking it down in mute reflection, his sea-blue eyes never leaving her face.

'Where's Sam?' she asked.

'He's at the lab looking at the first rushes.'

'Rushes?'

'The first film we've shot so far.'

'I'm sorry to say I've never seen one of your movies. I don't get to movies much.'

He laughed. 'I've only made two and the first one never left the can. I hadn't expected *Nam!* to be such a hit. My intention had only been to open the public's eyes. Who'd have thought a little eye-opening could be so painful?'

'Where did you get your degree in movie-making?'

Jonathan helped himself to a second bagel, spreading it generously with cream cheese and a strip of lox. 'I didn't. I'm a lawyer. Stanford, 1968.'

'You make movies in your spare time?'

'In my whole time. I went to law school to please my father. He had visions of me joining his Beverly Hills firm. It was never an ambition of mine, I always felt the tug of the cinema. I used to ditch classes to sit in dark movie houses. But I got the degree and passed the state bar like he wanted and fulfilled the contract, so to speak. Then I hung up my three-piece suit and bought a movie camera.' He took a bite of his bagel, chewed thoughtfully, washed it down with coffee, then said, 'My father hasn't spoken to me since.'

Mickey's cup stopped at her lips. 'I'm sorry,' she said quietly.

'He'll come around, he always does. My older brother rebelled the same way, going into marine insurance, but as soon as he had his first kid, my dad's first grandchild, all was forgiven.'

Mickey's eyes twinkled over the rim of her cup. 'Is that how you intend to get back into his good graces? Have a baby?'

Jonathan grinned, said, 'He'll be happy with whichever comes first, a baby or my first million,' and prayed silently that the wretched intercom wouldn't buzz.

By coincidence, Mickey was hoping the same thing, and it surprised her. Since she had said good-bye to Chris Novack that summer of '69, over two years ago, she'd plunged herself wholeheartedly into the study of medicine, to the exclusion of all else.

'What kind of doctor are you going to be?'

'A plastic surgeon.'

'Why?'

She told him about the birthmark and Chris Novack. She spoke unhesitantly where two and a half years ago she would rather have died than speak of it. Before she was through she found Jonathan frowning at her face.

'Which side was it on?'

'You tell me.'

He stood and came up to the exam table where Mickey sat swinging her legs. With a gentle touch, he took hold of her chin and turned her head this way and that, first with the eye of a man behind a camera and then just with the eye of a man. 'I don't believe you,' he said at last.

'Oh, it's true. And it's still there, really. Dr Novack didn't remove it, he just covered it. I have to be very careful of sunlight, and when I blush only one side of my face turns red.'

'Let me see you do that.'

'I can't blush on command!'

He moved a little closer to her, his legs touching hers, his fingertips still on her chin, and then he said quietly, 'I'd like to make love to you, right here on this exam table.'

She drew in her breath, and knew she was blushing.

'Ha!' he said, stepping back. 'You're right. Only the left side turned red.'

She stared as he went back to his chair, picked up a bagel and started to eat. 'So you want to be a plastic surgeon and rid the world of all ugliness?'

'People can't help how they're born or what nature gives them. Just because *you* were born with good looks –'

'Do you think so?'

'What I meant to say –'

'Half of your face is red again, Dr Long.'

Mickey put her cup down and stood up. 'I didn't make light of *your* life story.'

He was instantly on his feet. 'Hey! I'm sorry! I was teasing you, I didn't mean anything.' He reached out and took her arm. 'I really am sorry. Please don't go.'

Mickey looked up at him. 'I was never ugly, Jonathan – few people really are. But in my mind I was. The birthmark looked like nothing more than a sunburn, but since I was convinced I was grotesque, I acted as though I really was. When Dr Novack took away the stain, I became a changed woman. Another Mickey Long emerged overnight – the real Mickey Long. Nothing changed so much as my own image of myself. And that's what I want to do with my life, help other people with physical disfigurements to have better self-images and therefore happier lives.'

He stared at her, caught in the spell of her voice, her face. Suddenly he very much regretted his flippancy of a moment ago. 'You're something,' he said.

They stared at each other, and then she felt his hand tighten on her arm and she felt something else, a strong physical feeling, something she'd experienced only once before, two summers ago, in the arms of Chris Novack.

'You've heard my life story,' Jonathan said quietly, 'now tell me yours.'

'There's nothing to tell.'

'Family?'

'I have none. My father deserted us when I was little and my mother died two years ago.'

'So you're all alone.'

'Yes . . .'

When the buzzer broke the moment, neither of them reacted. And when the charge nurse's voice came over. 'Sorry, Mickey, got a spinal tap for you,' the two continued to stare at one another.

Finally Jonathan moved; Mickey cleared her throat and looked at her watch. 'I'll be right out, Judy, thanks.'

At the door she turned. 'Thanks for the brunch. It was lovely.'

'How about dinner Saturday night?'

She shook her head. 'I'll be on duty.'

'When are you off duty?'

'When I'm on call.'

'And the rest of the time?'

'I'm in bed.'

Jonathan sighed. With anyone else, he would have come back with something snappy – 'Then I'll join you in bed.' But not with Mickey Long. He was convinced she was someone special.

'I work long hours, Jonathan. I'm sorry. Thirty-six on and eighteen off. And then I have classes on campus and a lot of outside reading to do.'

'We seem to be nipped in the bud.'

'It looks that way.'

'Can't you *make* time? A little?'

She took a last look at him before opening the door. 'I'll try. I'll try.'

# Chapter Twelve

Ruth was running a race again, a new race. But this time the prize would not be a box of watercolours, or high grades or class standing.

It would be a baby.

Sitting in the October sunshine that streamed through the windows, Ruth occupied an easy chair of crushed velour, at the quiet end of Encinitas Hall. A calendar, spiral pad, and pencil were in her lap. She was in the process of calculating moon cycles and dates, when feminine voices distracted her. Looking up, Ruth contemplated the new group of first-years who were gathered about the fireplace; she took a minute to wonder where this breed of medical student had come from.

They sat cross-legged on the floor, some thirty young women with long straight hair hooked behind their ears, all in pants or slacks or jeans, in peasant blouses, men's work shirts, sweaters, and a T-shirt that said, 'A Woman Without a Man Is Like a Fish Without a Bicycle.' They were lazily familiar with one another, as if they'd been a group for years instead of having met for the first time just last month; four black women and two Chicanas nodded and communed with the Anglo woman in an ease that would not have been known a few years back.

They had unbalanced Ruth on the first day of Orientation four weeks ago when, having volunteered to give a welcome talk to the incoming freshman women, she'd arrived armed with the advice Selma Stone had given her three years ago. But Ruth had found her words meaningless. *They already knew.* How had it happened? What were the mysterious channels of feminine communication crisscrossing the country, putting out the word? How had these thirty arrived here from thirty different points, strangers but already knowing one another, agreeing, unified, bound together?

In a week they'd got the dress code rewritten. Moreno had pulled his cadaver stunt and then been made to apologise formally to the whole class. Dr Morphy quietly eliminated words like 'honey' and 'girlie' from his lectures. And, at this very moment, an old storeroom in Mariposa Hall was being converted into a women's room.

Why? Why had these thirty succeeded where their predecessors had failed? Was it merely a matter of their number, now accounting for one third of the class and therefore a force to be reckoned with, or were women really changing, more aware of themselves and their place in the world, bolder, a new breed indeed?

Ruth shook her head, mentally congratulated them, and returned to the project in her lap.

It was very delicate, determining the date for delivery. She had to time it just right, as precisely as nature would concede to science. If she were very pregnant when she tried to start her internship, the hospital wouldn't take her and they'd give her spot to someone else; but if, on the other hand, she waited too long to conceive she'd be pregnant through most of her internship and that wouldn't go over well either. However, knowing the staff with whom she'd worked the past three summers, in the hospital up in Seattle where she was going to start her internship in July, Ruth was fairly confident that they'd let her start if she had only a short way to go in her term, but not so far that she'd be of no use to them.

So Ruth estimated that her seventh month would be a good time to start her internship – that way all of the morning sickness and other incapacitations would be behind her, she'd be of modest size yet able to work, and would have it all over in September, at which time she knew they would grant her a week or two leave, not wanting to replace her at such a late date.

So.

Ruth picked up pen and paper and did the equation again. You take the date your last period began, add seven days, count back three months and you have your delivery date. Ruth was extremely regular, she was lucky in that respect, so she could look at the calendar and point right now to future cycle days. She calculated November 5 as when her next

114

period would start, added seven days, went back three months and came to mid-August for delivery. Too soon.

Her cycle was going to begin again on December 2. The equation this time brought her to September 9.

Ruth smiled, put down the pen and sat back. Perfect. Just the right time to have the baby. Now all she had to do was have sexual intercourse during the peak of her December cycle, which was the twelfth to the sixteenth.

And Arnie's cooperation.

In the nearly three years she'd been dating Arnie Roth, ever since first meeting him at the New Year's Eve party that heralded in 1969, Ruth and Arnie had seriously discussed marriage exactly twice – both times brought up by Arnie, both times rejected by Ruth. Her reasoning was valid, he hadn't been able to dispute that: with his office in Encino and Ruth's school in Palos Verdes, where would they live that was convenient for both? And besides, there seemed no point to getting married since they wouldn't be able to see any more of each other than they did now. The plan was to have the wedding in June, right after graduation, which would give them both four weeks in which to finalise the dissolution of Arnie's partnership, make the move up to Seattle, and get settled in a house before Ruth began internship on July 1. Arnie would not see the purpose in getting married now, in October, Ruth knew. 'We've waited three years, Ruth,' he would say. 'We can wait six more months. I don't want to live apart from my bride in the first months of our marriage.'

What Ruth had to plan next was how to talk Arnie into going along with her, to get him to agree to get married now and continue to live apart until graduation.

Ruth held a deep affection for Arnie Roth. His soft-spoken manner and gentle presence were the only balm in her life. There was a solid, well-anchored stability about him that lent ballast to her stressful life, especially when exams were coming up or grades were about to be posted. Arnie was always there. She had asked him one rainy night how he could put up with her craziness, her highs and lows, her placing school before their relationship, and he'd quietly, logically explained that what had to be done had to be done: 'No one graduates first in his or her class without putting blood and sweat and sacrifice into it. The time will come, Ruth, when all this will be behind us and you'll have earned a life of peace and ease. I'm willing to invest now against that future.'

It was so perfect, the dream they shared. Ruth getting her medical degree, the house in Seattle, three years of residency and then her own private practice in obstetrics; and finally, when they were financially secure, starting a family. Arnie was right, the future was worth it.

Except that now, everything had changed.

When Ruth had left Castillo last June to return for a summer in Seattle with her family, she'd gone away with the plum prize of fourth-place standing in her class. Out of seventy-nine students, she was fourth. *Now* her father had to admit finally that she could do it, that she'd shown him, that she was worthy after all. And, to her mild surprise, he had conceded. 'You did do it, Ruthie, I'm amazed. If you made it at all I thought you'd just squeak by. But fourth in your class, well, I'm impressed.' Ruth could have burst with pride. Not even Joshua had graduated from West Point with such a standing. 'However...'

Ruth replayed her father's words now as she sat staring out the windows of Encinitas Hall at the grey and white marbling of the sycamore bark, at the red and gold leaves swirling along the path in dust devils. She relived their conversation and saw once more her father's face darken, his voice turn solemn as he said, 'But what price did you pay, Ruthie? Are the sacrifices worth it? By the time you're all done and in practice you'll be thirty. That's late to be starting a family. You've sacrificed your femininity to be a doctor. You won't be a whole woman. It's an unnatural life you've carved out for yourself, Ruthie.'

Ruth had left Seattle early and returned to Southern California two weeks before school started, staying with Arnie in his Tarzana apartment, washing away her misery and bitterness with the antidote of his gentle love, his tireless strength. But now Ruth was recovered from the hurt of the summer and was coolly, rationally mapping out the plan to prove her father wrong.

The large double doors opened across the room and

Sondra appeared. She waved, walked over to a vending machine to get a Bit O' Honey bar, then came to join Ruth. 'How is it going?' she asked, glancing over at the discussion group by the fireplace. Where on earth did these women find time for discussion groups? Why weren't they over at Gilhooley's drinking beer and chewing their nails?

'I've got it figured out,' said Ruth, showing Sondra her calculations.

Sondra looked at the paper and nodded. She thought Ruth was making a mistake by starting a family at this stage. But Ruth was determined to carry out her plans, and Sondra had given up trying to dissuade her. 'I'm going over to Gilhooley's for a burger. Want to join me?'

'Can't. I have twelve chart reviews to do tonight and some research in the library.'

Most people would have been satisfied with fourth-place standing in class, ecstatic even; certainly Sondra was happy being twelfth and Mickey was pleased with her rank of fifteenth. But Ruth still was driving herself, and had even taken on a special project for extra credit. Sondra didn't understand how Arnie put up with it. But she admired him for sticking by Ruth, not insisting on seeing her, waiting for her to do the calling and arrange dates. Now she wondered how Ruth was going to talk him into getting married so soon and starting a baby.

'Try Mickey,' said Ruth, looking at her watch. 'I think she's free tonight.'

'Didn't you know? Mickey's got a date tonight. With Jonathan Archer.'

Ruth looked away from Sondra and started getting her things together. She had strong feelings on that subject but she kept them firmly to herself. Jonathan Archer had literally turned the hospital upside down. *Cinema verité*? A look inside a big medical centre as the public never sees it, gritty real life stuff, drama as it happens today? Ha! All the nurses were showing up in bright new uniforms with their faces made up and their hair done as if they were going to a party, always smiling, efficient, never addled, always serene and dedicated. And the men on the staff: suddenly no dingy white jackets were to be seen, no afternoon shadows, no cigarettes dangling from slack lips, no raunchy talk – a whole colony of fresh-scrubbed Dr Kildares. So much for *verité*.

Ruth didn't much like the young moviemaker. There wasn't a corner one could turn at St Catherine's without encountering Jonathan Archer carrying that monster of a camera on his shoulder; he was getting in the way, his assistant hovering with that bar of tungsten-halogen lamps, thrusting a microphone at you as you made a phone call and all you were doing was checking with the cafeteria to see if there was any corned beef left.

Well, Ruth hadn't told Mickey or Sondra but she'd been instrumental in barring Jonathan Archer, as far as was possible, from the Labour & Delivery suite.

'He's called every night this week,' said Sondra as she and Ruth walked towards the double doors. 'This is the first evening she's had free. He's taking her to see that antiwar picture of his, the one called *Nam!* It won a prize at the Cannes Film Festival this year and Mickey says there's talk of an Academy Award nomination.'

She might not like Jonathan Archer but Ruth did wish Mickey success with him. Tonight was their first date – you couldn't count that fiasco in the Emergency Room – and Ruth hoped it went well.

When Sondra and Ruth stepped out into the blustery October afternoon, Sondra said, 'You'll be on your own tonight, Ruth. I'm going to a lecture at Hernandez Hall. More tropical medicine.'

'I'll leave a light burning,' Ruth called after her, then added mentally: lucky Sondra.

Sondra's future was so neatly laid out, her goals so sharply defined, with no obstacles, no complicating relationships, no one to consider but herself. Having kept pretty much to herself and away from entanglements with men these past three years, Sondra Mallone was staying on the course she had set for herself years ago. This past summer, the Reverend Mr Ingels, the pastor of her parents' church in Phoenix, had asked her if she would consider donating time to a Christian mission in Kenya. Sondra had agreed, and after June, she would do a year of general internship in Arizona, then fly off to Africa for a life, her two roommates were certain, of adventure, discovery, and personal fulfilment.

Drawing her sweater closer about her, Ruth struck off down the path away from Encinitas Hall towards the medical library, where she would spend the next few hours. She needed to think, to work out how she would proceed with Arnie and the baby. And then she wanted to plunge into her extra-credit project, the one she hoped would nudge her up one more place in class standing.

June was eight months away and Ruth intended to graduate in first place.


Mickey met him at the door with an apologetic expression on her face. 'I'm sorry, Jonathan. I've been trying to get hold of you. I can't go out with you tonight after all. Something has come up.'

He stood in the doorway with the glow of the porch light falling onto his long hair. 'What happened?'

'I'm on ER call tonight.'

'So suddenly? You weren't when we talked this afternoon. Is this an assignment or did you volunteer?'

She shifted her eyes away from his penetrating stare. 'Well, they asked me . . .'

'And you didn't say no. Then can I at least come in and wait for your call with you?'

'Well, you see, I really should be at the hospital. When an emergency comes in –'

'You're not far. Besides, I can take you in my car.'

She thought a moment, then stepped back. 'I suppose it would be all right. But it's Saturday night, our busiest.'

He came in and took off his sweater, the bulky, cable-knit that fishermen wear. He had a rugged look about him tonight, in blue jeans and hiking boots. 'Why did you take it? Do they pay you?'

Mickey closed the door and went into the kitchen. 'Oh no, no money.'

'Then why?'

She opened the fridge door and called out, 'Beer, wine, or Fresca?'

'Beer, please. So why do you take emergency call when you don't have to?'

Mickey returned, handing him the beer with no glass and popping a can of Fresca for herself. 'For the experience. I want to be a plastic surgeon and for that you have to be damned good at suturing. When I'm in surgery, the most they let me do is hold retractors. It's the interns and residents who get to do the sewing.' She went into the living room, warmly lit against the October night, and took a seat on the sofa. Jonathan sat opposite her, in the easy chair. 'In the ER, too,' she went on, curling her legs under herself. 'The plastic surgery residents get first pickings, then the interns. We med students get the scut work. But on nights when they're really busy and the injuries are stacking up, they let us suture. Also, I've applied for an internship at a very choice hospital: competition is going to be tough, I want my record to hold up.'

He tasted his beer, then leaned back and looked around the room. 'Nice place you have here.'

'We've fixed it up over the years, added our own touches. It was quite bare when we moved in three years ago.'

'We?'

'My roommates and I.' Mickey went on to tell him how the three had met and become friends, then she was soon speaking in a soft, relaxed way about herself and her life at Castillo. Jonathan listened with interest, watching her; he found himself wondering if he could somehow manage to slip her phone off the hook and keep her with him.

'I'm sorry,' she said after a while. 'I've been running on, haven't I?'

'I think you're the most beautiful woman I've ever met. And I mean it literally, Mickey. In the physical sense. You're gorgeous. I took a look at my first rushes of you yesterday, from the filming we did in the ER last Wednesday, and you're incredibly photogenic. Even Sam was amazed. You're a natural on film. I think you're going into the wrong profession.'

She stared at him a moment, then laughed. 'Is this the way you sweet-talk all your dates?'

But he was serious and she knew it. 'It's every director's

dream to find a natural beauty like you. And it's not just your looks.' He set the beer aside and leaned forward, elbows on knees, hands clasped. 'You have a way of moving, of carrying yourself. You're *fluid*, Mickey.'

'Well!' She turned the Fresca around and around in her hands. 'Well . . .'

The silence was broken only by the distant sound of surf. Finally Mickey said, half to herself, 'They used to call me Mickey the Mud Hen.'

He got up and came to sit next to her on the sofa. She felt his energy coming across the small space between them; it was in his eyes, his body, his voice. 'Let me make a movie about you, Mickey.'

'No.'

'Why not? Yours is a great story and people will love just to look at you.'

'No, Jonathan,' she said. 'I'm not going into movies. I'm not going to go public. I'm going to be a doctor, plain and simple. Please don't try to persuade me otherwise, don't try to change me, Jonathan.'

He reached for her hand. 'Mickey, I wouldn't change you for a million dollars.' Then he was kissing her and Mickey marvelled at how easy it all seemed. Before, whenever she'd kissed a man she'd been frozen by an awareness of her face, the closeness of his to it; she would be wondering if he was attracted to her, yet also repulsed on another level. Mickey had never experienced an unselfconcious kind of kissing in which she could give herself up totally.

Jonathan was her first.

Then he pulled her to him and the kiss became demanding. Her pulse started to race: what were the rules?

Just then the phone rang.

Jonathan drew away and Mickey jumped up. The conversation was brief: 'Judy? Facial lacerations? You've got to be kidding! Of course I'll be right there!'

Jonathan watched her as she went into the bedroom, then emerged with sweater, handbag, a white jacket folded neatly over her arm. 'I'm sorry, Jonathan,' she said softly. 'I really do have to go.'

# Chapter Thirteen

The car radio was tuned to KFWB and Mick Jagger was singing, 'It is the evening of the day ... I sit and watch the children play ...'

Ruth gazed out of the window. To her right was a spectacular view: black velvet scattered with rubies and emeralds and diamonds, the San Fernando Valley at night, lit up for Christmas. But Ruth didn't really see it. Before her was the ghostly image of a young woman, not beautiful but pretty, with dark brown hair bobbed sensibly short, her dark eyes deep in thought. Before this evening was over, Ruth knew, she was going to have to tell Arnie, and finding the right moment wasn't going to be easy.

She felt warm fingers curl around her hand and lift it to a kiss. Ruth turned and smiled at him. 'You're rather free with my body, aren't you?'

He took the tricky curves of Mulholland Drive with one hand on the wheel. 'I can't get enough of you,' he said, biting her thumb.

'Better give that back, I'll need it tomorrow.'

He dropped her hand. 'I relinquish it gladly, fair maiden, as long as you don't tell me what you'll need it for.'

Ruth still couldn't get over it: Arnie hadn't exaggerated things the night they met, when he had told her he disliked hearing medical talk.

'Arnie, can we stop?'

He looked at her with raised eyebrows. 'Now? What do you want to do, neck?'

'I want to talk.'

He looked at the luminous clock face set in the dash. 'The family's expecting us, Ruth. Mother will have a fit if we're late.'

She sighed at the thought of Arnie's family. Mr Roth,

quiet and unassuming, an accountant like Arnie, two brothers, one the epidemiologist, the other in real estate, three sisters, all married with eight kids among them, cousins who lived in Northridge, an elderly aunt and uncle living in an 'active' retirement home, all presided over by the formidable and matriarchal Mrs Maxine Roth, a woman whose generous heart was as big as her enormous bosom. A family, in fact, not unlike Ruth's up in Seattle.

She rarely gave in, rarely let him have the final say, but she did now. 'Okay, Arnie. We can talk later.'

There was, as usual, more food on the table than an army could eat and Mrs Roth was constantly exhorting everyone to eat more. 'You don't like my cooking?' she would ask, while the kids ran around and the adults all talked at once. But Ruth loved it. It *was* like home.

Finally Mrs Roth released them all from the table, satisfied they were all well fed and happy, so Ruth took Arnie by the arm and gave him a significant look. The Roth house sat atop an Encino hill looking out over the glittering San Fernando Valley. While two TVs and a stereo down in the rumpus room blared and children's squeals mingled with adult talk, Ruth and Arnie stepped out into the blessed cool and quiet night.

The pool was lit, shimmering lime green, and tiki lights provided little cones of luminance for them to stroll through.

'Arnie,' Ruth said after a few minutes of silence, 'let's get married.'

'Sure.' He gave her hand a squeeze. 'We're going to, in June. Remember?'

'I mean now. Right away.'

Arnie laughed softly. 'Mad impetuous woman.'

'I'm serious, Arnie. I can't wait.'

He stopped and turned to face her. 'What do you mean, you can't wait?'

The words didn't come out at all as planned; the speech she had prepared, its calm delivery, fled in the emotion of the moment. She blurted it all, in half sentences, words run together, hands making sweeping gestures, about the *need* to have a baby soon, before her internship and residency made it impossible, about the race she ran with her biological clock, that she didn't want to be over thirty before having the first one, about how having a baby right now was so important to her that it was driving her crazy. Arnie listened to it all in perplexed silence, baffled by this sudden, new ambition in Ruth, after three years of agreeing they would wait to start the family. And while he took in the disjointed phrases and biological facts and the precise calendar Ruth had so amazingly worked out, Arnie heard something else, something that wasn't spoken in her words – it was the desperation in her eyes, the begging in her voice, the underlying trace of panic that seemed to have gripped her.

Why? he wondered. Because nothing in what she said really explained this sudden need to have a baby right away. Once again, as in the past, it fleetingly occured to Arnie that he didn't really know Ruth Shapiro, that there were hidden corridors and suppressed currents to her that were kept from him. On several occasions in their three-year relationship it had struck Arnie that Ruth was a mystery.

'If we get married now,' he said slowly, 'where will we live? My apartment is too far away for you, and I doubt we'll find any vacancies near the school at this time of year.'

Ruth looked down at the damp grass. This was the delicate moment. Because, what if he didn't agree to it, what if he insisted they wait, then what? Ruth knew she had to have a baby soon, to prove that she hadn't paid an unnatural price to study medicine, to show everyone she *could* be all things if she wanted – but how important was this need? Was it worth risking her relationship with Arnie?

'We would continue just as we are,' she said softly. 'It would only be for six months.'

His liquid brown eyes blinked in indecision. 'Are you sure the hospital will take you on as an intern if you're pregnant?'

Ruth spoke quickly. 'If we can do it so that I deliver in September, then I'll only be pregnant for two and a half, three months at the most during my internship, leaving the last nine months free.'

'But how will we manage? Me in a new job, you as an intern?'

'I'm sure my mother will help out until we can make

arrangements. We can get a student in to take care of the baby.' Ruth seized his hand. 'I know we can do it, Arnie. And it means so much to me.'

He frowned at her for a moment, torn between common sense and Ruth's pleading face, then he softened. Shrugging, he said, 'If it means that much to you.'

She went into his arms and buried her face in his neck. 'Oh, thank you, Arnie! It's going to be fine. You'll see. It'll all work out just fine...'

# Chapter Fourteen

'Happy New Year, Mickey.'

'Silly, New Year was three weeks ago.'

'It's still a new year.'

'And it's only eight o'clock. You're supposed to say things like Happy New Year at midnight.'

Jonathan leaned away from her, a look of mock disapproval on his face. 'I had no idea you were such a slave to convention.'

They were sharing a bottle of Dom Pérignon in Jonathan's Westwood apartment to celebrate the finish of his film, *Medical Center!* On the carpet between them were the remains of a picnic-style supper which had come in a cellophane-wrapped basket from Jurgensen's, and on the stereo Joan Baez sang the haunting 'Silent Running.'

Mickey bowed her head and looked deep into the golden bubbles in her glass. This was supposed to be a festive evening, they'd been trying to get together for days, but now that she was here, in Jonathan's world, sharing Jonathan's triumph, Mickey felt strangely cold.

A strong, square hand reached out and cupped her chin, and a voice that never failed to arouse her said, 'What's wrong, Mickey?'

She refused to meet his eyes. 'Why do you ask that?'

'You've been quiet all evening. Like your body's here but not your mind. Where are you, Mickey Long?'

She needed to think, to find the words. How could she explain that the new year had brought with it an unaccountable sadness? That the moment she had heard the distant chimes of the school belltower and the surgeon had looked up from his work and said to the team, 'It's 1972, everybody. Happy New Year,' Mickey had felt a cold hand embrace her soul? And that the chill was with her still, even tonight, even while they had made love?

It was all wrong. This was the year she had lived all her life for, the year for which all the sacrifices had been made, and now she dreaded it. *I need more time.* Time to figure out her feelings for Jonathan, to find a place for him in her life, and her place in his. Three weeks and one day ago it had been easy for her to love Jonathan because they would still have had another year together. But now she could see the turning point coming up before her, just six months away. Then she would come to the end of one phase and the beginning of a new one, and try though she might, she couldn't see Jonathan in that picture.

'I'm going to Hawaii tomorrow,' she murmured at last.

Through the heavy drapes, closed against the arctic January night, came the sounds of heavy traffic on Westwood Boulevard. People were rushing to the big movie theatres, heading for the intimate restaurants, circling UCLA for the impossible parking space. Life moved on, even in this moment of suspension.

Finally Jonathan said, 'Is it the internship interview?'

She raised her head. 'I got the telegram last week. They want to talk to me. I'll be gone two days.'

Jonathan pursed his lips, looked down at his champagne, then set his glass aside. 'So you're going to go?'

'You know I am, Jonathan, I haven't changed my mind. I told you a long time ago what Great Victoria means to me. It's the best hospital in the world for plastic surgery, it's been my dream for almost three years to go there. It's because of Great Victoria that I've worked so hard, taking all the ER and surgery call I can, making contacts at St Catherine's for references –'

Jonathan was instantly on his feet. Mickey didn't have to tell him about all the hospital calls; it had come between them often enough, caused her to cancel dates at the last minute, pulled them out of restaurants – Mickey's beeper had even once gone off while they were in bed together. 'Mickey, Great Victoria isn't the only hospital in the world. You could go to UCLA or stay at St Catherine's.'

'Yes, I could, but I don't want to. Great Victoria is the best, and one of the few places that counts the internship as

127

part of the residency. Anywhere else, right after internship I'd have to apply for residency all over again and I might not get what I want. At Great Victoria your year of internship is considered the first year of your residency, so this way I'm guaranteed both placements, if they accept me.'

'You aren't sure you'll get it.'

'No. It's one of the most sought-after internships in the country. I'll be competing with hundreds of applicants. That's one reason why I do all the scut work on the Plastic Surgery service at St Catherine's. I need all the ammunition I can get, and when I go for that interview, I'm going to try my best to convince them they want me.'

'If you don't get it, where will you go?'

'I'll get it, Jonathan.'

'Mickey, if you don't get it –'

'Then I might as well stay at St Catherine's. *But I will get that internship, Jonathan.*'

He touched her face. 'Starting in July, a year in Hawaii?'

'Six years; you're forgetting the five for residency.'

He turned away, pressing a fist into his palm. 'I can't live without you for six years, Mickey.'

'Then, come with me.'

He whipped around, a look of surprise on his face. 'You know I can't do that. You know what I'm trying to build here. You can't expect me to leave it all behind!'

'But that's just what you're asking of me.'

Jonathan breathed deeply, trying to control his frustration. This was not a new dialogue. They had been through it two weeks before, when they'd gone with Ruth and Arnie to City Hall. It had been a quick, civil ceremony at which Sondra Mallone had cried and which had made Jonathan and Mickey conscious of the painful truth neither wanted to face.

'I'm going to stay in our apartment by the school,' Ruth had said over the simple wedding lunch the five had shared in a small restaurant near City Hall. 'These last six months until graduation will be crucial. I can't be driving from Tarzana every day.'

Jonathan had turned to Arnie, who was his usual quiet self. 'When do you leave for Seattle?'

'Just as soon as I wrap things up down here. I sold my half of the accounting firm to my partner and he's already brought a new man in. I have to start looking for a job in Seattle right away. Ruth will join me in June.'

Jonathan and Mickey had exchanged a look: a mutual recognition of the sacrifices their friends were making.

Jonathan stood up abruptly, feeling his frustration turning into impotence. He was used to having his own way, to directing the scene. 'Let's go for a drive, Mickey,' he said suddenly, striding to the closet for his windbreaker. 'I feel claustrophobic.'

To her surprise, instead of heading towards the ocean and the school, Jonathan steered his Porsche onto the San Diego Freeway, heading north, and from there, onto the Ventura Freeway, going west. They drove in silence, each trying to manufacture new words, new persuasions, and when Jonathan drove through Woodland Hills and kept going towards the lesser populated corner of the San Fernando Valley, Mickey's curiosity mounted.

Presently, Jonathan took the Valley Circle off-ramp and headed west towards the hills, away from lights and traffic, and soon they were no longer on pavement but an old dirt road. The Valley fell away behind them; all was darkness. Finally the headlight beams turned onto a rusting chain-link fence and a rotted sign that said KEEP OUT. Jonathan stopped the car and turned off the motor.

'Where are we?' Mickey asked.

He turned to her in the darkness, reached out and touched her hair. 'I wasn't going to show you this yet. I was going to make a grand opening of it. But I think it's time. Come on.'

He led her by the hand as they crunched over the gravel, following the white circle of his flashlight. The night air was chill, and the dark seemed almost ominous. He stopped before a chained gate from which dangled a weathered sign that said PRIVATE PROP, and let go of her hand.

'What are you doing?' she whispered.

'You'll see.' He produced a key and a moment later the gate swung away from them. Jonathan took Mickey's hand again and led her forward.

At first it was like walking into nothingness, a large hollow

129

of blackness that was neither earth nor sky but, as Jonathan's flashlight illuminated patches here and there, Mickey started to see things. Buildings – massive, blocky warehouses; storefronts with broken windows and peeling paint, bits of sidewalk, a tilted street sign, an eerie deserted town.

'Where are we?' she whispered again, shivering, not liking the place.

'The old Morgan Studios. Closed down in the thirties and left to decay.'

'A movie studio?'

They went deeper into the darkness, passing odd shapes, stumbling over unidentifiable debris, sending tiny unseen feet skittering ahead of them. 'Old Alexander Morgan was a tyrant and a madman,' said Jonathan in a hushed voice, as if afraid to disturb the sleeping phantoms. 'But he made great silent films. He was a genius but towards the end of his life, when talkies came in, his films changed. They became warped and bizarre, and then the Hayes Office put him out of business.'

Mickey's eyes searched the night, trying to see what Jonathan saw, sensing in the shadows the forlorn spirits of the great movie past. 'Why did you bring me here?'

He stopped and turned to face her, and in the bit of star-glow that washed over him, Mickey saw the intensity in his eyes. 'I've bought it, Mickey,' he said. 'I'm going to bring this place back to life.'

'But . . . isn't it all in ruins?'

'A lot of it, yes, but there's a lot that's salvageable. And it's not just the buildings and the props, Mickey, it's the land. This layout is ideal. When the early moviemakers first came to California they came here because of the landscape and the year-round sun. In the daylight you'd see how perfect this place is for making movies.'

He turned away from her and waved the flashlight over the ghostly façades. 'If only you could see what I see,' he breathed. 'I'm not going to make amateur films all my life, Mickey, I want to do big things, give people something to see. Remember when we first met? You said you thought movies were made with lots of lights and canvas chairs and people all around. Come back in six months, Mickey, and you'll see just that.'

As so many times before, she felt his energy fill the air around her, spark her own imagination, and for just an instant she saw what he saw. Then it faded, because she suddenly knew why he had brought her here: to replace her dream with his own.

'Marry me, Mickey,' he said quietly, not looking at her, not touching her. 'Stay here, be my wife, and help me build this.'

'I can't,' she whispered.

'You *can't?* Or don't want to?'

'I want to, Jonathan. You know that. I want very much to spend the rest of my life with you. If you knew how often I think of it, how clearly I see that beautiful picture – you and me together, having children, sharing . . .'

He took her by the shoulders in a strong grip. His face was bent close to hers. 'I have that same vision, Mickey.'

'But how can it ever be?'

'It can if we make it so. You can stay in Los Angeles. We can both work at our dreams. Stay with me, Mickey. I'm begging you.'

She felt tears in her eyes, and then the moment was broken by a new, strange sound intruding into the night silence.

'What's that?' asked Jonathan.

Mickey thrust her hand into her purse. 'My beeper.'

His hands fell away from her shoulders. 'Did it go off by accident?'

'No.'

Jonathan was quiet for a moment and then his rage broke. Snatching the box out of her hand, he shouted, 'Mickey! Not even for one night? The night we planned, a night that was for *us?* Is this why you didn't drink any champagne – because you had to stay sober? We were making love and you *knew?* We were toasting my film and you *knew?* That at any minute you would leave me for the hospital –'

Before she knew what was happening, Jonathan's arm swung up in an arc and the beeper flew off into the night, signalling like a tiny UFO. Then he seized her, brutally.

131

'Are you so wrapped up in yourself that you can't give me one evening?' He shook her. 'Tell me what you were thinking about while we were making love! Surgery? The patient in Ward C?' He released her with an angry push and turned away.

She grabbed his wrist. 'Jonathan! Don't you see? My dream is no less important to me than yours is to you! And it's no less consuming! Being on emergency call is part of my work, just as everything involved with film-making is part of yours. It's what I have to do. If I give that up, then I give up what makes me *me*.'

Her voice grew softer. 'Oh, Jonathan, I love you. But don't you see? It can't work for us. We are too alike, we are two separate people in two separate worlds, with two strong and separate dreams. The only way we can stay together is if one of us gives up the very thing that makes us who we are. I must go to Hawaii, and you must stay here and build your studio, your films. I don't want you to give this up, I don't want to live with a shell of a man. Would you want to live with someone who was only half me?'

He took her in his arms then, burying his face in her hair, and Mickey began to cry.

It was a dazzling April day: lavender and scarlet bougainvillea had appeared overnight, the jacaranda trees had erupted in thousands of tiny purple blossoms, there were roses of yellow and orange, flaming cactus flowers. All stood out against the emerald lawns and white buildings of Castillo College.

At the very edge of the sheer cliff stood Mickey, her tall and slender figure leaning slightly into the wind. Out there, across thousands of miles of water, was Hawaii. In her mind's eye Mickey could almost see it. The hotels, the broad sandy beaches, the green lagoons, and at its heart, Great Victoria Hospital, where she so desperately hoped to go.

How could she leave Jonathan?

He called every day, asking to see her, but Mickey was afraid. Wounds don't heal if they're constantly reopened. It was better that they make a clean break. Jonathan did not agree. She knew what he was hoping: that Great Victoria would turn her down, for then she would stay and the decision would be made for them.

Deep in her soul lurked the suspicion that she, too, was hoping the same thing.

Mickey looked at her watch. It was time to go. Today was the day of 'matching', when the results of internship applications were announced. The ceremony would be held in Hernandez Hall where, with great pomp, Dean Hoskins would hand an envelope to each of the seventy-four students of the graduating class.

She sat between Sondra and Ruth, neither of whom was as agitated as the rest of the group. Due to her three summers working in their Labour & Delivery suite, the Seattle hospital Ruth had applied to had already assured her of the internship. All of Sondra's applications had been sent to hospitals in Arizona and New Mexico, so she was certain of spending some time with her parents before she moved on to pursue her dream in Africa.

Mickey could barely stay seated. She knew that three of her classmates had applied to Great Victoria too, and they were stiff competition; now she thought of the other great medical schools in the country – Harvard, Berkeley, UCLA – all turning out graduates who might also want to go to Great Victoria. As the envelopes were distributed, as cries of joy or disappointment erupted around her, she saw one of her three competitors whirl around and embrace his neighbour. Mickey's heart sank.

But at the same time she thought: *Now I can stay with Jonathan!*

Mickey's hands shook as she opened the envelope, and when she read the news she went into a kind of shock.

Most of the others stayed for a wine and cheese party in the reception room but Mickey, Sondra, and Ruth decided to go home. The phone was ringing when they got inside.

It was Jonathan and he was excited. 'Mickey! Guess what! I've been nominated for an Oscar! I just got the telegram! Best Documentary! My folks are having a celebration party for me tonight. I want you to come. Mickey, I want you to be here with me. Let me come and get you. Celebrate with me, Mickey.'

'I've been accepted by Great Victoria, Jonathan.'

He was silent for a moment, then he said, 'Mickey, I want you at my side when I get that Oscar. I want us to be married. I'll come and get you –'

'I can't, Jonathan.'

He was silent for another long minute, then he said, 'All right, Mickey. I'm going to leave it up to you. At eight o'clock this evening I'll be at the belltower on the school campus. I'll wait there for ten minutes. You make the decision. If you want to marry me, if you want to spend the rest of your life with me, *if you love me*, Mickey, you'll be there.'

'I won't be there, Jonathan.'

'Yes, you will. I know you won't let me down. Not at a time like this. Eight o'clock at the belltower.'

She went back to the ocean, drawn to the ancient sand and eternally rolling tide, as if answers might be found there. She sat in the company of sandpipers scurrying, digging into the sand with their needle beaks. On this curve of beach all evidence of civilisation was hidden; high above her the medical school stood behind Monterey pines and manzanita trees. Mickey felt she was sitting in an unsullied spot, a place on earth and in time untouched by troubled thoughts, a clean, virgin patch of space from which she could watch the ocean and try to set her soul free.

She drew up her legs and rested her forehead on her knees. She'd come so far, but had so far yet to go. Her life seemed full of paradoxes: to give up what she most cherished in order to have what she most loved; let go one dream in order to cleave to another.

But she knew what her decision would be. When Chris Novack had erased the stain from her face he had granted her a second chance in life. Mickey had vowed there and then to repay him in some way. But what she owed to Chris Novack couldn't be measured in wealth or words; it was a debt of the heart. It involved wanting to emulate him, to carry on his work and take that same hope and gift to other unfortunate people. There was more to all this than Mickey's dream to be a doctor; there was obligation and duty and the quest for perfection.

She would miss Jonathan. She would grieve the loss; she would always love him. But Mickey knew what she had to do.

It was possibly the worst evening of her life. She had to fight physically with herself, hold her body against a force that was reaching out to her like a magnet. As the arms of the clock crept to eight o'clock her torment mounted.

She imagined Jonathan, sitting alone at the foot of the belltower ...

*Run to him. Be truly loved for once in your life.*

*Go to Hawaii. Grab the future that you know is right for you.*

Eight bells rang out over the college campus and over the ocean to be carried away by the waves to the white-sand islands that beckoned. Still, not breathing, Mickey stared at the front door, half expecting him to burst in and take her in his arms.

She stared and stared, but he didn't come.

# Chapter Fifteen

It had been a beautiful ceremony. The June day seemed to want to honour the seventy-four new doctors and so had turned out nature's finest symphony of blossoms, clear summer sky, gentle sea breezes, the occasional tern straying from the beach. It was neither too warm nor too cool, a day for sleeveless dresses and ties worn with comfort, and the programme had not been taxing, well spaced with just the right amount of solemnity and academic humour.

And now the graduates milled around on the grass in the deep purple caps and gowns distinctive of Castillo College, and the satin doctoral stoles of pale blue and oyster white, visiting with friends and relatives on the quadrangle.

Ruth stood at the centre of a hive of activity; two nuclear and extended families paid homage to their graduate, taking turns laying gentle hands on her swelling abdomen. Two mothers and fathers embraced, meeting for the first time, and all the members of the Roth and Shapiro families took the first awkward steps towards acquaintance. Even Ruth's father appeared to be thoroughly enjoying the moment, congratulating himself on having produced a daughter who had graduated number one in her class. 'So, Ruthie, you fooled us all,' he said as he enveloped her in a demonstrative embrace. 'You came out on top. Well, well. I hope this means you're going to settle down now. You shouldn't be thinking of a medical practice now, what with the family you've started. Your place will be in the home. Still, maybe this wasn't all a total waste. Maybe you can put this diploma to use someday.'

A few graduates were alone, without visitors. Mickey was one of them. She strolled through the crowd, smiling, receiving praise and handshakes from staff and administration, being pulled into snapshots with fellow classmates, on the one hand envying them all the attention, on the other strangely glad to be alone. *This is how I will be from now on – alone.* Sondra, Mickey knew, would keep looking until she found the man who was right for her; Ruth and Arnie would grow together. But Mickey believed her road was to be a solitary one, and having accepted that, she believed she could live with it.

As she walked over the grass, she thought of the man she was leaving behind.

She recalled the last time she had spoken to Jonathan, the night he had called and asked her to meet him at the belltower, and she had stood him up. And then the last time she had seen him – on television in Encinitas Hall, accepting his Oscar for Best Documentary Film. How handsome he had looked, and dynamic. He didn't need her now, just as her own life must be free and unfettered. Still, Mickey knew he would go with her everywhere, all through life, because he had been her *first*.

Mickey walked to where her friends and their families were gathered. She felt electrified, charged with anticipation for the future. *Where are we going? What does life have in store?* The past four years, Mickey knew, had been but a preamble to the greater adventures ahead, and, happy that she was finally taking these last steps, Mickey could not help feel a bit sad: the three were going to be separated in just a short time.

As Mickey was introduced to everyone, she noticed how unusually quiet Arnie was. It was because of the diploma, she knew. Ruth had had her maiden name put on it instead of Roth, and Arnie was hurt.

There were Sondra's parents, expensively dressed, glowing with Arizona suntans. As he shook Mickey's hand, Mr Mallone said, 'I can't tell you how proud we are of you girls. Sondra tells us you're going to Hawaii. And our own little girl is going to Africa, to do the Lord's work.'

After the commotion died down, Mickey and Sondra and Ruth walked back to the apartment. They thought it was the last time they would walk this flagstone path together.

# PART THREE
## *1973 – 1974*

# Chapter Sixteen

One suitcase was filled with medical supplies that the hospital employees had collected for the mission, while the other, the small one, contained her clothes and the few personal effects she had chosen to take with her. Sondra kept an eye on the black porters who dragged dollies and dumped the luggage in the centre of the claim area. The scene was chaotic: tourists worrying that their cases had not made it to Kenya; men, sweating in business suits, anxious about making their connections; fretting mothers trying to control fractious children; a golf team from England shoving through other passengers to retrieve their monogrammed golf bags, faces deflated from long hours of flight, eyes rimmed with fatigue, and tempers very short. Sondra stood out from the crowd, a young woman in blue jeans, Western boots, and a faded University of Arizona T-shirt.

She looked at her watch. It was eight o'clock in the evening in Phoenix. The empty supper carts would be rattling down the hospital halls now, and Dr MacReady would be terrorising a new group of interns. He had surprised Sondra by asking her to stay, Dr MacReady, a walking slab of granite who, she had always thought, disliked her. And then he had surprised her by saying, 'You're a good doctor, Mallone. We need people like you. Don't go to Africa, stay here, train in a speciality. I'll see you get whatever you ask for.' Sondra had been flattered, and gratified to know that she had made MacReady's tough grade. But she was committed, to the Reverend Mr Ingels and this mission, to Africa, the land of her ancestors.

The Uhuru Mission was located in thornbush country about halfway between Nairobi and Mombasa. It was one of the oldest missions in Kenya and served a very large area, meeting mainly the needs of the Taita and Masai people.

When Sondra had told the Reverend Mr Ingels that she wasn't religious, that she wouldn't be able to preach, he'd said, 'We have preachers in abundance, Sondra, our list of evangelical volunteers is long. But what we're desperately in need of is doctors, especially ones like you who know general medicine. The mission hospital will need you to help teach the natives hygiene and basic health, to go out into the bush and tend to natives who can't make it in to the mission. Believe me, Sondra, you'll be doing the Lord's work all the same.'

The crowd started to thin as people drifted off to Customs and Immigration. Sondra had been told she would be met by someone from the mission, but by the time she had claimed her bags, no one had yet come for her. She was beginning to grow anxious. Finally, she spotted a man coming towards her. When he reached her he said abruptly, 'Dr Mallone?' Sondra said 'Yes,' and allowed him to take her two suitcases.

'I'm Dr Farrar,' he said curtly, turning sharply and pushing back into the crowd. 'Just follow me,' he said without looking at her, without smiling. 'Things will be better when the new airport is open.'

When they finally emerged from Customs into the cool, bright Kenya morning, they headed towards a Volkswagen van painted, to Sondra's surprise, in outrageous zebra stripes. Derry Farrar did not speak as he manoeuvred the awkward vehicle through the congested airport traffic, and Sondra, uncomfortable with his stony silence, could think of nothing to say.

Derry Farrar was a handsome man. In his khaki pants, khaki shirt with the sleeves rolled up, and with a ruddy tan, he looked to Sondra like the legendary white hunters of years ago. He held himself straight, and had the broad shoulders and back of a young man – yet he must be at least fifty, Sondra judged. He looked like a man caught between two worlds. His black hair was worn in an English country gentleman's fashion – neatly parted on one side and combed back, with a bit of silvering at the temples – and his speech was polished and genteel. Yet the sunburned chest exposed by the open top of his shirt would never be found on Fleet Street.

But it was his face that intrigued her most, an open and yet at the same time a very concealing face. His black brows, arched and heavy, gave him the look of a man who has been angry too often and for too long, and his cobalt blue eyes seemed stern and unfathomable. It was a face of ironies: Derry Farrar's good looks were almost as repellent as they were attractive.

The VW van followed a two-laned highway bordered with beautiful grassland and cascades of brilliant bougainvillea reminiscent of Castillo College. Along the roadside they passed what appeared to be a large bundle of sticks with legs; then Sondra saw that it was a woman bent beneath a heavy burden, trudging like a donkey behind a tall, proud man who carried nothing.

Sondra could barely contain her excitement. She couldn't believe she was here at last, after all these years, after all the dreaming and the hard work and determination.

When she saw a giraffe at the roadside nibbling the edges of an acacia, she said, 'My goodness, look!'

'That's Nairobi National Park,' said Derry.

'Will there be animals around the mission, Dr Farrar?'

'It's Derry. We're all on first-name basis there. Yes, there are animals. Have you been taking malaria tablets?'

'Yes.'

'Good. We've had some outbreaks. Keep taking them the whole time you're here.'

'I plan to,' she said cheerfully. 'I've brought a year's supply.'

Dr Farrar took his eyes off the road for one instant, to give her a look that said *you won't last a year out here*. Sondra quickly turned away and went back to staring out of the window.

The Volkswagen turned at a traffic circle, following a sign that said WILSON AIRPORT. When they drew up in front of yet another terminal, though not as crowded as the one they had just come from, Sondra frowned. 'Aren't we going to *drive* to the mission?' she asked as Derry started to get out.

'It's two hundred miles. Take us all day to get there.'

They paused briefly inside the terminal while Derry purchased a copy of the Nairobi *Standard*, then they crossed through to the tarmac where Sondra looked hopefully around at the large planes of East African Airways. But such was not to be her luck. She realised he was leading her towards a battered, dusty single-engine aircraft.

He jumped up on to a wing, opened the door, then reached down a hand to help her up. 'Oh dear,' she said with a small laugh. 'Will it make it, do you think?'

'Not afraid of flying, I hope. This is the mission's plane. You'll be going all over Kenya in it. Up you go.'

When she was settled in one of the small seats, Dr Farrar said, 'I'll be just a minute,' and jumped back to the ground.

The minute dragged into five, then ten, and ultimately into fifteen minutes as Sondra watched Derry do a thorough check of the aircraft, ending with sifting gasoline through a chamois into the tank.

He glanced up at her as he came around her side of the plane to check something underneath and again there was that look on his face, that he wasn't, for some reason, at all happy to see her.

Sondra didn't let it disturb her. She wasn't going to let one man's grumpy mood, whatever his reasons, spoil this special moment, her arrival, at long last, in Africa.

On impulse Sondra opened her purse and rummaged through the clutter of airsick pills, candy bar wrappers, passport, and documents, and withdrew an envelope that bore the postmark of Honolulu. Mickey's most recent letter was hastily written because she had just started her second year at Great Victoria and had precious little time for her personal affairs. Into the envelope Sondra had slipped mementos: a photograph of Ruth sitting on a sofa with eleven-month-old Rachel in her arms, and her stomach already big with the next baby; a Polaroid of Mickey on Waikiki Beach at sunset, looking back over her shoulder at someone in surprise. Sondra smiled down at the faces in the photographs and thought: I'm here, Ruth and Mickey. I made it.

Soon Derry was climbing into the pilot's seat and securing the door. Before starting the engine, he turned to Sondra and said, 'Want to pray?'

'I beg your pardon?'

'Do you want to pray before we take off?'

She blinked at him. 'I may be nervous about flying, but you needn't make fun of me for it.'

For a fleeting moment his face changed, smoothed out, the black eyebrows rose, and the mouth lightened into something almost resembling a smile. 'I'm sorry. I wasn't making fun of you. The mission people always say a prayer before departing, even if they're going on foot.'

'Oh,' said Sondra, embarrassed. 'I'm sorry, I didn't –' She turned away, flustered. 'No ... thank you.'

They soared above a counterpane of green rolling hills speckled with patches of red dirt. Sondra couldn't get her fill; she sat forward in her seat, trying to take in the whole vista with her wide eyes. Eventually the greenery gave way to tawny grass spotted with miniature trees. 'Look over there,' shouted Derry over the roar of the plane. 'You're lucky. It's usually cloud-covered, not many people get a chance to see it.'

Sondra stared ahead at the snow-capped mountain rising from the plains. 'Kilimanjaro?' she asked, spellbound.

'The Swahili word for it is *kilima*, which means "little hill" and its name is Njaro.'

Sondra gazed out in breathless wonder at the diorama-landscape of Africa, sweeping down from lavender hills and back up into them in carpets of red and ochre and lion-yellow. Dotted with flat-topped trees and roving patches of game herds, it was a glimpse into the past, a look at the world when it was still young and new. And comfortably secure in its dominance over the continent of Africa was eternally snow-capped Kilimanjaro, in nearby Tanzania.

Sondra was overwhelmed, she couldn't speak. A lighter-than-air feeling came over her, an almost paralysing elation. She'd experienced it once before, nearly five years ago, when Rick Parsons had unveiled the cerebellum of a little boy and excised the disease. It had been an almost mystical feeling, a discovery of place and purpose, of knowing beyond a doubt where she was going and why. It filled Sondra again now, just as then, and it made her shiver.

As Derry banked the plane eastward Sondra was rewarded with a dramatic view of a harsh, red desert below, a starkly primaeval landscape which reminded her of parts of the American Southwest. Over the noise of the Cessna engine Derry explained that it was Tsavo National Park, one of the largest animal preserves in the world. It went on for miles, it seemed, to the end of the earth. And then Sondra thought she saw something else. 'What's that?' she shouted, pointing straight down.

Derry reached for a pair of binoculars and searched the ground. 'It's an elephant,' he said, handing the glasses to her. 'And he's still alive.'

Sondra took one look, focused on it, then pulled the binoculars away from her eyes.

'He's dying,' shouted Derry. 'That's why he's on his side. Poachers got him. The bastards wait until the animals come to a watering hole, then shoot them like ducks. They send poisoned arrows into them and track the elephants as they wander off, sick and dying. It usually takes days. When the poor beast is finally dead, they come in and hack off its tusks and leave the rest to waste.'

'Can't something be done about it?'

'Like what? This park is eight thousand square miles of wilderness with just a handful of men to police it, while out there is a world greedy for ivory, for the horn of the rhino, the skins of leopards. As long as people like that pay good money for animal parts, these poor beggars don't stand a chance. I'll report this when we get to the mission, but it won't do any good. The poachers are down there now and they know we've spotted the animal. By the time a ranger gets to it they'll have cleared off, having sawed off the tusks before the poor elephant is dead.'

Soon Derry was bringing the plane down. 'Better hang on! Have to buzz the landing strip!'

Before she could hold on tight the Cessna went into a swoop.

'Damn hyenas!' Derry shouted. 'Never can get them off the landing strip!'

They buzzed once more and by the time the plane bumped along the dirt runway, Sondra was giddy. As Derry helped her down from the wing, he said, 'You'll get used to it.'

While he removed the suitcases, a packet of mail, and some sacks from the aeroplane, Sondra looked around at her new surroundings.

Behind her, yellow grass, twisted trees, thornbushes, and red dirt stretched away in a vast, flat plain; but in front of her, the landscape changed: green hillocks rolled away to the base of towering, mist-shrouded cliffs. Not far from the landing strip stood an orderly enclave of trees and hedges and clustered buildings – the mission – and just beyond, Sondra could see, round huts and small farming plots dotted the hills and valleys.

She felt Derry next to her, heard him say, 'That's odd. No one's come to meet you.'

She turned to see a puzzled frown on his face. Then they heard something like a shout, coming from beyond the barrier of trees and flowers, and suddenly Derry dropped everything and broke into a run. Bewildered, Sondra fell in behind him, also running.

They dashed through the wooden gateposts and under a carved sign that said UHURU MISSION. A crowd had gathered in the courtyard: Africans in brightly patterned cloth and white men in khaki, who seemed to Sondra either angry or frightened. The crowd parted as a man burst through, a large African dressed in khaki shirt and shorts, a slouch hat, and an official badge on his chest. First he ran an aimless zigzag course with two men chasing him, then he darted sharply to the left and headed straight for Sondra. She stopped short and he collided with her, knocking her down.

'Stop him!' she heard someone shout. Sondra saw Derry run by her, and then another white man, wearing a plaid shirt and blue jeans, with a stethoscope swinging from his neck.

As she got to her feet, brushing the dirt off her clothes, Sondra heard the shouts rise and saw two more men join the chase. The pursued man ran a crazed course, dodging hands that reached for him, and then, for no apparent reason, he collapsed, dropping to the ground as if he'd been felled by a bullet. He lay writhing in the dirt.

Derry and the man in blue jeans were instantly on their knees at the fallen man's side. Sondra ran to join them, while the rest of the crowd, gawking and murmuring among themselves, hung back.

'I don't know what happened,' the other white man was saying in a thick Scottish accent, shaking his blond head. 'I was about to examine him, hadn't even touched him yet, when suddenly he bolted out of the infirmary.'

Derry, down on one knee, stared at the black face, now twisted in agony. The man's eyes had rolled back so that only the whites showed, and spittle and drops of blood flecked his lips. Sondra fell to her knees next to him and immediately pressed two fingers to the stricken man's carotid pulse.

'He's having a seizure,' Sondra said. Then she raised her head and looked at the man opposite her. He was frowning down at the black face in obvious bafflement. 'What happened?' she asked.

'I don't know. I had barely had a look at the man. I don't even know why he came to the infirmary.'

'I do,' said Derry, as he stood up and brushed off his hands. 'I know this man. He's an official with the Department of Public Works at Voi.'

Sondra looked back down at the unconscious man whose seizure had subsided. 'It had to have been drug induced,' she murmured, thinking out loud. 'I don't know of any primary disease process what would cause a man to run about like that.' She lifted each of his eyelids and, noting that his pupils were normal, equal in size and reactive, felt her puzzlement mount. Any disorder she could come up with she had to discard, since they all involved impairment of motor coordination: alcoholic toxicity, on the other hand, or some sort of hallucinogen...

The Scotsman who knelt opposite Sondra stared at her for a moment, as if he'd only just noticed her, then he said, 'We'll put him to bed and have him watched closely. There's not much we can do for the man until we find out the cause.' Looking over his shoulder, he waved to two Africans hovering nearby. *'Kwenda, tafadhali.'*

But they didn't move.

'We'll have to carry him ourselves,' said Derry, reaching down for the man's ankles. 'They won't touch him.'

Sondra got to her feet. 'Why not?'

'They're afraid.'

She walked alongside as the two men carried the unconscious official to the infirmary. 'You would be Dr Mallone,' said the Scot as he struggled with the dead weight, his hand under the man's armpits. 'We've been looking forward to your arrival. I'm Alec MacDonald. Welcome to Africa.'

Once the man was laid upon a bed in the infirmary Sondra assisted Alec MacDonald in a routine neurological exam. Both continued to be mystified. The man's symptoms conformed to no disease process known to either of them. Although his pupils continued to be normal and reactive, he did not respond to the most painful stimulus. The two doctors started an IV and sent a nurse for a catheter in order to check for kidney function. Finally, taking the blood pressure again and finding it below seventy, Sondra said, 'He's going into shock. We'd better get him on dopamine for pressure support. We should also get blood levels right away and run a toxic panel –'

A short 'Ha!' caused the two doctors to look up. Derry had just come in and stood by the bed with his arms folded. 'Dopamine! Toxic panel! Where do you think you are, North London Hospital?'

Alec MacDonald said, 'What did you mean, Derry, when you said you knew why he had come to the infirmary?'

'Because I know this man and I think I've figured out what's wrong with him.'

Sondra curled her fingers around the bell of the stethoscope that hung from her neck, a stethoscope she had picked off a wall hook upon coming into the infirmary. 'What do you think is wrong with him?' she asked.

'He's had a curse put on him.'

'A curse!'

The cobalt eyes flickered; then, as if dismissing her, turned to Alec MacDonald. 'This man stole another man's goats. When he wouldn't return them the other man had a local witch doctor put a curse on him.' He looked at the head sleeping on the pillow of striped ticking. 'There isn't a thing we can do for him.'

Alec MacDonald said quietly, 'That must be why he came to the infirmary. He must have thought the white man's medicine could save him, and then at the last minute he panicked and ran out.'

'You mean this illness is just psychological?' asked Sondra.

'No, Dr Mallone,' said Derry, turning to leave. 'It's a Taita curse and something very real.'

She watched him go, feeling irritated and frustrated, then turned back to Alec MacDonald, who, standing on the other side of the bed, was now studying Sondra with undisguised interest.

'We have to do *something*,' she said.

Alec shrugged. 'What Derry says is true. I've read of cases like this. The poor bastard's beyond our help.' He smiled, and it was a warm, welcome smile. 'I expect you could do with a cup of tea right now.'

She laughed with relief. 'Those are the best words I've heard all day.'

'Let me find where that nurse has disappeared to and I'll take you to our elegant dining room.'

Before stepping out into the noon heat, Dr MacDonald pulled a straw hat off a hook by the door and settled it over his fair head. 'A highland laddie like myself wasn't born to live in sun like this!' He held the screen door open for her and added with a chuckle, 'You look as if you'll do all right in the equatorial sun. You'll be brown as a nut in a week.'

The courtyard was alive with activity, everyone having returned to duties that had been interrupted by the crazed man. All around her Sondra saw friendly faces, mostly smiling, but some staring in frank curiosity. Two mechanics with their arms deep into the motor of a Land Rover called a greeting in Swahili.

'They say welcome to the mission, Dr Mallone. You should learn Swahili as soon as you can, it's the *lingua franca* of East Africa.'

'You seem to do very well with it.'

'Oh no! I've only been here a month. I've learned what'll get me by and that's about it. You'll find that a few basic words will serve you well. And if you try to say Kenya instead of *Keenya* they'll love you all the more for it.'

'What's the difference?'

'Keenya offends their sense of national pride, ever since Independence. Keenya was the British colonial pronunciation. In Swahili it's Kenya as in pen.'

They came to a large, drab building of construction block and corrugated tin. Outside, on the vine-covered veranda, shaded by flowering jacaranda and mango trees, stood chairs and tables badly in need of paint. 'Our combination dining and recreation room. Not very luxurious, I'm afraid.'

When her eyes adjusted inside, she saw a plain room: walls of flaking plaster, the ceiling merely the underside of the corrugated tin roof, unmatched naugahyde chairs and sofa around a blackened fireplace, and at the other end several long tables with bench seats.

'A congregation in Iowa donated a television set,' said Dr MacDonald as he led her to one of the tables. 'But it's of little use to us. There's only one channel and it only comes on in the evening. And it's mostly Kenya news. Little from the outside. Please sit down. Njangu!'

Sondra settled on a bench and Alec MacDonald sat opposite. He pulled off his tattered hat and dropped it down. 'Dr Mallone, you don't know what a pleasant sight you are!'

'I'll say the same for you,' she replied, and meant it. Although Alec MacDonald was a nice-looking man, with fair colouring and evenly set features, it was his warmth and friendliness that most appealed to Sondra, such a contrast to the dark and imperious Derry Farrar.

'No one told us a beautiful young woman was coming,' he said. 'We were all expecting a man. Excuse me –' Alec MacDonald shifted around. 'Njangu! Tea, please!'

The doorway behind Dr MacDonald was covered with a curtain of African batik and presently a man stepped through carrying a tray. He was large and very dark, of an age Sondra could not determine, with a fierce, unfriendly eye. He wore dusty slacks and a faded checkered shirt, and on his head a skull cap, which Sondra learned later was made of sheep's stomach. She also learned later that Njangu was a Kikuyu, a member of the largest tribe in Africa. The Reverend Mr Sanders, director of the Uhuru Mission, had converted him

151

to Christianity years ago but everyone knew Njangu still secretly worshipped old Ngai, the Kikuyu god who lived on the peaks of Mount Kenya.

Njangu unceremoniously dropped the tray down and turned to go. 'Njangu,' said Alec MacDonald. 'Meet our new doctor.'

The black man halted, murmured, *'Iri kanwa itiri nda,'* and disappeared back through the curtained doorway.

'What did he say?' Sondra asked as Alec MacDonald poured the tea.

'You mustn't mind Njangu. He's a little brusque sometimes. His name is Kikuyu for "rough and treacherous" and I think now and then he likes to remind us of it.'

'But what did he say?'

A voice came from behind, startling them both. 'He said food in the mouth is not yet in the stomach.' Sondra turned to see Derry Farrar walking towards them. 'It's a Kikuyu saying which means don't count your chickens before they hatch.'

Sondra frowned slightly and turned back to Alec MacDonald, who shrugged and said, 'I don't speak Kikuyu.'

'Njangu meant that just because you're here doesn't mean you're going to be of any use to us,' Derry said as he, too, disappeared through the curtained door.

'Don't take all this personally, Dr Mallone,' said Alec as he set a cup before Sondra. 'The people here are so often disappointed that they don't get their hopes up any more.'

'Disappointed how?'

'Many people come, many good and well-intentioned people, but for various reasons they don't stick it out.'

'You mean they give up?'

'They bloody well cave in.' Derry reappeared in the doorway with a bottle of Tusker Beer in his hand. 'They arrive with their heads full of visions, flying their noble intentions like flags, and a month later they're packing, saying something about having to get back for Aunt Sophie's funeral.'

While he spoke there was the look of challenge in his dark blue eyes; Sondra had the odd feeling that Derry Farrar was at that moment making a mental wager with himself as to how long this latest newcomer was going to last.

She met his gaze boldly for a second, then said, 'Well, I don't have an Aunt Sophie, Dr Farrar.'

After he left, Sondra bit into a biscuit, and Alec MacDonald said gently, 'You mustn't mind Derry. He's really a good sort. But he's a bit on the cynical side, I'm afraid, doesn't know yet to put his trust in the Lord. And in a way I don't blame him. He sees so many people come through here. He orientates them, gets them acclimatised, and then they're overcome with something – homesickness, culture shock, disillusionment – and they leave. Especially the women. And especially the evangelists. They come here full of zeal and honestly believe the natives will flock to the mission to be saved. But it doesn't quite work out that way.'

They sipped their tea in silence for a few minutes, and in that time Sondra began to feel weariness invade her bones. She'd left Phoenix twenty-four hours before, had been constantly on the move, catching naps on aeroplanes and in terminals, and now finally she was in a strange and alien country, among friendly and not so friendly people, breathing new air, hearing foreign sounds beyond the cinder-block wall, with her body on night time while the day was only beginning.

'I intend to stay the full year,' she said quietly.

'Of course you do. And the Lord will give you the strength to do it.'

'How long will you be here, Dr MacDonald?'

'Like yourself, I've promised them a year. And please call me Alec. We're going to be friends, I know.'

'Are there any here who are permanent, besides the director and his wife?'

'There's a small permanent staff, those who make the mission their home. Like Derry.'

Sondra broke another biscuit in half and placed both pieces on her saucer. 'Is he always so rude? He seems so angry. It's a rather strange attitude for a Christian missionary.'

'Oh, Derry's no missionary, at least not in the sense you mean. He's an atheist and makes no secret of it.' Alec MacDonald shook his head. 'I understand that Reverend Sanders has tried for years to save Derry's soul. But God works in mysterious ways. Derry came here years ago when he married one of the nurses. Reverend Sanders thought it was a sign, that the Lord had brought this sinner here for salvation. He's got a rough manner, I'll grant, but underneath it all, Derry's a good man. And a damn fine surgeon.'

They shared a brief silence, both listening to the sounds of life on the other side of the window screens. Sondra noticed that Alec MacDonald had nice hands, smooth and slender, that looked as if they held a soft and gentle touch. Unlike the sunburned, calloused hands of Derry Farrar, which were probably as rough and blunt as the man himself.

'You must be terribly tired,' Alec said. 'It'll be jet lag for you for a few days.'

She looked up into his shy smile and, despite the fatigue she was indeed feeling, found herself wondering about him. 'I'm afraid I'm still on Phoenix time.'

'Is that where you're from then?'

Sondra was not too tired to detect from his tone that he was just as curious about her. Suddenly the pall cast over her arrival in Africa by Derry Farrar lifted. She wished now Alec MacDonald had met her at the airport instead.

'Have you ever been to Phoenix, Alec?'

'No, I've never been to Phoenix. I'm ashamed to say I've never been west of the Irish Sea!'

His thick brogue delighted her, the slight rolling of the Rs. 'Is your home in Scotland?' she asked.

'Aye. Do you know the Orkney Islands? Generations of MacDonalds have lived there. It's my ancestral home. And you?' he asked. 'You don't look Irish.'

'Irish? Oh, I'm not really a Mallone. That is . . .' She picked up her cup and then put it back in the saucer. Why did it fluster her now when it never had before? 'I was adopted by the Mallones when I was a baby.'

'I'm sorry, I wasn't meaning to pry.'

'It's all right, I don't mind talking about it.' *Except that you have an ancestral home and I don't belong anywhere.* 'In a way it has its advantages. I mean, I can be anything I want.'

Alec studied her in frank appraisal, his eyes taking in every detail, and his voice was oddly intimate as he said, 'Do you not know who your real parents are then?'

Sondra shook her head.

Their eyes met and held for ten beats of the heart, long enough for a Land Rover to hoot outside and a goat to bleat and an African voice to shout, *'Twende!'* And then Alec MacDonald stirred himself and said, 'Listen to me! Here you are dog tired and I'm keeping you talking. You'll want to go to your hut now and have a rest. The Reverend was to have been here to greet you but at the last minute he had to go into Voi. So I suppose I'm the official welcoming committee.'

Sondra rose with him, finding her joints very stiff. 'I can't think of anyone I'd rather have.'

Alec smiled and said, 'I'll take you to your hut. You can meet everyone tonight at supper.'

On the way Alec explained. 'The Uhuru Mission is on the Voi-Moshi road. That is, go far enough and you'll be in Tanganyika. I mean Tanzania. A few miles down the road is a new safari lodge built by Hilton. Back that way is Voi, not a very big town but it supplies us – apparently only when we can pay. These are the Taita Hills, and the Taita people are the ones we most see here in the mission. We also take care of the Masai, whom you'll be involved with when you go out on circuits.'

'When will that be?'

'When Derry decides you're ready. He's responsible for the medical staff here.'

They passed under an enormous fig tree that dominated the yard. Around its base were bits of food and small wood carvings. 'What's that?' asked Sondra.

'A superstition of many Africans. They venerate the fig tree; they think it's sacred. Njangu and others who work here believe a powerful spirit inhabits this tree so they leave it offerings. Now over here is the school...'

Like the rest of the mission's buildings, the schoolhouse was built of cinder block and had a corrugated tin roof. Through the open windows drifted a chorus of children's voices singing, 'Old MacDonald *ana shamba*, ee eye, ee eye, ohhh...'

'I'm sure they think they're singing about me!' said Alec with a laugh: 'There are two teachers, a lady from Kent who teaches arithmetic and geography, and Mrs Sanders, the

155

Reverend's wife, who teaches Christian education. She tells the small children about Creation and Genesis; they walk about outside and she points out all the wonderful things God has created. To the teenagers she teaches the Fall of Man. They have a different sense of morality, these people. Our task is to make them understand their relationship with the Lord and to accept Him as their saviour.'

They passed a vegetable garden, a cluster of fruit trees, four posts and a thatch roof that was the motor workshop, the plain cinder-block house of the Reverend and Mrs Sanders, and finally a small church, with a sign over its door that read: *'Kwa maana jinsi hii Mungo aliupenda alimwengu, hata akamtoa mwanawe pekee, Ili kila mtu amwaminiye asipotee, bali awe na uzima wa milele.'*

When Sondra gave Alec a puzzled look, he said, '"For God so loved the world, that He gave His only begotten Son, that whosoever believeth in Him should not perish, but have everlasting life."'

The air was becoming oppressive. What breeze there was carried wafts of queer odours, the smell of dust and animals and smoke and rotting fruit, a pungent, primaeval scent, intoxicating and repugnant at the same time. Sondra felt Alec MacDonald's hand come up and lightly touch her arm and was relieved when he said, 'Here's your place.'

They stood in a row, squat little huts like the other buildings – construction block, rough-hewn wood, and corrugated tin roofing. Alec pushed open a lockless door to reveal a black interior. 'You'll drink only the water that comes in the jugs,' he said, leading her inside. 'Njangu chlorinates it everyday. And when you visit the outhouse in the back, be sure to use a stick and rattle it around inside good and proper first. It gets the bats out.'

There was a metal-frame bed with hospital bedding, a wobbly table with a hurricane lamp and a jug of water on it, and a string stretched across the corner between two nails with a few wire coat hangers dangling. Her suitcases stood in the centre of the concrete floor.

It was hot inside despite the darkness, and rather claustrophobic. Alec smiled apologetically, as if he were responsible for the place, and held out a hand. 'I thank the

Lord that He sent you, Sondra Mallone,' he said quietly.

She took his hand and received an earnest, tight handshake in return. Alec lingered just a second longer than was necessary, holding her hand, then stepped back to the door. 'And I wish you a good sleep.'

# Chapter Seventeen

For all her exhaustion it was a short nap.

Sondra was startled awake by noise beyond her curtained window, car motors revving, children shouting and squealing, deep-voiced men calling out. She lay still for a moment on top of her bed, fully clothed, and wondered why the Lufthansa 747 was suddenly riding so smoothly. Then, remembering where she was, she rose and went to the door. She opened it on to a courtyard bathed in a coppery afternoon light, and bustling with life.

'Jambo!' called Alec MacDonald across the way. He was standing on the veranda of the infirmary where a dozen or so natives sat in the shade. Derry Farrar was there, too, bending over a child and peering into its ear through an otoscope.

Returning Alec's wave, Sondra stepped back into the hut, closed the door and took a moment to orient herself. There was a bucket of clear water under the table, and a chipped porcelain basin. She gave her hands and face a cool, vigorous wash, then changed out of her travelling clothes and into a light cotton dress that left her shoulders and arms bare. Feeling refreshed, she stepped outside.

Alec met her halfway, folding his stethoscope into the back pocket of his blue jeans. 'How are you feeling?'

'Like I could sleep another hundred hours!' She looked past him to where Derry was now down on one knee bandaging a woman's foot. 'Do you need help?'

Alec glanced back over his shoulder and shook his head. 'That'll be about it for today. Don't worry, you'll have your fingers in the pie soon enough. Come along now and meet the family.'

Everyone was gathered in the community room to relax and discuss the day's work. Sondra was introduced to the mission's residents: Kikuyu workmen, shy young nurses trained in Mombasa, another white doctor on temporary tour like Sondra and Alec, and several preachers from various congregations in the United States and Britain. With so many voices engaged in conversation, nearly drowning out the late afternoon broadcast of the Voice of Kenya, the community room took on a life it had not had that morning. Everyone greeted Sondra with friendliness, some shook her hand, and even the temporary whites hailed her with 'Jambo' and 'Salaam.'

She and Alec joined a group at one of the long tables for tea and biscuits. After introductions Sondra was assailed with questions, mainly for news of the outside, since the voice of Kenya broadcast little in the way of international news.

Njangu came out of his kitchen, fixed a frosty eye on her, and set a questionably clean cup before her.

'I don't think he likes me,' Sondra said quietly, accepting the teapot from Alec.

'Njangu's like that with everyone. The only person he likes is Derry, which is ironic considering they were once enemies.'

'Enemies?'

'Njangu was a Mau Mau rebel, one of the most feared, and Derry was a member of the police force fighting them.'

Sondra was familiar with Kenyan history and knew that Mau Mau had been a terrorist uprising in the 1950s, a bloody, black page in Kenya's book.

Suddenly an elderly, portly gentleman entered the room clapping his hands for everyone's attention. 'Good news!' He waved an envelope. 'The Lord has sent a hundred dollars our way!' There was applause and amens, and Alec MacDonald murmured, 'Praise the Lord.'

To Sondra's surprise, there followed a noisy exodus from the room. As everyone quickly filed out Alec explained, 'The post's come.'

The portly gentleman came towards Sondra with an outstretched hand. 'Oh my dear, I'm so glad to meet you! You're the very answer to our prayers. So sorry not to have been here when you arrived but there was a bit of trouble with our credit account in Voi.' The Reverend Mr Sanders lifted the straw hat off his head and ran a handkerchief over a bald spot.

159

He was dressed all in white – tennis shoes, slacks, collarless shirt buttoned right up to his throat – but it was a dingy, unrefreshing white. 'We'll be saying a special prayer of thanks for you at tonight's service, my dear. Have you met everyone?'

'Dr MacDonald has been taking care of me.'

'Ah good, good. Well, you must excuse me. So much to take care of in my busy little flock. It's Derry who'll be looking after you. *Kwa heri, kwa heri.*'

After the priest was gone, Sondra and Alec found themselves alone in the dining room. She toyed with her teaspoon a bit before saying, 'Don't you want to join the dash for the mail?'

He reddened slightly, as if she'd read his thoughts. 'The letters will wait. I didn't want you to be totally abandoned.'

'I take it the mail delivery is a big event here.'

'Aye, that it is, when it comes, which is very unpredictable. You'll find yourself wanting to read other people's letters after you've read your own!'

'Yes.' Sondra thought of the letters she would get from Ruth and Mickey, little islands of familiarity in this alien land. 'Do you have people writing to you, Alec?'

'I've lots of friends and family back in Kirkwall.'

'Is your wife there?'

His laugh was a little self-effacing. 'No wife. Had no time, I'm afraid. I'd only just got out of training and started in practice when I got the call.'

'The call?'

'To do God's work in Africa.'

'Oh.'

'And you? Do I correctly assume you are unattached?'

'You assume correctly.'

'Well then.' He placed his hands flatly and squarely on the table as if the most important business of the day had just been concluded. 'I shall have to look in on my patients now. Would you like to see the infirmary?'

Sondra said that she would. Her brief experience of the morning with the delirious Public Works official was a muddle in her memory. She hadn't had a good look at the place where she was going to be spending the coming year.

To her annoyance, Sondra found herself looking for Derry as she followed Alec up the infirmary steps.

The tiny hospital came as a shock. That Derry Farrar, a 'damn fine surgeon' as Alec had called him, could allow such laxity in order and hygiene was appalling. Where on earth had he trained in medicine? Drugs were stored in a most haphazard way, surgical instruments treated with less than proper care, records sloppily kept if at all, a crowded, noisy ward of twenty beds – some with two people in them – and an operating room that defied sanity.

'I know what you're thinking,' said Alec as they watched a porter half-heartedly scrub blood off the old-fashioned operating table. 'That you couldn't have imagined this in your worst nightmares. I know because that was my reaction when I arrived here four weeks ago.'

'These sutures are all outdated,' she said, thinking of the uproar the use of an outdated suture would cause back in Phoenix.

'I know. But it's all we've got. We make do here.'

Sondra picked up a blue Ethilon suture packet that was smudged with a big red thumbprint. This one had already seen service in the operating field! In Phoenix it would have been thrown in the bin. 'You mean this is *it*?'

'Aye, and we're glad to have it.'

'Oh, dear. And these instruments!' She drew a box towards her and riffled through the bent Kochers and toothless pickups. 'I can't believe these things are being saved for repair.'

Alec laughed and shook his head. 'Repair! Bless you, lass, these aren't waiting for repair, these are the ones we work with.'

Sondra gasped at the box in horror, as if the instruments had turned into snakes. 'But this is terrible!'

'What is?' came a voice from behind. Derry was coming out of the washroom drying his hands and forearms on a towel.

Alec said, 'I'm afraid Sondra is suffering a bit of a shock.'

Tossing the towel into a wicker hamper, Derry planted himself before Sondra, towering over her, and said as he rolled down his sleeves, 'And just what did you expect to find here, Doctor? A hospital the likes of the one you just left in America?'

Sondra felt her irritation flare up. 'No, Dr Farrar, I didn't expect that. But I can't imagine you would find *this* acceptable.'

A very awkward silence followed her words, a storm of emotion clouded Derry's eyes. Alec shifted on his feet and Sondra wondered if they could hear the pounding of her heart. Then Derry, saying nothing, turned and walked out.

Alec said with a low whistle, 'I don't believe I've ever seen two people get on so badly from the start.'

'I want to know what I've done to warrant such rudeness from him.'

'Well, in a way I see his point. This infirmary is his. He's had the run of it for years and he defends it like it was his bairn. Derry doesn't like strangers to come in and criticise the pride of his heart and soul.'

Sondra frowned and looked over the counter of old instruments and sutures, at the yellowed packets of dressings, at the antique operating table, and she remembered the Reverend Mr Ingels' words back in Phoenix: 'The Uhuru Mission is supported solely by contributions. You'll find it very poor and quite a contrast to the medical environment you're used to.'

Well, Sondra had to admit that perhaps she had been hasty in criticising Derry's infirmary, expecially after having been within its walls only a few minutes. But that didn't excuse his almost hostile behaviour towards her. When she said as much to Alec, he explained: 'This mission is desperate for all the help it can get, but sometimes *inept* help can be more of a hindrance than a help.'

'Is that what he thinks I will be? Inept?'

'I imagine he's thinking you're too inexperienced for a rough place like this. You're awfully young. He'll have to teach you a lot before you can work on your own and take some of the burden off the rest of us. And he's no doubt thinking you'll be giving up before you've got to that point. I'll have to admit,' Alec's voice lowered, 'when I myself first set eyes on you my thought was: how will a frail thing like this get on here?'

She looked up into his kind eyes and encouraging smile and felt her fury evaporate. Alec MacDonald was right. Derry Farrar was no doubt looking for older, more experienced doctors of the rugged stripe, field doctors who were used to mean conditions and could carry their own load. Maybe she did give the appearance of someone who would be of no use to him at all. Well, first appearances are often incorrect: in no time at all, Sondra was certain, Derry Farrar would realise his mistake.

Towards sunset there was a service in the small church. As far as Sondra could determine, all mission residents attended except for Derry and the nurse who was sitting watch over the infirmary ward. There was a long prayer of thanks for the arrival of Dr Mallone; no one sang the closing hymn louder than Alec MacDonald. Dinner consisted of roasted goat, a native bean stew called *posho*, and mounds of fresh strawberries. Alec MacDonald sat next to her and told her how strawberries grew all year round in Kenya but that she'd never see an apple. Dinner conversation seemed to revolve around one subject, the dearth of favourite foods, with the Reverend Mr Sanders asking Sondra in a hopeful voice if she'd brought a jar of Tang with her and looking crestfallen when she said she hadn't.

Sondra couldn't help noticing the division of people by colour in the dining room, that all the whites sat at one table and the Africans at the other. She asked Alec if this was a rule.

'Oh no, people can sit where they like. They just seem to favour their own groups.'

Derry Farrar, she noticed, sat at the very end of their table, eating in singular silence. She wondered about his wife.

'Say, Doctor,' said the Reverend Mr Lambert, an evangelist from Ohio who was sitting across the table from her, 'what's the latest on Watergate?'

A few stayed behind after dinner to listen to the Armed Forces Radio, to write letters or read the *Standard* brought by Derry that morning. One group gathered in a healthy discussion of Corinthians. Sondra and Alec MacDonald strolled out into the African twilight.

'It's difficult at first,' Alec said in his soft spoken way. 'Coming here, getting used to it all. I still haven't quite settled in myself.'

'What will you do when your year is up here?'

'I'm going back to Scotland to set up my practice. We haven't much population on our little islands but it'll be enough to keep me comfortable, and my family too, should I marry. It'll seem a quiet life to me after this, I suppose, but my home's there, and my roots.' He thrust his hands into the pockets of his jeans. 'And I'll have the satisfaction of having done the Lord's work here.'

Sondra looked up at the rough cross of jacaranda wood topping the crude church, etched against the lavender sky. Religion was something that had never reached her, she had never felt its stirrings, despite her parents' involvement with God. 'Do you preach as well as practice medicine, Alec?'

'Oh, I'm no preacher, but I do let those I help know it's the Lord healing them, not me. That's what our purpose is here, to bring these people to God. And it's not easy. It takes a long time to bring people to Christ, although sometimes there are instant successes. Only last week a Masai was mauled by a lion and brought to the infirmary. After Derry and I did what we could for him, everyone formed a prayer circle around his bed and prayed through a whole day and night. The Lord granted the man a miraculous recovery and that next night he witnessed Jesus Christ as his saviour. But they aren't all that easy. Like old Njangu, our cook. He witnessed the Lord ten years ago when Reverend Sanders visited him in prison, but have you seen what he wears around his neck? Besides the cross that the mission gave him, there's a string that dangles some heathen talisman meant to ward off sleeping sickness. They're the most superstitious people on the face of the earth, the Kikuyu.'

He paused beneath a flowering jacaranda tree and turned to look down at Sondra. 'What do you think of it all so far?'

'I'm anxious to learn more.'

'You'll have the best teacher in Derry. When I got here four weeks ago, what did I know of tropical medicine? I've been out with him twice now on circuits, setting up camp in the wilderness and turning a thorn tree into an instant clinic. He's marvellous with the natives.'

'How is it he knows this country so well?'

'Derry was born here, in a place near Nairobi. I'm told his father was one of the original settlers, owned a plantation or something like that. It was the practice of the colonials to send their sons to England for higher education; that's where Derry got his medical training. While he was there the war broke out and he enlisted in the RAF. Derry's a war hero, you know. He fought in the Battle of Britain, they tell me, flew dangerous missions and received the Victoria Cross. According to Reverend Sanders, Derry came back to Kenya in 1953 just when Mau Mau was starting and he volunteered to fight the rebels.'

Alec turned away and resumed walking; Sondra fell into step at his side. 'It's a fascinating story, Derry's. The terrorists were hiding in the Aberdare forest. They were doing terrible things, to their own people as well as to the white farmers, butchering and torturing. As the story goes, although Derry was in favour of African self-rule, he was opposed to the tactics of Mau Mau, so when the police asked for a volunteer to fly a plane over the forest and spot the terrorist camps, Derry stepped forward.

'They say his plane was shot down by the rebels and they took him prisoner. They tortured him... that's why he limps. But he gained their respect and eventually became a negotiator between the Mau Mau and the British. Derry was one of the few men the rebels would allow freely in and out of their secret camps. That was how he met Njangu.'

'How did he come to the mission?'

'When he met his wife, Jane, she was working here as a nurse. She wouldn't leave the mission so he came here to live. That was, I believe, twelve years ago, just before Independence.'

When Alec stopped speaking there seemed to be a void in the hollow African night, a void filled with queer, unnamable sounds. Sondra listened for a moment to the Eden beyond the compound, to the cry of a solitary bird, and beyond that, beyond the bushes and trees and green grass, to a silence stealing across the land, leaving behind a wake of such stillness that, for an instant, she was terrified; then she said quietly, 'Which one of the nurses is his wife?'

'I beg your pardon? Oh, Derry's wife. She died some years

ago, in childbirth, I believe. Right here at the mission. I expect he stayed on because of the infirmary he'd built up.'

They stopped short, their way suddenly blocked by the appearance of Derry Farrar. He stood with hands on hips, a scowl on his face. 'Hell of a way to go about at night,' he said.

'What do you mean?' asked Sondra.

He pointed to her bare arms. 'Mosquitoes. The malaria carriers start biting at this time of night. And trade those useless sandals for real shoes. You'll pick up spirillum fever ticks going about like that.' He turned to Alec. 'I've just looked in on our Public Works man. His condition has remained unchanged. If his family comes to claim him we'll let them take him.'

'But you can't!' Sondra cried.

'We need the bed, Doctor, and our medicine is of no use to him. Good night to you both.'

When they came to stand at last on the wooden step of her hut, Sondra found herself welcoming it as if it were a mansion. She felt as if she could sleep for ever.

Alec stood close to her. 'Derry's right about the mosquitoes. The malaria carriers start biting right after sunset. I should have thought to tell you.'

She offered him her hand. 'Thanks so much, Alec, for helping me through my first day here.'

He held her hand in both of his, then said as he released it, 'I'm only next door if you need anything.'

She got ready for bed by the light of the hurricane lamp. She knew she was too tired to give much thought to her new circumstances; time enough tomorrow and the next 364 days to ponder it all. All she wanted to do right now was sleep the dreamless sleep.

She was snuffing the lampwick and pulling back the covers when her head brushed against something – the knot of mosquito netting suspended above the bed, which Alec had made a point of reminding her to use. After a few ineffectual attempts to unravel it, Sondra fumbled in her suitcase for her bathrobe.

All was dark outside. In a short time, the mission seemed to have closed in upon itself. Few lights glowed from windows and silence filled the night. Tiptoeing quickly with her robe clutched at her chest, she rapped lightly on the door of the next hut. A bit of light coming around the curtains told her Alec MacDonald was still awake.

When the door opened she blinked first in confusion and then, realising her error, in acute embarrassment. Derry Farrar stood on the other side and he wore no shirt.

'I, uh . . .' she began, feeling her face burn and wishing she could vanish. 'The mosquito netting. I don't know how to . . .'

He stared at her for a moment, then said, 'They're tricky at first. Take some getting used to.'

As he stepped out into the night and walked past her, Sondra glimpsed the interior of his hut; it was almost as spartan as her own, as if he hadn't inhabited it long. But there was a naugahyde easy chair with a blanket thrown over it and a book face down on the seat.

She hovered uncertainly in the doorway of her own hut as she watched him untie the netting and bring it down. He was showing her how to undo the knot but all Sondra could stare at were the muscles of his bare back and the tight sinews of his shoulders and arms. 'All right,' he said, fanning out the netting as it fell to the bed. 'This is the tricky part. You tuck in three corners, then climb into the bed and tuck the last one in behind you. You must make absolutely certain you haven't missed a spot and left a doorway for a mosquito. I'll do it for you this time.'

He straightened and looked at her expectantly. 'Come along then,' he said softly. 'I haven't got all night.'

Sondra haltingly shrugged out of her bathrobe and folded it with care into the suitcase. Derry stepped back as she got into bed, then he proceeded very swiftly to tuck her in all around. She lay on her back and stared up at the gauzy circus tent rising over her, trying to keep Derry out of the edge of her vision, feeling the gentle rocking of the mattress as he secured each corner. When he was done he went to the door and rested his hand on the knob. In the darkness she couldn't see his expression, but he sounded almost as if he was smiling as he said, 'You'd better practise it, I can't be tucking you in every night. Good night, Doctor.'

Sondra settled into the stiff sheets that smelled of strong

hospital soap and hoped sleep would quickly claim her. But it didn't. She was beginning to wonder if she would ever experience normal sleep again. It was the internship that had done it, never a night of uninterrupted sleep, never a stretch of eight blessed hours because if the phone wasn't ringing or the beeper going off, then there were the dreams to plague you and make you sit bolt upright with your eyes snapping open. Her internship had ended two months ago and despite the eight weeks' rest in her parents' house before coming to Kenya, Sondra still had not got back into normal sleep.

Internship. Medical school didn't prepare you for it. In fact, medical school was nothing like the 'real thing' because at St Catherine's the third and fourth-years always had doctors overseeing their work; someone higher up always made the ultimate decisions. Knowledge in medical school was textbook knowledge, and medicine had seemed a breeze, no sweat at all. And then all of a sudden, internship, and the naïve new doctor suffered every shock from disillusionment to black depression to terror to soaring elation. It was Vulcan's forge; they received the fresh, raw material and pounded it mercilessly into an efficient, skilful, decision-making medical machine. On July 1st of last year Sondra had walked on to her assigned ward and a weary-looking man in dingy whites had said, 'You the new intern? Here.' He had thrust a pile of charts into her arms. 'Thirty-five patients. Make rounds as fast as you can, you have seven new admissions waiting.' Then he'd walked away, leaving a startled, disbelieving Sondra staring after him. And then exactly one year later – just two months ago – a cheery young man with a spring in his step had walked onto Sondra's ward and she had said to him, 'Are you the new intern? Here.' She had delivered the charts into his arms and said, 'Thirty-seven to be seen, five waiting to be admitted. Good luck.'

Sondra closed her eyes and listened to the African silence beyond her walls.

It had been a strange year, a year difficult to describe to anyone who had never lived through it. Twelve months of no friends because there wasn't time, of no recreational reading or movies or TV; not a day spent outside those concrete walls, no normal relationships with people, no levelling out of emotions, no minute to stop and let your shadow catch up. Your teacher is fear and your tools are panic and sweat, because mistakes aren't forgiven in medicine, you do it right the first time or you attend the post-mortem. So many things Sondra's hands had learned to do that she'd never believed them capable of: sternal punctures, liver biopsies, surgical cut-downs. So many split-second decisions when there wasn't anyone else around to tell her what to do: 'Get her up to surgery; we're going to have to sacrifice the baby.' So many failures, so many successes. Had it all been worth it?

As Sondra felt the gradual melting of her muscles that meant sleep was encroaching, she cut her mind loose from its mooring and let it drift into the night silence. From a distance she heard MacReady saying, 'Thank God you caught the error, Mallone. That blasted nurse was about to give our hypertensive patient something to raise his pressure!' Sondra smiled sleepily. Another voice crowded in: 'Thank you, Doctor, for saving my little girl.'

She was no longer awake but not quite deeply asleep. Sondra was still smiling. Yes, it was worth it. All of it. Because now here she was, where she had said so many years ago that she must be, and she was ready to help. As a Board Certified and licensed physician she had so much to offer, so much to give; those twelve months of heartache and sacrifice had all been for this, for tomorrow and the 364 tomorrows after.

As sleep finally took her, Sondra dreamed she was back in the Phoenix hospital and they'd just brought Mrs Minelli in with her mysterious rash and Sondra was ordering a panel of blood tests and suddenly Derry Farrar was there, in his khaki shirt and pants, hands on hips, scowling. And he was saying, 'Where do you think you are, North London Hospital?'

In her sleep, Sondra laughed softly.

# Chapter Eighteen

'The blood's a little dark, don't you think, Doctor?'

Mason threw down a clamp and thrust out his hand; the scrub nurse slapped a pair of Mayos into it.

Mickey Long lifted her eyes to look across the operating table at him. 'Dr Mason?' she said. 'Don't you think we should do something about it?'

'Give her more oxygen,' he barked to the anaesthetist.

Mickey exchanged glances with the man behind the anaesthesia screen.

'Sponge, for Christ's sake!' snapped Mason. 'Pay attention!'

Mickey saw blotches of sweat spreading on the front of Mason's surgical cap, and above his damp mask, anxious eyes. The ashen pallor of his face and the tremor in his hands told Mickey that Dr Mason was hung over again.

'Dr Mason,' she said quietly and calmly. 'I think her pressure's dropping. We should check.'

'This is my case, Dr Long,' he growled. 'Keep out of it. And clear the field, for Christ's sake! Where the hell did you learn to handle a sponge!'

Mickey suppressed her anger and turned to the anaesthetist. 'What's her pressure, Gordon?'

Mason jerked his head up, his eyes dark and thunderous. 'Who the hell do you think you are? You're here to assist me, Doctor. I could have done better with an orderly!'

'Dr Mason, I think this patient's –'

Throwing down his instruments and leaning menacingly towards her, Dr Mason said in a tone that usually struck terror in his residents, 'I don't like your attitude, Doctor. And I don't like the way you work. If I had my way I'd bar you from the operating room.'

'Holy shit!' shouted the anaesthetist. 'She's arrested!'

Six pairs of eyes snapped to the cardiac monitor, held there for a stunned moment, then all chaos erupted.

'Oh, Jesus,' whispered Mason, his hands fumbling ineffectually with the clumsy drapes.

Mickey, way ahead of him, took up the Mayo scissors, snipped a notch in the paper lap sheet, grasped it firmly with both hands and tore it all the way up to the patient's neck, exposing a bare chest with electrodes attached. She acted without thinking, her mind moving mechanically and expertly through the steps: external massage, call for the crash cart, syringes of epinephrine and bicarb, take up the paddles, each order just a microsecond ahead of Mason's order. The room was instantly full of people and over the commotion could be heard the robotic voice of the hospital operator: 'Code Blue, Surgery. Code Blue, Surgery...'

'Jesus Christ, Mickey!' shouted Gregg, slamming the door behind him. 'What the hell is the matter with you?'

She pushed herself wearily up to a sitting position and swung her feet off the couch. 'Please don't shout, Gregg. I'm at death's door.'

He came to a standstill in the centre of the living room, his face bright red all the way up to the roots of his sandy hair. 'I'm surprised you're not *dead!* Mason's out for your blood!'

'I'm sorry,' she said quietly. 'The man's an incompetent. I did what I had to do.'

'*What you had to do!* Just what do you call storming into the doctors' locker room and accusing Mason, *in front of a dozen surgeons*, of gross negligence?'

'Only because he accused me of interfering. Gregg, the man practically told me to my face that *I* was at fault for that arrest!'

'Well you just don't march into the men's locker room and start shouting!'

'He's an incompetent, Gregg!'

'For God's sake, Mickey, you're a second-year resident, not Christian Barnard! Why can't you remember that? I can't be constantly bailing you out.'

Mickey shot him a furious look. 'I've never asked you to bail me out, Gregg. I can fight my own battles.'

'Yeah,' he said, turning away. 'You're good at starting them, too.' He took off his white hospital jacket and draped it over the stereo on his way to the kitchen.

Mickey heard the refrigerator door open and close, then she turned towards the balcony where she could see a spectacular Hawaiian sunset set the sky afire. What was the use of having an apartment on the Ala Wai Canal if you were always too dog-weary to enjoy it?

Gregg reappeared, leaned his lanky body against the door-frame, and popped a can of Primo. When his eyes met Mickey's again, they both saw that the anger was dissipating – they could never stay mad at one another for long. 'I'll say one thing for you, girl, you certainly take the boredom out of life.'

Mickey smiled. That was what she liked about Gregg Waterman. Anger wasn't one of his hobbies.

She had moved in with Gregg six months ago when, after a few months of trying to keep up a relationship, it had become too much of a hassle to try to get together on their odd schedules, both working over a hundred hours a week and rarely having the same time off. Gregg was then a fifth-year surgical resident and Mickey was still in her first. The move had seemed the perfect solution: no more trying to meet somewhere and missing, no unanswered phone calls, no figuring out whose bed to use. Sharing an apartment, they were bound to cross paths at some point during the week and, if they were lucky, to share a meal and maybe even make love, if they didn't fall asleep first.

'You've got the whole hospital thinking that if you hadn't been there the patient would have died,' he said, making his way across the shag carpet to settle into a wicker chair.

'*I* don't have the hospital thinking that, Gregg. They reached that conclusion themselves. They have eyes and ears, especially the nurses who were in the room with us. They saw what was happening. They saw him almost kill that patient.'

'Hell, Mickey, it's surgery. It happens.'

'Gregg, it was a routine hysterectomy. He was ignoring the signs.'

'Look, anaesthesia idiosyncrasy, or something the pre-op

172

work-ups can't detect. It happens. It wasn't Mason's fault.'

'No, it wasn't his fault she arrested, but dammit, Gregg, he wasn't *prepared*.'

Mickey got to her feet. She'd been standing continuously for the past sixteen hours, yet she paced the room, trying to jog some life into her body. She was on surgery call again in just five hours, and should be catching up on sleep. But she was too agitated.

'Mickey,' said Gregg, frowning down at his beer can. 'Mason is demanding an apology.'

She swung around. 'I won't do it.'

'You have to.'

'Gregg, I won't apologise for doing what was right.'

'That's not the issue. The issue is Mason is a surgeon who's been with Great Victoria for nearly twenty years and you insulted him. He's got clout, you haven't. It's politics, girl, you've got to play the game to stay alive.'

'Gregg, he shouldn't be allowed to teach. He's a dreadful surgeon. He only uses residents as automatic retractor holders. He never lets us operate. And he's showing us bad techniques.'

Gregg took another draw on his beer and settled his eyes on the view beyond the balcony. It was a travel-poster sunset with silhouettes of palm trees and hotel towers. Waikiki was just across the canal. Watching the rolling motion of the water, Gregg tried to sort out his thoughts. Life had seemed simple before Mickey Long had come into it! Why me? he asked himself now. And why, he wondered, watching her reflection in the glass of the sliding door, *her?*

She was standing to one side, like the statue of an ice goddess in the midst of ferns and bamboo, the most beautiful woman he'd ever met, and the most exasperating. Didn't she see the spot he was in? Her lover and her chief, two irreconcilable poles.

His fingers tightened around the beer can. Damn it, Mickey was right, Mason *was* an incompetent. Gregg himself had agonised through some wretched surgery with the man. But he had kept his mouth shut and now he was chief and in a few months he'd be out and in his own surgical practice.

'I can't do it, Gregg.'

'Mickey,' he said evenly, trying not to get mad again. 'You've broken the cardinal rule in residency – you refused to obey the order of an attending surgeon. Think back to your interview, for Christ's sake. The first question they asked you was *can you take orders?* And you promised the review board that you could take orders like a trouper. Now you're saying you can't – or won't!'

Gregg clenched the empty can in his hand, bending it with a resounding *clunk*. 'And as if that weren't enough, you followed it up by committing the most mortal sin a resident can commit – you complained about Mason to the Chief of Surgery.'

'That's because he was the only one available at the time. And besides, he was in the locker room.'

'Mickey! You know damn well the hierarchy and the correct protocol! A *junior* does not go directly go to a senior with a gripe! There are established lines of authority. You should have come to me. I would have taken care of it. Instead, you've created a sticky situation for yourself. Mickey, you *have* to apologise to Mason.'

'No.'

'Then you risk getting kicked out.'

She wrapped her arms around herself and resumed pacing. 'Not if you back me up.'

'I can't.'

'You mean you won't.'

'All right, I won't. I only have eight months to go. I'm not going to throw it all away now.'

A breeze wafted through the open balcony door, a breeze that smelled of salt and gardenias and pit-roasting meat. It made Mickey shiver. Music drifted in, the orchestra of a hotel down the way was entertaining tourists in tiki light. It was a rare moment that Mickey was dissatisfied with her life and this was one of them.

She knew why Mason was pressing the issue. He'd been looking for an opportunity to clash horns with her ever since the morning of their first embarrassing encounter. Mickey had been at Great Victoria just a month and was in the nurses' locker room of the surgery suite. Dr Mason had pushed the door open, dropped a case of instruments on a bench, said, 'Flash these for me, honey,' and then disappeared. Half dressed, Mickey had run out after him and caught him, handing his case back. 'You'll want a nurse to do these for you, Doctor.' He'd looked her up and down in confusion and barked, 'Then what are you, an X-ray tech?' To Mickey's reply, 'No, I'm a doctor,' Mason had first shown surprise, then had frowned, and finally a flush had come over his jowly cheeks and he'd marched off without a word. It was a short time later that Mickey learned Dr Mason couldn't tolerate being caught in an error or an embarrassing situation.

'It won't kill you to apologise.'

*Yes it will.*

They sat in silence for a while, watching the sky wax from peach to maroon and finally to black. At last Mickey murmured, 'The man must be stopped.'

'Yes, well...' Gregg got up, stretched, flicked on a light, and headed back towards the kitchen. 'You're not the one who's going to do it.' She listened for a moment to the sounds of kitchen cupboards opening, the can opener humming, a pan being set on the stove. Then she wandered out onto the balcony.

It was a balmy October evening. The air was gravid with sultry smells and tropical melodies, lulling, tranquillising; silent now were the jackhammers and power saws that filled the daytime as yet another hotel inched up towards the sky. In their place throbbed the pulse of a hundred island drums and, closer in, the orchestral strains of 'Beyond the Reef.' Down on the Ala Wai Canal, six floors below her, mullet fishermen sat on the grassy banks beneath the artificial night lighting and idly watched energetic young men, flaxen-haired and brown as nuts, work on shell and outrigger canoes. Farther down, houseboats bobbed and glowed like Japanese lanterns. It was a world so far removed from Mickey that she might as well be watching a movie.

Only once, in the sixteen months she'd been here, had Mickey stepped outside the walls of Great Victoria, just down the street from the apartment, and tasted the carefree world of frosty rum drinks, mahi mahi, and postcards; it had been on her first date with Gregg. 'You've *never* been to Waikiki?' he had asked last October, just a year ago, as shocked as if she'd said she had just dropped down from Mars. That had been when she was living in the hospital's staff quarters on the grounds of Great Victoria. 'A thirty-second walk across a street and *you've never been?*'

His immediate solution had been to plan an outing, one of those freak days when their twenty-four hour off-time coincided. But Mickey had pleaded her deathly fear of the sun, so they'd gone at sundown, when he'd snapped a Polaroid of her, catching her by surprise, and she'd chased him along the warm white sand, past the open terraces of beachfront hotels from which poured songs like 'Pearly Shells.' They'd had dinner at the charming Halekulani Hotel in an atmosphere redolent of the island's monarchical days. Mickey wore a scarlet hibiscus in her hair, and Gregg had literally swept her off her feet and on to the dance floor. Possibly it was then that Mickey had decided she wanted to fall in love with Gregg, or perhaps it had been later, during their moonlight swim in the seventy-degree ocean water so still and buoyant that it had been almost impossible to touch her feet to the sandy bottom. Other midnight bathers had shared that idyll, and folks on trimarans, splashing out to the distant breakers while they plucked newly bought ukeleles and dropped coconut drinks into the Pacific.

It was a single, treasured moment cut out of the canvas of her life, a canvas of work and study and worry and rush. She wondered if such luxury would ever come back.

She embraced herself now as she looked down on that lively, night-lit world and tried to fight off the unwanted thought that so often nettled her mind: *If only Jonathan were here.*

It had been exactly a year and a half ago that she'd last seen Jonathan Archer, on television, accepting his Oscar, a year and a half since she'd vowed to go it alone, to commit herself to no man. And it had worked for a while, in those first hectic, no-time-for-thinking weeks of her internship. But then something unexpected had happened, taking her totally by surprise.

It had happened during her three-month surgical rotation

last year when she had assisted Dr Gregg Waterman on a varicose vein ligation. To her surprise he had turned clamp and ties over to her and had proceeded to walk her through every step of the operation, helping where needed but generally letting her do it on her own. The episode had filled Mickey with a profound sense of accomplishment – her first 'real' operation done almost on her own – and at the same time it had awakened in her something she had thought laid to rest long ago.

She had looked into the smiling brown eyes of Gregg Waterman and had felt an old familiar warmth.

He wasn't Jonathan, no man would ever be Jonathan. Mickey still cherished his memory, and when she'd gone to see *Nam!* she had cried, knowing who had stood behind the camera. But Mickey was also a realist. She had chosen not to go to the belltower; this was her destined path. When *Medical Center* had come on TV as a three-hour special she had made a point to miss it because the past was gone and this was the present and Gregg Waterman occupied it.

In time, Mickey hoped, she would love him as deeply as she had Jonathan.

A nurse came into the patient's room and said, 'ER's on the phone, Mickey. They've got an acute abdomen. Think it might be surgical.'

'Thanks, Rita. Tell them I'll get right back to them.'

Mickey removed the last of the sutures, replaced it with a butterfly strip, then rose up from the bed and pulled off her gloves. 'You're healing very nicely, Mr Thomas,' she said to the gentleman in the bed. 'I see no reason why you can't go home tomorrow.'

The patient, a lively old sailor with bright blue eyes in a weathered face, winked at Mickey. 'With you as my doc, I think I'll develop complications and stay on!'

Laughing, she left the room and went to the nearest house phone. 'I think it's appendicitis,' said Eric, the intern currently covering the emergency room.

'What's her WBC?'

'Only slightly elevated but she's in acute pain.'

'Okay, I'll be right there.'

As a second-year resident on general surgery, Mickey was expected to cover the two major pre- and post-operative surgical floors of Great Victoria, admit and discharge surgical patients, scrub on cases all day long, and be around for twenty-four-hour emergency call. Of course, it was humanly impossible to do all that – all hospital rotations were impossible – but she got around to as much as she could. Mickey loved surgical residency. It was a vast improvement over the year of internship, which had been so wearing and so dehumanising that, like most doctors, she preferred to put that one year out of her mind. Now she was in surgery (as a second-year resident because Great Victoria counted the internship as the first year of residency) and for the first time others were giving her credit for knowing something.

As she ran down to the ER she hastily ate an apple along the way. Mickey had missed breakfast and, with morning surgery starting in an hour, did not doubt she would be scrubbed straight through lunch and probably even through dinner. Surgery required a stamina that no other service demanded. Only yesterday she'd scrubbed on a stomach resection with Dr Brock – second assist, which meant Mickey did nothing but hold retractors – and she had stood for five insufferable hours, her hands cramped and numb around the Deaver handles, her feet turning wooden on the cold floor, her legs aching, her back hurting. She hadn't dared move. Brock was doing some tricky suturing deep in the abdomen and needed all the exposure Mickey could give him. If she had eased up an inch on those big metal retractors a vital error could have been made. Just when she'd started to feel a sharp pain between her shoulder blades and a headache coming on, Dr Brock had said, 'Okay, let's close,' and Mickey had had to grab the table to keep herself from collapsing. Some residents she knew had developed the ability to sleep while holding retractors – wedging themselves into the angle of table and anaesthesia screen and closing their eyes for a few minutes. The miracle was the way their fingers never relaxed their grip on the retractors they were holding, on the same principle, no doubt, as a bird's talons cling to a perch when he falls asleep.

'How can you do it?' Toby, the intern on Four South, had

once asked her. 'I could never be a surgeon.'

Doctors were divided into two groups: medicine and surgery. No one in either camp could see the sense in being in the other. Those in medicine – that is, internists – thought surgeons were cut-happy while surgeons thought of internists as living by the Four Ps: promises, pills, prayers, post-mortem.

Mickey loved surgery. She couldn't imagine herself anywhere else.

'Hi, Sharla,' she said as she came into the Emergency Room. 'Where's my abdomen?'

Sharla nodded to her left. 'She's in Three, Mickey. And in a lot of pain.'

Mickey had thought it odd at first, to hear the nurses call her by her first name. They automatically addressed all the women doctors by first name but would never dream of doing so with the men. Mickey had wondered if it was a sign of unconscious contempt or jealousy, women resenting women in higher authority. But she'd come to realise it was simply sororal friendliness, a way of demarcating this special sisterhood within a uniquely men's world.

Eric the intern was outside Room Three smoking a cigarette. 'Put that out,' said Mickey as she walked past him and through the door. Mickey didn't care for Eric Jones. Only in his fourth month of internship and already he was getting smug and cocky. Eric had declared that he was going to go into medicine with strictly nine to five hours and Wednesdays off.

Back at St Catherine's Mickey's work-ups had taken as long as two hours. That was because the medical students had been taught to be painstakingly thorough. They always began methodically with the 'chief complaint,' followed by a detailed history of that particular complaint. Then came a history of the patient's illnesses, of parents, siblings, ancestors. Next, 'system review,' a verbal going-over of all body systems – heart, lungs, nervous system, etc. Lastly came the actual physical exam. What Mickey had learned, as all do in their year of internship, was how to compress all of this into a matter of minutes.

Since Eric had already done the major history and physical

work-up, Mickey needed only read the chart and then do a specialised examination of the patient.

Mrs Mortimer had been brought into the Emergency Room two hours earlier by her husband, the poor whey-faced man who now hovered outside the exam room wringing his hands. She lay on her side on the gurney with her knees drawn up to her chest. Mickey introduced herself then asked a few questions while she checked the vital signs.

'When did this come on, Mrs Mortimer?'

'About a couple of weeks ago,' gasped the woman. 'It came and went. I thought it was gas. But then it came on real strong last night and I nearly passed out.'

Mickey listened to the heart: the pulse was weak and rapid. Mickey also noted that the woman was clasping the area above her right groin. 'Did you have nausea at any time?'

'Yes . . .' She started to breathe in pants. 'A few weeks ago.'

Mickey looked at the chart. Mrs Mortimer had classic signs of appendicitis. She also had the signs of ectopic pregnancy. Mickey read further down the chart. Eric's notes described a pelvic exam which showed no indication of pregnancy. Mrs Mortimer was forty-eight years old. 'When was your last period?' Mickey asked as she gently felt the patient's neck nodes.

'I told the other doctor,' she said breathlessly. 'I don't remember. I know I went through menopause. I got very irregular. And I had hot flushes. And then my period stopped altogether – Oh, it hurts!'

'We'll take care of that right away.' At least Eric hadn't rushed in and given Mrs Mortimer morphine. He had done that on a patient last week so that by the time Mickey examined him all the symptoms were masked and a diagnosis couldn't be made.

'Mrs Mortimer, whenever a woman comes in with pain in that area we have to consider tubal pregnancy.'

The woman started to cry. 'It's not possible. My husband and I . . . we haven't, you know, for a long time . . .'

Asking a nurse to stay with Mrs Mortimer, Mickey went to a house phone and had Jay Sorenson paged. He was a fourth-year surgical resident; he would do the surgery since Mickey was not yet able to scrub on her own. 'Jay,' she said when she had him on the phone. 'I think we have a surgical abdomen. Are you free?'

Mickey described Mrs Mortimer's condition and answered Jay's few questions. 'She doesn't remember when her periods stopped. She said she's had some spotting in the last few weeks, but that might just be menopausal. No relations with her husband in a long time. She has a mild temp elevation and WBC slightly elevated. But the pain is severe and she's shocky.'

'Bring her up. I'll get a room.'

It took a while for the blood typing and crossmatching to be done, and for an operating room to be set up for this emergency; and since the anaesthetist wasn't yet ready to take over the patient, Mickey decided to stand with Mrs Mortimer until everything was ready. It was a busy morning in the OR suite, chaotic as usual, and Mickey's patient was lying wide awake on a stretcher looking around with frightened eyes.

'Dr Brown will have you snoozing in no time,' Mickey said as she laid a hand on Mrs Mortimer's arm. Like St Catherine's, Great Victoria had a rule about keeping masks up in the OR suite but surgeons always made necessary exceptions. With children and frightened patients, they kept their faces exposed.

Mrs Mortimer pulled a feverish hand out from under the blanket and grabbed Mickey's wrist. 'Doctor,' she gasped. 'Doctor, it *is* my appendix, isn't it?'

'We think so. Don't worry, Mrs Mortimer, you're going to have one of the best surgeons –'

'No, no.' The grip tightened. Mrs Mortimer looked up at Mickey with enormous eyes. 'I mean what you said about the other thing. The tubal pregnancy. I mean, I'm too old for that, aren't I?'

A small alarm went off inside Mickey's head. She spoke gently as she asked, 'Why are you concerned about tubal pregnancy, Mrs Mortimer?'

Tears started to spill from the frightened eyes. 'I'm scared, Doctor. I'm so scared.'

Mickey looked quickly around, saw a rolling stool in the

suture closet, pulled it out and sat on it, close to Mrs Mortimer, at eye level. 'What are you afraid of?' she asked quietly.

'I mean, it *has* to be appendicitis, doesn't it?'

Mickey spoke carefully. 'Actually, Mrs Mortimer, although adults can come down with appendicitis, we don't often see it in a woman your age.'

'But it *can* happen?'

'Is there any reason why it should be anything else?'

Mrs Mortimer ran a dry tongue over her lips. She plucked at her covers with nervous fingers. 'Please don't tell anyone, Doctor. I'm so ashamed.'

'What is it, Mrs Mortimer?'

'It's my husband. You see, we've been married for thirty years and we love each other dearly. I've always been faithful to him. We've always been devoted to one another.' She rolled her head away and looked up at the ceiling. 'Two months ago I went to Kona to stay with my sister for a week. I met this man . . .' Mrs Mortimer rolled her head back and regarded Mickey with panicked eyes. 'He didn't mean anything to me. I don't even remember his name! I met him at a party and . . . Doctor, my husband is a diabetic. He hasn't been able to, well, *function* for the past few years. We've been told there isn't anything that can be done for us. I love him very much. I don't know why I did it.' She broke down and cried in earnest.

Mickey patted her shoulder and said, 'Don't worry, Mrs Mortimer. I don't think you're pregnant. When Dr Jones did the pelvic exam on you he didn't find anything.'

Mrs Mortimer looked at Mickey with tear-filled eyes. 'What pelvic exam?'

Mickey stiffened. She kept her voice calm. 'In the Emergency Room, the doctor who took a look at you before I did. Don't you remember him doing a pelvic exam on you?'

'How could he do one, Doctor? I can't even straighten up!'

A green figure came into the edge of Mickey's vision. It was Jay Sorensen, walking up and tying his mask. 'Hi,' he said with a smile. 'I'm Dr Sorensen. You're going to be in my care while you're here.'

'Jay,' said Mickey quietly, rising to her feet. 'Can I talk to you for a minute? Over there?' She nodded towards the scrub sinks.

He said, 'Sure,' and walked away. When Mickey started to follow, her wrist was seized again by Mrs Mortimer. 'Please,' whispered the woman. 'Please, Doctor. If it should be a tubal pregnancy, if that is what I have done, then let it be *my* punishment and not my husband's. It would kill him to know what I've done. Promise me you won't tell him, Doctor.'

Mickey looked down at the hand curled around her wrist. 'Mrs Mortimer, I will have to tell him the truth –'

'*Please*. It would be the end of him. Please don't tell him!'

# Chapter Nineteen

The story goes like this: One day, many years ago, a god named Lono decided to become a farmer and so took human form. He accidentally struck his foot with a digging stick and inflicted a terrible wound on himself. Kane appeared, Kane the Creator, greatest of the Hawaiian gods, and taught Lono how to heal his wound with the laying on of a poultice of *popolo* leaves. Kane then imparted to Lono, who became Lono-puha, Lono of the Swelling, all his knowledge of medicinal herbs and the healing arts, thus making Lono-puha the patron god of all doctors who came after him.

On the place where Kane worked his miracle a house of worship was constructed, a house where the lame and the infirm could come and have the evil spirits of sickness driven out of their bodies, a simple house constructed of *koa* branches and the sacred *ohia* wood. But with the passing of time, as the gods gradually retreated before the tide of a new world and a new age, and as memory of the gods dimmed, the spot sacred to Lono-puha eventually saw a new house raised for the worship of another medicine god, a white medicine god. It began in the year 1883 as a small missionary hospital built by the British and was called, rather ostentatiously, Great Victoria Hospital.

By the time Mickey Long came to Great Victoria, this memorial to the healing gods rose ten stories from the lush soil of Oahu. It was made of concrete and glass and all that remained of the past was the missionaries' sundial rooted at the edge of a giant weeping banyan. This was where Mickey now sat, on a marble bench set back from the concrete path that bisected the immaculately kept hospital lawns. It was a beautiful day, but a hot one: the island was suffering under the spell of *kona* weather, one of those autumn freak periods when the trade winds die and a leeward wind sets in, bringing high humidity with the October heat.

Mickey was enjoying an unexpected thirty minutes between scrubs and so she sat in the sun and ate a cup of yoghurt while she read Sondra's letter, a letter she'd been carrying around for three days.

Hello, Mickey. How are you? Well, I hope. I'm afraid I'm still having trouble settling into this place. In the past six weeks I've had to *unlearn* an awful lot of my training from Phoenix. While I was there as an intern I thought we were all worked mercilessly hard and I couldn't wait to get out. Now I look back and see how easy we had it! The mission has no X-ray machine, No EKG, no handy diagnostic equipment to give us our answers. There are no lab technicians to do the blood work for us; *we* have to do everything, and with very basic equipment. For instance, our lab here is rudimentary to say the least! One microscope and one centrifuge. We do all the work ourselves, reading blood smears, doing grams stains and urinalysis. We even have to type and crossmatch the blood ourselves.

Everything here is hopelessly outdated. We use paraldehyde suppositories for sedation. Weren't those discontinued years ago? I'd never even seen one before. And in the operating room there's a tank of cyclopropane – illegal where I came from! I can't seem to get out of the habit of relying on the things I was trained with. Like respirators. I ordered a patient put on a respirator and Dr Farrar asked me if I intended to drive the patient into Nairobi for it!

We clash all the time, Derry and I. He won't let me go out into the bush yet and I haven't touched a scalpel in the six weeks I've been here. And now I'm having a problem with the nurses. They don't know what to make of me, a female doctor. For the most part they either ignore my orders or go to Derry or Alec for confirmation. They are all trained on the old British system in Mombasa, which calls for a class division between doctors and staff. For instance, when a doctor enters a room a nurse must stand and offer him her chair. They are suspicious of my attempts to make friends with them.

Likewise, the natives who come in as patients don't trust me. They've learned that the white man is the healer; white women are good only for making tea.

I still don't know what to make of Derry. He's a very quiet, private man, and he isn't going to any great efforts to teach me anything; I must rely on Alec MacDonald for that.

Mickey pulled the photograph out of the envelope. It was a peculiar scene, five people standing stiffly in the shade of a fig tree with a queer-looking bird strutting in the foreground. On the back Sondra had written: 'From l. to r. Reverend Sanders, his wife, me, Alec MacDonald, and Rebecca (Samburu nurse). The bird is Lulu, a crested crane who cries "Waffle!" Njangu is taking the picture. Derry walked away when we called him to join us.'

Mickey went back to the letter.

We're praying for the rains to come soon. They say it's been an unusually dry year and we're terribly short of water. As a result, the wildlife is coming very close to the compound; elephants, rhino, buffalo. At night we hear lions prowling all around.

I'm afraid I sound like a bit of a grouch in this letter. I hadn't meant to. On the whole, I'm quite happy and just as determined as ever to help these people. It's just going to take a little longer than I had expected. What do you hear from Ruth? The last letter I got from her she said they think this next one might be twins! How on earth is Ruth doing it, I wonder? When I was an intern it was all I could do to keep myself upright some days; how does she manage with a house and a husband *and* a baby?' ·

Mickey let the letter rest in her lap as she settled her eyes on a group of oriental nurses eating lunch on the lawn not far away.

*A house and a husband and a baby.*

Mickey might not have given the subject much thought if people weren't always bringing it up all the time. She got an awful lot of it from patients. 'Are you married, Doctor? No? A beautiful girl like you? Well, being a doctor is nice and all but you also need a husband and babies.' Even some of the nurses had expressed a similar sentiment: 'You know, Mickey, I thought of going to medical school, but I also wanted to have a family. I mean, four years of med school – and that's *after* four years of college – and then a year of internship and then residency, which can last anywhere from one to six years more. It's okay for a man. He has a wife at home cooking his meals and taking care of the house and having the babies for him. But no way can a woman do it. So I settled for two years of nursing school and now we own our own home and have the three kids we wanted.'

Ruth was managing it. But at what price? Her letters were always spare, to the point, and written during stolen moments. She rarely mentioned Arnie; it was all Rachel this and Rachel that. Were things going all right for them? Mickey remembered the look on Arnie's face when Ruth got her diploma as Ruth Shapiro instead of Roth.

Mickey folded Sondra's letter into her pocket. *We walk the paths we choose.*

'Hi. I've been looking for you.'

She looked up and shielded her eyes from the sun. 'Hi, Gregg. I'm on the beeper.'

'Oh, I knew I'd find you out here.' He sat next to her on the bench. 'I have a breast biopsy and possible mastectomy at four and I was wondering if you'd like to help me on it.'

'You're kidding! I'd love to! You know, the others are going to accuse you of playing favourites. That will be the third choice case you've given me this week. Parker still hasn't stopped fuming over that gall bladder.'

'Let him fume. I'm doing it for selfish reasons. I want my future partner to be the best surgeon in town, next to me!' Gregg bent down, plucked a blade of grass, and twirled it between his fingers. 'I was talking to Jay Sorensen a few minutes ago. He told me about your hot abdomen this morning.'

'Yes, that,' said Mickey, her anger flaring again. Right after the surgery Mickey had gone down to the ER and read the riot act to Eric Jones.

'Maybe this'll get Nakamura to kick him out. It won't be the first goofing off Eric's been caught at. You should have done a pregnancy test on her first, Mickey. You know it's routine in all suspected ectopics.'

'I know. I just took the patient's word for it that she hadn't had sexual relations, and I believed Eric when he said he'd done a pelvic. It didn't occur to me that he faked most of that history to grab a few extra minutes of coffee and a cigarette. All I could think of was getting her up to surgery fast. It won't happen again.'

Gregg nodded. That was what he liked about Mickey, she took criticism well and never got sulky or resentful like some of the other residents did. 'Always keep two things in mind: don't rely on the patient to tell you the truth, and don't rely on interns like Eric Jones to do an accurate H and P.'

'You know, Gregg, Mrs Mortimer asked me not to tell her husband if it was a tubal pregnancy. She wanted me to lie and tell him it was her appendix.'

'Then it was lucky for you it *was* her appendix. If it hadn't been, what would you have done?'

'I don't know . . .' She turned to look at him. 'What would you have done?'

He returned her stare, then quickly turned away. 'There's something I want to discuss with you, Mickey.'

She caught the gravity of his tone. 'What is it?'

He plucked another blade of grass and twisted in into a knot. 'It's Mason. He wants your apology in writing.'

Mickey held herself perfectly still. 'And what did you tell him?'

'That it would be on Nakamura's desk this afternoon.'

'No.'

'With your signature on it, stating that you were out of line.'

Mickey clasped her hands tightly in her lap. 'I won't do it, Gregg. I'll meet with him in Nakamura's office if he wants, I'll face any mediating board he chooses, I'll even fight it out with him, but *I will not apologise.*'

'Look, Mickey, you're going to *have* to. Think of your career here at Great Victoria. If you get kicked out, think of the setback that would be for you and me.'

'I won't sacrifice my ethics, Gregg. I was right and he was wrong.'

Gregg tossed the twisted blades of grass to the ground and strummed his fingers on his knee. He knew how stubborn

Mickey could be; he had butted his head against that impossible wall more than once. After a minute of weighing everything, he snapped his head up, smiled the smile that always mended their rifts, and said lightly, 'I know you'll do it, Mickey. You won't let me down, you won't let *us* down. Now get up to surgery, and I'll see you at four.'

'All right, Koko,' he said to the Polynesian scrub nurse, giving her a wink. 'I hope you got us a sharp scalpel today.'

The young woman's mask shifted and stretched, indicating there was a big smile behind it. All the nurses liked scrubbing for Dr Gregg Waterman, he was always cheerful and patient and fair. They liked working with Dr Long, too; she wasn't fumbly like other residents, or nervous, and never tried to cover up her inexperience by shouting at the nurses.

'I'll take the knife, please, Koko,' said Mickey quietly, holding out her right hand while with her left she held the breast skin taut.

It was an inch-long incision and Mickey worked quickly but deftly, locating the lump and excising it with minimal trauma to the surrounding tissue. While she worked, Gregg sponged and cauterised for her, only once repositioning her placement of a clamp, and he left it to her to call for pathology and choose her method of skin closure. Mickey needed all the practice she could get, Gregg knew, to perfect her cosmetic closures. This patient was a woman in her fifties and the incision was close to the nipple, it would never be seen; if it were Gregg's case he would close it with interrupted silk. But Mickey was taking her time and working as carefully as if she were sewing up a movie star's face, using a buried nylon suture to create a hairline, almost invisible scar.

They had time to do it because they were now waiting for the verdict from the pathologist who was doing a frozen section on the lump. 'Art says we can use his boat this weekend if we want to,' Gregg said, sponging a little as Mickey sewed. 'He said he'll leave the dock key in the house.' Art was an orthopod who'd been a year ahead of Gregg in residency and now lived in a Kona condo earning a fabulous yearly income fixing up the injuries of water skiers, scuba divers, and volcano climbers.

Mickey didn't respond. Most surgeons, once the patient is

asleep and the case is underway, become chatty, discussing everything from stocks and bonds to golf scores, even to how they were scoring in bed, but Mickey preferred silence.

She always did delicate work, using mosquito clamps instead of Kellys where she could, her long, slender fingers mindful of the tender tissue. Whenever he watched her, Gregg always felt his pride swell; Mickey had come green and virgin to Great Victoria sixteen months ago, and he'd seen how, in that short time, she'd latched onto every new thing like a limpet, not letting go, always asking for more, and never flagging like the others but welcoming all the emergency work she could get. She was becoming a crackerjack surgeon. In practice together, they were going to make a heck of a team.

Dr Yamamoto shuffled into the room in paper boots as Mickey was applying the sterile dressing to the wound. Like all people temporarily in the OR, he wore a white paper 'bunny' suit over his street clothes, a complete overall that he slipped into when he was called up from Pathology to do a frozen section in surgery. In his hands he held a square of gauze upon which lay several slices of breast lump.

'Okay, Gregg,' he said, coming as close to the operating table as he could, showing the two surgeons the specimen. 'What you guys have here is lobular cee-ay.'

'Mm, minimal cancer.'

'What's her age?'

'Fifty-six. What would you do, Mickey?'

She thought a moment. Behind her, Dr Yamamoto was handing the frozen tissue to the circulating nurse, who then dropped it into a jar of formalin. 'I'd do a simple,' Mickey said. 'And a mirror biopsy on the other side, just in case.'

He nodded. 'Okay, team, let's go!'

The changeover was quick, Koko and the other nurse having been prepared for the possibility of a mastectomy. While one set of instruments was being wheeled out and the next uncovered, Gregg and Mickey changed into clean gowns and gloves and redraped the patient. Once the team was reassembled at the table, with fresh towels and shiny instruments, with the gentle rise of a breast, yellow from the Betadine, exposed through a hole in the top sheet, Gregg looked across at Mickey and said, 'Do you want to do it, Doctor?'

'If I may.'

'Koko, give Dr Long the scalpel.'

Yvette, the circulating nurse, silently groaned and pulled a crossword puzzle out of the pocket of her green dress. When a resident did the surgery, even if it was Dr Long, it always took two or three times longer than normal – one of the drawbacks of working in a teaching hospital. Dr Scadudo, behind his anaesthesia screen, slipped a cassette into the player on his machine.

Mickey flipped the scalpel upside down and first ran the blunt handle over the breast along the line her incision would make. She studied the invisible scar for a moment, making sure of the anatomy, then turned the blade around and got ready to cut.

'What are you doing?' asked Gregg.

She looked up. 'A transverse incision. Level of the fourth rib.'

'Why?'

'Because it's a hidden incision. The scar won't show.'

'And where did you learn this?'

'Last week when I scrubbed with Dr Keller. He showed me how to do it. We remove just as much breast tissue as –'

'I remember that case. The patient was thirty-five and had told Keller ahead of time she was going to undergo reconstruction later. *This* patient is in her fifties, Mickey. We can't take the time to worry about cosmetic work.'

'But the usual incisions will leave a scar that will show above a bathing suit, Gregg. And if she should decide to have reconstruction later, it'll be more difficult.'

'At her age? A silicone breast? I hardly think so! Shoulder to xiphoid, Mickey. Come on, you're learning general surgery here. Save the Michelangelo stuff for your plastic residency.'

She stared at him, then shrugged and commenced a standard incision for simple mastectomy. The day would come, Mickey reassured herself, the day would come . . .

'I'll go talk to the husband,' said Gregg as he peeled off his damp gown and gloves. 'I'll meet you in the cafeteria in half an hour.'

Since she was writing orders in the patient's chart, Mickey nodded absently, but a second later looked up and said, 'What?' Gregg was already out of the room; she followed him. 'Why the cafeteria? I have patients to see, Gregg.'

Now she saw in his eyes what she had not seen during her three-hour immersion in the surgery. 'We have to talk, Mickey,' he said.

'There's nothing to talk about.' She looked up at the clock on the green-tiled wall. 'It's past seven, Nakamura knows by now that letter isn't showing up.'

Gregg glanced up and down the hall of the OR suite, deserted now except for two maids with mops and buckets, and took Mickey by the arm to draw her away from the doorway they'd just come through, to get out of earshot of the nurses inside getting ready to wheel their patient out. He steered her to an alcove that held sutures and skin staples and said quietly, 'Nakamura got the letter, Mickey.'

She blinked up at him. 'What do you mean?'

'I mean that it's all over. You can relax and forget it.'

'I don't under –' Mickey felt a shock go through her body, a jolt that turned her rigid. '*You* wrote it?' she whispered.

'I had to, Mickey, I knew you would never do it.'

'Oh, Gregg!' She whipped away from him, strode three paces, then spun back around. 'That's the most terrible thing you could have done to me!'

'You'll thank me for it, Mickey, I promise. When we're in practice together, and you look back and see what I saved you –'

'You had no right!'

Gregg looked over at the maids who were watching them surreptitiously. 'Damn it, Mickey, I was worried. Not just for you but for *us*. I wish you'd understand that. If Nakamura fired you, where do you think you'd find another surgical residency? Stop thinking of just yourself and your goddamned personal principles!' He held up a hand. 'No, don't come high and mighty with me, turning *me* into the villain. You're the one who got herself into it. And don't try to convince me and the world that you're the only one with ethics!'

His voice echoed after that last shout, bringing a few nosy faces to peer out of the recovery room. Mickey was trying to keep from trembling, but the more stiffly she held herself the more she shook. It took her some moments and a great deal of effort, but she finally spoke. 'I know why you were so anxious for me to apologise to Mason, Gregg,' she said in an even tone that carried undercurrents. 'It has nothing to do with saving *my* reputation, has it? It's yours you're worried about.'

'Mine!' Gregg forced a nervous laugh and shifted on his feet. 'What the hell are you talking about?'

'You're afraid Nakamura is going to wonder what kind of surgical chief you are if you can't get a second-year resident to obey your orders. It's not *my* image, Gregg, *my* career that had you worried ... it was your own.'

Mickey managed to turn and walk steadily away from him, leaving Gregg to stare after her, stunned.

Mickey was deep inside herself as she looked out of the open window of the doctors' lounge. She watched the sky darkening to a deep purple, inhaled the scents of blossoms and barbecues on the sultry air, heard the sounds of music and laughter pour out of other open windows down the street. It was a beautiful scene, a fantasy scene, and she hated it.

Mickey was leaning against the window frame, her arms crossed, her face marble-white. Her green eyes burned brightly with anger; her lips were pressed bloodless. Gregg had had no right to do what he did. It was unforgivable. He had betrayed her and now there was no way they could go on living together, even being friends; and their professional relationship was going to suffer from now on because there would always be the mistrust and suspicion.

Mickey felt suddenly very tired. There was a throbbing ache in her legs and her stomach growled. When she looked at her watch she realised that, with the exception of the half hour on the bench at noon when she'd eaten yoghurt and read Sondra's letter, she had been on her feet for almost twenty-four hours.

Last night, in the middle of dinner with Gregg in their apartment, Mickey had got a call from the paediatric ward to put a cut-down catheter in a leukaemic patient. Immediately after that she'd been called down to the ER to admit a possible gall bladder patient to the surgical ward, then had had to run back up to Paediatrics because the cut-down was infiltrating. It had taken her the better part of the night to get it started again while two nurses held the hysterical child and Mickey battled tiny veins and milky blood. Towards dawn a post-op patient on Three East had ruptured her abdominal wound and had had to be rushed back to surgery to be reclosed. After that, Mickey had managed a shower and a cup of black coffee and then had only started rounds when the ER had called her down to take a look at Mrs Mortimer. Almost twenty-four hours since she was sitting at that dinner with Gregg, arguing about Mason; twenty-four hectic, ridiculous hours in which the half hour grabbed by the sundial was literally so outweighed as not to have happened at all.

Pushing away from the window, Mickey went to the sofa, sank down on it and buried her face in her hands.

She was in the doctors' lounge on Three East because she was on call and had to be near a phone. Out there on the ward thirty-two post-operative patients were waiting to be seen by her: thirty-two dressings to be checked, sutures removed, meds ordered or discontinued, charts written in. Thirty-two patients with pain and anxieties and a hundred questions each, all waiting for Mickey to come smiling brightly into their rooms.

A sob escaped her throat. She couldn't do it. She just couldn't face them.

As she cried softly into her hands, Mickey was aware of the foot traffic in the corridor beyond the closed door: gurneys whispering by, rubber-soled shoes squeaking on the linoleum, voices growing loud and then fading as they passed. Only once before had Mickey done this, only once had she succumbed to her weariness and depression and had a good cry; but even then she had hoped nobody would come in and catch her at it. This time she didn't care. She wanted to cry it all out, long and loud, and then sleep for a week. She wanted to run through that door and away from these imprisoning walls and away from the thirty-two who were lying there waiting for her to come and mend them and cheer them up without themselves stopping to think that maybe the doctor needed mending and cheering up.

Suddenly Mickey resented them, she resented their illnesses and their dependence on her. She resented this hospital, *hated* it; and she hated Gregg and Jay Sorensen and Sharla in the ER. *How can they stand it?* How can they come here day after day, living in artificial light and breathing artificial air and repairing an endless assembly line of malfunctioning bodies like technicians in a robot factory? Where was the satisfaction in it all? Where was the dignity?

*Five more years of this.*

Mickey's gentle crying turned to weeping. She was sobbing out loud now, possibly loud enough to be heard through the closed door, but she still didn't care. *Let them hear. Let them discover that I'm not a machine.* Because that was what sixteen months at Great Victoria had done to her, turned her into a cold, efficient, emotionless machine. Twelve months as an intern had knocked useless sentimentality out of her, had taught her to regard death as just another clinical phase of illness, and had conditioned her not to become attached to patients, but to look upon them as 'cases.' Her natural instincts had been snuffed.

*When I leave here I will be thirty-one years old.*

The phone rang on the desk. Mickey looked at it. For a fleeting instant her mind shouted: Leave me alone! Then, pulling a handkerchief out of her pocket and drying her face, she answered it.

'Is that you, Dr Long?' came an anxious voice. 'This is Karen in Paediatrics. We have an emergency.'

'What is it?'

'A post-op tonsil haemorrhage.'

'Who's the intern?'

'Toby Abrams. He told me to call you. We need you *stat*.'

Mickey hung up and moved mechanically to the door. She was going because she was programmed to go, moving the way she was trained to. But inside she felt cold and lifeless.

When Mickey arrived on the paediatric floor she found pandemonium. An hysterical woman was being subdued out in the hall, and inside the patient's room two nurses and the intern were holding down a child. Bed, clothes, and floor were all covered in fresh blood. Rushing to the little girl, who lay on her side, Mickey asked, 'What happened?'

Toby, the intern, turned a pale face to Mickey. His hospital whites were drenched and he had one hand around the child's wrist, holding an IV in place. 'She's Bernie Blackbridge's patient. He did a tonsillectomy this afternoon. She was doing fine until about an hour ago when she suddenly vomited up a stomachful of blood and went into shock. I drew blood for typing and crossmatching and tried to get an IV started. But she wouldn't hold still and her veins are so small –'

Mickey checked the child's pupils and then looked down her throat with a light.

'It took three of us to hold her down,' Toby said bleakly. 'I got the needle in and then she threw up more blood. We got the transfusion started but –'

'Damn it, Toby,' said Mickey, jumping up from the bed. 'All she needs are a couple of stitches. Have you called Dr Blackbridge?'

'His wife said he hadn't got home yet but that she'd send him right back to the hospital as soon as he did.'

She turned to the nurses. 'Have you tried Gregg Waterman?'

'He's up in Labour doing a Caesarian section.'

'All right. Page Jay Sorensen for me. *Any* surgical resident. Let's get this kid up to surgery right away!'

By the time she showered and changed out of her bloody clothes, it was midnight. But, curiously, Mickey wasn't fatigued. After calling Three East to say she would be making rounds as soon as possible, she went back down to Paediatrics where she looked in on the child's mother, to whom Mickey had given a sedative, and found her sleeping peacefully in the interns' call room.

In the doctors' lounge there was fresh coffee, orange juice, doughnuts, and fruit, and cold cuts in the refrigerator, just brought up from the kitchen for the night shift. Pouring a cup of thickly creamed coffee, Mickey sank into a vinyl chair and methodically polished an apple on the lapel of her clean white jacket.

It was strange. She was tired, but not tired like earlier, when she'd been about to cash it all in. That had been a different kind of tired; *this* was an almost invigorating one. Mickey hadn't felt this good in days.

The door opened and a gloomy face looked through. 'Hi,' said Toby. 'Can I join you?'

'Sure. Come on in. There's some great salami in the fridge.'

But Toby shook his head and sat on the edge of the sofa, his face hang-dog and forlorn. 'Thanks for saving the kid, Mickey. You saved *my* life as well.'

'All in a day's work, Toby.'

He shook his head again. Toby Abrams was a big bear of a guy, with shaggy looks and pawlike hands, and the temperament of a St Bernard. Everybody liked Toby. 'I almost killed that kid, Mickey. I made a terrible mistake. I'll never forgive myself.'

When she saw the bleak look in his eyes and the way his shoulders curved down, Mickey laid aside her coffee and apple and leaned forward with her elbows on her knees. 'Toby,' she said quietly, 'you're only four months out of medical school. Nobody expects you to know everything.'

'Yes, but all she needed was a couple of stitches. I didn't know that. I farted around for an hour while she bled into her stomach. I should have called you right away.'

'That's how we learn in this business, Toby. Now you know it, you'll never forget it.'

He regarded her with eyes that were two wastelands. 'And what about the next time? What about my next mistake? I'm scared, Mickey. That kid really frightened me.'

Mickey recognised the terror in his eyes; she had seen it often, in her own and in others. Suddenly Mickey was reminded of another intern, Jordan Plummer, who had entered Great Victoria the same time she had: a young, ambitious, and conscientious man full of idealism and dedication. About a year ago Jordan Plummer had been rotating through the Medicine service and had admitted an elderly gentleman in severe respiratory distress. Thinking the man was in heart failure, Jordan had given him an injection of morphine and the man had died shortly after. The post-mortem had revealed the patient had not been in heart failure at all but had had obstructive bronchitis so that the morphine had suppressed whatever respiratory reflex he had left. Although the only consequence had been a harsh reprimand from the Chief of Medicine – because, after all, Jordan was brand new and acting correctly according to what he thought was the right diagnosis – Jordan never got over it and, six weeks later, committed suicide.

There was a little of Jordan Plummer's ghost on Toby's face right now.

'Toby,' said Mickey gently. 'You're a good doctor. You're one of the best interns we have. Don't let one mistake rule your life. Listen,' she shifted to the edge of her chair and clasped her hands together. '*I* made a few errors last year, and one big one that nearly put me away. It was right here on this floor. Little Richard Grey, I'll never forget him. A cute sixteen-month-old with the looks of a cherub. He was brought in after several days of severe diarrhoea, dehydrated and lethargic. I was very careful about the whole thing, calculating electrolyte levels and water and salt necessary for maintenance, and then I started an IV on him. He did all right for a little while, improved with the IV, so I kept it going. But the next day he went into convulsions. I tried everything – calcium gluconate, concentrated salt solution – but nothing worked. So I called Jerry Smith, he was my chief at the time. He took one look at the baby, one look at the input sheet, and screamed at me that I'd put the kid into congestive heart failure. I had literally doubled the fluid volume in his little body. Jerry stopped the IV, gave the kid a shot of sodium Amytal, and after a while little Richard Grey started to improve. But it was close, Toby, really close. I almost lost him. And for no other reason than my ignorance.'

Mickey paused and studied the intern's face. He didn't seem to be listening. After a moment, Toby stirred and said with a sign, 'I can't cut it any more, Mickey. I just wasn't meant for this. You've got to have a spine made of steel and galvanised rubber for muscles and no nerves at all. Let alone a heart. I cried after you took the girl up to the OR. I came in here and sat down and bawled like a baby.'

When he sniffed and dashed a hand against his cheek, Mickey got up and went to sit next to him on the sofa, laying an arm across his broad back. 'When was the last time you got some sleep, Toby?'

'What day is it today?'

Mickey laughed softly. 'Okay, you haven't slept since last March and you've been living on Twinkies and you almost lost a kid today while you were trying to save her. I'd say you've earned a session of feeling sorry for yourself.'

But he resolutely shook his head. 'It's not just the kid, Mickey. It's everything.' He waved his large hands as if to encompass the hospital, the science of medicine, the whole world. 'Do you know how often I see my wife? Every other weekend if we're lucky. And then I'm too tired to do anything with her. I just sleep the whole weekend away. It's unnatural, Mickey, this life. Running ragged thirty hours at a stretch, catching naps on cots, gobbling down junk food on the run. Not to mention balancing a whole floor full of patients and trying to make the right decisions. Even when I do sleep I dream I'm running down the halls and I wake up all cramped and exhausted. No, Mickey,' he shook his big head. 'I can't go on.'

Mickey stared at him. She studied every bowed line of him, every dejected curve and droop, and knew she was looking at a version of herself as she had been a short while before. *A bug is going around the hospital. I had it a few hours ago and now Toby has it. Pretty soon it'll move on to infect someone else.*

Only three hours ago Mickey had sat in this same posture thinking the same thing: I can't go on. But she had snapped out of it, in the OR; all her depression and gloom and lack of hope had been dispelled with the anchoring of a single suture and in that instant her old sense of purpose and dedication had come flooding back.

That was all it took. Just a gentle reminder, a nudge of the old common sense and the pall lifted. Bernie Blackbridge had come into the OR just as Mickey was finishing up and he'd said, 'Thank God you took care of it. It's not often one of my sutures slips, but when they do . . .' Mickey had done it alone, by herself. Jay Sorensen was already in another operating room doing an emergency and there wasn't another surgical resident to be found in time. So Mickey had gone ahead on her own. And then later, down in Paediatrics, Mickey had assured the mother her child was going to be all right and Mickey had wanted to climb out on the roof and shout it all over Honolulu that *the child was going to be all right*.

'How can you stand it?' Toby was saying, working his hands into fists. 'How can you come here day after day and work in this factory like a robot? It's all so *meaningless*.'

'It's not meaningless, Toby, and you know it. Try to conjure in your mind's eye a pair of scales, like the ones Justice carries, and in one plate heap all the successes you've had, and in the other put your failures. Which way are the scales tipping?'

'That's not a fair comparison, Mickey. One fatal error has to outweigh a hundred successes.'

'Wrong. Because every success you had came into this hospital as a potential failure.'

'You sound like Dr Shimada.'

'How so?'

'He says not to list the patients we save but the ones we don't kill.' Toby released a short, dry laugh, then he straightened up. 'I can't stick out eight more months of this, Mickey. July is just too far away.'

'Okay, so you quit now. In eight months it will still be July, whether you stick it out here or not.'

Withdrawing her arm, Mickey settled back against the sofa cushions and heard an echo of her own earlier thoughts. *By the time I get out of here I'll be thirty-one years old.* Now she responded with: And if I quit now, how old will I be in five years?

The door opened and a nurse poked her head inside. 'Dr Abrams? We need you for an infant spinal tap.'

He stirred his large frame, trying to coax life into it, and as he rose to his great height said to Mickey, 'I'm just tired. I always get cranky when I miss my afternoon nap.'

'You're a good doctor, Toby. This is your proving ground. When you get through here you're going to be one nice new addition to the world.'

He smiled down at her, said 'Yeah,' and shambled out.

Returning to her coffee and apple, Mickey thought about Gregg. She had been where Toby was now, on the day she'd met Gregg, feeling useless and inept and wondering if she should go on. And then Gregg had looked at her in a way that reminded her she was still a woman and young and attractive, and she'd fallen into his arms as much out of gratitude as attraction to him. Not much to base a lifelong relationship on. Especially when she had tried for twelve months to really fall in love with him and it just hadn't come.

When the phone buzzed Mickey reached for it with renewed energy. This coming weekend was her weekend off. She was going to use the precious time to move back into the staff quarters on the hospital grounds. And then maybe she would look into buying a secondhand car for going out on drives whenever she was free. Explore Waimea Bay on the other side of the island. Invite Toby and his wife along. Have a picnic. Find space to breathe . . .

'Mickey,' came the ER nurse's voice over the phone. 'Mr Johnson, the man you discharged post-op two weeks ago, the one Mason did a gastrectomy on, has just been brought in. Acute abdomen, shocky . . .'

Mickey grabbed a second apple and ran out of the lounge.

# Chapter Twenty

Derry Farrar stepped out of his hut into the fresh January sunshine and surveyed the chaotic scene with his usual cynicism. The safari was almost ready to leave.

Pulling a pack of Crown Bird cigarettes out of his pocket, he lit one, took two puffs, threw it to the ground, and stamped it into the dirt with the sole of his boot. Then he looked over at the next hut. Its door was still closed. She hadn't come out yet.

He pulled another Crown Bird out of the pack and lit it, filling the air space around his head with pungent blue smoke. Derry thought about Sondra Mallone.

She had wanted to go on this safari. That was what their argument yesterday had been about – Sondra going out on circuits. She was starting to get insistent and Derry still didn't think she was ready. That had been just one of the many clashes they had had in the past four months, ever since her arrival on the day the Public Works official had gone berserk and Sondra Mallone had had the audacity to criticise Derry's handling of it. After the poor man had been collected by his family and then died a day later, Sondra had voiced her opinion that *something* should have been done here at the mission even though, when Derry had pressed her, she hadn't been able to come up with just what.

Sondra Mallone's problem, Derry decided, was that she was too zealous. Out to save the world single-handedly. And even though Derry had to admire her dedication and enthusiasm, she simply wasn't practical. She hadn't got inside the native mind yet, still wasn't able to stand in their footprints. She stubbornly stuck to her modern, scientific training without the least bit of resilience, trying to force the African native through centuries of evolution in one day.

One issue Derry and Sondra had clashed on was the business with antisepsis. She ignored his assurances that these people had built-in immunities, and she took so long sterilising everything and trying to explain hygiene to the natives that she saw one patient to Derry's three. And then there had been the episode over the infirmary's dietary practice. She'd been appalled to discover that many patients were fed by their own families who brought food in everyday; Sondra had tried to talk Derry into setting up some sort of regimen with the patients' food cooked hygienically and nutritionally in the mission kitchen, establishing 'scientific' menus for each and every patient. Derry had tried to make her understand that the scientific approach wouldn't work in this environment. 'They convalesce better in surroundings they're familiar with,' he had explained to her. 'They do better with their own food, prepared the way they're used to and fed to them by family members.'

And then there was the problem with the nurses. How had *that* mess got its start?

It was a nuisance, this lack of cooperation from the nurses. It slowed things down. They questioned Sondra's every order, going to Derry or Alec for confirmation; often they ignored her altogether and proceeded just as they pleased. Derry would admit that the nurses could be a bit of a problem sometimes, preferring to do things their own way and at their own pace, but they generally heeded the temporary doctors who came through. And they helped as well, explaining idiosyncrasies peculiar to this or that tribe, often acting as diplomatic go-between when ignorance had offended tribal custom. But Sondra they let fend for herself and as a result a few problems had arisen which had required Derry's instant attention.

So how could he possibly consider sending her out into the bush?

Sondra Mallone was a mystery to Derry. Why was she here? Every doctor who came through the mission came armed with Bible as well as stethoscope. But not Sondra. She wasn't the least bit religious as far as he could tell and not at all inclined to want to preach. In fact, her dedication was not to Jesus but to Africa itself, and while this mystified Derry it also earned his admiration. They might occasionally lock horns and she might try his patience, but Derry had to admit one thing about Sondra Mallone: she loved Africa.

To Derry, that meant a lot.

Born in Kenya, Derry drew his first breath in the high, pure air of Nairobi, and his first milk was from the breast of a Kikuyu woman who had sat on the veranda of the Farrar cattle ranch suckling her own new babe in the crook of one arm, the master's baby in the other, because the *memsabu* was too frail to feed him herself. His first steps were taken on Kenya's red dust; the equatorial sun browned his *mzungu* pinkness; his first words were a child's pidgin of Swahili and English; and his first playmates were black, Derry having not yet, at that time, been taught the British colonial colour bar.

At his mother's funeral, it was that same Kikuyu nanny who took his grief into her sturdy arms while his father stood apart, grim and remote, a stranger in a white suit, refusing to show sorrow in front of colour. Later, hungering for the love that his parent was incapable of giving, young Derry sneaked down into the Rift with his closest friend and companion, Kamante, where they tracked lion and shared the thorns and the stars and the bully beef of another Kenya, and where Derry found his first sense of belonging.

But those had been brief days, a quick taste of identity and unquestioning love, before Reginald Farrar looked at his boy seemingly for the first time, saw the unforgivable social crime he was committing, and thrashed 'better sense' into him. That was when it was arranged that Derry should be removed from this unhealthy atmosphere and highly improper commerce with blacks; on the eve of his departure for England, Derry went back to the Rift one last time with Kamante, simply to watch the animals, having lost his adolescent thirst for the hunt, to find deep masculine satisfaction in saluting their superiority and letting them go their way.

He had hated England, had no place there; it was too late to imbue in the youth the sense of British identity that the father should have seen to years earlier. Derry's valiant heroics in the RAF had not, as people liked to think, been on behalf of England but rather had been one man's personal effort to end the blasted war that was keeping him from his true home.

When Derry finally returned to Kenya, it was to bury his father. And then he found a troubled and divided country, a Kenya that no longer had a place for the son of a hated white colonial. And it was on that October day of 1953, when thirty-one-year-old Derry was staggered with the realisation that he was a man trapped between two worlds, belonging in neither, wanted in neither, that the poison began to flow.

Jane had rescued him from that dreadful limbo for two short years, had given Derry a sense of place in the universal scheme, and then she, too, had left him to founder once more.

'*Kwenda! Kwenda!*'

Shouts brought Derry out of his thoughts and he saw Kamante, his old friend from boyhood days, waving to the other driver, who had paused for a cigarette.

It had surprised Derry, back in England, to find blacks thought of as shiftless and lazy. He knew that there were no more industrious and hardworking people in all the world than the Kikuyu. They may have been responsible for Mau Mau, but on the other hand they had produced the brilliant Jomo Kenyatta and brought him to power, had restored African sovereignty to Kenya, and had rejuvenated the people with a unifying, forward-looking national pride. *Harambee!* they cried, the motto of Kenya: Let's pull together.

Kamante, although Derry's age, fifty-one, had not a white hair on his ebony head and, like Derry, was in prime physical condition. The black muscled arms that swung now in the early January sun were the same as when they'd prised a very unhappy and humiliated young Derry from the trap of the wait-a-bit thorn. Kamante strode over to Abdi, the other driver, a Muslim Swahili from the coast, shot a barrage of words at him, and had the man working again.

Kamante called, gesturing to Derry. 'You can inspect now.'

Derry waved back and headed across the compound.

In her hut, Sondra was making her bed. The sound of Derry's voice beyond the curtained window made her pause and then pound the pillow a little too hard. She was angry. She should be out there now, getting ready to make the circuit into Masai country. Unfortunately, Derry didn't agree with her.

They didn't agree on anything, it seemed. It wasn't as if she was trying to change things here, she was only trying to improve them – there was a difference. But Derry was a stubborn man, not the least bit open to new ideas. He was too fatalistic, Sondra thought, too accepting without putting up a fight first. His thinking was archaic, that, what cannot be cured must be endured.

Turning from the bed, she took a last look at herself in the mirror.

She was darker now; after four months in the equatorial sun, Sondra possessed a glowing nut-brownness that contrasted beautifully with the African dresses she had taken to wearing. After purchasing several lengths of brightly patterned cloth at the native market, Sondra had put away her blue jeans and T-shirts and started dressing like the local women with a colourful scarf binding up her long black hair. The effect was remarkable. She looked as if she'd been born to this land.

More voices drifted through her window, drawing her away from the mirror. The Reverend Mr Sanders was asking Kamante if he had enough tins of butter, Derry was shouting something in Swahili, Alec MacDonald was asking if this was all the ice they had for the polio vaccines, and Rebecca was calling out to another nurse.

Sondra relaxed. She was glad Rebecca was going on this safari. Rebecca was the senior nurse, a Samburu woman in her forties who had been converted to Christianity as a child and who spoke excellent English. A woman who made Sondra very uncomfortable.

If only things were better on that score then maybe Sondra wouldn't begin each day with the feeling that she was swimming against an impossible tide. When precisely had it begun? Probably on the first day when the nurses had taken one look at the new doctor and were startled to find she was a woman. But perhaps that small hurdle could have been overcome if she hadn't committed the blunder of trying to make friends with them. 'These nurses have a very strong sense of place,' Alec had explained. 'And they can't quite make out where to put you.' Sondra had learned that doctors and nurses simply didn't mingle and she'd apparently committed some professional breech when she had tried to sit with the nurses in the common room. Even so, Sondra knew now that those early obstacles might have been smoothed over if it hadn't been for the disastrous incident with the catheter.

It had happened two weeks after she arrived. Sondra had been alone in the infirmary, bent over the bed of a tribesman recovering from an appendectomy when she had glanced over and seen Rebecca in the process of committing a terrible error. Sondra couldn't believe it. The sterile tubing had rolled off the bed and hit the dusty floor; Rebecca had picked it up and proceeded to use it. 'Stop!' Sondra had cried, getting the attention of everyone in the ward. She then told Rebecca to break out new tubing, explaining, in front of everyone, what the nurse had done wrong, and Rebecca, after a brief, hot glare at Sondra, had thrown down the catheter and marched out.

From then on, the resistance had grown. And Rebecca, being the senior nurse, had got the rest of the nurses to follow her.

But Sondra refused to be daunted. One way or another, she was going to overcome it.

Opening the door now and stepping out into the bright morning sunlight, she paused to let her eyes adjust. The three Rovers were about ready to leave, and the safari members – Alec, the Reverend Mr Thorn, Rebecca, and the two drivers – were gathering for the departing prayer. Sondra went to join them, standing next to Alec with her head bowed while the Reverend Mr Sanders led them, and out of the corner of her eye she watched Derry stride away from the Rovers and into the infirmary.

An impossible man and an impossible situation! Now made worse by a new and, for Sondra, very unwelcome complication.

The dreams had started one rainy night back in October. She had been sitting in the common room with Alec

MacDonald. Sondra had been writing a letter to Ruth, congratulating her on the birth of the twin girls, when the door to the outside had blown open and a rain-drenched Derry had entered, complaining about the Rover getting caught in the mud down the road. But Sondra hadn't heard a word. She had stared at the havoc the storm had worked on him, the way his dishevelled black hair curled slightly at the ends and flopped onto his forehead, the deep musculature of his chest seen through his rain-soaked shirt, his bare arms caked with mud, the angry, snapping motions of his body, the way his voice deepened in fury, but ultimately, ultimately she was captured by the storm in his eyes.

The dreams had started then, sexual and erotic dreams involving Derry. Sondra didn't want them, wished they would go away. They worried her: certainly it was absurd to think she was attracted to the man, when he exasperated her so.

After the Reverend Mr Sanders recited the final blessing, everyone said goodbye and moved towards the Rovers. Alec paused to take Sondra's hand and clasp it warmly.

'Good luck,' she said. 'I envy you.'

'It's you who'll need the luck. I'm leaving you with all the work.'

Sondra couldn't help a reflexive glance towards the infirmary where already a small crowd of patients was waiting to be seen, and Alec caught a look in her amber eyes that Sondra was not aware she transmitted.

It was the look of challenge. Alec knew of the conflict between Derry and Sondra, the unfortunate clash of two enormously stubborn people from two very different worlds, each determined to impose his or her ways upon the other. Derry was old-fashioned, having left London twenty years ago and having barely kept up with medical progress, but he had all those years of hard experience behind him and the ability to 'read' a patient like a book, making quick and accurate diagnoses that modern technicians would be hard put to match. Sondra, on the other hand, was green and new, with only three years of clinical experience (and two of *those* in medical school) but she possessed a store of brand-new knowledge and familiarity with the latest in lifesaving techniques of which Derry was ignorant. Together they could make a considerable team if their headstrong pride would permit.

Today was the first time Sondra was going to work alone with Derry in the infirmary and Alec hoped they would get on all right. 'I'll be back tomorrow afternoon to relieve you,' he said, still holding her hand.

Sondra studied his face, the kind smile and gentle features. Why couldn't the dreams be of Alec? 'Take care,' she said. 'God go with you.'

She waited to wave the Rovers off, then continued on to the infirmary where she found Derry already at work tapping fluid off a knee.

The infirmary used a simple system: when the natives arrived at the mission they waited on the veranda and as each person was seen and sent away, the next in line went in. The dispensary was a large, thatch-roofed room divided down the centre by a curtain on a string. Each half contained an old-fashioned examining table, a cabinet of instruments, a cupboard of dressings and medicines, and a small rolling tray; a sink in the centre was shared by both sides. Since it was January the morning air was warm and the ceiling fans were in motion; the windows were propped open and already flies and wasps were droning in and out.

Sondra was well acquainted with the regulars, those who came for weekly treatments or to have pill bottles refilled; by now they were accustomed to the *memsabu daktari*. But in the main Sondra still saw only women and children while the men chose to wait for Derry. After four months her Swahili was good enough for her to work without an interpreter.

The first patient Sondra saw was a Taita woman with a baby in her arms. The woman indicated that there was something wrong with the infant's mouth but, on examination, Sondra found it to be perfectly healthy. As she started to hand it back to the mother, the woman protested frantically by pointing to her own mouth.

The nurse who was assisting said, 'She tells you to look at the baby's tooth, *memsabu*.'

Sondra opened the infant's mouth again and inspected the single pearl embraced in a ridge of pink gum. 'It looks fine,' she said, puzzled.

'No, no,' said the nurse. 'Baby's tooth must always come

209

from the bottom first. Tooth coming from top first is bad sign for family. Disaster coming. She asks will you pull the tooth.'

'Pull it! Why should I do that?'

From the other side of the curtain came Derry's voice: 'Since it's bad luck for the baby's first tooth to come from the top, they think that pulling it will fool the gods.'

'Tell her I'm sorry. I won't do it.'

Taking her baby back with much protesting, the Taita woman went straight to a chair against the wall and parked herself firmly on it, glaring at Sondra. When Sondra was in the middle of examining her next patient, the Taita woman ducked behind the curtain and there followed a barrage of rapid Swahili that Sondra could not translate. The infant started crying; the woman's voice grew shrill. Then Derry said something and suddenly all was quiet.

Sondra concentrated on the young woman lying on her exam table.

She couldn't feel the girl's spleen, and when she listened to the girl's chest, Sondra thought she detected an enlarged heart with a murmur. The young woman said that this was an episodic problem, that the abdominal pain and vomiting came and went in attacks, and was usually accompanied by painful, swollen joints. Sondra was mystified: the symptoms individually pointed to a variety of conditions, but together they added up to a puzzle.

'Draw some blood, please,' she said to the nurse as she helped the girl to sit up. 'And prepare a bed for her in the infirmary.'

'That won't be necessary,' said Derry, coming around the curtain; the Taita woman and her baby hurried out of the dispensary behind him.

'Why? This girl should be on observation. This might be a surgical abdomen.'

'It isn't.'

'But you haven't even looked at her!'

Derry turned to the nurse. 'Prick her finger and get a few drops of blood on a slide for me, please.' To Sondra he said, 'Come on, I'll show you.'

The small lab was off the dispensary, a room barely bigger than a walk-in closet, with a workbench along one wall, sink and refrigerator along the other. Derry went to the workbench where he picked up a small vial of sterile distilled water, drew out 10 ml by syringe, and squirted it into a test tube. Then he reached for a bottle of tablets and dropped one into the test tube.

'What's that?' asked Sondra.

'Point two grams of sodium metabisulphite,' he said, holding up the test tube to watch the tablet dissolve.

'What is it for?'

'You'll see in a moment.'

The nurse came in with the glass slide. Using an eyedropper, Derry added two drops of the test-tube solution to the blood on the slide, placed a cover glass over it, removed the excess by gently pressing the cover glass with absorbent paper, then fixed the slide to the microscope. 'We wait fifteen minutes,' he said, looking at his watch.

They left the lab. 'What did you do to quiet the Taita woman?' Sondra asked as she went to the sink to wash her hands.

'I pulled the tooth.'

She looked up. 'What?'

Derry opened the instrument cabinet and took out an ophthalmoscope. 'I had to. If I hadn't she would have knocked the tooth out herself. The baby's jaw would have become infected and the child would have died.'

Sondra's next patient was a routine case, the cleaning and suturing of a scalp laceration, and by the time she was finished Derry was heading for the lab, saying, 'Let's look at that slide now.'

While Sondra sat on the high stool and swivelled the microscope mirror to catch the morning light, Derry leaned casually against the workbench with folded arms and said, 'Use the high dry objective.'

Sondra brought her right eye over the lens and adjusted the focus. After a moment, she said, 'Oh, I see...'

'You've never seen one of these before?'

'No.'

'The reason we treat the blood first with sodium metabisulphite is because it prevents the sample from drying out. Dry stains don't sickle.'

'Is this the trait or the anaemia?'

'She has the anaemia. If only the trait exists, then sickling takes up to twenty-four hours and doesn't affect all the cells.'

Sondra stared into the microscope, at the distorted red blood cells shaped like crescent moons, which, because of their sickle shape, couldn't pass through arterioles and therefore plugged up vital blood vessels, and also which, being more fragile than normal red blood cells, disintegrated in the bloodstream, thereby literally starving the victim to death.

Sondra looked back up at Derry. 'And the prognosis?'

'Therapy, if any, is purely symptomatic and temporary. Sometimes prednisone can ease the pain. But nothing much else can be done. There's no cure for sickle cell anaemia. She'll get worse and worse and sicker and sicker until she finally dies of pulmonary embolus or thrombosis or tuberculosis. I doubt she'll live to see her twentieth birthday.'

As the morning moved on, the gathering on the veranda grew. Sondra and Derry worked with the help of a nurse, bandaging and injecting and explaining how a medicine was to be taken (Sondra had discovered that many natives, instead of swallowing pills, hung them in little sacks around their necks as protective amulets) until by noon, it seemed they hadn't made much of a dent in the crowd outside. While they were pausing for tea and cucumber sandwiches, Sondra and Derry were told by one of the infirmary nurses that there were no more vacant beds.

The steady stream continued, the infections and cuts and parasitic illnesses. A little Taita girl was brought in by her mother, severely dehydrated from diarrhoea and vomiting. The illness had passed but the child could not be encouraged to eat, and force-feeding had proved useless. So Sondra decided to admit the child at once to the infirmary and put her on intravenous therapy. Derry stepped around the curtain and vetoed the order.

'We haven't a bed to spare and our supply of IV sets is too low to be wasting one on something we can remedy right here and now.'

Before Sondra could protest Derry sent the nurse over to

the kitchen to fetch a bottle of Coca-Cola and a bag of potato crisps. 'Children can get stubborn and turn away from nutritional food,' he explained while they were waiting. 'Even when severely ill. But no child can refuse treats.'

He was right. No sooner did he uncap the warm Coke and tear open the 'crisps' than the child was gobbling and drinking with delight. 'On that diet,' Derry said, 'she'll have her sugar, salt, and fluid back up to normal in no time. Discharge her.'

It was early afternoon when the baby was brought in. Nine months old with a very high temperature, she had sore-looking eardrums and a red throat and screamed when Sondra tried to bend her knees. This was an FUO – fever of unknown origin – and could be treated only after blood tests determined the cause.

'I'll have to draw a blood sample,' Sondra told the nurse. 'We'll take it from the jugular vein.'

Just then Derry's patient came hobbling by on crutches and Derry was coming around the curtain. 'I'll do it,' he said, 'Nurse, take the mother outside.'

Sondra stared at him. 'I can do it, Derry. I did a lot of these back in –'

'Yes, I know. But if you make one mistake you'll have an angry tribe on your hands. I know how to handle these people.'

'And *I* know how to do a jugular puncture.'

But he ignored her. While the nurse started bundling the baby like a mummy, binding it tightly so it couldn't move, Derry selected his instruments from a basin of sterilising solution.

After the baby was good and mummied and couldn't wiggle, he was laid on the table with his head over the edge and turned to one side. The trick was to get him hollering because that distended the neck veins and made them an easy target. If he stopped crying, however, the vein would collapse and no blood would be taken; so the child had to be given a painful stimulus to keep him upset, which was why the mother was sent out. While the nurse flicked a finger against the soft skull, Derry guided a two-inch needle into the bulging vein and smoothly drew off the desired amount.

The instant he was through Derry took the baby from the nurse and cradled it in his arms until it was quiet.

'Tell the woman to bring the child back tomorrow,' he said to Sondra as he walked to the sink. 'We'll have the first results by then.'

Twice more Derry stepped in, changing her orders on one case and doing another procedure himself. Towards teatime Sondra felt her impatience coming to a peak.

And then a child named Ouko was brought in.

He was seven years old, a handsome boy, long-limbed like his Masai parents, with big solemn eyes that watched Sondra. Ouko was deposited gently on the examining table by his father, who had carried him in, a tall Masai herdsman with noble features and skin glowing red with ochre. Ouko sat quietly while the lady doctor heard about the headaches he'd been having the past three days. He let her take his temperature; he stoically allowed her to check his eyes with a penlight. But when Sondra tried to feel the nodes in his neck Ouko let out a howl.

The father said in Swahili, 'The boy says his neck hurts. His eyes hurt. His cheeks hurt.'

Sondra gave Ouko a long look, then asked him if he could bend his chin down to touch his chest. The boy tried, but instead of moving his head, sprouted big tears from his eyes.

'He cannot move his head, *memsabu*,' said the father.

Sondra carefully laid a hand on either side of Ouko's head and tried to bend it herself. He howled again.

Sondra then tried to look down his throat but to open his mouth, Ouko said, hurt his cheeks too much. She smiled reassuringly, patted his bare shoulder and told him in Swahili that she wasn't going to force him to do anything he didn't want. To the nurse she said in English, 'It looks like an early meningitis. Tell the infirmary we need a bed. Double up if they have to.'

Derry was coming around the curtain and drying his hands as Sondra was adding, 'And I'll need to do a spinal tap.'

He came up to Ouko, said a few words with a smile, then said to Sondra, 'Could be mumps. Watch for parotid swelling. We'd also better rule out polio. If it is polio, we'll

214

see the paralysis in three or four days. And just in case he *is* contagious, let's isolate him.'

Since Derry became immediately involved in treating an ear infection in a screaming infant, Sondra was left to do the spinal tap on her own, with the nurse's help.

Typical of his proud race, the Masai boy silently suffered the painful arching of his back, but he wept nonetheless, in silent, pitiful sobs. He was lucky that Sondra was very practised at this procedure because it was over quickly: just a moment of being braced on his side in the nurse's strong arms, Sondra's fingertips gently probing his spine for the right vertebral interspace, and then a deft in and out of the needle.

The fluid came out clear – which ruled out possible intracranial bleeding – and a moment later, a microscopic count in the lab showed no evidence of pus cells.

Since they had no idea what sort of organism they were dealing with, and since the report on the blood cultures wouldn't come back from Nairobi for two weeks, it was decided that Ouko would be settled in a bed at the end of the ward and partitioned off by portable screens.

By then the sun was close to setting and the mission was winding down its busy day. As Sondra walked wearily to her hut to wash and change her dress for supper, she couldn't shake the nagging thought that there was something they had overlooked with Ouko.

## Chapter Twenty-one

She was in the middle of writing letters to Ruth and Mickey when there came an anxious knock on her door. It was a nurse from the infirmary. The boy Ouko had got worse.

Slipping into a sweater, Sondra ran across the silent compound towards the infirmary. At the entrance end of the long thatch-roofed building a nurse's desk was bathed in the glow of a solitary hurricane lamp. The long ward of twenty beds stretched away into darkness – ten gauzy circus tents along each wall with dark heads slumbering upon pillows.

Picking up the lamp, Sondra walked swiftly but silently to the far end where Ouko's bed stood behind two folding screens. The instant she came around the screens the boy flinched.

Setting the lamp down, Sondra bent close and softly said, 'Ouko.'

He nearly jumped out of bed.

She studied him with a deep frown. When the nurse started to speak and Ouko jerked again, Sondra's bafflement turned to chilling alarm. *Not polio or meningitis at all!* Her blood ran cold. *Dear God . . .*

Motioning to the nurse to be very quiet and to follow her, Sondra turned and walked softly back to the nurse's desk. 'I'm sure it's tetanus,' she murmured, trying to keep her voice steady. 'We'll need sixty thousand units of antitoxin. Do we have it?'

'Yes, *memsabu*,' whispered the young nurse, her large round eyes starkly white in her black face.

'We'll need 1,500 units per cc in horse serum and give it in doses of 3,000 units every half hour. Let's get started.'

Ouko received his first injection of the horse serum in the left thigh, and he jerked so violently he almost fell out of the bed.

Sondra's mouth ran dry. She'd never dealt with tetanus before; it was rare in a city like Phoenix where vaccines and boosters were available. She knew the antitoxin she was giving to Ouko wasn't going to help much; all it would do was neutralise the poison that had not yet got into his nervous system. But the toxin already fixed into Ouko's central nervous system wouldn't be touched by the serum. And that was what now terrified her.

She pulled a chair to the bedside and sat to watch. Pretty soon, Sondra knew, Ouko was going to start suffering the attacks that were characteristic of tetanus: powerful spasms of the neck and jaw muscles, clenching them tightly shut, every muscle in his body jerking painfully and bending him back in an arc. The greatest danger was to the respiratory muscles: a severe spasm would literally suffocate the boy.

Gazing down at Ouko's frightened face, glistening with perspiration and fear, Sondra knew they were in for a bad night.

Derry came in a short while later, gave Ouko a long, thoughtful lookover, then said as quietly as he could, 'Did you locate the wound?'

Sondra nodded. 'The bottom of his foot. It's already healed.'

Derry picked up the syringe of antitoxin on the night table, studied it, then put it back down. 'Has he had an attack yet?'

She shook her head. Sondra didn't take her eyes off Ouko. The first attack was coming soon and they had to be prepared.

Derry continued to stand over her in mute deliberation, his face hidden in the shadow beyond the circle of lamplight. He said nothing more but Sondra sensed his tension, could feel his worry as acutely as she felt her own.

Suddenly, from the other side of the screen, somewhere in the dark ward, a patient cried out in his sleep and Ouko was thrown into a spasm. His jaw clamped shut, his mouth pulled back in the sardonic grin, his back arched unnaturally, and his arms and legs stiffened so that Ouko was literally lifted off the bed and touched the mattress only at his elbows and heels. Sondra looked on in horror.

And then, just as suddenly as it had come on, the spasm

stopped and Ouko collapsed exhausted onto the mattress. Sondra turned her wide eyes to Derry, who was tapping his watch and opening and closing his hands with fingers outspread. Twenty seconds the attack had lasted. Twenty seconds of intense pain and agony. Twenty seconds of imprisonment in a body that felt as if it were being twisted by demons. And Ouko had been conscious the whole time.

Outside, somewhere in the African night, a bird swooped low and called out. Immediately Ouko's body tightened again and arched off the bed.

Sondra caught a sob in her throat.

Then she felt Derry whip away and heard him stride down the ward; a moment later he was back with a syringe in his hand and the instant Ouko's attack subsided Derry injected him in the thigh.

'Seconal,' he whispered to Sondra. 'But I doubt it will do any good.'

They stared down at Ouko a moment more; the poor boy on the bed looked up with big, uncomprehending eyes. Then Derry took hold of Sondra's wrist and drew her away from the bedside. Back at the nurse's desk he told the nurse to go and sit with the boy. 'Be careful to make no noise or sudden moves. That's what triggers the spasms.' Then he took Sondra out into the cool night air where they could talk in normal tones.

'What can we *do*?' she asked, wrapping her arms around herself.

'There's nothing we *can* do,' he said quietly, his eyes fixed darkly on a spot above Sondra's shoulder. 'All we can do is ride it out. The boy really has no chance of making it. The spasms will kill him first.'

'But we can't just leave him to suffer those attacks!'

Derry's angry eyes focused on her face. 'I've seen a hundred of these cases. There's no cure for tetanus. Nothing works – Demerol, Seconal, Valium. It's a matter of holding on until the toxin runs its course and eventually is expelled from the body.'

'Then all we have to do is keep Ouko alive long enough for that to happen.'

Derry shook his head. 'You're hoping for the impossible.

He has one of the severest forms of tetanus I've ever seen. Very soon one of those spasms is going to either freeze his respiratory muscles and he'll die of asphyxiation, or his spine will snap and that'll be it.'

'We could paralyse him,' Sondra said quickly. 'Curare will paralyse his muscles and stop the spasms.'

'It'll also stop his breathing.'

'We can put in a tracheostomy tube.'

'That wouldn't work. He'd need positive respiration and we don't have a mechanical respirator.'

'We can do it manually, have the nurses –'

'It still won't work.'

'Why not?'

'Because even if we could support his respiration, how will we feed him? This disease runs a course of weeks. We wouldn't be able to support him on IV therapy for that long. Sondra, we're going to have to let him go. It's the best thing for the boy.'

She blinked at him. 'You're not serious! We can't just give up on him!'

'Don't you think I want to save him?' Derry said, almost shouting, 'Don't you think I've tried before with dozens like Ouko? First the sedatives and then the tracheostomy and then we stand by and watch him slowly starve to death. And in between, we watch him suffer those spasms again and again, putting the child through the worst torture imaginable until finally, mercifully, he dies!'

Derry glared down at Sondra; the air between them was charged. Then he said quietly, 'There will be no heroics on Ouko. The first time he arrests, let him go.'

She stared at him in disbelief. 'You're sentencing that boy to death!'

'My orders are final.' He turned and walked away.

Derry went as far as the compound fence would allow, to the perimeter of the mission's safety because beyond that fence was a world that didn't belong to men and their weaknesses; it was a feral world where even now paws padded close to the fence and eyes blinked golden in the dark. Derry stopped and turned to look back at the infirmary, a long, low building with squares of gently diffused light, a building that he had designed and built and made workable. The sum of his life.

It was not often these days that Derry thought of Jane and the baby that slept with her in her grave; he'd learned over the years to temper his grief and accept what had happened. But there were times when something triggered the memories – like pathetic little Ouko – and the past and the sadness came rushing back. Jane had been the first and only love in his life; it was for her he had first come to the mission, and for her unhappy ghost that he had stayed. He rarely questioned his life, rarely gave much thought to himself and his work. But he did now.

*You're sentencing that boy to death*, Sondra had said. And he was. But only because he couldn't sentence him to life. *We're powerless*. For all our learning and knowledge and science, we really don't count for much in the final analysis.

The night was cold, the breeze cutting, but Derry didn't feel it, didn't care. He was thinking about Sondra. Thinking, and wishing she had never come to the mission.

Why did he let her get to him like this? Why did what *she* said matter more than what all the others have said? *Because she reminds me of how I once was*. Twenty-one years ago, a young and idealistic Derry had returned to Kenya full of plans and visions and propelled by the same blind optimism that now made Sondra Mallone think she could change the world. When had he lost it, that youthful hope, when had the sweet electricity died and the jaded cynicism crept into its place? It hadn't been any one event, any one hour, but a slowly eroding process like a one-toothed lion gnawing the carcass of a zebra. Without his even being aware of it, Derry's once large store of idealism had gradually crumbled away until all that was left was this walking, talking hollow shell.

He gazed at the infirmary. A shadow appeared in one of the windows, a shape moving behind the drawn blind. Sondra was tiptoeing back to Ouko's bed to take up her vigil again. It reminded Derry of similar nights years ago when he had sat the same useless vigils. He felt sorry for Sondra. A hard blow was coming her way and he was powerless to protect her from it.

The cry of a night bird brought Derry out of himself.

Reaching into his shirt pocket for a cigarette, Derry forced his thoughts aside. Enough was enough. Nothing to be gained from feeling sorry for oneself, or worrying about the tender psyche of a naïve young woman. Tomorrow would be a day of work, and sleep was the most important thing right now.

Still, Derry thought as he crossed the compound to his hut, he wished there was some way he could spare Sondra the pain.

She was prepared. On Ouko's night table everything lay in readiness: the scalpel, the clamps and gauze, the metal endotracheal tube, and the respiratory bag for artificially inflating his lungs.

The nurse refused to help. She knew Derry's order, that no heroics were to be performed, and she didn't trust the *memsabu*'s judgment. So when a loud snore from the next bed sent Ouko into another spasm, this one more violent and of longer duration than the others, Sondra worked alone.

His lips turned blue and his skin went an alarming purplish colour and Sondra thought: *This is it. The one that kills him.*

Instantly she was up on a knee on the bed and forcing Ouko's head back. Her hands shook as she brought down the blade and cut a vertical line down to the third tracheal ring, split it open, slipped the cannula down the windpipe and inflated the cuff with a syringe of air. Once she was sure it was firmly seated and the airway clear, Sondra quickly attached the respiratory bag to the end of the cannula and gave it a few squeezes. Ouko's chest rose and fell each time.

Her hands still shook terribly. She had had so little time. There was blood on his neck and down on the sheets, but he was breathing now, with the help of the bag. 'Nurse!' she called out, risking another spasm. 'Come help me!'

The nurse appeared so quickly Sondra suspected she had been just on the other side of the screen. 'Come here,' she said. 'Bag him while I stop the bleeding.'

But the woman didn't move.

'Please! It's *my* responsibility. You won't get into trouble.'

The nurse took a step back. 'Dr Farrar said not to do that.'

221

Ouko went into another spasm and nearly knocked Sondra off the bed. When his chest and hips rose off the mattress as his back arched like a bow, she heard the creak of bones starting to give away.

'Dear God,' she murmured, blinking sweat out of her eyes and trying to keep the bag attached to the tube. 'Nurse! Suction! Quickly! He's bleeding into his trachea!'

The nurse stood in frozen indecision, her eyes wide with fear.

*'Help me!'*

And then suddenly Derry was there, pushing the nurse out of the way and plunging a hypodermic needle into Ouko's rigid thigh. As the curare went to work paralysing the straining muscles, Derry seized a rubber catheter off the night table, attached the air syringe to its end, looked at Sondra, gave her a nod, and when she pulled the bag off the tracheostomy cuff he sent the catheter down the tube and pulled back on the syringe. Blood filled the barrel. He emptied it into a basin and suctioned again, bringing up more bright blood. By this time Ouko had gone limp and Sondra was rapidly working to staunch the bleeding at the incision. Their four hands worked together as if they belonged to one person, with Derry aspirating, then pausing to let Sondra inflate Ouko's lungs a few times, then aspirating while she finished cleaning up the wound.

Finally, after what seemed an eternity, they were rolling clean sheets under the unconscious boy and washing him off while continuing to assist his breathing with the bag. When they were done and the nurse was carrying everything away, Derry and Sondra sat on opposite sides of the bed, facing one another; Derry's strong hand kept up a rhythmic squeezing of the bag while Sondra listened to Ouko's chest through her stethoscope.

'His lungs are clear,' she said at last, sitting back and removing the stethoscope.

'How long was he without oxygen?'

'I don't know. Two minutes, maybe three.'

'He should be all right then.' Derry had to change hands; the constant squeezing of the bag was cramping his fingers. 'Well, Doctor, it looks as though we're committed to seeing this thing through.'

Sondra looked up at him. His handsome face was cast in shadow. 'We can get the family to help,' she said quietly. 'Brothers, sisters, cousins. They can all take turns squeezing the bag.'

Derry's dark blue eyes were deep in thought. 'I'll call Voi Hospital and see if they can spare a respirator. If not, I'll try Nairobi. We'll get an IV started right away, and then we'll try stomach feeding him through a nasal tube.'

Sondra studied Derry's tired face, the slope of his broad shoulders, the rhythmic flexing of the muscles of his arm. Then she said softly, 'I'm sorry for what I said earlier. About you sentencing Ouko to death. I was frustrated.'

'I know. It's all right. We all go through it.'

Their eyes held for a long time as the African night closed in around them.

# Chapter Twenty-two

By sunrise Ouko was still unconscious. An IV solution of salts and sugar was running into a vein, and one of the missionary mechanics, a strong man, was stationed at the bedside diligently squeezing the respiratory bag.

Derry came into the community room to find Sondra desultorily stirring a cup of tea. Laying a hand on her shoulder he said, 'Go get some sleep.'

She roused herself as if from a dream, and asked if he had had any luck with Voi Hospital.

'I'm afraid they don't have a respirator available. I'll have to fly to Nairobi. But I won't go until Alec returns tonight. In the meantime we'll keep Ouko on the oxygen and the bag.' Derry sat down next to her and spread his hands flat on the table. 'I'm worried about feeding him. He was malnourished when he came in. He can't last long on an IV.'

Sondra was weary beyond belief. She had never before ached so totally, so all over and through and through, not even during her internship. It was a ragged fatigue, as if she had come apart everywhere. And her mind was just as flagged as her body. Right now she was thinking: What have I done? We'll never be able to keep Ouko alive for three weeks!

But she didn't voice this to Derry. Not now. Not now that they were committed. Sondra had performed the 'heroics' that Derry had forbidden and now there was no going back. 'I'll tube feed him first and then I'll get some sleep.'

Derry studied her. A few black filaments had escaped from the brightly patterned bandana around her hair; the white sweater covering her bare arms was rolled neatly at the wrists, offsetting the brown of her skin. Derry realised he was noticing something for the first time.

Sondra had a soft profile. A high forehead, slightly slanted eyes, and high cheekbones, but her nose was small and rounded, her lips full, her chin firm but not prominent and sloping down to a long neck. She was beautiful. He had always known that. But now he saw something else, something which he had been blind to until now but which, recognising it, he saw was very obvious. Derry finally knew why Sondra Mallone had come to Africa.

'I'll do the tube feeding,' he said quietly. '*You* get some sleep.'

She turned a faint smile to him. 'Orders?'

'Orders.'

To everyone's amazement, all was going well. Ouko's veins accommodated the IV drip, the morning stomach feeding through a nasal tube had worked, and now, by sunset, he continued to sleep peacefully and free from spasms. But this was only the first day. There were many more to come.

The compound was in commotion. Half of Ouko's tribe, it seemed, had taken up residence outside the infirmary – twenty or so Masai squatted in the dirt and sang magic chants. At the same time, the Reverend Mr Sanders was leading a prayer group on the infirmary steps. All this was disrupted by the return of the Rovers from the overnight safari, sending the compound into chaos. Derry ran out to meet them, quickly told Alec what had happened, then led him into the infirmary where Sondra was explaining Ouko's nursing management to one of the nurses. Immediately behind the two men came Rebecca, the senior nurse.

'He must be turned every two hours,' Sondra was saying, using her hands to demonstrate how the boy must be rolled from side to side. 'Back rubs. Very important. And his eyes must be irrigated.' She held up a small bottle of ophthalmic saline. 'And add a few drops of mineral oil.'

Sondra looked up to see Derry and Alec come into the ward. Alec was covered with dust and his sandy hair was windblown.

When the nurse saw Rebecca come in, she moved back from the desk like a child caught with the cookie jar. 'I will take care now, *memsabu*,' Rebecca said to Sondra, her tone cool and hard.

Sondra turned to her. 'It's important we outline a strict nursing management for the boy. He's in critical condition. Now, I've written here –' Sondra picked up the sheet of paper on which she had outlined Ouko's bedside care.

But Rebecca didn't look at it. Her hooded eyes, looking out from an expressionless black face, were fixed on Sondra. '*I take care now, memsabu,*' she said more firmly.

'Come along,' said Derry, touching Sondra's elbow. 'Let's look at him.'

Sondra hesitated, locking eyes with the hostile nurse, then turned sharply and led the way to Ouko's bed.

After a few minutes Alec MacDonald was gravely shaking his head. 'I wouldn't have done it myself. Best to let the boy go. I don't see how we can keep him alive.'

'He's being oxygenated,' Sondra said, indicating the $O_2$ bottle at the head of the bed.

Alec shook his head. 'He'll be dried out in no time. He needs humidification.'

'That's why I'm going to Nairobi at once,' said Derry. 'I only waited until you got back.'

'You're flying out now?' asked Sondra. 'But it'll be dark soon!'

A smile briefly curved his lips. 'I've done it before. Don't worry about me. I'm leaving the infirmary in your care, Alec. Sondra's got her hands full here.' He paused to watch the way the large hands of the Masai, a member of Ouko's family, faithfully squeezed the bag. The boy's chest rose with each insufflation. Then Derry's eyebrows came together. Ouko didn't look good. He wondered if he would get back from Nairobi in time.

Alec stayed with the boy while Sondra ate a hasty supper and then showered and changed her clothes. Ouko was going to require a twenty-four hour vigil; his vital signs were going to have to be constantly monitored. As Sondra brushed out her long damp hair she thought of how this case would be handled in Phoenix: the cardiac monitor, the intra-arterial pressure line, the tests for blood gases.

All she, Alec, and Derry had were their eyes and ears.

'How is he?' she asked softly as she stepped around the screen. Ouko's corner was darkened and carpets had been laid around the bed to muffle footsteps. The boy had wakened earlier but so far had not suffered a spasm.

Alec rose up from his chair, gave a nod to the Reverend Mr Thorn, who was now squeezing the respiratory bag, and walked back around the screen with Sondra. 'I don't know how we're going to do it,' he murmured as they walked to the end of the ward. 'The boy won't last another day on that IV solution. He's undernourished. He'll starve to death.'

'He's tolerated two stomach feedings so far.'

But Alec's face darkened. 'We need proper equipment to monitor his blood. We've no idea what his electrolyte balance is. Salts, potassium. We can't keep him down with the curare because then we're asking for pulmonary oedema. But if we let him spasm then he'll lose the IV.' Alec shook his head. 'And we can't transfer him to another hospital. He's not strong enough for such a move. I just don't know, Sondra.'

*I* know, she thought. *I kept him alive when he would have died. And now it's up to me to see that he makes it through.*

When they reached the nurse's desk, Rebecca looked up from the newspaper she was reading. There was an instant spark in her eyes as they met Sondra's, cold and challenging. 'Go and sit with Ouko, please, Rebecca. Reverend Thorn is alone with him.'

Slowly, deliberately Rebecca slid her gaze to Alec and stared at him expectantly. He nodded tiredly and said, 'Go sit with him, please.' She did so.

At midnight Ouko went into spasm. He lost the IV. Sondra worked until dawn to get another one started and ended up having to resort to putting a cut-down IV into one of his ankles. By the time the sun was climbing and the compound was coming to life, Ouko's vital signs were worse.

Alec had to force Sondra to go to her hut for a rest, but it was a fitful sleep and she woke unrefreshed to the sound of Derry returning in the Cessna. By the time she had washed and put on fresh clothes, the respirator was installed and a green transparent tube was carrying moist oxygen into Ouko's lungs. But his vital signs were still getting worse; the cut-down had infiltrated; and a feeding at noon of eggnog and broth had come back up.

As Derry had predicted, Ouko was slowly starving to death.

'You did your best, Sondra,' Alec said as he sat with her by the bed. It was late at night, the mission was asleep, and Ouko had been on the respirator for seven hours. No one could budge Sondra from the bedside.

Her amber eyes were settled wide and unblinking on the boy's face. Ouko looked peaceful. He looked like any boy lying on his side, propped up by pillows. But the look was a lie. Inside his body the tetanus toxin was winning the battle.

'I won't give up, Alec,' she said quietly. Her voice was level, without emotion.

Alec reached over and took hold of her hand. 'Sondra, you've done all you can. There's nothing more to be done. No human being can be sustained on IV fluids indefinitely, you know that. He's losing calories everyday. The tube feeding isn't enough. We're at the end of it.'

But Sondra wasn't listening. She was staring at Ouko's gently rising and falling chest. The respirator was doing its job. And the nurses were keeping Ouko's body comfortable and free from bedsores. All he needed, *all he needed*, was to be kept alive until the toxin had run its course and was washed out of his system. And for that he needed to be fed, he needed nutrients. Something more than the IV and the tube feeding could supply.

Sondra stared at his chest. His ribs were straining beneath the reddish brown skin. His collarbone stood out in sharp relief.

His collarbone...

'Alec,' she said suddenly, turning to him. 'Alec, have you ever heard of hyperalimentation?'

'Hyperalimentation?' He rubbed his jaw. 'I believe I read about it somewhere. Some sort of experimental feeding technique. Designed for premature infants, isn't it. And very risky I understand.'

Sondra grew excited. 'Have you ever seen it done?'

'No, but –'

'I have. In Phoenix. An internist and a surgeon were pioneering in hyperalimentation in the hospital where I trained and I had the good luck to observe the procedure several times.' Sondra withdrew her hand from his and stood. 'I think we should try it on Ouko.'

'You're not serious.' Alec also came to his feet. 'You've only observed, that's a long mile from actually doing it. You want to try inserting a catheter into that boy's heart *here*? Under *these* conditions? From what I read, I understand we have nowhere near the capability of such a procedure.'

But Sondra was afire now. 'Stay with him, Alec. I'm going to talk to Derry.'

Before he could protest further she was gone. Alec sat back down in the chair, lifted one of Ouko's limp wrists and counted the weakening pulse.

Halfway across the compound, under the bower of the sacred fig tree, Sondra's way was blocked by the sudden appearance of Rebecca. The nurse stepped out from the shadows as if she'd been waiting for Sondra; her eyes were luminous and hard in the moonlight. 'Let him die, *memsabu*,' she said in a low tone that sounded almost threatening. 'God calls to him. Let him die.'

Sondra stared at her for one heartbeat, then she stepped around and continued on to Derry's hut.

Although the hour was late a light glowed in the window. Sondra tapped on the door.

'I've come up with an idea,' she said in answer to his questioning look. 'It might work. At least it's a chance. Have you ever heard of hyperalimentation?'

A furrow appeared between his heavy brows. 'What is it?'

'A way of providing complete nutrition entirely by an intravenous route. Only it's not the usual IV, it's done through an indwelling catheter placed in the superior vena cava.'

Derry gave her a long look. He had never heard of hyperalimentation, and the idea of keeping a catheter in the superior vena cava, the large vein that fed directly into the heart, sounded preposterous. But he didn't miss the new life on Sondra's face, could not deny the energy he felt emanating from her.

'How does it work?' he asked, tucking in his shirt.

'You know the reason we cannot feed Ouko totally

through an ordinary IV is because the small peripheral vessels don't tolerate concentrated solutions. And concentrated solutions are what he needs to stay alive. But this new procedure, introducing a catheter into a large vessel and keeping it there, has shown that the superior vena cava permits a continuous infusion of concentrated nutrient solution *for as long as is necessary*. It was begun a few years ago as a means to sustain newborns with intestinal disorders, but in Phoenix we started trying the new method in adults who were undergoing multiple bowel surgeries and could not take any food by mouth. Derry, Ouko could be kept alive on hyperalimentation for weeks!'

His look remained skeptical. 'Do we have the equipment to do it?'

'I don't know. But we could improvise.'

'What are the solutions?'

'We'll have to make them up ourselves. I would think a pharmacy in Nairobi would help us.'

'Do you know how to put the catheter in?'

She hesitated. 'I've seen it done.'

'And what are the risks?'

She held out her hands. 'There are probably a hundred of them. But Ouko will die if we don't take them.'

Sondra and Derry walked back across the compound together, circling the prayer vigil led by the Reverend Mr Sanders under Ouko's window, and passing through the encampment of Masai who sat around cooking fires and shared gourds of sour milk and cow's blood. In the infirmary, things were not as peaceful as Sondra had left them. Ouko had wakened and gone into spasm. The cut-down IV had infiltrated again and the boy had started coughing up fluid from his lungs. Derry and Sondra arrived to find Alec and Rebecca suctioning the tracheostomy and bandaging the IV sites. An injection of curare had Ouko unconscious again.

Alec drove his hands through his hair. 'He's in vasospasm. There isn't a vein that'll take an IV.'

Sondra bent over the boy and listened to his lungs through a stethoscope. She didn't like what she heard.

'We have to try the hyperalimentation,' she said, joining

Alec and Derry at the foot of the bed while Rebecca rearranged Ouko between clean pillows.

Derry looked to Alec, who was shaking his head. 'I've heard of it being done, Derry, but only under *ideal* conditions. It's highly experimental; the risks are too great. From the catheter alone we could get septicaemia, thrombosis, cardiac arrhythmia. And then there are the metabolic complications: glucosuria, acidosis, pulmonary oedema.'

Derry turned to Sondra with a raised eyebrow.

'I didn't say there were no risks,' she said.

'What about the procedure itself? How risky is that?'

'We could go through the thorax and puncture the chest wall, collapsing his lung. We could think we're in a vein but actually get into the pleural space and pour gallons of fluid into his chest. We could hit an artery and he would be dead before we even knew it. But,' she waved her hand towards the boy sleeping innocently between white sheets, 'if we do nothing he won't last much longer.'

The look in Derry's eyes as he weighed the situation was unmistakable. Should they put Ouko through more suffering, prolong his pain? And was it fair to those people outside to give them false hope?

Derry looked into Sondra's wide, pleading eyes and said quietly, 'All right. We'll try it.'

# Chapter Twenty-three

They didn't have the equipment or the properly balanced solutions or the sterile conditions for insertion or a person trained in the procedure, but that didn't stop the three doctors of the Uhuru Mission.

Sondra worked all night to improvise a set-up as best she could, despite Derry's orders that she get some sleep. She was beyond sleep; that would come later. Right now her adrenalin was running and her mind was racing ahead of her.

The equipment was basic and easily assembled with what could be found around the infirmary: it was the sterility of it that worried her. Opening a vein and keeping it open, especially one that connected directly with the heart, was inviting rampant infection. Once the surgical part was done, once the catheter was inside the superior vena cava and anchored with sutures, then a continual monitor of the site where the catheter came out was going to be necessary. Great care was going to have to be taken that the catheter was neither dislodged nor under tension, that the catheter and the wound were kept clean at all times, that there was no rough handling of Ouko, that the solutions going in were sterile and fed in under sterile conditions, and that Ouko was watched around the clock for the first sign of infection.

This all came under the care of the nurses.

Sondra would tackle Rebecca when that time came. Right now, while the mission slept and the Masai kept up their soft song outside, she went through the infirmary's supplies and put together a makeshift hyperalimentation set-up: no. 18 Silastic catheter, sixteen-gauge needle, intravenous tubing, forceps, scissors, syringes, hypodermic needles, haemostats, scalpel, gauzes, and black silk suture. Sondra ran it all through the infirmary's ancient autoclave three times to ensure sterility.

While Sondra was at work in the infirmary, Derry was on the radio with an emergency room in Nairobi. The formula for Ouko's hyperalimentation solution was no simple thing: together with the pharmacist at the other end Derry determined the vitamin requirements, protein needs, electrolytes, sugars, salts, and Ouko's daily caloric requirement. The sterile solutions would be ready late the next day, when Derry would pick them up by aeroplane.

They performed the operation in the first light of day.

Since minimal movement of Ouko was essential the three doctors agreed it would be best to do the procedure with the boy in his bed.

They brought in another screen and covered it with clean sheets. A spare lamp was set on the table by Ouko's bed with the light focused on the area of his right collarbone. Alec sat behind Ouko's head holding a stethoscope to the boy's chest to monitor his vital signs. Derry and Sondra worked together on opposite sides of the bed. And at the foot, Rebecca stood in silent watchfulness, her eyes above the cloth surgical mask heavy-lidded and unreadable.

After putting on sterile gloves, Sondra and Derry covered Ouko with sterile drapes and towels, leaving an exposed square only a few inches wide to reveal the boy's neck and collarbone, streaked red with iodine paint. When this was done, Sondra looked first at Alec, who nodded to indicate vital signs were stable, then across at Derry, whose eyes were grave but showed no trace of doubt. As she picked up the syringe with its long hypodermic needle, Sondra said quietly, 'What I have to do is find the subclavian vein. Through that we will introduce the catheter.'

The three doctors looked down at the square of reddish brown skin, rising and falling slightly with respirations; Ouko's neck veins were standing out – this was caused by the foot of the bed being slightly raised on blocks in order to engorge the vessels and render the subclavian vein easier to find. Sondra was suddenly scared. To hit one of those veins, or an artery . . .

She kept her hands steady as she felt beneath the slender collarbone. When she found the sternal notch – a small indentation in the top of the bone – she brought the tip of the needle to the skin. Then she hesitated. Her mouth had run dry. She heard a roaring in her ears. Sondra had watched this procedure several times, but now, to actually do it herself –

She jabbed the needle into the skin. 'Derry,' she murmured.

At once he reached over and steadied the cumbersome glass syringe on the end of the needle. As Sondra slowly and cautiously advanced the needle under the skin, Derry's hand moved with hers, guiding the syringe.

'Draw back,' she said.

Derry pulled back slightly on the barrel of the syringe; nothing came up.

They were looking for blood. Smooth, dark blood that would mean the needle was in the vein. If they came up with nothing, they had missed their target; if they came up with air, it would mean they had hit a lung; and if they drew up bright red, pulsing blood...

Sondra swallowed hard. Feeling the sternal notch with her fingertips as she guided the needle, she went deeper and deeper into Ouko's chest.

She felt a fine moisture sprout on her forehead. So much could go wrong! If she should hit the axillary artery, or the brachial plexus! 'Draw back, please,' she murmured.

Derry pulled up on the barrel. Nothing.

From her place at the foot of the bed, Rebecca watched with veiled eyes.

Alec listened to Ouko's heart.

'Draw back,' said Sondra.

Still nothing.

Sondra started to tremble. Surely she should be there now! Had she gone too far? She was dangerously near the apex of Ouko's right lung. *Should I draw the needle out and try again, targeting at a different angle?*

'Draw back.'

The syringe remained empty.

Her hands froze. She couldn't go on. Nor could she pull out. *Something's wrong! I shouldn't have attempted this!*

Sondra whispered, 'I don't think I can –' and then Derry's hand was over hers, guiding the needle again, and when he drew back on the plunge a tide of maroon blood rose up in the barrel.

All four people around the bed sighed together.

'All right,' said Sondra, taking a deep breath. 'We are in the subclavian vein. Now we must introduce the catheter through the needle and place it in the superior vena cava.'

While Derry held the syringe Sondra picked up the coil of Silastic tubing, straightened it, and held it along Ouko's chest. Noting the red line that marked the distance to the heart, she said, 'All right, Derry, remove the syringe, please.'

A bit of blood bubbled out as the syringe came off; Sondra sponged it with a gauze and then proceeded to slide the tubing into the end of the needle.

Her hands were shaking now and she felt a trickle run down between her shoulder blades. If she miscalculated, the tubing could go into the heart, or it could go up into the neck, killing Ouko.

They worked together, Sondra and Derry, his strong and steady hands assisting her delicate touch. As the tubing went into the needle and followed its shaft, Alec leaned forward in concentrated attention to the heart. With the stethoscope in his ears and his hand under the sheets on Ouko's chest, he listened for the first sound of cardiac trouble.

Bit by bit the tubing went in, guided by the collective skill of Sondra's and Derry's fingers, and when the red mark on the tubing reached the skin, Sondra stopped and said, 'We should be there.'

All three doctors stared down at the reddish brown patch of skin, as if to see through it and down to the large vein underneath. All three, in their minds' eyes, could picture the catheter sitting in the great vessel that fed into the right atrium of the heart.

Even Rebecca, leaning forward from her vigilant spot, seemed to see into Ouko's chest. Her eyes flickered and she leaned away.

Sondra looked at Alec. 'How is the heart?'

'It sounds fine. No arrhythmia.'

She looked across at Derry, whose eyes were pensive above the white surgical mask. 'Shall we remove the needle now?' she asked.

They anchored the catheter to the skin with black silk suture and then covered the site with sterile gauze and tape. After removing her gloves, Sondra connected the free end of the tubing to an IV bottle of 5 per cent dextrose that had been hung in readiness. She then opened the flow and four pairs of anxious eyes watched the drip begin.

Derry came around the bed, took hold of Sondra's arm, and said quietly, 'Go get some rest. Alec and I will take over now.'

Just as she had expected, the fatigue of the past three days swept over her, sending Sondra into a deep and dreamless sleep, stretched out on her bed, fully clothed. Her orders to be wakened at noon were countered by Derry so that when Sondra did stir on her bed and blink up into darkness, she had to take a minute to orient herself. Outside, the compound was strangely quiet.

Then she remembered. Ouko!

The ward was dark, all the patients were asleep. A solitary nurse sat at the desk, her Bible open to Revelation. Sondra found Derry at Ouko's bedside, holding the lamp up to the IV's bottle and inspecting it.

'How is he?' she asked, coming around the screen.

Derry turned, startled. 'You're awake.'

'How is Ouko?'

'Fine, so far.' Derry gestured towards the bottle and Sondra came up close to see it. 'I came back from Nairobi a little while ago with it. If we calculated correctly and if we have no trouble with the catheter, this should keep Ouko alive long enough.'

Sondra examined the upside-down bottle. Right after the operation they had started a drip of 5 per cent dextrose, to make sure the catheter worked and to give Ouko something while Derry flew to Nairobi. The formula hanging here now had not been an easy one to come up with, nor was it a proven one: time would tell them that. They had calculated Ouko's daily caloric need at two thousand. The usual 5 per cent dextrose provided only four hundred calories per day, which was one of the reasons a concentrated solution had to be manufactured. This bottle also contained nitrogen, potassium, salts, sugar, vitamins, protein, amino acids, magnesium, and calcium – all calculated according to Ouko's weight, age, and nutritional needs.

'We'll know tomorrow if it's working,' Derry said, lowering the lamp and turning to face Sondra. They stood close together in the semidarkness, surrounded by silence and a watchful night. 'We'll start him on a bottle a day and increase it as he tolerates it, replacing with supplemental IVs in between. We should do blood sugar every week, serum electrolytes three times a week, and blood counts periodically.'

He paused, looking down at her with enigmatic eyes. He opened his mouth to say something further; then, as if changing his mind, turned to look down at the sleeping child. 'I've told Rebecca to keep a nurse here around the clock,' Derry murmured. 'And I've told her that they are to take their orders directly from you.'

Ouko became the focus of attention of the entire mission. Other patients continued to be treated as usual, but it was the Masai boy everyone watched. His course was rocky.

Four days after the operation, the skin around the catheter became inflamed and the whole set-up had to be replaced. During periods of consciousness Ouko spasmed so violently that he was nearly lost. On the tenth day an alarming gurgle was heard in his lungs and antibiotics for pneumonia were started. The three doctors rotated turns watching him, checking vital signs, doing the lab work. The nurses, following Sondra's strict bed-care outline, kept Ouko clean and comfortable and free from bedsores. The Reverend Mr Sanders prayed at the bedside every morning, and each evening candlelight vigils were held for Ouko.

He lost a shocking amount of weight. The formula was changed with an increase in calories. He showed sugar in his urine. The formula was changed again. When he could tolerate it, tube feedings of cream and egg were given. His urinary catheter became infected and had to be replaced; more antibiotics were given. The pneumonia held fast; frequently suctioning of the tracheostomy was carried out. Lab work went on around the clock. There was someone at his bedside every minute. And the prayers never ceased.

Finally, on the eighteenth day, just two weeks and four days from the afternoon he was brought in, Ouko stayed awake for a full twenty-four hours without spasm. The tracheostomy tube was removed.

On the nineteenth day the hyperalimentation catheter was removed.

Sondra was going to be doing an amputation in the morning – the ulcerated foot of a Taita elder. She was in the infirmary lab mixing blood samples in a saline suspension in preparation for the operation and just finishing up when Alec came in.

'How about a walk before supper?' he asked.

It was a beautiful February evening with a spectacular sunset: first the entire sky was pink, then orange, and now a liquid lavender was inching up from the four horizons. The compound was busy as everyone was hastily making use of the last light of the day.

Sondra liked Alec MacDonald. There was something reassuringly stable about him; she liked his easy smile and comfortable presence, the faint mixture of Old Spice and pipe tobacco that was always around him. As they strolled around the periphery of the compound in the late afternoon, they waved to other people who were collecting the children to be taken back to their villages, or who were rounding up the animals into their pens. The mission was starting to close up for the night.

'I took a look in on old *Mzee* Moses a little while ago,' Alec said as they passed the fig tree. 'He has stopped coughing blood and his chest sounds clear. Thank the Lord.'

Sondra nodded and settled her hands into the pockets of her bulky sweater. There was no end to the variety of patients the infirmary saw, never a let-up of the steady flow. She loved it.

They strolled under jacaranda and bougainvillea. Alec turned to the subject of the weather. 'The long rains should be starting soon. You can smell the old grass the Masai have been burning off.'

Sondra called out to people they passed; bid good evening to Mrs Whittaker, the teacher, as she closed up the schoolhouse. Sondra looked for Derry, but he was nowhere around.

It was some minutes before she realised Alec had skilfully

shifted the conversation while still holding to the subject. 'We can have punishing winters there sometimes. No doubt, coming from Arizona you would find my islands at the top of the world somewhat rough and primitive. But they have a rare beauty. I think you could come to love them.'

They came alongside the church, on the sun-side so that they stood in the final, golden rays of the disappearing day. Alec stopped suddenly and turned to face her. 'I can't think of any other way to approach this, Sondra,' he said impulsively. 'I've been on it for days and all I keep coming up with is weather.'

She looked up at him, puzzled.

He put his hands on her shoulders and looked down into her eyes. 'I'm asking you to marry me,' he said softly. 'I'm asking you to go back to Scotland with me and share my life.'

Sondra stared up at him. All of a sudden she could see it, just what Alec had been talking about: the starkly beautiful islands and centuries-old ancestral home and the brothers and sisters and cousins and the comfortable and secure life he was offering along with name and family. *Family*.

'You don't need to answer me now, Sondra. I know it's come as a surprise. I won't pressure you. We've seven months to go here yet, plenty of time to think about what I'm offering. All I can say is I love you very much and want you to spend the rest of your life with me.'

It was like a dream. And when he bent his head to kiss her Sondra didn't resist. But as the kiss grew passionate and Alec pulled her tightly to him, Sondra knew that Derry was still there, in her thoughts, in her dreams, and it wasn't right, kissing Alec and not telling him the truth.

The dusky stillness was disturbed by the heavy crunch of footfall. Sondra and Alec drew apart to see Derry come to a halt as he rounded the church. He hesitated a moment, then, as if he had seen nothing, said to Sondra, 'I've been looking for you. There's someone who wants to see you.'

She followed him back across the compound, Alec close behind, and when he led her into the infirmary she wondered who Derry was taking her to see.

Sondra had her answer the instant she stepped into the ward. Down at the far end was a bed that had not been seen in nineteen days – the screen was gone now and there was a little boy sitting up eagerly eating porridge and honey spoon-fed to him by Rebecca.

When the three doctors came up, Ouko stopped chewing and stared up at them with wide eyes. Rebecca wiped his chin with a napkin. Ouko stared in particular at the *memsabu* in the centre, the lady who had been in his strange dreams.

'Hello, Ouko,' Sondra said softly, smiling.

The boy smiled shyly and finished swallowing. He was still woefully thin and too weak to lift a spoon, but there was no mistaking the liveliness in his eyes and smile.

'Ouko,' said Derry in Masai dialect. 'This is the *memsabu* who saved your life.'

The boy murmured something and his face blushed a reddish brown.

Derry turned to Sondra. 'Ouko thanks you. He says he will never forget you.'

Sondra felt her eyes sting.

And then Rebecca, laying aside the porridge bowl, came to her feet, fixed an eye on Sondra, and said, 'Does the *memsabu* have any new orders for Ouko's care?'

Sondra looked at her. Rebecca had put in more hours at this bedside than any of her nurses, had been the one to detect the pneumonia, had overseen the hourly turnings to make sure the catheter was not disturbed, and had dismissed one nurse for not properly taking the vital signs. She was a good, solid woman and the one a doctor wanted on hand in an emergency.

'Use your own judgement, Rebecca,' Sondra said.

There was the barest trace of a smile on Rebecca's lips. 'Yes, *memsabu*,' she said, and resumed her seat.

While Alec stopped at the bed of *Mzee* Moses to listen to his chest once more, Derry and Sondra stepped out into the darkening night. A breeze had picked up, carrying animal smells and the perfume of flowers and the aroma of burned grass. Derry looked straight ahead at the Taita Hills turning purple against the sky and said, 'You've made a few friends. And well earned, too.'

Sondra didn't speak, couldn't speak.

'I'm going out on safari up north into Masai country in a few days,' Derry said. 'Will you come with me?'

## Chapter Twenty-four

They were to travel over four hundred miles with a stop in Nairobi to pick up refrigerated supplies. Sondra rode in the first Land Rover with Derry; the Reverend Mr Thorn rode with Kamante in the second; and the third vehicle was occupied only by Abdi, the Swahili driver.

The three Rovers bumped and bounced along the dusty track from the mission to the Voi-Moshi Road, cutting a straight swath through flat red desert spotted with green trees and man-high balls of thornbush. By the time they turned northward on the Mombasa Road, meeting heavier traffic, the sun was climbing and the day was growing warm. Sondra looked right and left at the flat, expansive Tsavo West and Tsavo East, rusty deserts occasionally thrusting up lava rock and a tree that looked as if it had been planted upside down.

'The baobab tree,' said Derry. 'The Africans believe that tree once made God angry so He plucked it up and shoved it back into the ground upside down, which is just what it looks like. The Africans believe that the branches one sees are really the roots, and that the leaves are growing underground.' From the myth of the baobab Derry went on to tell other tribal lore – legends and tales that explained many mysteries to the primitive African mind.

By the time they reached Nairobi, just before noon, Sondra knew more about Kenya and its varied people than she had learned in the past five months.

After a pleasant lunch at the Thorn Tree Restaurant in the New Stanley Hotel, and then a pick-up of supplies at the World Health Organisation Immunology Research Centre, the three Rovers headed out of the city along a busy road. Derry became increasingly more animated and lively, and as they followed the heavy traffic on the two-lane tarmac, Derry told Sondra more stories.

She was intrigued by the change in Derry, and as she studied his smiling profile she realised what it was about him that was different: she had never seen him so lively.

They followed a rough road between farms and plantations, a road the Africans called 'Mussolini's Revenge' because it had been built by Italian prisoners of war and was in disastrous condition. Forty-five minutes out of Nairobi the road reached a mountainous summit in an area called Kijabe, and around a curve, a spectacular view of the Great Rift Valley came into sight.

'My father's ranch was down there,' Derry said as he slowed the Rover and pulled it to the roadside. 'That's where I grew up.'

He got out of the car, came around, opened her door, and offered her a hand. 'You have to see this.'

Derry led Sondra to the edge of the world. At their feet, far below, stretched a wheat-yellow valley contained in a bowl of mauve hills. It was vast and breathtaking, its floor etched with a patchwork of farms and ranches, the wind cool and silent, carrying martial eagles on stilled wings. Sondra was mesmerised. Next to her, Derry said quietly. 'The ranch was down there. It's carved up now. I sold it years ago. The old house is now a *harambee* school.'

Sondra turned to look at Derry; she saw how his eyes embraced all of it, saw the wind stir his hair as it surely stirred his soul.

It embarrassed her slightly, to see him so open and exposed, almost vulnerable, but at the same time it answered all her questions about him. This land, this wild, untamed land of wheat-coloured valleys and verdant mountain slopes was the explanation for Derry Farrar; he was no more and no less complex than this savage world. Its pulse was his, its breath was his. She could almost feel his yearning soul reach out and embrace it all, like the returning son embracing his family. And she envied him. Derry had his place; he knew who and where he was and possibly even why.

At the foot of the escarpment they turned on to a long ribbon of highway that bisected green plantations and farms;

they passed women in colourful African prints with babies slung on their backs; children in uniforms spilled out of schoolrooms. The Rovers came upon lopsided trucks loaded with sugar-cane and coffee sacks and overtook them, Kenya fashion, on blind curves, passing 'black spots' where traffic deaths had occurred. And then the farms started to give way to wilderness and the population dwindled and finally there were no more utility poles. Traffic thinned out and the landscape grew flatter and warmer and *older*.

They reached Narok in the late afternoon, a sprawl of concrete-block buildings, corrugated rooftops, and acacia trees dominated by a Mobil station congested with about twenty tourist safari vans. The three Rovers pulled into Loita Traders for petrol. Derry strode into the trading post with a youthful gait; his entire character and physical bearing changed after the stop at Kijabe. He laughed and joked with the Indian proprietor behind the counter, exchanged greetings with a group of old Masai gathered to share a bottle of Harvey's Bristol Cream, and when Sondra accepted the chilled Tusker he handed her, she thought: *He's come home.*

From Narok the road changed from macadam to dirt and then, as the sun started its descent on the other side of the Masai Mara and the Rovers turned off the road to Keekorok Safari Lodge, the dirt degenerated into just two ruts formed by previous tyres through the tall grass. Ahead, the golden plains of Tanzania were washed in coppery-orange and the fever trees threw longer and longer shadows. A pride of lions, belly-full and dozing beneath a thorn tree, barely lifted their noses to the three vehicles bumping past.

Ahead and all around, a level plain of lion-coloured grass and flat-topped trees stretched away to the distant horizon; Sondra had a sense of moving through time rather than space, of leaving the civilised world behind her not in miles but in years. A family of giraffes sailed alongside the Rovers, then an elephant, startled, bolted away from the tree he had been bark-stripping. A grey and white goshawk etched exaggerated circles in the sky, then dived and swooped up, its talons no longer empty.

After a teeth-jarring hour over torturous terrain, the Rovers came to a stream that was a small offshoot of the Mara

River. They found a cluster of yellow-barked acacias, which would serve as their outdoor clinic, circled them with the Rovers, and proceeded to set up camp.

They sat down inside the protective netting of a tent to enjoy a supper of catfish, which Kamante had caught in the stream, stewed in new potatoes and a savoury sauce. Then there was a short period of winding down before they went off to their bedrolls.

'Tomorrow the patients will start arriving,' said Derry, lighting a Crown Bird and leaning back in the folding canvas chair with his long legs stretched before him. 'In this part of the country the Masai are spread far and wide, but there's a communication network. By morning we'll have our hands full.'

Sondra nursed a tin cup of coffee heavily laced with Nestlé's canned milk as she watched Kamante bank the open campfire. The Reverend Mr Thorn was already snoozing on his cot under netting draped from a tree branch. Across the small circle stood the tent that was to be their dispensary by day, Sondra's sleeping quarters at night. Derry would sleep in the cooking and storage tent, while the two drivers slept on cots under trees. She listened to the profound stillness that she had not only become used to but had, in fact, come to love.

'What's that sound?' she asked.

Derry listened. 'It's the call of the honey guide. He's a nice little bird who loves honey but whose beak is too fragile to peck out the comb. So he calls for help. Sometimes the honey badger helps, sometimes man. You follow the honey guide and he leads you to the hive. You gather as much honey and comb as you need and leave the rest for him.'

'What a handy system,' said Sondra, smiling.

Derry took a long draw on his cigarette, exhaled it slowly, then pressed it out in the metal ashtray clipped to his chair. 'Yes, well, not any more. Now that man is getting his confection from sugar and jam and chocolate he doesn't need honey like he used to. Now, the honey guide calls out and calls out but no one follows.'

Sondra felt a kind of sadness come over her then, sadness for the futile calls of the honey guide, for a vanished Africa and with it a man's cherished boyhood.

'I hope we encounter Ole Seronei,' came Derry's quiet voice. 'Now there's a Masai worthy of legends. You won't find a nobler, more dignified chief than Ole Seronei. He was in this area last year, but his *enkang* could be far away by now.'

Sondra heard the wood and canvas of Derry's chair creak as he pushed himself to his feet. She watched him walk to the wall of netting, first peer out through the mesh, then part it slightly to look straight up at the sky. 'I wonder where they are,' he murmured.

'Where what are?'

'The slums of heaven.' He gave a short laugh. 'Because that's surely where *I'm* going.'

She stared at him as he watched the sky, studied every line and angle of his body as it stood silhouetted against the dark camp, quiet now that the others had crept off to bed.

'There's a new star up there tonight,' he said softly. He turned and looked down at her. 'Want to see it?'

Putting her cup down, Sondra came to stand next to Derry, very close to him, and looked up at the black sky. 'See it?' he said. 'That tiny bit of light, moving slightly faster than all the rest?'

Sondra said, 'Yes,' but in truth she saw nothing but the awesome wash of diamonds against black velvet, the silvery celestial dust scattered by God's indifferent hand. Derry pointed out things she couldn't see, didn't want to see, not wanting to find order in that accidental universe. 'There,' he said softly. 'You can see the Southern Cross. It's the doorway to Tanzania and the southern hemisphere. Over there you can see the Great Bear upside down on his head. And straight up overhead, Sondra, look,' he put his hand on the small of her back, 'that's the Centaur and those are Alpha and Beta.'

'Where is the new star you mentioned?'

'Just up there, crowding the Pleiades. It's a communication satellite. After you've memorised the African sky like I have, you can easily pick them out.'

He looked down at her, the trace of a smile on his lips. 'You love Africa, don't you?'

'Yes.'

He hesitated for a moment, then stepped away from her and said, 'We'd better get some sleep. As soon as the Masai know we're here we'll be very busy.'

The morning air was sharp and chill; it invigorated the marrow, uplifted the spirit. Sondra ate a heartier breakfast than was her habit. She had slept well, deeply and dreamlessly, on her cot inside the other tent, and had washed in fresh water brought up from the stream.

As the drivers washed the dishes and began to arrange the camp into a clinic, Sondra saw the Masai start to appear, materialising from the red earth as if God had just created them.

They stood shyly a few yards from the camp: tall and handsome young warriors leaning on spears, their long plaited hair and slender, red-painted bodies gleaming in the morning sun; beautiful, long-limbed girls in cowhide cloaks, their breasts seductively bare, their heads shaven smooth, also red-smeared and glowing like redwood statues, with arms and ankles and necks heavy with colourful beadwork. There were older women with babies slung on their backs and across bare breasts, chatting like birds, smiling and gesturing, gossiping and exchanging the latest news. Old men were already squatting in the dirt and digging holes for the game they would play all day long; and children, their heads shaven like all the Masai, except the young warriors, playing naked in the dirt or holding on to mothers' tanned hides, watching the *wazungu* with great round eyes. Within an hour a large crowd had gathered from miles around, all talking and laughing, touching and kissing in the typical fashion of the affectionate Masai – the white man's tree-clinic was always an occasion for entertainment and diversion.

The Reverend Mr Thorn placed himself beneath a tree and began to read Genesis. Few paid him any heed; the natives' attention was collectively fixed on one more curious object.

Then Sondra became aware of it, when she turned away from the card table on which she was spreading thermometers, medicines, and syringes, she turned to find all eyes on her.

She looked at Derry. 'What is it?'

'They're curious about you.'

Through heat and insects, language barriers and native superstition, Derry and Sondra worked their medical skills. The Masai presented them with malaria, sleeping sickness, and parasites, while under his tree, the Reverend Mr Thorn tirelessly intoned his Gospel.

After an hour of working at Derry's side, of looking into the ingenuous smiles of the Masai, of listening to the deep silence of the bush – so unlike the beehive that was the mission – Sondra started to feel a special peace descend upon her. She paused at one point, a syringe in one hand and a bottle of Quinacrine HCL in the other, and lifted her face to the wind. Fifty yards to her left a bull elephant stood planted in the tawny grass like a small grey mountain, lazily stripping a tree and flapping his enormous ears; to her right, a pair of Masai *moran*, young warriors, handsome and long-jawed, leaned idly on their spears and watched Sondra with studied interest. Someone played a simple wooden flute, a handful of notes in a repetitive, haunting melody. There were flowers: the Nandi flame of dark green leaves and huge scarlet blossoms, the white frangipani like bits of fallen cloud, the mustard-bloomed yellow fever tree. There were also birds to splash colour against the dun landscape: golden-breasted starlings, little Melba finches with white breasts and ruby heads, and, perched on a termite hill the height of a man, a lemon-coloured barbet.

Through the blond grass came a small, lively group led by an old Masai chief who was carrying a *rukuma*, a short black club that was the symbol of his authority. Seven tall and beautiful Masai girls followed behind, their tanned leather cloaks draped over their shoulders, leaving full, sensuous breasts bare. They laughed as they moved through the crowd, receiving kisses and bestowing them, jumping up and down, a bouncing, singing group mingling ecstatically with everyone. Derry explained to Sondra that they were *olomal*, unmarried girls who had worked themselves into a state of physical and mental bliss and who were undulating through the crowd for blessings, for luck, hoping to get fertile, looking for love. One in particular, a tall, ripe young woman with long, inviting eyes seemed to have set herself on Derry and she danced for him, chanting words that made the crowd smile approvingly.

When the chief said something to Derry and Derry laughed, Sondra asked Kamante what it was all about. 'The chief says to Derry, she has her eye on him. She likes Derry. Does he want her?'

Sondra watched Derry smile and shake his head, and then the group moved on, back into the high grass that had created them, their primitive song riding away on the wind.

Supper consisted of tinned beef and hard biscuits in gravy and again there was a winding down period before the early retirement to bed. All five safari members sat inside the protection of the main tent, the drivers to play cards, the Reverend Mr Thorn to engage Derry in a discussion of African politics. Sondra sat slightly apart, sipping her coffee, looking up at the stars through the tent's netting.

She was filled with the strange sense of having come to the end of a long road.

Finally she said good night and went across to her own tent. Sitting down amid boxes of medicines and bandages, she brushed out her hair by the light of the hurricane lamp. When she heard footsteps come near her tent Sondra thought it was the priest on his way to his cot under the tree. Then she heard Derry's voice say, 'Are you awake, Sondra?'

He sat down on one of the crates and folded his arms. 'I haven't properly thanked you for what you did for Ouko.'

'We all did it.'

'Yes, but you gave us the means for saving his life. And further lives. One of the biggest problems the mission sees is severe malnutrition. With hyperalimentation we stand a greater chance of saving lives that would otherwise be lost.' He regarded her for a long moment, then said quietly, 'I misjudged you, Sondra. I'm sorry. I didn't treat you with much kindness when you first arrived.'

She stared up at him, held by the spell of his dark blue eyes.

'What do you plan to do after your year is up here?'

'I don't know. I hadn't really thought about it.'

'Are you going to marry Alec?'

'No.'

'Why not? He's a decent chap, has a lot to offer you, and he's plainly mad about you.'

'Shouldn't I be telling you that it's none of your business?'

'But it *is* my business.'

Sondra smiled faintly. 'Why? Because you're director of the infirmary?'

'No. Because I'm in love with you.'

Her smile faded. She looked up at him.

'I think it was the night you came knocking at my door with a crazy scheme for keeping Ouko alive. I don't know. Or maybe it was the very first night and you couldn't manage the mosquito netting and you came knocking at my door, thinking you were at Alec's hut.' His eyes flickered. 'I suppose I should try to sweep you off your feet or something, but I'm afraid I'd make a bloody fool of myself.' He paused and said more quietly, 'Or have I already made a fool of myself?'

Sondra whispered only one word: 'Derry.'

And then he was taking her into his arms and placing his mouth over hers, gently at first, then hungrily. Their kissing became urgent, frantic: Sondra felt his two strong arms draw her against his hard body and she clung fast to him, finding in Derry's love the end to her search. There would be no more seeking, there was only here and now and Derry; and she knew, as he knew, that they had both come long and circuitous roads to find an ending at last.

# PART FOUR
## *1977 – 1978*

# Chapter Twenty-five

Ruth was furious.

As if swatting a fly, she slapped the newspaper with the back of her hand. 'Listen to this, Arnie. "Home birth is nothing more than child abuse."' She let the paper drop to the cluttered table and fixed hot eyes, like the coals now glowing in the kitchen fireplace, on her husband. 'Child abuse! What utter rot!'

Arnie didn't look up from his steady, rhythmic feeding of ten-month-old Sarah. If he paused at all she'd start to fuss. 'What's it about, Ruthie?' he asked, dipping into the bowl of warmed, creamy cereal and lifting the tiny spoon to the bud that was the baby's mouth. 'What triggered it?'

'Oh, that insane trial in California. You remember, the midwife accused of murder after a baby she delivered at home died. What hogwash!' Ruth slapped the paper again, rattling her breakfast plate and silverware that lay beneath it. 'It's been proven that the baby would have died under the most ideal conditions! But no, they've latched onto this case like a pack of starved dogs on a bone. And the tragedy is, they'll convince people.'

'Mommy!'

Ruth looked up from the Letters to the Editor and at once the fury dissolved from her face. 'What is it, honey?'

Rachel, five years old – five years *and two months,* she liked to remind everybody – stood in the doorway that led from the cavernous brick kitchen to the living room. 'This,' she said in a very grown-up voice, 'is what I will wear to school today.'

Ruth smiled. Rachel had just started kindergarten and was taking herself very seriously. 'But, sweetheart, you have it on backwards.'

Rachel had managed to squeeze her plump little body into one of her new school dresses without having undone the

253

buttons. The smocking that Ruth had stitched across the chest was now hidden beneath a fall of black hair. 'But *Mommy*,' she said, putting her hands on her hips the way Miss Salisbury did, 'this is how I want to wear it. That way, you see, when I come home today I can, um, undress myself and you and Beth won't have to help me because, um, the buttons are right *here*.'

Ruth had to laugh. 'You go back upstairs and have Beth put it on the right way for you.'

Rachel sighed the sigh of sophisticated suffering, said, 'Oh, very well,' and exited primly.

Arnie joined Ruth in her laughter as he lifted Sarah out of her high chair and settled her on the rag rug under the table. He glanced towards the window over the kitchen sink and said, 'Looks like rain, Ruthie. Be sure to dress well.'

While Arnie started cleaning the egg-crusted plates off the table, Ruth bent down to rest her hand on Sarah's fluffy head. Although she didn't have favourites, Ruth had found in each of her four girls a unique and endearing quality, and she cherished each one separately: Rachel had courage and aggression; Naomi had a quick wit, her twin sister Miriam, an inquisitive, exploring nature; and little Sarah was showing signs of being a thinker. Unlike the other three who'd enjoyed noisy infancies, the ten-month-old would sit for long periods in contemplation, her unfathomable eyes looking far too old for her baby face.

What will this one be like? wondered Ruth as she straightened and placed a hand on her abdomen. Will you be an artist, a politician, a setter of trends? Or possibly, she thought, looking at Arnie's back as he stood at the sink scraping dishes, this time you might even be a boy.

A crash from overhead brought her to look up at the beamed ceiling, but not in alarm. Noise was the norm in the Roth household; these hundred-year-old walls hadn't heard a moment of silence in five years.

She loved this old house. Back in 1972, when Ruth was in her first month of internship and as big as a bus with Rachel, Arnie had protested that they couldn't possibly afford it; but Ruth had set her mind on it and had, as always, got her way. Not that Arnie minded. For one thing, he loved giving in to

Ruth, for another, he loved this old Victorian farmhouse on the south shore of Bainbridge Island as much as she did.

They'd soon filled the nine rooms with warmth and love and mouths that needed feeding. On the heels of Rachel's birth had come the second pregnancy – the twins – while Brandy, the Labrador, had synchronously produced puppies. The several cats had come over the next five years on their own schedule, appearing individually at the back door and setting up the yowl that meant this family's been adopted. The cockatiel, a small white parrot that liked to ride on shoulders and nibble earlobes, had come home with the guppies; the hamster was Rachel's five-year birthday present, and Ruth had bought the lop-eared rabbits on a Saturday shopping impulse. Beth, the fifteen-year-old runaway who was now upstairs helping Rachel get dressed, had come home in the car one day with Ruth. Sooner or later, Arnie often thought, all the strays of Bainbridge Island found their way to the Roth house.

He looked up from the sink and frowned at the threatening sky. Yesterday had been bright and blue and crisp, but during the night some celestial hand had slapped a pewter bowl over the Olympic Peninsula, as if to punish malefactors. He shook his head. What was a San Fernando Valley boy like him doing in this cold, wet place?

The month before last they had decided to end the summer with a bang and to take their first real vacation now that Ruth was out of residency. They'd gone for a week over Labour Day to camp in the mountains and *it had rained the whole time*.

Leaving the dishes – Beth would wash them later – Arnie dried his hands and then turned to look at Ruth as he rolled his sleeves down.

God, she was beautiful. She seemed to grow more beautiful, if that was possible, with each pregnancy. What a picture she was, sitting at the table, framed in the soft glow from the brick fireplace behind her, head bowed, her look contemplative, reminding him of little Sarah, who now crouched between her mother's legs, exploring Ruth's bare feet. She had put on a few pounds, but they were good pounds, Arnie thought, round and soft and sexy.

It wasn't often they shared a suspended moment like this; all too frequently there was a rush to get dressed and dash out of the door. The phone would be ringing – a patient in distress. Now that Ruth was in her own private practice, Arnie hoped such quiet moments as this would become a regular feature in the Roth household.

An ominously familiar sound behind him brought Arnie to glare at the old kitchen sink faucet. It was dripping again. He tried to think: had they paid the plumber yet for the last bill, when the upstairs bathroom had had to be pulled apart because Rachel had stuffed a washcloth down the drain? He shook his head. How was it that the more money he earned the more they were short of it?

Another drip-sound joined the faucet. The November rain had begun. He gazed through the window as if mentally to curse the weather, but his annoyance waned at the sight of the little jungle in the foreground of the rain. On the kitchen windowsill was a miniature garden of green life: every broken stem, every snipping, every seed and pip found its way into one of Ruth's jars and ended up here, to spread new shoots and roots and lacy filaments. The newest additions were four milk glasses filled with water and supporting avocado stones pierced with toothpicks. Each glass was labelled with a child's name and every morning Ruth lifted each girl to inspect the progress of her seed – even baby Sarah, who couldn't possibly understand.

Arnie suddenly realised he'd been fumbling for some time with the right cuff of his shirt. Lifting his wrist he saw that the button was gone and a thread dangled. He frowned. He'd lost that button weeks ago. And he couldn't go upstairs now and change his shirt because this was the last one; the laundry was piling up to the ceiling again.

'Sarah darling, you mustn't put pencils up your nose.'

He turned back around to see Ruth bend and pick the baby up, cradling Sarah in the hammock her caftan created between her knees. Ruth gathered the small pink fist into her hand and pressed it against her belly. 'There, Sarah, your new brother or sister. Say hello, Sarah, she'll hear you.'

Sarah gurgled and drooled down Ruth's caftan. Arnie shook his head again. How did she do it? Back in 1972 he had suspected it couldn't all be juggled at once – the marriage, the new house, the family, Ruth's medical career. She had often had to put in a week of over a hundred hours and, in fact, had gone into labour with Sarah while making rounds at the hospital. Ruth had continued seeing her patients, pausing now and then to lean against a wall until the contraction subsided, then she'd gone calmly up to the OB suite, informed the nurses of the imminent birth, and had stretched out on a labour bed right next to one of her own patients.

Of course, when you're juggling a lot of things at once and you stop to scratch your nose something is bound to fall. At first the constant messiness of the house had irritated Arnie, and the occasional shirt-shortage in the morning getting ready for the office, and coming home after a headachy day over undecipherable tax records to have to cook dinner and put kids to bed – not seeing his wife sometimes for days at a time – but Arnie had got used to it; and now he gave it no second thought, being breadwinner and housekeeper at the same time. These had been five very full years and they'd gone by in the wink of an eye. Arnie's job with an accounting firm across the bay in Seattle was paying well, and he took extra jobs – preparing tax forms, giving investment counselling – to bring home the additional money they always needed. And now Ruth was out of her residency and starting her own practice in Winslow; soon they would have more money coming in and he'd never run out of clean shirts.

'You won't be late, will you dear?' Ruth asked.

Arnie looked over at the clock on the wall, nearly buried beneath a haphazard display of fingerpaintings and crayon drawings, and saw that it had stopped again. It was one of those new ones, more fancy than practical – a mirror in a frame with a small clock set up in the corner; no wires, no plugs, just batteries that were always running down. It had been a gift from Ruth's sister last January, when five million Shapiros and extended relations had descended on the Roth house to celebrate Ruth's and Arnie's fifth wedding anniversary.

Five years. Five years of sacrifice and doing without and putting-up-with. But worth it now. Just as soon as Ruth got settled in her practice and had regular working hours like everyone else she would be home every night and spending more time with her family. Yes, Arnie decided after thinking about it again for the thousandth time: it was worth it.

He had been taking stock of himself with increasing frequency these days. Primarily, he inspected his hairline, which, yes, he was sure of it now, was starting to recede. Every morning, a few more hairs on the pillow; every night, a few more in the comb. Well, after all, he'd had his fortieth birthday last month, he was getting a small paunch over his belt, and he'd finally started wearing the inevitable bifocals.

He pushed away from the sink, crossed the flagstone floor of the kitchen, and tapped the clock with a fingertip. It didn't come back to life. In the mirror he saw Ruth's reflection. She had put Sarah back on the floor and was now rubbing her abdomen. He'd vowed to himself that he wouldn't show her any alarm, but he felt it nonetheless. 'Are you sure you don't want me to go with you?' he asked as casually as he could.

'No, it's all right, honey. You go on to work. I'll call you when it's over.'

*When it's over.* The test to find out if they should keep this baby or not.

Ruth had been very calm about it from the start. Last month she'd come home from her pre-natal checkup with her new gynaecologist, Dr Mary Farnsworth, who had taken over old Dr Pott's practice, and had said very matter-of-factly over a dinner of roast lamb and child-chatter, 'Oh, by the way, Mary wants you to go in and give her a blood sample.'

'What for?'

Ruth had shrugged, but the way she'd avoided looking at him had betrayed her worry. 'Well, it seems that she tested my blood for a particular factor and found it, and now she wants to check yours, just in case.'

'What are you talking about? What factor?'

Ruth had a rule of No Unpleasantness During Meals, and that extended from world news to squabbles over who got to pick the evening's bedtime story. Meals had to be pleasant for good digestion; serious talk was saved for later. But on this particular night Ruth had had a patient in labour and she

258

was due back at the hospital in an hour. So she'd had to bring it up.

'Just a factor, Arnie, you know you don't like medical details.'

'Christ, Ruthie –'

'Mary will explain it to you, all right?' She'd shot him a look that was supposed to say *Don't alarm the girls* but which had really said *I'm upset, don't make it worse.*

So Arnie had gone to Dr Mary Farnsworth's office and she had indeed explained. 'I tested your wife on a hunch, Mr Roth, because of her ancestry. The gene she carries shows up in about one in two hundred, but in Jews, especially Jews of Eastern European extraction, it is about one in twenty-seven. On her own she cannot transmit the disease to her child, but if you also have the gene, then you and Ruth have a twenty-five percent chance of having a Tay-Sachs baby.'

*Of having a baby that had no chance of living beyond its fourth birthday.*

'And if I have the gene?' he had asked.

'Then we test the foetus to see if it indeed has Tay-Sachs, in which case the pregnancy should be terminated.'

Last week, Arnie's blood had come back positive. He and Ruth were both carriers and it was a wonder, Mary Farnsworth had said quite frankly, that they had given birth to four healthy girls.

The next step now was a procedure called amniocentesis. As a baby is developing in the womb, skin cells slough off and float in the amniotic fluid surrounding it; this water is drawn out through a needle, cultured, and examined for an enzyme called *hexosaminidase* (HEX A). If the enzyme is absent, the baby has the disease.

Ruth was undergoing amniocentesis today and in two weeks they would have their answer.

'I can take the day off,' Arnie said now, wanting to go with her to the hospital, and not wanting to go. 'You shouldn't be alone.'

'Nonsense.' Ruth shoved her chair back, careful first that Sarah was out of the way, and stood up, sending a shower of toast crumbs to the floor. 'It won't take long and I'll be going on to the office afterwards.'

Contrary to one of his most rigid rules, Arnie had asked Ruth what the amniocentesis was going to be like and he'd instantly regretted it. First they locate the position of the baby ('foetus' she'd called it, slipping from mother to physician) and then they insert a long needle into her abdomen. Were there risks to the test? he'd asked. Yes, there were risks. But it was better to know now whether or not the baby was normal.

'Go on, Arnie. You'll miss your ferry.'

As he plodded up the stairs to get his breifcase (and a safety pin for the shirt cuff) Arnie felt that odd, achy feeling start to thrum deep inside him again. What was it? Whenever it materialised he always tried to identify it, but never quite could. Sometimes it tasted of frustration, others, impatience; and now, this morning, there was the taint of resentment. Against what, whom?

Ruthie's a doctor. She'd known all along the possible risks we carry in our heritage. But she's never brought it up before, never had us tested for it.

In the master bedroom Arnie absently straightened the covers of the bed as he always did, because if he didn't the bed wouldn't get made.

Doctors hid their heads in the sand just like everyone else, Arnie had learned. They were just as afraid as other people. Like Ruth's paediatrician, Dr Mary Walsh, walking around with a lump in her breast and telling herself it was only a harmless cyst and would go away and now she'd had both breasts removed and was receiving radiation treatment.

Well, maybe the more you know the more you hide from it. He supposed he couldn't really blame Ruth.

Downstairs, Ruth listened for the sound of Arnie's car pulling out of the gravel driveway, then she went to the fridge, and pulled out a pitcher of orange juice she'd squeezed that morning. She would have preferred coffee but caffeine was one of her personal taboos during pregnancy. Like cigarettes and aspirin and alcohol, even drugstore cough syrup, coffee was a luxury Ruth would indulge in after next April.

As she drank she consulted her watch and saw that she had a few minutes before Mrs Colodny was due to arrive, so Ruth resumed her seat at the table, Early American maple like most of the furniture throughout the house, and idly pushed the bills around as she listened to the heavy rain.

She was hoping her new practice was going to start paying off soon so they could start getting some of these bills out of the way. It was a comfortable set-up: Ruth had rented a modest storefront on the corner of Winslow and Madison, and she had one nurse and one receptionist and enough patients to keep busy all week. The problem now was, getting them to pay.

A cream-coloured, important-looking envelope lay beneath the utility bills: Arnie's invitation to join the Caribou Lodge, a prestigious men's club on Bainbridge Island. It would be a boon to his career; he'd certainly gain good-paying clients from his association with the Caribou. But where to get the two-thousand-dollar initiation fee?

The familiar thunder of feet came pounding down the stairs and in the next instant three little girls were bursting into the kitchen and piling into their mother's outstretched arms.

Rachel, whose dress was on properly now, also wore galoshes and a thick wool sweater over which would go a slicker. The twins were also dressed up, a practice they'd started in imitation of lucky Rachel, who now had the much envied status of *going to school*. Each morning Naomi and Miriam went through an elaborate ritual of 'getting ready for school,' chattering about their make-believe teacher Miss Pennies, and going out to the school bus with Rachel. Ruth even packed them little lunches in brown sacks, which they brought back inside with them after the yellow bus had disappeared down the road; then Naomi and Miriam would settle down in front of 'Sesame Street,' eat their lunches, eventually discard the dresses that they secretly disliked, don Levi's and T-shirts and spend their day playing.

'Angels,' Mrs Colodny, the baby-sitter, called them. But Ruth knew better. Her girls could also be terrors when they put their minds to it.

Beth appeared in the doorway, shy and hesitant as always, even though she'd lived with the Roths for three months now, anxious to please, hopeful for praise. Like a dog, Ruth thought as she tried to accommodate three girls on her lap, who's been whipped too many times.

Ruth and Arnie knew very little about the girl. That she was fifteen, had run away from a home in the Midwest, and was pregnant was all they really knew. Ruth had found her panhandling in Seattle one smoggy day and there had been something in the hollow, frightened eyes, skinny arms, and ropy blonde hair that had made Ruth stop and look more closely. Seattle was no stranger to runaways, to wild kids who existed in their own world, but there had been something about this child that had made her stand out. The pregnancy hadn't shown then. She'd confessed it after Ruth had brought her home and put a meal of meat loaf and gravy and home-baked corn bread into her. For a while Ruth and Arnie had tried to convince her to go back home, to make her see how worried her folks must be, but the firmness with which Beth had held her ground, her promise to run again, had made Ruth grasp something of the nightmare the girl must have run from.

The authorities had been no help. 'Thousands of runaways flock to Seattle every year, Mrs Roth. We haven't the manpower to go chasing after the older ones, or the housing to hold them if they've committed no crimes. We put them in homes and they run again. Fifteen is too old. Right now we're concentrating on eleven and under.' So Ruth had just let her stay.

'Do you want me to make the roast today, Mrs Shapiro?'

'That would be very nice, Beth. And some new potatoes and carrots. Gravy, too, very thick the way Mr Roth likes it.'

Beth had by chance and luck brought a valuable asset into the household: she was a marvellous cook. Her speciality at stretching a dollar, turning bland into spicy, and cooking in quantities large enough to feed a small army, were clues into Beth's former life, the life of hardship and crowding she must surely have run from.

'I'll scrub the bathrooms today, too, Mrs Shapiro.'

Ruth smiled gently. 'Don't push yourself, dear. Remember the baby. You're due in two months.'

'Yes'm.'

As Beth waddled to the sink and started filling it with suds and hot water, Ruth thought: *And then what? What do we do after her baby's born?*

But that was not high priority right now; there was another unborn to worry about.

Mrs Colodny and the school bus arrived simultaneously, creating a brief vortex of chaos, but soon the bus was slogging off down the muddy road, and the twins were on their cushions next to a roaring fire, watching TV and eating boloney sandwiches, Mrs Colodny was dandling Sarah on her lap, and Beth was dishing out Kitty Queen and kibble, fish food, and birdseed. Ruth moved slowly up to the master bedroom.

'Okay, Dr Shapiro, if you will please, just lie back and relax...'

They draped a sheet over her legs to make up for the dehumanising immodesty of the patient gown she wore, and then beneath the bright cold lights and in the cool, recirculated air repeatedly exhorted her to relax.

How could she? How could she relax while something like this was happening to her body? Ruth closed her eyes. She hadn't been successful in fending off the incipient and familiar depression that had been nudging her for days. During the drive through the island and then on the ferry crossing over to Seattle, she had kept up a running battle against the demons that plagued her. Primarily, they centred around the memory of the recurrent dream. It had come back again.

When was the last time Ruth had had the nightmare? She couldn't remember. Although she'd been beleagured with it and its recurrent sequences during her adolescence, the dream had abated during her years at Castillo College. And now it was back, just when she'd thought it had gone for ever; back in full force and full fury, keeping her awake during the night while her family slept.

Before the amniotic fluid could be drawn, an ultrasound had to be done to locate the position of the placenta and baby. This was done by placing a small transducer, about the size of a cigarette pack and pointed at one end, against Ruth's bare skin, which was covered first with conductive gel; then the instrument was run back and forth across her abdomen. An image appeared on the ultrasound monitor, like a bad TV picture, fuzzy and spotty and totally nonsensical if you didn't know what you were looking for.

But Ruth had an expert and trained eye; she saw the curves and spaces that formed the body of her fifteen-week foetus, nonhuman, fleshless, a shrimp-like space alien floating in blackness and stars.

Ruth had to look away. That little not-yet-formed person was depending on her, on all these people, to give it a life's pardon, to find it clean and free of contamination, contamination passed unwittingly along through mother's and father's chromosomes. *I had no right to start you, if I must soon end you.*

'How are you doing, Ruth?'

She gave him a low kilowatt smile. 'Fine . . .'

The man who was performing the test was Dr Joe Selbie, himself an OBGYN, trained specially at UCLA in amniocentesis. He patted Ruth's shoulder. 'It'll be real quick, Ruth. The baby's in a good position.'

She returned to staring up at the ceiling, at the white, arctic lights set in white acoustical squares. The room was greenish white with a shiny white linoleum floor and cold, hard stainless steel equipment. She could have been lying on any table in the hospital – the operating room, nuclear medicine, the morgue. It was all so *impersonal.*

When she heard the small tray being wheeled up she closed her eyes. Ruth was no innocent to this procedure, she'd handled the long needle herself; but there was a difference between which end of the needle you were on. A vast difference. And try though she did, Ruth could not get herself mentally to reverse roles, to divorce herself from the lower half of her body and put herself in the objective place of physician.

She felt the transducer, like a small animal, crawl across her naked abdomen, heard Dr Selbie murmur, 'We'll go in here,' then she felt the chilly swab of antiseptic on a patch of her skin.

'This is the Xylocaine, Ruth,' he said, and she felt a prick followed by a numbing.

She wanted to open her eyes and look at the monitor, at the picture of her baby, like a watch dog, making sure nothing happened, but she couldn't bring herself to do it. As if on their own her eyelids clamped tighter shut and she thought: *Will my baby be aware of the invasion of cold metal into her warm, liquid world? Will she be frightened? Do unborn babies cry? Will she hate me for allowing this invasion? She can't be nameless at a time like this. She must have a name. I'll call her Leah. Leah, don't cry, Mother's with you.*

'Okay, Ruth, here goes. Just relax now, you won't feel a thing.'

Ruth felt a dull puncture and then nothing; but her mind's eye saw the needle descend through skin and flesh and muscles; it pierced peritoneum, then uterine wall, and then –

Poor little thing! Poor little defenceless thing! I'm powerless to protect you from this violation. Oh, Arnie, I'm afraid, I'm so alone. I wish I'd given in, I wish I'd let you come and be here with me, with us, and let you be strong for me.

*Daddy...*

Ruth began to cry.

# Chapter Twenty-six

Ruth was mystified. By all the laws of nature and science this patient should now be pregnant. Ruth was not only mystified, she was frustrated. It seemed to her that the elusive answer was at her fingertips, that if she could stretch out her hand an inch farther she would have the solution in her grasp. But it was no use – Ruth had reached the limit of her knowledge and skill.

They were sitting on a wicker sofa in her office, white wicker with pale green and yellow cushions; the struggling November sun washed over the fabric like a light rain. In the corner, a rubber tree stood in defiance of the northern climate beyond the windows, and tropical fish glinted scarlet and gold in their aquamarine world. Ruth's office, all her own design, brimmed with life. In the waiting room hung the poster that said, 'War Is Not Healthy for Children and Other Living Things.'

'I'm afraid I don't know what to tell you, Joan. I've done all I can.'

Mrs Joan Freeman, two years married and desperate to have a family, twisted a handkerchief in her hands. 'Can't you inseminate me artificially, Doctor, with my husband's sperm?'

'Your post-coital tests are normal, Joan. There's nothing *I* can do to improve on what your husband is doing.'

And that was the maddening thing about it all. When Mrs Freeman had come to her four visits ago, Ruth had done the routine exam and asked the routine history, all of which had presented a normal, healthy young woman of twenty-three. She had never had pelvic inflammatory disease or pelvic surgery, had never used any form of birth control prior to marriage because of religious beliefs, had never been pregnant, was on no medication now; her menstruation was regular and normal, ovaries normal-sized and uterus properly positioned; blood tests and Rubin test, all normal. Sex with her husband was conducive to pregnancy: intercourse at least three times a week using no lubricants and not douching afterwards. And Mr Freeman's sperm count was normal.

So why wasn't she conceiving?

It was now five months since that first visit, and they were no nearer a solution. After all the standard therapy – the temperature charts, the pillow under the hips, the fertility cycle graphs – Ruth was now asking herself: Should I do a laparoscopy? Invade her body with foot-long instruments to see if there are adhesions or undetected endometriosis? Ruth hated unnecessary surgery, hated resorting to anything mechanical or requiring drugs. But without it she could do nothing more for the woman.

'I can only recommend you go to a fertility specialist.'

'You mean, go to someone *else*?'

'I've done all I can for you, Joan. You might wish to put off seeing someone else for a while, just keep trying the way you have, relax more, put the spontaneity back into your love life . . .' Her voice trailed off as she spread her hands out to finish her point.

It was an unfortunate side effect of fertility treatment that patients often complained of the magic and romance going out of their sex lives. The couple became so intent on doing the 'right thing' at the 'right time' and producing a baby that impulsive sex, spur of the moment lovemaking, vanished. They came together when the temperature chart called for it, they had sex in the morning when neither felt like it so she could rush off to her doctor's for yet another post-coital test; the rising tension brought occasions of impotence, which in turn triggered further episodes of limpness. Sex became a robotic act, the purpose of it reduced to mere manufacture of a product.

Ruth rose from the sofa and walked over to her cluttered desk. After rummaging through folders, charts, and pamphlets, Ruth found the referral list. 'Here,' she said, turning and smiling encouragingly. 'He's in Seattle. You shouldn't have any trouble –'

'He?'

The look on the woman's face spoke volumes. All Ruth could do was shrug apologetically and say, 'I'm sorry, he's the only one I can recommend. I hear he's very good.'

Mrs Freeman looked down at her hands. 'And I'll have to start all over again?'

'I'm afraid so. I'll send your chart over, of course, but I'm sure he'll want to repeat a lot of what I've done, to get to know you better.'

A silence descended over them, freezing the scene into a stopped movie frame: the pretty young woman in blue jeans and lumberman's shirt, head bent, small-looking; the woman next to her, slightly older but centuries wiser, in creamy silk blouse and tweed skirt. A cold northern Pacific wind swept through the tiny town of Winslow, encircled the humble storefront doctor's office, tested the windows to see if it could get in, rattling them, then moved on to menace the Douglas firs and western hemlocks.

'I don't think,' began Joan haltingly, 'my husband's going to like it. As it is, Dr Shapiro, we can hardly pay *your* bills, let alone another doctor.' She raised bereft eyes. 'If you don't mind, Doctor, I'd like to keep coming to you.'

*But I've done all I can, I can do nothing more!* 'All right, Joan, if that's what you want. I'll see if there's something else we can try.' *Because I want to fulfil your wish, just as I want my wish to be fulfilled. I want Mary Farnsworth to tell me my baby's all right.*

It had been two weeks since the amniocentesis and in that time Ruth had undergone a slight change. And so had her medical practice.

It had started the day after the test when she and Arnie and the girls had gone to Port Angeles to Ruth's parents' house for dinner. It had been while she was standing at the sink helping her younger sister wash the dishes that the miracle had occurred. The baby had moved. It was a sensation familiar to Ruth: a flutter, like the rumble of gas in the bowel, a pause, and then a flutter again. What in olden times was called 'quickening.' She had felt it with her four previous babies, but it hadn't been the same, not the same at all.

Ruth had dropped a glass and burst into tears. A crowd

had come running: Mrs Shapiro, Joshua's young wife, Max's wife, David's girl friend, a gathering of worried women, steering Ruth to a chair. When they had all asked her what was wrong Ruth hadn't been able to reply. She didn't know herself what was wrong.

And then she had looked up and seen him standing in the doorway. Her father. For a split-second Ruth's eyes had locked with his, and in that brief moment a message had been passed along. It had made her stop crying at once. Ruth had pushed herself to her feet, assured everyone that she was all right, and had gone back to doing the dishes. But she would never forget her father standing there, the look on his face. It had said, What's the matter, Ruthie? Can't you handle it?

From that moment Ruth had felt strange new seeds sprout within her, frightening, ominous seeds: the kernels of self-dislike, the pain of betrayal, the hating of this Judas body of hers. Her spirit was strong but her body was fallible; it wasn't *her* fault she hadn't been able to come in first in that race so many years ago – she had *wanted* to. Didn't that count for anything? Not in Mike Shapiro's eyes. Only performance counted, only trophies and accomplishments. The desire to do good didn't win medals.

Out of this revelation, this new anger with her body, came a heightened awareness of the same self-loathing in other women. She saw it in many of her patients: the depression following a miscarriage, the discovery of cancer in a breast, the loss of a baby to crib death – all resulting in a malignant grief that turned inward, spinning a web of guilt and self-blame, confusion and fear.

Ruth had wasted no time. Two weeks ago she had started her group. She had invited patients to meet with her in the casual atmosphere of her office, to talk about their physical problems and the spiritual torment they shared, to come to grips with their bodies. Just as Joan Freeman now, Ruth saw, was starting the ugly process of hating herself and despising the body that was betraying her, so did Heidi Smith find it impossible to live with only one breast, Sharon Lasnick to cope with three miscarriages, and Betsy Chowder to accept her hysterectomy. They met once a week and talked it all out late into the evening. 'I am no longer desirable to my husband.' 'I'm useless, I can't produce a child.' 'My husband won't want to have sex with me any more.' Ruth took up the role of counsellor; she was not only the one who removed the uterus, she was also the one who said it was natural to feel cheated. Last week the group had been five; tonight it would be twelve.

'Joan,' she said as she walked the young woman to her door. 'Why don't you come back here tonight, at seven o'clock? We have a group that meets to talk out problems...'

When she returned to her desk, Ruth heard the voice of her receptionist come over the intercom. 'Dr Shapiro? Your husband is here.'

Arnie? Here? 'Tell him to take a seat, I'll be with him in a minute. Who's left, Andrea?'

'Mrs Glass. Then you're free.'

'Put her in the exam room for me please, Andrea, and have Carol collect a urine specimen.' Ruth looked at her watch. She was due at Dr Farnsworth's in an hour. She hadn't known Arnie was going to go with her.

Arnie looked at his watch. She was running late again. Well, Ruth had warned him before they got married: obstetricians can't go by clocks.

Still, he thought as he tried to settle into a chair designed to accommodate rounder bodies. He had thought that was all behind him, the long hours and the calls in the night. He had put up with it through Ruth's residency because he had known there was a light at the end of the tunnel: her private practice, regular hours, and a normal family life at long last. Except that it wasn't turning out that way. In fact, instead of slowing down and balancing her hours between patients and family, Ruth seemed to be trying to fill up her hours with yet more projects.

Like this group that met every Friday evening. She didn't spend enough hours at home in the evenings as it was. Why did Ruth have to add this new involvement?

'Arnie?' she said, coming into the waiting room. 'I hadn't expected you to be here.'

He shot to his feet. 'I decided I should be with you when Mary Farnsworth gives you the news.'

She slipped her hand into his, gave it a squeeze, and smiled. 'I'm glad.'

And Arnie thought: *It's this baby. It's worrying about this baby that makes her want to fill all her hours. After this is over . . .*

As they headed towards the door, Ruth said, 'Do you know what? She'll be able to tell us the sex of the baby. Five months before it's born!' She squeezed his hand again. 'I hope it's a boy.'

# Chapter Twenty-seven

Jason Butler knew he was dead. He knew it because he heard someone say so. But if he was dead, then how come he still felt pain? And how come a beautiful blonde was working him over as if he was still alive?

As Jason's consciousness started to ebb, he knew the answer: *Not dead. Dying. I'm dying.* The result, he realised as blackness washed over him, of the ultimate wipe-out.

'I've lost the pulse, Doctor!'

The team went to work at once to resuscitate the young man on the stretcher. Mickey massaged his chest while the defibrillators were being prepared; then she said, 'Stand back,' and the body on the stretcher jerked. Everyone looked at the cardioscope. 'Again!' said Mickey. And this time it worked.

Out in the hall of Great Victoria's emergency room, while the team inside worked to save their friend, two teenage boys stood shivering with towels around them. Their long hair hung in salty strings and their baggy surfing shorts clung to them. They weren't shivering from cold but because they were scared. They weren't sure they had dragged their friend out of the water in time.

It had been a freak accident. Eighteen-year-old Jason Butler, an expert surfer, and his friends had been challenging the forty-foot combers at Makaha. Nobody could say what really happened: one minute Jason was up on the board and taking the wave with his usual confidence and skill, the next, he was down in the water and being dragged out to sea by a rip. By the time his friends got to him, Jason had been badly injured by his surfboard as it had churned in the water. When they pulled him out and saw what the Semi-gun had done to his face, the two friends thought they were rescuing a corpse.

But now the emergency team was working on him and Jason Butler was still alive, if only barely so.

When Mickey came out of the surgical suite four hours later, Jason was on his way up to the Intensive Care Unit. Three surgeons had worked on him, Mickey one of them. All they had been able to do for the boy at this time was to stabilise him. While Mickey had wired together the shattered bones of his face and sutured the many lacerations, two orthopaedic surgeons had removed Jason's right leg from above the knee. He was still unconscious and in critical condition, but his vital signs were stable and the massive bleeding had been controlled.

Mickey had been told there was a parent waiting in the visitor's lounge outside surgery. She found a man sitting by himself and staring blankly. 'Mr Butler?' She held out her hand. 'I'm Dr Long.'

He was on his feet at once and shaking her hand. 'How is my son, Doctor?'

'He's doing as well as can be expected at this point.'

'Then he's still alive.'

'Yes, he's still alive.'

Mr Butler said, 'Thank God,' and sank back down onto the sofa.

Taking a seat in the matching easy chair, Mickey explained Jason's condition and everything that had been done for him in the operating room. 'Your son suffered extensive damage to his throat and jaw, Mr Butler. We took care of those first, to ensure his breathing. But I'm afraid we're not out of the woods yet. Before we can do any more tests Jason must be stable. He has a skull fracture and possibly other injuries. We don't yet know the extent of it all.'

Mickey studied the man opposite her. His name, she knew, was Harrison Butler; he owned Butler Pineapple, the second-largest pineapple producer on the Islands. She estimated his age around sixty years, but he was a physically fit, athletic-looking sixty. And he was very handsome. 'Are you all right, Mr Butler?' she asked gently.

He finally focused his grey eyes on her. 'When may I see him?'

'You'll have to wait a while. He's been taken up to ICU where he'll be under constant observation. He's still unconscious, Mr Butler.'

Harrison Butler nodded. His face took on a faraway look and his eyes lost focus again.

'Would you like some coffee?' Mickey asked him.

'I never did approve of that surfing,' he said almost to himself. 'Last year it was hang gliding, and I put my foot down on that. But the surfing is in his blood. He's been on a surfboard since he was five years old. I knew this was going to happen someday.'

Mickey sat in silence with him for a little while; she had found it often helped. And while she did she watched him for signs of distress. Some patients' relatives required sedation. But Harrison Butler showed no such inclination. He merely sat staring.

Mickey thought he was an elegant-looking man, distinguished and refined in his expensively tailored suit and French cuffs and burgundy silk tie. Patrician, she thought, with that silver hair and high forehead. Mickey saw a strong resemblance to Michael Rennie, the actor.

When she heard her name being paged over the hospital public address system, she said, 'I'm Jason's primary physician, Mr Butler. If you have any questions, or if you just want to talk, please call me. The hospital can get in touch with me wherever I am.'

Over the next fourteen days Mickey could count on seeing Harrison Butler in one of two places: in the small visitor's lounge attached to the ICU, or at his son's bedside. He was always polite, never intrusive, and very appreciative of the care Jason was receiving. When an artery in Jason's abdomen ruptured and Mickey opened him up and held the pulsating vessel until a vascular surgeon arrived, Harrison Butler departed the ICU at once and waited patiently through the ensuing six hours for Mickey to seek him out and report on the boy's condition. Butler blamed no one, didn't vent his anger and frustration on the staff as some relatives were prone to do, but understood that Jason was receiving the best possible care.

Sometimes Harrison was there with a tape recorder,

dictating business letters; at other times he was on the telephone discussing contracts and deals. But there was never anyone with him, no other relatives came to see Jason, and no friends. Early in the morning or late at night, Harrison Butler could be found in either the lounge or at the bedside, impeccably dressed, calm and in control. A man, Mickey thought, who had never known a moment's lack of self-confidence, a man who had an immutable sureness of his place in the universe.

One day he sent a large basket of fruit to the nurses in the ICU; another time he sent flowers to the nine other patients in the unit. And whenever he encountered Mickey, he always stood, shook her hand, and asked after her own well-being. Everyone liked Harrison Butler. Everyone fought for his son's life.

'Hello, Mr Butler,' said Mickey as she came into the lounge.

'How is Jason?'

They had just repaired the ruptured artery with a knitted graft and Jason had received twelve units of blood. He was back in the ICU and in shaky condition.

'You won't be able to see him for a few hours, Mr Butler. Why don't you go home and get some rest?'

He did look tired. Despite his own natural refinement and attention to his appearance, the fourteen days of vigil were starting to tell. 'I don't want to leave the hospital, Doctor. I want to be near my son.'

'But there's nothing you can do right now. I think you'll feel better after some sleep. And when was the last time you ate?'

He sighed and looked at his watch. 'Breakfast, I think.'

'It's late, Mr Butler.'

'When was the last time *you* ate, Doctor?'

She smiled up at him. 'Doctors aren't expected to eat normal meals like everyone else, Mr Butler. I'll grab something down in the cafeteria.'

'Please call me Harrison. I feel as though we're members of the same family. May I take my son's doctor to dinner?'

She thought a moment. The look in his eyes said so much – the worry, the anxiety. Finally she said. 'There's a little

Italian restaurant across the street from the hospital. They cater to people with odd hours and people in a hurry. Let me change into my regular clothes and I'll meet you down in the lobby.'

It was the sort of place that had checkered tablecloths and candles stuck into wine bottles. The menu was simple and inexpensive. Quite a few employees from Great Victoria were there and it was not uncommon to hear a beeper sound and to see someone run out.

'Thank you for joining me, Dr Long,' said Harrison after they had given their orders. 'I'm used to eating alone, but tonight, well –' He opened out his hands.

Mickey found herself wondering about him. In the ICU or in the visitor's lounge he had been Jason's father, one of the many worried parents Mickey frequently dealt with. But here, in this nonmedical setting and romantic lighting, Mickey suddenly saw Harrison Butler as a man. A very charming, attractive man. 'Please call me Mickey,' she said with a smile. 'As you said, I feel as though we're members of the same family.'

He nodded solemnly. 'Tragedy does bring people together, doesn't it?'

There was so much Mickey wanted to ask – Where was Jason's mother? Were there no brothers and sisters? But she refrained from asking. Theirs was still a professional relationship, despite its ironic sense of intimacy.

'I can't tell you how much I appreciate everything you're doing for my boy,' Harrison said quietly. 'I don't know what... I would do without Jason. He's all I have.'

Mickey didn't say anything. She knew now that everything was going to come out and that Harrison was going to tell it in his own time, at his own pace.

Mrs Butler had left Harrison and their one-year-old son seventeen years ago, had since remarried, and now Harrison had no idea where she was. She had never written, never expressed any interest in the boy. Harrison and Jason divided their time between two houses: the Oahu house near Koko Head, which Harrison used when he had business in Honolulu, and the family home on the island of Lania, an old ancestral mansion named Pukula Hau.

'Jason was born at Pukula Hau,' Harrison said in his quietly modulated voice. '*I* was born at Pukula Hau. My father built the house in 1912, and brought his bride there in 1913. In 1916 he went off to the war and never came back. I was born the next year. My mother did the job of raising both me and the pineapple on our plantation. When she died twenty years ago I inherited the company. I expect to pass it on to Jason.'

Mickey knew Harrison was a millionaire. The Butler name could be seen all over the Islands, in streets and on buildings; it was a name nearly as legendary as Dole. Over the years, however, Harrison had got away from personal involvement with the company and had become a private investor in a variety of interests. His latest enterprise, he explained now, was putting money into movies. Harrison had already backed one box office success; he hoped to be financially involved in future films.

Harrison soon left the subject of himself and his heir and asked Mickey questions about herself.

'You're a woman who knows what she wants and goes after it,' he said after hearing about her five and a half years at Great Victoria. 'To pursue such a long residency at the cost of other things must take a lot of courage.'

The 'other things' that were the price of Mickey's residency in surgery were husband and family. Although her hospital schedule was no longer as hectic and demanding as it used to be, now that she was a senior resident, Mickey still did not want to divide her energies.

'When will you be finished with it all?'

'Next June. It will seem strange, after four years of medical school and six at Great Victoria to be suddenly on my own.'

'Will you go into private practice?'

'I hope to. After the New Year I'll start looking for an office.'

He studied her for a moment, watching the way the flickering candlelight played on her classic features. Mickey still wore her platinum hair the way Ruth and Sondra had first combed it, over eight years ago – pulled tightly back into a bun at the nape of her neck. Like a ballerina, Harrison

277

thought now, a *prima* ballerina. Jason's doctor was stunningly beautiful; why wasn't she married?

'May I ask you to dinner again some time?' he asked.

Mickey was about to reply when the beeper in her purse sounded. 'Excuse me, please,' she said and went to the back of the restaurant where the telephones were.

She was gone a few minutes, during which time their food arrived. When she came back to the table, Harrison had but to take one look at her face to know what the call had been about. 'It's Jason,' he said simply.

'I'm sorry, Harrison. A blood clot went to his lung. It was sudden.'

He nodded and stood. 'Will you walk back to the hospital with me?'

Mickey loved her apartment. It had a view of Diamond Head and a balcony where she could sit in the fresh tropical breeze. Inside it was furnished tastefully and comfortably with items she had collected since the day she'd left Gregg Waterman four years ago: a vicuña rug, leather and chrome chairs, brush drawings by Tseng-Yu-Ho, sculpture from Tonga, and draperies of Polynesian batik. She had books and records, a small colour TV, and, most importantly, quiet neighbours on either side. Because Mickey liked to live a quiet life. She spent her time off from the hospital reading medical books and listening to classical music, or taking drives around the island in her small car. She had friends but she shied from frequent socialising. Her closest friends were Toby Abrams, in private practice now, and his wife; occasionally they tried to fix Mickey up with an eligible bachelor.

Mickey didn't mind their matchmaking efforts, but so far none had been successful. They were always professional men, intelligent and pleasant, but there was never a spark. Perhaps there never would be.

On this windy March morning, the beginning of her 'off' weekend, Mickey was getting her things together for a drive around the island. She had only recently begun to get acquainted with her tropical home, exploring Oahu like a tourist, armed with camera, picnic lunch, and suntan oil.

There was still so much to see, so much to savour. Today Mickey was going to visit the Polynesian Cultural Centre, a re-created South Sea colony on the north-east side of the island. She planned to stop along the way and take photographs of the Blow Hole and Chinaman's Hat.

But this time, there would be no photographs of surfers.

Only last year that had been one of Mickey's favourite pastimes, driving to Waimea Bay or Banzai Pipeline and sitting on the sand with her Nikon to take pictures of the young men on their surfboards. But that had been before Jason Butler was brought into the emergency room last November and Mickey had fought harder than she ever had to save a life.

His death had been a blow to them all – to Mickey, to the other doctors on the case, to the ICU nurses. Since those first moments in the ER when Jason had blinked up at Mickey in pain and confusion and then had passed out again, he had not regained consciousness for even a second. His father had sat diligently by the bedside through those fourteen days, hoping, Mickey knew, for a flicker of life in his moribund son, watching for a sign that Jason's soul still inhabited that broken body. But Jason had never come out of his coma and had died not knowing the love that had surrounded the last moments of his life.

She thought about Harrison Butler now as she zipped up her carry-all. The last time she had seen him was at the bedside, when they had been called from the restaurant. The nurses had already disconnected all the wires and tubing and had brought the sheets up to Jason's neck. His face was bandaged, little of him could be seen. It could have been a stranger lying there; anyone's son. Not dead, just asleep. Mickey and the nurses had left Harrison alone in the cubicle, drawing the drapes over the glass walls and closing the door. He was in there a long time with the boy, and when he came out his face was pale and drawn, but there were no tears. Harrison had shaken everyone's hand and thanked each individually for trying to help his son. And then he had left.

That was four months ago. In that time there had been only one communication from Harrison Butler – a gift to Great Victoria Hospital in the form of a CAT scanner, one of the new, revolutionary diagnostic machines for detecting brain damage. It was donated in the name of Jason Butler.

Mickey called her answering service and told them she was going to be unavailable for two days. Then she picked up two letters to mail on the way down to her car. One was to Ruth, congratulating her on the birth of Leah, a healthy little baby girl whose life had hung in the balance back in November. But the amniocentesis had shown her free of Tay-Sachs and she'd been brought to term. In the other envelope was an anniversary card for Sondra and Derry. In two weeks they would be celebrating four years of marriage.

As she closed and locked the sliding glass door that led to the balcony, Mickey paused to look out at the view. It was breathtaking. The majestic rising of Diamond Head against an incredibly blue sky; and below, white buildings and palm trees and gardens in springtime bloom. Down on one of those streets Mickey's new office waited. She had already furnished it with the help of a bank loan and had hired a receptionist and a nurse. In three months she would be going there. She would be getting up in the morning and heading away from the hospital instead of towards it, as she had these past six years; she would walk the short distance in the bright Hawaiian sun, hang up her purse and sweater in her own office, and sit down with patients that would be totally her own.

In only three short months.

*Does it frighten me?* she asked herself now. *Yes, a little. It's what I've worked all my life for, that office down there. And now that I have it, I'm a little afraid of it.*

It was almost here, the day she and Jonathan could not wait for, the day that had been too far away. Six years ago he had said to her, 'I can't live without you for six years, Mickey.' And she had said, 'Then come with me.' But that had been impossible; the future had seemed insurmountable. Six years was too long. The end would never come. And yet, here it was at last, the end of the six years, the end of an era of sacrifice that had seemed, back then, so long and so far away.

In three months Mickey would be free at last, free to live where she wanted, work where she wanted, and love whom she chose. But there was no one waiting for her.

As she was turning away from the view, Mickey's phone rang. She frowned at it. The hospital knew she wasn't on call. She picked it up. 'Hello?'

'Mickey?' came a familiar voice. 'It's Harrison Butler. I was wondering if I could see you today.'

'Harrison,' she said.

'I need to talk to you, Mickey.'

The evening was hot and humid, *kona* weather, when Oahu's psychiatrists saw their greatest numbers of patients. As they departed from Mickey's apartment, she and Harrison heard a radio warning: a storm might hit the southern side of the island around midnight.

They were going to attend a governor's ball in honour of Cary and Barbara Grant, which was being held at Washington Place, formerly the home of Queen Liliuokalani, now the residence of the governor of Hawaii. Mickey sat silently at Harrison's side as their limousine inched along in the slow procession up to the entrance of the mansion. She looked out at the magnificent house set amid green lawns and neat rows of *pili* nut trees. It was a mansion built in the last century and it stood as a symbol of an elegant, exotic, and vanished past, Mickey could hardly contain her happiness. She was in love with the man at her side.

They had been seeing each other for six months, ever since his unexpected phone call back in March and his need to talk to her. Mickey had immediately dropped her plans to explore the island and had spent the day walking an isolated beach with Harrison, listening to him talk about Jason, about his pain, about the four months of mourning, the loneliness, the grief, hiding away in his house on Lanai, taking no calls, seeing no one, trying to come to terms with his son's death. Then, he had come out, looked around himself, and had found within him a tremendous need to seek out Mickey Long and talk to her. He knew she would understand; she had been a part of it.

And Mickey did understand. She listened for a while, and then she talked. They covered a great distance that day, isolated on that lonely beach with only the seagulls and the breakers. They had both been able to release their pent-up emotions about Jason, the father losing a son, the doctor losing a patient. And when, by sunset, they were spent, when there was nothing more that could be said, Mickey and Harrison both realised that a special bond had been woven.

Theirs was a comfortable relationship, undemanding, nonconditional; a sharing of afternoons, an occasional evening concert, a Sunday drive to Waimea Bay for lunch. There had been no instant stars-and-skyrockets falling in love for Mickey; it had been a slow, gradual thing, a sharing of philosophies and interests while a growing mutual respect started to send down roots; then a barely perceptible reaching out, a small concession here and there of need, a baring of the soul, confidences exchanged, a bit-by-bit giving way beneath the advance of something that appeared inevitable.

Harrison Butler was a kind and generous man, as considerate as he was handsome, always smiling, ever thoughtful. And their age difference – Harrison was sixty to her thirty – had not preoccupied Mickey as she had thought it would; Harrison's own vigour and youthful outlook had bridged that gap.

But the relationship remained somewhat ambiguous. After six months they were friends, not lovers, gently skimming the surface, but pulling back when involvement seemed imminent. Days would pass without a phone call from him and then she would hear and they would have a wonderful time together, they would become close for an afternoon, an evening, a little like old friends. And on rare occasions they were like lovers-to-be and Harrison would take hold of her hand and look at her quietly. But then, when intimacy threatened, when the brink of deeper involvement seemed within reach, Harrison would pull back abruptly, as if afraid of something; and distance would be placed between them again. The word 'love' had never been spoken and so far they had never even kissed.

When Harrison had taken her once to see his home on the island of Lanai, a magnificent colonial mansion set high on a cliff, Mickey had hoped it meant something serious. But it had turned out not to be so, although for totally unexpected reasons.

On that day back in July when she had flown to Lanai with

Harrison in his private jet, Jonathan had come back into her life. It had been a shock to Mickey because she hadn't been expecting it, a double shock because it had been Harrison Butler's doing.

Mickey had arrived at the Lanai mansion, Pukula Hau, to find that a party was planned for that night. A hundred guests in black tie and *holoku* evening gowns were soon sipping champagne and nibbling Hawaiian hors d'oeuvres while a six-piece band played island melodies under the stars. At midnight there had been a lavish *luau* complete with *kalua* pig and fire and hula dances. Afterwards, when the guests had finished the *lomi* salmon and taro-wrapped meats, when the *haupia* pudding was gone and the *imu* stones of the roasting pig were growing cool, Harrison had unveiled his surprise of the evening: a preview showing of the not yet released movie *Invaders!*

They had filed into the small movie room in the east wing of the house, the tired and giddy guests, and they had sunk wearily into the thick velvet seats facing the screen. Harrison, because of his financial connections with the studios, was known for getting choice movies before official release, so his guests knew they were in for a treat. But the *luau* had been draining and quite a few feared they would nod off as soon as the lights dimmed.

But once the film started, they knew there would be no danger of nodding off.

As soon as the room was dark, the screen exploded with fire. A cinematic masterpiece of fireworks kaleidoscoped before the viewers' startled eyes and before they were consciously aware of it, a swirling inferno meant to depict the Big Bang engulfed them. Someone in the darkness muttered, 'Oh, science fiction,' but that was to be the only comment heard for the next three hours. When the film came to a climax, stars and planets imploded in a backward-run of the opening sequence. The room lights came on and no one moved.

As the audience began to stir Mickey heard bits and pieces of comment: 'Science fiction! I thought it was dead and buried.' 'Who is the director – someone named Archer.' 'Didn't he used to make documentaries?'

Snatches of conversation had ebbed around Mickey: 'He's

married to that French actress, Vivienne. Archer's over on Kahoolawe right now scouting the military target-practice sites for his next picture. The word is it's going to be a sequel to this one.'

Now, on this warm September evening, as Harrison's limousine neared the front steps of the governor's mansion, Mickey went back to the night Jonathan had driven out to the abandoned movie studio in Calabasas, and she saw again the ghostly façades and storefronts, heard the echoing crunch of their footsteps on the gravel as they followed the frail spot of the flashlight. 'I'm not going to make amateur films all my life, Mickey. I want to do big things. I want to give people something to see. And I want you to help me do it.' Then she heard the terrible intrusion of the beeper signal and saw the little box sail overhead.

Is that where he made that exquisite film, that phenomenal space opera that had, since the night of Harrison Butler's party, broken all box office records? In that rusted, dilapidated, and forgotten old movie studio?

*He's scouting Kahoolawe right now.*

At the time she had briefly considered trying to get in touch with him, telling herself it was just out of friendship, for old times' sake. And then the impulse had passed, reality had set her back on her feet; she focused again on the year, the place, the circumstances. *He's married to Vivienne. We're no longer the two people we used to be.*

She had recently seen his face on the cover of *Time*, a slightly older face, the hair now stylishly short, and a new, arresting confidence around the crinkled eyes. One of Hollywood's new *wunderkind* directors. 'A face that should be *before* the cameras instead of behind them,' one female columnist had quipped, going on to say that if he were an actor instead of a director, Jonathan Archer would now be numbered among Hollywood's new 'hunks.'

Mickey was happy for him. And for herself. They had both reached their goals. After only three months in private practice she knew there had been nothing to fear. She had made the right decisions, all down the line. The sacrifices had been worth it. She had been right not to go to the belltower, because now she was a board eligible surgeon in plastic and reconstructive surgery, with her own office and a growing

284

patient load, receiving referrals from other doctors, starting to make a name for herself. And she was sitting at this moment beside a man with whom she had fallen deeply in love.

All that was needed now to make her life complete was for Harrison to tell her he felt the same for her.

People stared at them as they entered: Harrison Butler, tall and straight and smartly cut in Andrade and Reyn's, stepping into the chandelier-bright foyer like a visiting nobleman; Mickey, also tall, willowy, in ice-pale, and sky blues. It was as if they stepped into a tropical dream. Starting in the foyer and throughout the mansion were clever arrangements of colourful and fragrant blossoms, from the common, year-round plumeria and fiery red African tulip to the delicate, white bauhinia. Doorways were festooned with yellow amanda and wood rose; crystal bowls held blood-red anthuriums and rare sunset-orange roses. The air was a dizzying fragrance of jasmine and frangipani. Finally, *leis* made of white orchids and lavender bougainvillea were draped around the necks of the arriving guests.

From the terrace came the throbbing rhythm of music; hula dancers performed the intricate *Kaimana Hila*. Lace-covered tables held massive ice sculptures, heaps of crimson Haden mangoes, Bluefield bananas, chilled papayas, yellow and purple passion fruit, and, of course, pineapple picked that day out of Oahu fields. Brass and wood ceiling fans were rotating speedily to circulate the gravid air. This was *hoo-ilo* season, the time for rain and wind, and tonight's atmosphere lay heavy over the governor's guests.

There were many people to speak to, to nod to, to be introduced to; Harrison and Mickey moved through the sea of guests as if the gentle trades were at their backs. Occasionally he would touch her arm, take her elbow. As always, he was courteous and solicitous, ever mindful of her glass, her plate, her comfort. And if she thought there was something slightly different about Harrison tonight, something slightly out of character, Mickey knew it was only her imagination.

She was giddy with happiness. The evening was something out of a fairy tale. Would she have believed this could ever happen to her, that blemished Mickey of years ago

285

who hid behind her hair? She laughed a lot throughout the evening; the champagne was like an elixir and Harrison had cast a spell on her. She wanted it to go on for ever.

They danced under the night sky to fluid island melodies, a beautiful couple who looked as if the world was theirs. Close to him like this, in Harrison's strong arms, Mickey felt her love for him swell until she thought she couldn't contain it. And the *desire*. It was a delicious ache that she hadn't felt in many years. Not since... But she wouldn't think of Jonathan now, at least not in that way. Am I still in love with him? she wondered as she twirled in Harrison's embrace. No, not with Jonathan, not any more. Or, at any rate, I *mustn't* be; I must let that go as all past things must go. If anything, he will be a cherished memory, because he was the first.

And if I should ever meet him again? Mickey put that thought out of her mind. Tonight she was with Harrison and, for tonight at least, she belonged only to him.

Halfway through the waltz Harrison stopped suddenly and looked down at Mickey with a masked expression. He took her arm and led her off the terrace, down a path that wound among trees and flowers, and when they were alone and the sounds of the ball seemed far away, he turned and looked long and thoughtfully into her face.

Mickey became tense. All evening, she had thought she'd imagined an aloofness about Harrison, a slight stiffness that she'd never seen in him before. But now, looking up into his pewter grey eyes, which were dark and grave, she realised she had not imagined it – Harrison *was* different tonight.

'Mickey,' he said at last, placing his hands gently on her bare arms. 'There's something I have to say.'

A wind came up, hot and damp; the storm was gathering.

'I have been searching for some time for a way to say this, the right time, the right words. This isn't easy for me, Mickey. I want you to understand that.'

Branches and leaves started to stir around them. Heavy blossoms dropped to the ground. Mickey gazed up at him, waiting.

'When my wife left me, almost eighteen years ago,' he said quietly, 'it was the worst loss I had ever suffered. She was much younger than I. She was twenty and I was forty when we got married. And I thought she was happy at Pukula Hau. I thought she loved our life together on the island. I had no idea she thought of it as a prison and me as her gaoler.'

The wind rose suddenly; palmetto leaves slapped together.

'After Jason was born she became moody, restless. I had my work on the plantation and I thought she had found fulfilment in caring for our new son. But I was wrong. I came home one day to find a note. She didn't want anything from me, just her freedom. She had run off with an island boy. Two years passed before I started divorce proceedings. I always hoped she would come back.'

Harrison's hands tightened on Mickey's shoulders. 'When Jason turned six I hired a private detective to find her. She had remarried and was living a nomadic life in the States. And then I lost track of her and gave up altogether. Jason and I made a life for ourselves.'

Harrison's voice broke. His handsome face showed pain. Mickey reached up and clasped his hand.

'When Jason died,' he went on, 'it was that same awful loss all over again. It was almost more than I could bear. I thought I wouldn't live through it this time. And when I realised what I was doing to myself, destroying myself with grief, I remembered you, how you had taken care of my son, and those fourteen days in which we shared Jason.'

The wind was fierce now. Through the trees came the sound of laughter as guests and musicians were forced to abandon the terrace. From far away a chandelier tinkled. Harrison's grip on Mickey's shoulders tightened as if to prevent the wind from stealing her away. Her platinum hair came partially out of its knot and whipped about her face.

'I couldn't stand another loss, Mickey,' he said urgently. 'I must know tonight, *now*, how you feel about me, if there is any hope of our having something together, if you will stay with me and never leave me. Because if there is no hope of that, then I want us to part now, while I still have the strength.'

Before she could reply, a palm frond, torn loose by the wind, crashed to the ground inches from where they stood. Harrison instantly put his arms around Mickey, protectively. Monstrous elephant-ear leaves whipped and snapped in the angry wind; a maelstrom kicked up stones and flowers and gravel. Nearby, a crash was heard through the trees. Burying her face in his neck, Mickey stood safely in Harrison's strong embrace. The wind tried to topple them but Harrison stood firm and unswayable. Mickey clung to him. It felt good to be vulnerable for once, to let someone else be the strength and courage. Ten years of standing alone, of having to be brave, of fighting, of having to manufacture new strength each day – and now Harrison would be her stanchion; he would be her support and her safe harbour.

They stood in the garden for a long time, Harrison holding her against the wind, shielding her with his hard body, and Mickey pressed against him, safe, loved, cherished.

Then the first drops of rain started to fall. Warm, tropical rain that instantly brought mist up from the loamy earth. Finally Mickey raised her head, pressed her cheek against his, and said into his ear, 'Take us home, Harrison.'

The party was still going strong inside the mansion, with the band now set up in the grand ballroom and the windows and doors shut against the storm. Mickey and Harrison pushed through the gay crowd, holding on to one another as if afraid their new thread could be easily broken, and when they reached the entry foyer, they found a minor chaos as a few guests were trying to depart with borrowed umbrellas, while many more still-arriving guests rushed in out of the rain.

It took a few minutes to summon Harrison's limousine. They waited impatiently, urgent now to get on with what they had started, anxious to get to the Koko Head house where they could be alone. Mickey's cheeks blazed brightly; her eyes flamed peridot green. Harrison's arm circled her waist possessively and with a strength that held sexual promise.

Mickey couldn't believe this was happening. And yet it was: her dreams all come true, her life now complete.

As she and Harrison hurried down the steps towards the limousine with its door being held open by the chauffeur, Mickey turned her face away from the wind and rain, turned it against Harrison's shoulder and therefore did not see, as she slid gracefully into her own limousine, Jonathan Archer emerge from the car behind, himself just now arriving at the ball.

# PART FIVE
## *1980*

# Chapter Twenty-eight

Mickey paused in her writing to look out at the view from the veranda where she sat.

November in Hawaii was like a season nowhere else on earth, but November on the island of Lanai, especially from the lush promontory that cradled Pukula Hau and its thirty acres, was particularly unique – God's brushstroke had painted a sky of the headiest blues, orchids, and anthuriums, so bright as to be almost blinding, a panorama too beautiful to be real.

The first time she had seen Pukula Hau, when Harrison had brought her here two and a half years ago, Mickey had been speechless. The house was a perfect white jewel set in a bed of emerald and jade, a masterpiece of white columns and gabled windows. Norfolk pines and weeping banyans ringed the mansion, giving it a timeless quality; its name was Pukula Hau because that was the closest the Hawaiians, seventy years ago, could come to pronouncing Butler House.

This autumn morning, under the shade of a frangipani tree, ever mindful of the sun and her sensitive complexion, Mickey sat on the hillside plateau that looked out over a tapestry of silver-green pineapple fields, palm trees, cream puff clouds and blue-jade ocean. Behind her, the mountain slope rose to a craggy and verdant summit of three thousand feet, old Lanaihale, an extinct volcano from whose peak one can see on a day like this the sister islands of Molokai, Maui, little Kahoolawe, Oahu, and the Big Island.

As was her habit, Mickey was breakfasting at a caramel-coloured wicker table on Earl Grey tea, fresh pineapple slices, and lightly buttered toast. Spread on the glass tabletop were her notes on her patients; it was for Dr Kepler, who was going to cover her practice while she was away.

Mickey was waiting to be taken to Lanai Airport. Living

on this island sixty miles from Honolulu had proved no inconvenience for Mickey when she had moved here just over two years ago. She made a thirty-minute flight in Harrison's Lear jet every morning and evening; and if she had a patient in unstable condition, she stayed overnight at the Koko Head house. Today, the jet was going to carry her to Honolulu, for her flight to Seattle. To Seattle and Ruth.

Mickey poured some Earl Grey into her cup and stirred in a spoon of honey.

In just a few hours she would be with Ruth. All of Mickey's hopes were resting on the upcoming visit.

These past two years with Harrison had been almost dreamlike, so nearly perfect had they been. Their life together in this house, the deep love they shared; his growing list of film successes, Mickey's prospering medical practice. Could it be more perfect?

She felt a cold wind blow through her soul. A wind that had started almost a year ago but which now seemed never to give her respite. It came from the one cloud in their otherwise ideal life together: *childlessness*.

At first they had been relaxed about it, making the sometimes gentle, sometimes violent love of newlyweds, never really thinking of babies, just loving one another for the immediacy of it, for the delicious physical gratification of it. Then there had come the casual wondering each month, the bantered what-ifs and wouldn't-it-be-nices followed by a slow building up of expectations, a rising of hopes, the monthly disappointments deepening, the very subject segueing from happily aired speculations to real concern.

Finally, last March, Mickey had found the courage to ask, 'Could there be something wrong?' And Harrison, relieved that their unspoken anxiety had surfaced, had readily agreed that they should 'look into it.'

And now it was nine months later – a mocking figure, Mickey thought – and the specialist in Pearl City had tossed up his hands. 'I don't know what the problem is. You're both normal. You should be having no trouble.'

That was when Mickey thought of Ruth.

Ever since the amniocentesis three years ago, the focus of Ruth's practice had shifted from general OBGYN to

292

specialising in fertility. And so, to her old friend and helper Mickey would fly.

She looked at her watch; she should start getting ready soon. Harrison would be up from the fields to take her to the airport.

Laying aside her patient notes, Mickey picked up one of the sample Christmas cards she had earlier been looking through. This one would be for the workers on the plantation: it formed a money envelope which said *Mele Kalikimaka* under a Santa Claus arriving on a surf board with his sack on his back – the popular Hawaiian concept of Santa.

'I wonder how outrageous Harrison will be this year,' an acquaintance of theirs had been overheard to say at one of their parties. In his joy to have taken Dr Mickey Long as his wife, Harrison Butler had the past two Decembers enclosed triple the usual workers' holiday bonus, creating a hardship on the already straining Butler Pineapple accounts. If this kept up, Mickey had overheard the friend quip, Harrison's new wife was going to be the ruin of the company. Which wasn't too far off the mark: Butler Pineapple, because of world oversupply, wasn't as prosperous as it had been in former days. Following Dole's example, Harrison had cut back on acreage and was now going into diversification.

'Madam,' came a discreet voice. It was Apikalia, the Filipino housekeeper whose mother had come to Pukula Hau long ago as a 'picture bride' for one of the workers. 'Mr Butler asked me to tell you he is here.'

'Thank you, Apikalia. I'll be right in.'


'Excuse the mess,' Arnie said as he followed Mickey into the house with her suitcases. 'I didn't have a chance to tidy up before I left for the airport. We have a cleaning lady come in once a week but it doesn't last long, not with this crowd!'

Mickey looked around the farmhouse living room. Two big unmatching sofas, a green easy chair, and an orange lounger, all littered with Golden Books and dolls, were arranged around a fireplace where two cats dozed. Arnie led her into the vast, cluttered kitchen where empty Triscuit boxes lay on their sides, a child's security blanket was snagged under a chair, and a bowl of forgotten something stood in the open microwave. 'I'll make some coffee,' he said, clearing a chair for her to sit on. 'I know you're not used to this cold!'

Mickey laughed. 'I think I'll keep my coat on until my bones thaw out!'

He scooped up a measure of coffee beans and dropped them in the grinder. While the whirring momentarily filled the air, Arnie tried to find somewhere to settle his eyes.

It had been a long time; Mickey was little more than a stranger to him. Arnie hadn't been able to go to the wedding with Ruth but had heard all about how rich Mickey was now, and with her sitting there at the crumb-strewn table he was suddenly embarrassed for this messy house.

While the coffee brewed he came and joined her at the table. He was a little awkward, a little uncertain. 'The older girls are in school. The little ones are upstairs with Mrs Colodny, the baby-sitter.' He gave a nervous cough. 'Ruth really feels awful she couldn't meet you at the airport. She had an emergency delivery at the hospital.'

Mickey rested her eyes on Arnie Roth, noticing how he fidgeted with the corner of the scouting manual that lay on the table. He was a neat, compact man with thinning hair, thick glasses, and shy smile. A comfortable man, in brown suit and brown tie and white button-down shirt with a plastic protector in the pocket full of pens and pencils. She didn't really know him, had not seen him since medical school when he and Ruth were dating, and Ruth rarely mentioned him in her notes that accompanied birthday and Christmas cards. Arnie was a scoutmaster now and he'd joined Big Brothers and was very active in his men's lodge.

'I'm glad you're here, Mickey,' he said quietly, pouring two big mugs of coffee. 'It'll be nice for Ruth. She doesn't have many friends around here, she's so busy . . .'

Another silence expanded between them until it was broken, some minutes later, by the sound of the front door opening. A rush of crisp autumn air blew in a knot of persimmon-cheeked girls, their wispy hair escaping knitted hats, with knees bitten red and saddle Oxfords trailing in orange and gold leaves. Coats and sweaters went into the closet, books went *plunk* onto the sideboard, shoes went back and forth across a scruffy brown mat.

They came to a sharp halt in the kitchen doorway, standing as if their picture was about to be taken, short ones in front, tall ones in back: eight-year-old Rachel, seven-year-old Naomi and Miriam, and eighteen-year-old Beth. All staring at the lady sitting at the kitchen table.

'Come on, girls,' said Arnie. 'Don't be rude. Say hello to your Aunt Mickey.'

Good Lord, she thought a little anxiously. They're so intimidating in person.

'Hello, Auntie Mickey,' said the twins in unison.

A little unsure of herself, Mickey opened out her arms and was startled by the instinctive response: two warm bodies smelling of wool and pencils threw themselves at her and wet her cheeks with kisses.

'Are you really going to live with us?' asked Rachel, coming forward for a closer inspection.

'For a little while.'

'We're going to share a bathroom,' said Beth with pride. 'I've cleared a whole shelf and a towel rack for you.'

Mickey was laughing when the front door opened again and the November gusts brought in the one person she'd been waiting for. 'Ruth,' she said, rising.

Through the closed doors came the sounds of muffled squeals and bedsprings creaking. There was an occasional *whump* as a swung pillow found its target. Ruth said, 'They'll settle down soon. They're awfully excited.' She crossed the bedroom and settled herself into the bow of the window seat. 'Beth positively *adores* you. She's going through a phase of watching old movies on TV, you know, and she swears you look just like Grace Kelly.'

Mickey shook her head and drew neat piles of satin and lace lingerie from her suitcase. What an evening it had been! In the noise and mayhem there had been a curious order to it all – the march upstairs with school books, the change into long pants and sweaters, the gathering around the fireplace for milk and cookies. Then, chores to be attended to: the twins feeding the animal population that occupied the below-knee space, Rachel setting the table and arranging a centrepiece of pumpkin and ears of speckled corn; Beth peeling and dicing. Ruth spent an hour upstairs on the phone and Arnie settled himself in front of the downstairs TV to catch the news. While Mickey was monopolised by the little ones of the tribe, Sarah, Leah, and Figgy, Beth's little girl.

Dinner was a production with simultaneous talk and arms reaching across your plate and a glass of milk going over and legs kicking underneath; then, dishes washed and dried, floor swept, little ones bathed and put down by the fire, animals let in and let out, homework whined over, TV channels fought over, more telephone work for Ruth, and Arnie hidden behind the sports section. With Mickey once again the nucleus of a band of demanding little girls.

Finally, now, as she unpacked her suitcases while Ruth watched from the window seat, the house was starting to settle down. Arnie was downstairs watching the late news and the girls were trying very hard not to go to sleep.

'They'll pass out soon,' Ruth promised. 'They're worn to a frazzle.'

As she transferred folded clothes from her suitcase to the emptied dresser, Mickey compared this house to the stately silence of Pukula Hau. Like a museum, Pukula Hau seemed, with antiques and polished floors and maids that moved about in whispers.

As Ruth watched her friend unpack she was taken back to a balmy February almost two years ago.

What an affair that had been, those three hectic days in Hawaii, reunited once more with Sondra and Mickey for the wedding; flying to Honolulu first class, paid for by Mickey, the Butlers' private jet taking them to the island of Lanai, the drive through the pineapple plantation, and then seeing Mickey standing on the white steps of an old colonial mansion. Ruth and Sondra had spent three heavenly days with their friend, reminiscing, laughing and crying, giving advice and taking none, standing together at the altar under a bower of tropical flowers and palms, Ruth the matron of honour, Sondra the first bridesmaid, wearing apricot chiffon dresses Mickey had bought. And then that fairylike outdoor reception: the hundreds of guests, the glitter and gold, the orchestra and champagne beneath a spread of tropical stars. Mickey and Harrison had danced the first dance alone, and as they had twirled out onto the patio a helicopter had materialised and showered them with a rain of perfect white orchids, hundreds of them.

'So!' said Mickey. 'Did you suffer much from Mount St Helen's?'

'Not a speck. We didn't hear it or feel it or smell it or get one dot of dust. It all got blown into Idaho!'

'Ah,' said Mickey, straightening and turning. 'Here's something for you.' She held out a thick airmail envelope. 'It's from Sondra.'

Ruth was on her feet. 'I haven't heard from her in ages!'

They sat next to each other on the bed and bent their heads close over a photograph. A grinning Sondra and Derry were waving and showing off a small bundle in Sondra's arms. 'Jesus,' murmured Ruth. 'Just look at that man. What a hunk!'

But Mickey was staring at the tiny features of two-month-old Roddy, and the one pink fist that waved out of the blanket. 'We named him after Derry,' Sondra wrote on the back of the picture, 'whose real name is Roderick. But we call him Roddy so we can tell father and son apart!'

Dear Mickey,

Sorry it's been so long since I've written. So much has been happening, as you can see! Roddy's a little handful right now, but I love every minute. The only drawback is that I can't go out on circuits with Derry. But as soon as Roddy can be taken care of by one of our native helpers, I shall join my husband in the bush.

It is night now and I've just put Roddy to bed. Derry is up in the Taita village seeing to some emergency. So I'm all alone. The compound is quiet. Beyond my window I can hear the curious cry of the hyrax, which sounds like a toy being wound up and let run down, over and over.

I can't believe my happiness. What did I do to deserve this?

It is paradoxical, I suppose, that Derry and I are so

rootless, so nomadic, and yet we feel as permanently attached to this soil as a baobab tree. We could never be tied down to one spot, to one house – all of Kenya is our home.

Mickey, please pass this letter on to Ruth. I'm sure she thinks I've forgotten her! I would love to hear from you. How is married life? How are Ruth's kids?

God bless and *kwa heri*.

They sat in silence for a moment, listening to the cold Pacific Northwest wind beyond the heavy curtains, then Mickey went back to her unpacking.

'So,' said Ruth, shifting around so she could lean against one of the bedposts that supported the old-fashioned canopy. 'How's your practice?'

'It's going well. It felt strange at first, after so many years of school and residency. It felt strange to be out and on my own. I have an office not far from Great Victoria, with two nurses and a receptionist. And I'm very busy. No lack of referrals. But look at you now. That big clinic of yours!'

Pushing away from the bedpost, Ruth walked over to the fireplace and idly stirred the glowing embers. That big clinic of hers... when the Speedie Market next door went out of business Ruth bought the building and had it remodelled. Her clinic now took up the entire corner of the block, had a staff of twelve, and complete facilities which included X-ray, labs, and 'home environment' delivery rooms. Ruth recalled the day her father had come to see it, his only visit to her clinic. And all he had said was, 'Don't you find it rather limiting, to be restricted to such a narrow speciality?'

There was a tiny knock at the door and a small, heart-shaped face peered around, puffy with sleep. It was two-and-a-half-year-old Leah, the God-sent child, and she was holding a doll. 'Mommy, I thought Auntie Mimmy will want to sleep with Wobbwy.'

Ruth went to scoop up the child. 'That's very thoughtful of you, Leah. I'm sure Auntie Mickey would love to sleep with Lobbly.' Over her shoulder she said, 'I'll put her back to bed. Don't worry, this won't be happening all the time.'

Mickey laughed and insisted it was okay, she didn't mind,

and as she heard Ruth go down the hall, Mickey thought: *I really don't mind, to be wakened during the night by a child . . .*

Ruth returned with the doll, a soft, hairy little creature with four arms and two tails. It was one of the characters from Jonathan Archer's sequel to *Invaders!*

'Here's irony for you, sleeping with Jonathan's brain-child,' said Ruth, tossing the Lobbly onto Mickey's bed. 'Do you ever think about him?'

'Not any more. I used to, a lot. I wonder if he's still angry with me for standing him up at the belltower that night.'

'I'll bet you sometimes wonder what your life would be like right now if you *had* gone to the belltower.' Ruth returned to the window seat. 'My girls are mad for the Invaders series. They can't wait for the third one to come out at Christmas. They've seen *Starhawks!* five times. Have you seen Jonathan's films?'

'*Invaders!* and *Nam!* are the only ones.'

'Now that he has three Oscars on his shelf I imagine his ego is the size of –'

'Ruth, can you help me?'

November brushed its frosty breath on the panes beyond the drapes and a pocket of orange heat in the fireplace belched a shower of sparks. 'Tell me what you've done so far.'

Mickey sighed. 'Last February Harrison and I went to a specialist in Pearl City. He said we should be conceiving.'

'Did you bring your records?'

Mickey reached down for the burgundy leather briefcase between her suitcases and hefted it up and down. 'The Manhattan telephone directory!'

'What about Harrison?'

'He's normal. It's all in here. He passed every test with flying colours. Apparently,' Mickey's voice tightened, 'the problem is with me. But Dr Toland couldn't find it.'

Ruth sat next to Mickey on the bed. There were a thousand questions she could ask but she already knew what the answers would be. Mickey's posture, the movements of her hands, the telltale strain in her voice – Mickey had joined a sisterhood with which Ruth was intimately familiar.

'Have you discussed adoption?'

'It's not the same, Ruth, another woman's baby. I want

the experience, I want to know what it's like to give birth. And I want Harrison to have a son to replace the one he lost. Can you help me?'

There was that look again. All too hauntingly familiar – not from what she'd seen in her patients' eyes but in her own. Looking in the mirror lately, Ruth was seeing the same mute plea, that adrift-look of fear/hunger/confusion. *I feel it, too, Mickey, I want to have another one.*

'It's a terrible thing,' Mickey went quietly on, 'to have a useless womb. To think of each monthly blood flow as a death in the family. To ache and ache until you think you'll just *die* from the wanting!'

'I know, Mickey, I know. I have a group that meets on Friday evenings and every fear and anger has been uttered in that hour. Loss of femininity, a feeling of bodily betrayal, self-hate, a feeling of uselessness –'

'Yes,' said Mickey. 'Oh yes.'

Ruth got up and went back to the fireplace to give the embers a few more pokes. *But, Ruthie, you can't possibly, seriously consider having another!* Yes I can. You don't know how badly I want one, Arnie. *But the risks, it isn't fair.* We've had five healthy babies, Arnie, we can have one more. *It's an insane gamble, Ruthie, and a selfish one.*

She straightened and replaced the poker. Arnie, why are we arguing so much lately?

'Ruth?'

'Sorry, Mickey, just thinking. I'll read the records over the weekend and then do a complete work-up on you. It's possible your doctor overlooked something.

Mickey smiled and sagged. 'Thanks, Ruth.'

'As you know, Mickey, the one risk in this procedure is that you might unknowingly be pregnant right now and I would trigger a miscarriage.'

Mickey thought a moment, looking out the window at the red and gold trees. 'No, there's no chance that I'm pregnant.'

'Okay.' Ruth closed the chart and stood up from her desk. 'I'll have my nurse get everything ready.'

They were going to do an endometrial biospy in Ruth's

300

office to determine whether or not Mickey was ovulating. Dr Toland had performed the same test back in Pearl City and had found that she was – but Ruth wanted to make sure.

Statistically, the causes for infertility were found about 40 per cent with men, 30 per cent with women, about 20 per cent with both partners together, and the remaining 10 per cent to mysterious, unknowable circumstances. According to the records Mickey had brought, there was nothing wrong with Harrison: his sperm count was high, with good motility and morphology. Dr Toland's post-coital tests showed that Mickey's cervical mucus contained no spermicidal antibodies or hindered progress in any way. And according to Mickey, nothing in their love-making inhibited conception. Therefore, the problem must lie somewhere within her, although Dr Toland had been at a loss to find it.

While Ruth was out of the office, Mickey looked around. She had been both surprised and not surprised by Ruth's office. Surprised because it was so different from her own or any other doctor's office she'd seen, not surprised because it was so like Ruth. Plants, toys, handmade pillows, and pictures, pictures, pictures: of probably every baby Ruth had delivered, of beaming mothers in hospital beds, of flushed husbands in surgical greens, of little screwed faces and chins awash with drool. And of Ruth's own seven, Beth and Figgy included, at various ages and in various stages from mud to frilly dresses. Strangely, there was only one picture of Arnie – a small Polaroid in a simple frame, taken eight years ago – Arnie holding newborn Rachel.

Mickey thought about this now. In her week at the Roth house she'd seen something emerge, something that disturbed her and that was all the more disturbing because of Ruth's apparent blindness to it.

Arnie.

Arnie Roth lived at the centre of a female world, a world of Tampax boxes in the bathrooms and bras on doorknobs, of dolls and curlers and barrettes, a world in which even the cats and dogs were female; and there was quiet Arnie, as if in an unconscious effort to stem this feminine tide, fabricating an un-Arnie-like fanaticism for sports, working up an obsession with his lodge and scouting and Big Brothers, and now – yesterday – the purchase of a hunting rifle.

Not Arnie Roth, not Arnie at all. But he was pressed into a corner. A man being set aside, pushed out, redundant. Didn't Ruth see what she was doing to him?

'Okay, Mickey, we're ready.' Ruth had come back in and was holding the door open.

An endometrial biopsy is the taking of a small piece of the lining of the uterus; it is performed in a doctor's office without anaesthesia, takes only a few minutes, causes a pain similar to a menstrual cramp, and is done to determine a number of things, primarily if the patient is ovulating.

Lying on her back while Ruth worked, Mickey closed her eyes and tried to relax. She knew what the laboratory would find: that she was indeed ovulating. That is, that each month, on or around the fourteenth day of her cycle, one of her ovaries produced an egg, which was then carried along a Fallopian tube where, hopefully, it would meet a sperm and be fertilised.

Mickey knew the answers to all her tests: her hormone levels were normal and cyclical, her cervical mucus was also normal and conducive to assisting the sperm, her uterus was perfectly formed and in the right position, both Rubin and HSG tests had shown her tubes clear, and finally, a laparoscopy in the hospital had revealed her abdomen to be free of endometriosis or adhesions.

'Okay, Mickey,' said Ruth, drawing the paper sheet down over Mickey's legs. 'That's it. Now we wait for the pathologist's verdict.'

# Chapter Twenty-nine

'As you already knew, Mickey, you do ovulate normally and on the same day every month.'

They were sitting in a small seafood restaurant near the ferry harbour, enjoying crab and white wine and a flawlessly clear day. 'What next?' asked Mickey.

'I thought first of doing a hysterosalpingogram, but I've decided to skip that. Dr Toland did a thorough job on that test, repeating it won't show us anything else. I'd like to take a direct look through a laparoscope. How do you feel about that?'

Mickey shrugged. In her nine months with Dr Toland, Mickey had become used to thinking of her body as an object, to be probed, examined, tapped, and studied by others. This body that refused to give her a baby. 'You're the doctor.'

Ruth reached across and touched her hand. 'Don't be depressed, Mickey.'

'I'm not, Ruth, honestly. Just tired, I guess.'

'I'm sorry about that. I keep telling the girls to leave you alone. But you *are* visiting royalty, you know.'

It wasn't *that* that was making Mickey tired, the attentions of seven star-struck girls. Mickey couldn't tell her friend the truth – that the overwhelming evidence of Ruth's own fertility, being swallowed up by it day and night, was contributing to her depression.

'So when do we do the laparoscopy?' she asked.

'First I have to talk to Joe Selbie, he's the one who'll be doing it. Then I'll have to coordinate that with my own schedule and what's available on the OR schedule.' It is an unspoken tradition in the medical profession that surgeons don't operate on relatives or close friends.

'And after the laparoscopy?'

'It depends on what Joe Selbie finds. Mickey, how do you feel about fertility drugs?'

'No.' Dr Toland had brought this up also and both Mickey and Harrison had decided not to try them. Although, of all the products currently being used to increase fertility, only bromocryptine showed evidence of having harmful side effects. 'I prefer not to take drugs.'

Ruth reached for the wine carafe and refilled their glasses. This was a rare luxury, to drink wine in the middle of the day; but it was a rare day: no patients in labour or even near labour, no patients in the hospital, and none to be seen in the office. She had cleared the day for Mickey.

'What do you think of another go at artificial insemination?'

Mickey sighed.

'All right then,' said Ruth. 'First let's see what the laparoscopy reveals. Maybe Dr Toland missed something after all.'

They fell silent and both turned to stare out the window at the view of the bay. As she watched the stately progress of the *Walla Walla*, the ferry they had taken over from Bainbridge Island, Mickey returned to thoughts that had been nagging her since almost the night of her arrival – thoughts of Ruth and Arnie.

Their life together had not turned out as Mickey had imagined it would be. After only two days in the Roth house she had seen the signs and symptoms, had felt the crosscurrents that were at work. But, strangely, Ruth seemed oblivious to the problem.

Mickey recalled now the conversation she had had with Arnie three nights ago when she had helped him do dishes – Ruth had been at the hospital. Unexpectedly, Arnie had said to Mickey, 'So what do you think, Mickey, of me and Ruth?'

She looked at him, her hands poised over a casserole dish. 'What do I think about what?'

Tossing the rag into the sink, Arnie turned and folded his arms. 'Would you say we're a happy couple, looking at us?'

'I don't know. Aren't you?'

'I can't answer that. Isn't that crazy. I can't tell if we're happy or not. I have nothing to compare it to. What are other couples like after nine years?'

Mickey stared at him. After nine years? I don't know. I've only been married for two. Jonathan and I would have been married almost nine years now, if I had gone to the belltower. But I'll never know what that life would have been like.

'She's mad at me because I won't let her have another baby. I don't understand why she's so obsessed with having kids, Mickey, I mean, we've got five. Why press our luck? You know,' his voice grew quiet. 'I've even thought of divorce. Oh, not actually considered it but, you know, I sort of looked at it like a stock prospectus or something. Like, *what if*. But I don't know if that's the answer. Because I don't know what I *want*. I know that I want my girls and this house and Ruth and a life together, but not the way it is now.'

'Have you two talked about it?'

'We've shouted about it. I don't know, Mickey, I don't seem to count anymore, I don't feel like I'm important to her or needed. She's not the same girl I married.'

Mickey had to bite her tongue. When did the rose-coloured glasses come off, Arnie? Ruth has always been like she is now – driven.

'She's got so many things going,' he went on. 'I thought when her residency ended and she got into private practice that we'd settle down to a normal life. But no sooner was she on her own than she started taking on other projects, like her Friday night support group and her Lamaze classes and her private counselling. It seems that just when it looks like she's got some free time coming up she fills it right away with something she doesn't really need to do. It's like, she's trying to be so busy she won't have time to think. I don't know, Mickey...'

Mickey didn't know either. It had dismayed her to find Ruth, after all these years, living a parody of marriage. She and Arnie were almost like two strangers occupying the same house, each moving on a different plane. They shared the children but that was about all. Ruth was phenomenally busy, Mickey had discovered; she packed more into a day than seemed possible, living a peripatetic life so that a husband was almost vestigial. And there was Arnie, watching ball games, going hunting when he could, filling his free time with masculine diversions. Like the business with the fireplace logs. Those logs were Arnie's hobby. Last weekend, during a football game half time, he had pulled on his lumber jacket and earflaps, slipped into combat boots, and gone out back to the woodpile where he attacked the large logs with his power saw. He spent every Saturday afternoon out back, sawing wood.

Mickey didn't know what to make of it, hadn't known what to say to him. Ruth was just the same as when Mickey had first met her, twelve years ago – ambitious, determined, racing against time. But *why?* To what end?

Mickey now turned to look at her friend. Ruth was plump with a few silver strands in her dark brown hair. But still the same Ruth. When Mickey was on her way to Seattle she had been prepared to meet some of Ruth's friends, but none had been produced and none were ever mentioned, It occurred to Mickey now that maybe Ruth had no friends. When would she have the time for them?

'So, Ruth,' she said now, sipping her wine. 'Is everything going all right with you? I mean, we haven't really *talked*, have we?'

Ruth seemed to pull her attention from a great distance, as though she had drifted far from this restaurant. 'Everything's fine! Why do you ask?'

'You're so busy. I can't imagine how you manage it all. Where do you find the time?'

'I *make* time,' Ruth said.

And it triggered a memory for Mickey, a conversation of long ago in which Sondra, following Ruth into her dormitory room in Tesoro Hall, had asked, 'How did you find the time to buy your books so soon?' and Ruth had said, 'I *made* the time.'

Make time for what, Ruth? What is lacking in your life that you need to fill it up with so many other diversions?

Now another conversation came to Mickey's mind, one that had taken place only last night. She and Ruth and Arnie had been sitting in the living room with amaretto coffee when the girls had come downstairs to say good night. While the others had clustered around Mickey and their mother, eight-year-old Rachel had gone straight to Arnie and climbed into his lap.

Ruth had scowled and murmured to Mickey next to her,

'Look at that. Look how she slave-worships him. Why are little girls such submissive masochists, taking anything Daddy dishes out? Arnie could doormat Rachel and she'd come back for more!'

Mickey had looked at Ruth in surprise. 'But I think Arnie is a good father.'

'Of course he is. But she'll have her disillusionment someday. When it's too late.'

Mickey hadn't had the chance to ask Ruth to explain, and now, sitting across from her in this sun-lit, busy restaurant, Mickey wondered if this was a good time. But now that she thought about it, hadn't Ruth had some problems with her own father back in medical school? Hadn't she had to pay her own way while her brothers had received financial assistance from their father?

Ruth picked up a breadstick, started to eat it, changed her mind, and dropped it onto her empty plate. 'Did I tell you, Mickey, that I'd like to have another baby? It's true. One last one. While I still can.'

'Do you think it's wise?'

'You sound like Arnie. I want another baby and he's scared to death. You know what bombshell he dropped on me last week? That he's going to get a vasectomy if I stop taking the Pill. Is that fair?'

'Is he going to do it?'

'No. I'm staying on the Pill. It makes me seethe, though. Every time I look at my little Leah I think: what if we knew about the Tay-Sachs when I was pregnant with Sarah? Arnie would have put his foot down then and Leah never would have been born.'

Ruth picked up the breadstick again and this time ate it in earnest, her jaw snapping angrily as she chewed. 'Vasectomy! Another form of male tyranny. Vasectomy is just a variation on the chastity belt. By robbing his wife of control over her own conception and *contra*ception, a man can rest secure in the knowledge that she isn't playing around. I personally know two women who used to dabble outside the marriage bed but who had to stop when their husbands' tubes were tied, because naturally they had to throw away their pills and foam. And they can't risk getting pregnant because there's no way they can pass the kid off as *his*.'

Mickey opened her mouth to say something but was cut off by the intrusion of another voice. 'Ruth! What a pleasant surprise. How are you?'

They both looked up to see a woman standing by their table. She was in her fifties, dressed in a conservative pantsuit, her greying hair in a French roll. Ruth smiled. 'Hello, Lorna. Please join us. I want you to meet my friend Mickey.'

Lorna Smith was an editor on a Seattle newspaper and had first met Ruth as a patient; but they were now socially connected through Arnie's accounting firm partner.

'So you and Ruth knew each other in medical school,' Lorna said after ordering a Bloody Mary. 'Those must have been interesting times, in the days before women's lib.'

Thinking of some of the men in her class and Mr Moreno in anatomy, Mickey had to smile.

'May I ask you a *very* ignorant question, Mickey? Why are you called a *plastic* surgeon? Do you use plastic in your operations?'

'We don't use plastic. The word comes from the Greek *plastikos*, which means to mould.'

'There,' said Lorna, nodding to Ruth. 'I've learned something new today. Now I can relax.'

The waitress came by with the Bloody Mary and coffee for Ruth.

'So,' said Lorna after tasting her drink. 'We missed you at the Campbell's barbecue last month.' Jim Campbell was Arnie's partner and Lorna's husband's financial consultant.

'I was called to the hospital. Did I miss anything?'

'Not much, except that I must *warn* you, dear, that Wisteria Campbell is stalking your husband.'

'What? You must be kidding!'

'I am not. That black widow spider has her eye on your husband.'

'On Arnie? Come now, he's not the type of man women *go after*.'

While Ruth chuckled, Mickey and Lorna exchanged a glance. Then Lorna, turning serious, said, 'Actually I'm glad I ran into you, Ruth. I've been meaning to call you. I have some business to discuss with you.'

'Yours or mine?'

'It's both. My business and yours. Do you ever read Dr Chapman's column?'

'You mean "Ask Dr Paul"? Sometimes, although he's very often off the mark. He's about twenty years behind the times.'

'I know, we've been aware of it for some time. He's old; he's been with the paper since Columbus landed. The old management kept him on because they liked him, but big changes are being made at the *Clarion* and we've decided we need someone new, young, and up on the latest in medicine.'

'You want me to recommend someone?'

'And since most of our letters are from women, we thought we'd switch to a woman doctor. Rename the column "Ask Dr Ruth."'

'What? You want *me*?'

'You answer questions all the time in your office, Ruth, and probably many of the same questions Dr Chapman gets. The general ignorance is appalling.'

'You're telling me!'

'Dr Chapman gets a lot of inquiries about the oestrogen therapy controversy, and letters from women who've taken up athletics and have questions about their bodies, and people who want to know the latest on drugs and surgery. What do you say, Ruth? It's only a weekly column, we'll give you a desk at the office, and an assistant. The pay is small but it could be fun.'

Mickey did not mistake the spark in Ruth's eyes, the sudden excitement, the eagerness to take on yet another project, more responsibility. And Mickey thought: *She's crazy to take it on.*

At the same time, Ruth was thinking of her father: *A newspaper medical column. He wouldn't be able to say* that *was limiting!*

The operating room was still decorated with cardboard pilgrims taped to chrome cabinets and crepe paper turkeys crowning the anaesthesia gas; no holiday, no matter how minor, went neglected because of the relief each afforded to break the monotonous green.

Mickey smiled up at the nurse anaesthetist, a pretty young

woman with big blue eyes that smiled over the top of her mask. 'When I give you the pentothal, Doctor, I'm going to ask you to count backwards from a hundred,' she said, opening the IV drip going into Mickey's arm. 'And if you make it to eighty you win a free trip to Hawaii.'

'I already live in Hawaii,' said Mickey groggily.

'Then we'll make it the North Pole.' The anaesthetist swivelled around in her chair. 'Dr Shapiro, we're ready.'

Ruth had been at the back table looking over the laparoscopic instruments set out by the scrub nurse. She went to Mickey's side and took hold of her free hand. 'Pleasant dreams,' Ruth said through her paper mask.

Mickey's fingers made a feeble attempt to curl around Ruth's hand, her heavy eyelids drooped over her green eyes, and, tasting the garlic at the back of her throat, which meant the pentothal was in her system, she whispered, 'One hundred, ninety-nine, ninety-eight, ninety-seven . . . ninety-seven . . . seven . . . seven . . .'

The anaesthetist flicked Mickey's eyelashes, gave Ruth a signalling nod, and murmured, 'They never even make it to ninety-five.'

Joe Selbie worked with the help of a scrub nurse. After the sterile drapes were on, the uterine instruments were introduced into Mickey's vagina – a tenaculum for manipulating the uterus, a cannula for injecting dye. Then he came round to her side, made a small incision adjacent to her navel for the introduction of a trocar, and inserted the insufflating needle just at her pubic hairline. The first step was the introduction of carbon dioxide gas, to lift the abdominal wall up off the pelvic contents. As the gas went in and Mickey's abdomen slowly swelled, Ruth standing close but not touching the sterile field, recited a silent prayer.

When the insufflation was complete, Joe Selbie introduced into Mickey's pelvis the fibreoptic scope, through which he would do his exam. Bent over the sterile drapes, he brought his eye close to the eyepiece and the room fell silent. While Joe Selbie did a careful inspection of the hidden world beneath the flesh, his scrub nurse stood ready to hand him an instrument if necessary; the nurse anaesthetist listened to Mickey's heart through a stethoscope taped to Mickey's chest; the circulating nurse spread a sheet on the floor to receive the bloody sponges, and Ruth held her breath as she stared at the rise of iodine-brown skin as if to penetrate it and see what Joe saw.

'Looks normal,' he murmured, moving the sterile shaft of the scope with his gloved hand. 'No adhesions. No endometriosis. No scarring. Your friend has textbook anatomy, Ruth.'

She slumped a little and pulled in her lower lip to give it a couple of bites. From the wall speaker 'Moon River' joined the whisper of the recirculated air.

'Okay, Doris,' Dr Selbie said to the scrub nurse. 'Methylene blue now.'

The scrub nurse, carrying a large plastic syringe full of purplish dye, went around to stand between Mickey's raised legs. She attached the plastic tip of the syringe to the end of the metal cannula and, on a signal from Dr Selbie, started a slow push on the plunger.

Ruth felt herself tighten as she stared at Joe's curved back. With his eye over the scope he watched for the emergence of the dye as it made its way up through the uterus, along the two Fallopian tubes, and eventually out the fimbriae from where it would scatter and be absorbed harmlessly into the body.

Joe Selbie's head rocked slightly. 'Normal, Ruth. No blockage. Good flow.' He straightened up and said almost apologetically, 'I'm afraid her tubes look clear and normal.'

Ruth experienced a brief tremor of fury – a fury born of frustration and tension and towering hopes. But it quickly passed and she was stepping up to the table to look for herself.

While Joe Selbie held the scope for her Ruth bent forward with her arms wrapped around herself to keep her scrub dress from contaminating the sterile drapes; the nurse pressed the plunger again and Ruth saw, a moment later, the dark blue tide spill from the ends of Mickey's tubes.

'Damn,' she whispered.

After she stepped away from the table, Dr Selbie picked up the scalpel, made a second puncture at the pubic hairline, and drove in another trocar. Picking up one of the long laparoscopic graspers he said, 'I'm going to try something.'

Standing away from the table – she might as well be miles away for all she could participate – Ruth watched him slide the grasper into the second incision, replace his eye over the eyepiece, and heard him say, 'Okay, Doris, more dye, please.'

The world was suspended in a silent, taut moment as he watched the dye trickle through the delicate fimbriae, the gentle 'fingers' that nature had provided to coax the newly released ovum up into the tube. Then he took hold of the left tube with the grasper, rolled it a little for better visualisation, and signalled for more dye. As on the right side, the methylene blue seeped out and washed over the white ovary beneath the fimbriae. Except –

It didn't!

Jerking his head up and blinking to clear his eyes, Joe said with a frown, 'Again, Doris,' and returned to the eyepiece.

There was no doubt. The dye was missing the ovary.

'Ruth, come and look at this!'

With her eye over the scope and Joe Selbie operating the grasper, Ruth saw, when the dye came through, the slight 'miss' between tube and ovary. A miss so scant and negligible that, without the manipulation of the tube, it couldn't have been seen.

She looked up. 'What do you think? A scar?'

'Or a slight congenital deformity.'

Ruth felt electricity rise up through her legs and invade her body. *It was a chance!*

Mickey had already signed a pre-op consent to have herself opened up in the event they found something, so the team wasted no time. The laparoscopic instruments were taken away, the drapes pulled off, and the two nurses got to work setting up for an abdominal case. While the circulator brought Mickey's legs down and repprepped and the scrub nurse started opening packs of instruments and sutures, the anaesthetist took the oxygen mask off Mickey's face and slipped an endotracheal tube down her throat. In eight minutes Dr Selbie was making a Pfannenstiel, 'bikini,' incision and Ruth had sponge and cautery ready.

They found the tiniest deformity at the end of the tube, almost too small in fact to see with the naked eye, but big enough, in comparison to the microscopic ovum, to cause infertility.

In normal ovulation, when an egg is expelled from an ovary, it floats, for a brief time, in liquid space. The fimbriae of the nearby Fallopian tube, triggered by hormones, begin a primal dance, a series of contractions that create a current which draws the egg towards the oscillating fingers. Once in the entrance of the 'trumpet' end of the tube, the egg is gently urged along the narrow passage where it will either be fertilised by a sperm or disintegrate and be carried away in menstruation. In the case of Mickey's left tube, however, Dr Selbie and Ruth were able to ascertain with the aid of an operating microscope that had been positioned over Mickey's pelvis that due either to some mild infection in her early years of which Mickey was never aware, or a case of endometriosis, the fimbriae were all tangled and enmeshed. Instead of reaching out for the egg and drawing it into the tube, they acted as a repelling barrier. A small opening retrograde to the fimbriae, created most likely when scarring set in, was the outlet for the dye, making it appear on such diagnostic tests as the Rubin and HSG that the tube was functioning normally.

Ruth was almost giddy with relief. As Dr Selbie worked silently through the microscope, freeing up the fimbriae with the most delicate of instruments and sewing up the secondary hole with ophthalmic suture, Ruth could hardly contain her excitement.

'My guess, Mickey, is that you probably ovulate mostly on the left side. Or possibly entirely on the left side. It happens in some women.'

They were taking a slow, refreshing walk through the bracing December day. The acre on which Ruth's farmhouse sat was a woodland pastiche of evergreens, barren trees, tall green grass, and patches of hard, frosty earth. The wind bit their cheeks.

'All the tests showed you to be normal. You ovulated, yes, but on the blocked side. The ova never made it to the tube.'

Mickey watched Ruth's breath as it came out in little jets when she spoke, something you never saw in Hawaii! She was noticing things like that lately. She had heard of such a phenomenon from back-to-life patients; people who had died and been resuscitated reported a heightened keenness of their senses. *I died and was brought back.* She noticed everything now, like the prickly texture of the weave of her coat, the tinkling sound of the old creek at the bottom of the Roth property, even the sprinkle of pungent cinnamon Beth had put on the pumpkin pie she'd taken out of the oven a while ago.

Mickey was going back home to Hawaii tomorrow. In order to safeguard against the newly sutured tube scarring and closing up, Dr Selbie had left in a 'stent,' a tiny morsel of harmless silicone around which the tube would grow and strengthen; in a month she would come back so he could remove it and then, as he'd told her in the hospital, 'there's no reason why you can't conceive right away.'

Still she held herself back. It was too tempting, too easy to let those old hopes and dreams soar again. Caution was the best path, a guarding of the emotions. She still hadn't told Harrison; she wanted to tell him in person.

'You understand, of course,' Ruth went on, 'that there are no guarantees.'

They came at last to the creek at the foot of the acre and found a boulder strewn with pine needles to sit on. Winter sunlight came through the branches and speckled their faces as they spoke. 'There are no guarantees in anything, Mickey, you know that. But I can honestly tell you we've done our best and I think there's good reason to hope.' She reached into the pocket of her car coat and pulled out a small bundle. 'I want you to have this, Mickey.' Resting in the palm of her hand was a plain box with string around it. Mickey took it and opened it. Snuggled in the nest of tissue paper was a blue-green stone, a turquoise, about the size of a silver dollar.

'It's very old, Mickey. Centuries old. A patient gave it to me last year, a woman who was in toxaemia and who almost lost her baby. This stone is supposed to be very lucky for the bearer, but you can use the luck only once. She said it turns pale after the luck's been used.'

Mickey examined the stone. A robin's-egg blue, it had a curious brown veining down the centre that looked, at first glance, like a woman with her arms outstretched but on more careful inspection like two snakes coiling up a tree. On the back was a casing of yellow metal and some sort of foreign inscription, too worn now to be readable.

'I swear, Mickey, it was pale when she gave it to me. But now it's bright blue.'

'Then you haven't used the luck, Ruth.'

'I have all the luck I can handle. I want you to have it.' Ruth reached out and curled Mickey's fingers around the turquoise. 'I want you to wear it the night you get back together with Harrison.'

They both grinned as tears tumbled down their cheeks.

# PART SIX
*1985 – 1986*

# Chapter Thirty

Sondra reached into the old steriliser, grasped the hot egg, then cracked it against the wall. It was very hard-boiled. That meant the instruments were sterile. Slipping on old-fashioned gloves, she drew the tray of steaming instruments out and carried them to the side of the operating table.

It was a gorgeous June day outside; the operating room windows were open to admit the gentle, perfumed breezes – a cardinal sin in 'real' hospitals! – and the lazy ceiling fan overhead worked to keep flies off the sterile field.

Sondra was working alone. She was preparing to clean an infected wound in the arm of a Taita elder.

Her old friends from years gone by might not have recognised the woman in the tropical surgical costume of short pants and sleeveless tunic; Sondra's skin had tanned to a brown, the deep shade seen on many natives, and her long black hair was twisted in a coil and wrapped on top of her head in a bandana of colourful African cloth. And when she spoke to the elderly man on the operating table, she spoke in an almost flawless Swahili. 'All right, *mzee*, a little juice from the spirit of sleep to make your arm slumber.'

When, a minute later, she heard the drone of the Cessna as it buzzed the landing strip for animals, Sondra looked up and smiled. *All right, Dr Farrar,* she thought, *you're going to take a nap this afternoon if I have to tie you to the bed!*

Poor Derry. Running here and there, taking medicines to outposts that were suffering from the drought, assisting government teams to clear malarial areas, hardly taking a minute for himself. 'I'll have plenty of time to rest in the Seychelles,' he assured her repeatedly. The Seychelles, the islands in the Indian Ocean where they were going to spend their first real vacation together.

Somewhere she'd got the notion that, after a time,

husbands and wives got tired of one another, complacent, the honeymoon ended and a life of comfortable toleration set in. That could never be the case with her and Derry! Here they were, married over eleven years, and still the sight of him excited her, just as it had long ago.

She ran to meet him on the dusty landing strip. His hands were full with mail pouch and sugar sacks, but he still flung his arms around her and kissed her.

As they walked arm in arm back to the compound, Sondra noticed that his limp was bad today.

'What's new, Dr Farrar?' he asked, giving her a squeeze.

'Not much, Dr Farrar.' Sondra could hardly contain herself. She had a secret, a wildly wonderful secret and she was bursting to tell him. But not now, not until the red dust had been washed off him and a hot bath had eased his bones.

'Daddy! Daddy!'

An amazing little replica of Derry came bounding out from the school-house. Five-year-old Roddy was so stamped from his father's mould that anyone could see what the boy was going to look like grown. Except for the amber eyes. Those were his mother's.

Derry scooped his son up; Sondra pressed her hands to her abdomen. Her secret: there was going to be a second baby to steal their love.

'Come along now, Roddy,' she said, relieving her husband of the squealing child. 'Daddy must rest.'

Roddy skipped ahead of them, flashing dirty legs below khaki short pants. 'Njangu says we can have jam for tea today! He says he stole it from nasty old Gupta Singh!'

Sondra shot him a look but the boy was already running off to announce his father's return. 'I do wish Njangu would watch what he says around the children,' she complained.

Derry shrugged. It was something that couldn't be helped. Prejudice against Indians among the African population was a deeply ingrained fact of Kenya life. Gupta Singh was the proprietor of the trading post the mission did business with. An old Indian who had elected to stay in Kenya when thousands had fled back to India upon Kenyatta's seizing power, he was Njangu's fiercest enemy. 'They breed like rabbits,' the old Kikuyu often declared. 'And they live off the smell of oil rags!'

Sondra's worry had been increasing of late. Roddy was picking up some unhealthy ideas from Njangu, and learning some wild ways from the native children. When she'd voiced her concerns to Derry, wondering if this was a good place to raise their son, Derry had rejoined with, 'Well, growing up in Africa did *me* no harm.'

She hoped the spell in the Seychelles Islands would do the child some good. And then, sometimes a baby sister or brother injected a child with a sense of responsibility.

She wondered when to break the news to Derry. Tonight, after supper.

In a world where giraffes and elephants and lions roamed his backyard, it was not surprising that a little boy should find the most fascination in an ordinary rodent. So they stalked one now, armed with sticks and imaginations, Roddy and Zebediah, Kamante's son.

They were a month apart in age, the two boys, but it was a big month, and Roddy took advantage of it. Being the older, it was up to him to outline the plan of the hunt. They were creeping around the back of the church, crunching over Elsie Sanders' strawberry patch. As their fathers were, the two little boys were like brothers; just as Derry and Kamante had once been inseparable and shared the adventures of their youth, so did Roddy and Zebediah spend their every free moment together, with Roddy, being the one-month-elder and the tiniest-bit-taller, always in the lead.

'You go round that way, Zeb,' he whispered to Zebediah, motioning with his stick. 'It's gone under that bush. You flush it out and I'll whack it one!'

Zeb did as told, feeling very important because he was, after all, next in command after Roddy.

The adults were in the common room, hearing what news Derry had brought from Nairobi, reading long-awaited letters, drinking tea. While in Nairobi Derry had stopped at the travel agent and picked up the tickets for their trip next week; he now handed a copy of their itinerary to the Reverend Mr Sanders. 'We'll be back in two weeks. The infirmary will be in capable hands. Dr Bartlett is quite qualified to take care of things in our absence –'

A scream cut the warm air. All heads swivelled to the open

windows; Derry was the first on his feet. As everyone ran to the door, more screams filled the lazy afternoon, high, child's screams, full of panic and terror.

Roddy was stumbling across the compound waving his arms. 'It got Zeb!' he cried. 'It got Zeb!'

Derry didn't stop. He ran past the boy in the direction Roddy was waving. Sondra fell to her knees and took hold of her son by his thin shoulders. 'What is it, Roddy? What happened?'

Roddy's face was white; his eyes were two black holes in his head. 'A monster! It got Zeb. It *killed* him!'

Now Kamante, having been startled by the shouts, was running behind Derry, his young wife hanging back in the doorway of their hut, looking dazed.

By the time a small crowd had gathered, Derry was emerging from behind the church with a sobbing Zebediah in his arms.

Sondra ran up to him. 'What happened?'

'A rat got him.'

She took hold of the black, round face and saw the several tiny red gnashes and thin streams of blood. 'It's all right, Zeb,' she crooned, running alongside as Derry carried the boy to the infirmary. 'You'll be all right. You're just frightened.'

As soon as the boy was laid down on a table, Sondra got to work cleaning the wounds. Her hands trembled. Nothing had been said but she knew what Derry was thinking. Rabies.

By the time Derry had the medicine kit out and was loading a syringe, Kamante was at his boy's side, holding one of his small hands, speaking softly in Swahili.

Derry had done a rapid mental calculation: half a milligram of duck embryo serum per kilogram of body weight. First, infiltration around and under the bites; then the routine initial dose to begin anti-rabies treatment. In multiple bites of the head and face, especially in children, time was vital.

When he was done and a nurse was bandaging Zebediah's head, Derry took Sondra by the arm and led her out of the room. 'We haven't enough,' he said quietly. 'I'll call Voi and see what they've got.'

Rooted to the spot, she watched him go, then Sondra turned back to look through the doorway. Zebediah was calmer now, he wasn't in pain, only badly scared. Apparently the boys had cornered the rat and it had gone for his head. As there was a chance it had been rabid, Zebediah must now face a series of twenty-three injections.

When she came out of the infirmary she found Roddy standing self-consciously under the fig tree, digging his toes into the dirt. One look at his hangdog posture, at the shame-faced expression, and Sondra knew the rat hunt had been his idea.

She squatted before him and wiped the tears off his cheeks. 'Zeb will be all right, Roddy. You mustn't feel bad. Let this be a lesson, all right?'

'Yes, Mummy.'

'No more going after the wild animals. We've a very nice little dog here who could use some company.'

'Yes, Mummy.'

'Now,' she gave him a hug and stood up, 'first we'll go see Zeb and promise to save him some jam, then we'll think about what a lovely present we'll bring back for him from the Seychelles.'

With that the five-year-old brightened and, taking hold of his mother's hand, proceeded to offer her a string of promises to be a good boy.

Sondra joined Derry in the common room just as he was getting up from the radio. 'It's no good,' he said wearily. 'They haven't any serum.'

'Call Nairobi then. Have them send some.'

'I'll do better than that. I'll go myself.'

'But they can send it!'

'I don't trust it to come in time.'

Sondra nodded reluctantly. They frequently had trouble with medical shipments; either the wrong medicine was sent or it had been allowed to sit in the hot sun, or it came days too late. And she saw Derry's heavy thoughts written plainly on his face; this was his best friend's son, just one step away from their own, really.

'We've got to start him on the series in the morning, Sondra. I'll go now.'

'Let one of the drivers take you.'

'There won't be a soul awake in Nairobi when I get there. I'll take the plane.'

'Derry, give yourself a rest.'

He smiled and patted her arm. 'Won't take me long. I'll be back in time for supper.'

Despite the hurry he was in, Derry still carefully checked out the aircraft and refilled it with fuel. By the time he was ready to take off, Sondra was coming out to the landing strip.

'How is he?' asked Derry, taking the bush jacket she had brought out.

'He's asleep. I gave him a sedative. I hope the vaccine isn't necessary, Derry.'

He took Sondra in a strong embrace. 'Keep supper warm for me.'

'I'm worried about you, Derry. You overwork yourself.'

'Think of all the rest I'll get in the Seychelles!'

She stood back and shielded her eyes as the propeller started turning and the plane began to roll. Derry headed to the end of the strip, got into position, waved to Sondra, and opened the throttle.

He bumped and rattled by in a whirl of noise and dust. Sondra waved with both arms as she watched the Cessna pick up speed. At seventy miles per hour Derry pulled back on the stick. Sondra saw the shadow before he did, a black hump that was startled out of a deep sleep by the approach of the aircraft and sprang up on four legs. Sondra saw the left wheel catch the hyena, sending the animal tumbling; she saw the plane tilt dizzily, unbalanced by the snag, saw the left wing dip and touch the ground, the plane fly into a crazy flip-flop spin, and then all in an instant smash into the ground and burst into flame.

She stared in frozen horror, then she started running. 'Derry!' she screamed. 'DERRY!'

# Chapter Thirty-one

Arnie found himself looking for her again. He didn't want to but he couldn't help it. The young woman who had been staring at him these past few weeks.

It had begun innocently enough. When you take the same ferry every morning of your life you start recognising the 'regulars,' people you wave to each day, with whom you exchange opinions about the weather but whose names you never learn. This one had been like all the others; she'd started riding the *Walla Walla* to Seattle about six months back, coming down the ramp with everyone else and taking a place in the smoking section, then spending the thirty-minute trip across the Sound behind her *Post Intelligencer*. Arnie hadn't paid much attention to her then, being, like the rest of the commuters, mentally involved in the day ahead, running his schedule through his mind, ticking off clients to see, what to do about Stan Ferguson's tax audit, until one day he'd realised she was staring at him. Well, it *was* possible he had started it; he'd been gazing absently in her direction. It was like one of those silly staring things one gets into with a total stranger: one stares for no reason, just blankly looking, and then the other notices. Pretty soon, both are sneaking little glances to see if the other is watching.

That had been several weeks ago, and since then they'd played the game, morning and evening.

Arnie's curiosity about her was growing. Who was she? What did she do in Seattle? He decided she must be a secretary or work in an office because although she was always dressed nicely, there was none of the heavy-handed 'dress for success' look about her that was so appallingly blatant among the female executives who rode the ferry. Did she live on Bainbridge Island or did she drive from Suquamish or Kitsap? Because she looked like she could live on the reservation there. Most of the Indians taking the ferry did.

And she was beautiful. A perfect round face, like a harvest moon, coppery and framed by long black hair; a face that was paradoxically innocent and exotic at the same time, a face that he placed around twenty-five or twenty-six. She was petite, small-boned, and she was shy, but not, Arnie suspected, timid. There was something in those big liquid eyes with their thick black lashes, something that shone through the shyness that made him think she was bold at the core, and brave.

So, on this unparalleled Pacific Northwest morning, with the sun coming up pink and salmony over Seattle's fogbank, which stood at the edge of the Sound, with the water a deep indigo and the distant skyline a slash of indistinct grey a-sparkle with lingering lights, on this early morning of new air and new possibilities, Arnie Roth climbed out of his station wagon and found himself once again, watching for her.

He looked at his watch. He was becoming preoccupied with time and he knew it. Marking the passage of years is one thing, but when you get down to days and hours, when you wake up thinking about how rapidly the minutes are trickling through your fingers, when your first waking thought is, *We sleep away one third of our lives*, then you know you're in trouble. When had this obsession with time started? On his last birthday, the forty-eighth, when he'd blown out his candles and had seen through the bluish smoke the big Five-O that waited for him two scant years down the line.

I'll be fifty and what do I have to show for it? Where did my youth go?

Arnie Roth was beginning to think he was born middle-aged. Looking back, he saw the unremarkable childhood in Tarzana, a quiet little boy sprouting up at the centre of mediocrity; the calm, almost boring transition through puberty and adolescence – no acne, no wet dreams – and then college and (yawn) accounting school, a life painted in browns and tans with few peaks and valleys, just an ordinary guy tapping out an ordinary existence on his calculating machine. And then Ruth Shapiro had walked in and changed all that.

Arnie had known, for a little while, a short term of excitement, a quick taste of the unconventional – dating Ruth, going to bed with her; she was so outspoken and crazily liberal *and* she was going to be a doctor – and for a while Arnie Roth had thought his middling life was going to change for good. But it had turned out not to be so. Exchanging a quiet bachelor existence for a mortgage and diapers had turned his life on to a very predictable course.

There it was, the blue Volvo. Jerking to life, Arnie slammed his door, locked the car, and marched with briefcase in hand towards the ferry terminal.

The crowd was growing now, all the commuters from Bainbridge to Seattle were gathering to be herded down the ramp on to the ferry. Joining the front of the mob, Arnie could feel her back there, hanging at the tail end, her pretty face contained halo-like in the circle of scarf around her head. He had to fight the impulse to turn and look for her.

*Blat* went the ferry. 'Ferry farts' everyone called them. One short one meant the boat was leaving; a longer *blat* meant it's just left and anyone running down the ramp was too late. Arnie stayed out on deck for a change, having no taste this morning to sit with the white collar types in their drooping socks, or the Joe Lunchbuckets with ther legs stretched out over the seats. On this flawless, crisp morning, Arnie wanted to watch the passing scenery as the *Walla Walla* cut a silver swath through water smooth as glass; he needed to look, really *look* at the mountains, sharply visible on each horizon, the Olympics and Cascades all freshly dusted with snow from yesterday's storm.

Today the boat was bucking and rocking as if it rode a storm tide, and yet the water was perfectly calm. Must be something wrong with the engines again. Arnie shivered with the cold but refused to go inside. *She* was in there and her large, soulful eyes would settle on him like a pair of trembling moths.

His thoughts went to Ruth. In fact, he was thinking a lot about Ruth lately, probably because this newcomer kept intruding on his thoughts. Whenever he found himself pondering the enigma of the young woman (he turned now on impulse, saw her staring at him through the salty glass, then he turned away), he would chase her out with visions of his wife.

Ruthie, Ruthie, where are we going? Is this what we started out to do, was this our intention thirteen years ago? Did we enter into our marriage with visions of monotony and humdrum? It wasn't her fault; Arnie wasn't blaming Ruth. It took two to make a marriage drab. No, that wasn't fair. He couldn't exactly say their life was drab – if anything it was *too* predictable, being called out of movies, away from restaurants and parties, never knowing when he got home if his wife was going to be there or if he was going to have to be nursemaid to the girls. There was a time when they'd fought a lot about it, when Arnie had got fed up with buttonless shirts and burned suppers and interrupted evenings. But he'd soon learned that fighting didn't help, that nothing was going to change, and so, somewhere along the line he'd acquiesced, and found a certain bland peace in resignation.

Even on the issue of sex. Ever since the birth of Leah, seven years ago, when they had agreed not to have any more kids (well, it had been a shaky, tentative agreement) Ruth and Arnie's sex life had gradually diminished, until now, it was almost nonexistent. Arnie never pushed it. If it happened, it happened, sometimes by accident, sometimes because one of them was in a rare mood. It was a comfortable, old-married sex life and Arnie suspected that this was how it was with most couples after this many years.

He slowly swivelled his head and looked over his shoulder. She was reading the newspaper and smoking; all Indians smoked. When she raised her head he quickly looked away. *Is she married? Does she have a boyfriend, a lot of boyfriends?*

It's midlife crisis, Arnie Roth, plain and simple. When a man starts counting the hairs on his head and buckling his belt below his stomach and noticing beautiful young women on the commuter ferry...

*Where does she go every night? Always, into the Volvo and out of the parking lot before everyone else...*

The girls were growing up at an alarming rate. It wouldn't be long before they were out of the house for good and he and Ruth were alone, for the first time in their life together.

God, am I *afraid* of that?

A gust of wind against Arnie's chilled face made him think it was time to go inside. As he pushed through the doors and into the stuffy, smoky air, he forced himself to avoid looking in her direction.

He settled into a seat and marched his thoughts along a decorous line. This weekend they were going to celebrate Ruth's birthday and he still hadn't got her a present. Today's lunch hour would be a good opportunity to shop for it. The Pike Street Market. And something special. After all, Ruth was facing forty soon. Did women go through midlife crises, too? Or did they have to cope with menopause instead? *A menopausal woman can't help herself but a forty-eight-year-old man staring at Indian girls on the ferry is making a fool of himself.*

The ceiling panels rattled as the boat rounded the final corner into Eagle Harbor. There was a long *blat* and two short ones signalling arrival, and everyone started getting up and stretching. He glanced over. Her eyes brushed his.

They both quickly looked away.

'Mrs Livingstone, the problem lies solely with your husband. His sperm count is too low.'

The woman sitting on the wicker sofa in Ruth's office started wringing her hands. 'He won't like that, Doctor. He's very ... proud.'

Ruth bent her head over the woman's chart to hide her scowl. Men. They were eager enough to blame a wife for lack of children in the family, even though in 40 per cent of the cases of infertility the fault lay with the husband; they scowl at their wives, or pity them, or pat them condescendingly on the head, but just hint to them that the problem lies with *them* and they raise a shout.

'Mrs Livingstone, your tubes are clear, you ovulate regularly, your mucus is not too acidy and contains no sperm antibodies. You are, in fact, one of those women who gets pregnant very easily. If you would like, I'll explain it to your husband for you.'

The woman blanched. It hadn't been easy coming to Dr Shapiro in the first place, and then getting a sperm sample out of Frank had been nearly impossible. 'What's she questioning *my* potency for? *You're* the one who can't get pregnant!' And now, to tell him *this* . . .

'Think it over, Mrs Livingstone,' said Ruth, closing the chart. 'If you think it would be easier, I can recommend a male specialist to your husband –'

'Can it be cured? Can something be done for Frank?'

Ruth folded her hands on the desk top. 'Unfortunately, Mrs Livingstone, recognition of the man's contribution to a couple's fertility is fairly recent and because of this, research hasn't yet developed treatments the way it has for women. Now, it's possible your husband has a hormone deficiency in which case there are drugs on the market to raise a low sperm count. There is also the possibility of a varicocele, which is a varicose vein on the spermatic cord and which can cause a low sperm count plus diminished mobility. Surgery can correct that in most cases . . .'

Fifteen minutes later Ruth was alone once again in her office, having seen the last patient; a pile of paper work faced her. She'd sat up late last night with the latest batch of letters for 'Ask Dr Ruth' and had sifted out four of the most representative ones. She occasionally got crank letters, once in a long while an obscene letter, plus several that weren't germaine to her column (lovelorn advice); of the rest, she had to determine which had the widest appeal to the newspaper audience, and also which she could consolidate into one 'letter' asking several things.

For Monday's column she had decided to spotlight the hazards of certain hygiene products, such as soap and shampoo and deodorant, urging her readers to pay attention to ingredients listed on labels and at the same time avoiding specific mention of certain brands. It was something she often resorted to when pressed for time – devoting the whole column to a single theme – because it made research easier and the writing a lot faster. It was also a gimmick she was resorting to a lot lately because the work seemed to be piling up faster than she could get to it.

If she didn't get some of it done this afternoon, tomorrow would be her next opportunity since tonight was her support group. And then, tomorrow was her birthday, and she suspected she wouldn't be allowed too much time to herself.

Maybe Sunday, if Arnie took the girls out of the house for a few hours . . .

When the telephone buzzed Ruth frowned. She had told her receptionist not to disturb her unless it was an emergency. 'Yes?' she said into the phone.

'Sorry, Doctor, but your sister is on line one.'

With her frown deepening – in her eight years of private practice Ruth had never received a phone call at the office from her sister – Ruth punched the next button and heard a soft sobbing at the other end. 'Judy? What is it?'

'It's Dad. His heart. Just an hour ago.'

Ruth's arms and legs turned into solid stone. 'Where is he? Which hospital? Is someone with Mom?'

'They put him in CCU. Mom is with him, and Samuel as well. Ruth, he hasn't regained consciousness.'

'Keep Mom quiet. Get her to lie down if you can and have Samuel take care of her. I'll be right there.'

Arnie liked the Pike Street Market. Whenever he came here, which wasn't often, he would take his time and stroll among the little shops, stopping in at the Athenian Café and squeezing into a tiny booth next to the window so he could look out over the Sound as he enjoyed pitta bread stuffed with lamb and rice. Although today there wasn't time enough for the Athenian, he still didn't hurry up and down the stairways, along the crowded walks, through courtyards filled with artsy-craftsy people selling candles and quilts and etchings. It reminded him of Farmer's Market in LA except this was bigger and, being just a block from the waterfront, had a very 'shippy,' wharfy atmosphere to it.

What on earth to get Ruth for her birthday? She disliked totally decorative things, like plastic plants and knickknacks. An object had to have some use or it had no place in her house. Well, that was no problem. Most of these cottage industry handicrafts served some useful purpose, like the batik skirts and the macramé plant holders. Still, after thirty minutes' stroll it was all beginning to look the same to Arnie. He wanted unique. Practical, but unique.

He was just about to give up and head back to the office when he came upon the art gallery. Actually, it was an oil painting in the window that caught his eye, a strikingly dramatic portrait of an old Indian chief, a masterwork of chiaroscuro and mood. It wasn't exactly practical, but it *was* breathtaking. Arnie bent forward and squinted at the price. Twelve hundred dollars. He leaned away and surveyed the rest of the objects in the window. Another oil painting, a dramatic eagle carved in wood, sandstone whales, scrimshawed ivory, handwoven Indian blankets. Arnie didn't know how Ruth felt about native American art. But it wouldn't hurt to have a look around inside.

He could see at once that this gallery was out of his league: there were very few objects displayed, and those that were were spotlighted discreetly and tastefully. A peek at the first few price stickers confirmed his suspicion. He couldn't afford this place.

He was just starting to turn back to the door when a voice came from the back of the gallery. 'May I help you?'

He turned back around. *I'll be polite. Look at a few things and then tell her I have to think it over.*

Arnie froze. It was *the girl*.

If she was as surprised to see him as he was to see her, she gave no sign. In fact, she showed no sign of recognition at all. 'Is there anything in particular you're looking for?'

God, her voice was beautiful. And the way she walked! A fluid glide over the thick carpet, bringing her to a rest just three feet from him, so he could see her close up, every tiny, gemlike detail of her. And what was that perfume she was wearing?

'Yes,' he mumbled. Arnie had to clear his throat. 'A gift. I'm looking for a gift.'

'I see.' She folded her hands delicately before her. 'Is this person a collector?'

'Um, no. Just someone's who's ... birthday is coming up and I ...' Arnie couldn't bring himself to utter the word 'wife.'

She turned slightly and held out a slender, brown arm. 'Most of the objects in our gallery were made by local artists. Some of these artists are very famous and their works are recognised world-wide. We also carry some fine old pieces. For instance, if you like Kwakiutl wood carving, we have some very nice works done by Willie Seaweed.' She began walking slowly away from him, pointing first to this painting, now to that kachina doll. 'Perhaps you would be interested in something from a particular tribe rather than a particular artist. Or possibly you prefer a certain region. We aren't limited to just Northwest Coast Indian art; we also have some fine examples of Pueblo and Plains art.'

She turned to face him; Arnie felt his face burn from his collar up to his far-back hairline. He hadn't heard a word she'd said; he'd been watching how her long, straight black hair swung like a silk curtain as she walked.

'Well,' he gave a little laugh, 'I know this is going to sound odd, but it would have to be something practical. You know, have a use besides standing there and looking pretty.'

She didn't seem to find his suggestion silly at all. 'We have some very nice Navajo blankets. And handwoven baskets.' She took a few steps to her right and rested her slender hand on a magnificent piece of pottery, elegantly displayed on a tall, white pedestal.

'Oh, that's beautiful,' said Arnie, going to it. 'Is it Northwest Coast?'

'Well actually, the Northwest Coast tribes do not have a traditional pottery style as such; usually we work in pueblo-style pottery and incise Northwest Coast motifs on them. This, for instance, is Thunderbird-Stealing-the-Sun.'

Arnie, starting to relax a little, laughed softly. 'I'm afraid my ignorance of Indian lore is appalling.'

She smiled. 'There is a legend that when the skygod possessed the sun he kept it in a box and would only let daylight out on a whim. So the Thunder-bird stole the sun from the box of daylight and gave it to mankind. You see, he has horns and a short crooked beak.'

Arnie stared at the pot. It *was* beautiful. Into reddish brown clay had been engraved an intricate motif all around, depicting the myth; the black and turquoise paint against the rust-coloured clay was eye-catching. And it was huge. It would hold one of Ruth's benjamin trees.

Arnie was just wondering if it was tacky to ask the price when, seemingly reading his mind, she very gently picked up the pot and placed it in his hands. 'You will notice that it was signed by the artist at the bottom.'

Arnie tipped the pot and saw a signature engraved in the clay. *Angeline, 1984.* And next to it a sticker that said five hundred dollars.

'Ah –' He handed it back to her. 'Yes, well, it is sort of what I'm looking for . . .'

As she placed it back on the pedestal she said, 'This pot was hand-thrown on a wheel. Very few artists today work in the traditional coil method, and then firing in a dung oven. Now, over here I have some Joseph Lonewolf if you're interested in –'

'No, no. This is perfect. I just have to think about it.' *Christ, what am I saying? There's no way I can afford this and she no doubt gets a commission on everything she sells. So here I am getting her hopes up on a big sale when I have no intention –*

'Perhaps that one is a little bigger than you would like. We have a few others by the same artist, smaller pieces, less intricately painted.' As she walked away Arnie tried in a thousand ways to think of how he could calmly, casually, ask her if she'd like to go to lunch with him. No, you fool, coffee, yes, coffee. Just, you know, to sit by the water and listen to the seagulls and talk . . .

The telephone rang at the back of the shop and it startled them both. 'Excuse me, please.'

He watched her walk away, felt a lump start to gather in his throat, and knew exactly what he should do next. Which was what he did do. When she wasn't looking Arnie turned and left the gallery.

Ruth gazed coolly down at the man in the hospital bed as if he were a stranger. Her mother, slumped in a chair next to the bed, was weeping noisily. 'He said last night he wasn't feeling well. I didn't listen, God strike me dead, I thought your father was complaining about my cooking again. He was getting ready to go to the office this morning and just like that he went to the floor and me all alone with him!'

Outside, beyond the electronic door that separated the Cardiac Care Unit from the rest of the world, a crowd of Shapiros was gathering. Two visitors at a time only was the CCU rule and since Ruth's mother refused to give up her vigil at her husband's bedside that meant they had to take turns, one by one, to see him.

The tubes and monitors didn't frighten Ruth as they did the others; what did frighten her now was what she felt inside, terrifying, knife-sharp emotions that sprang out of her like ghosts in a fun house. They dizzied her. She felt the floor tilt. She took hold of the cold metal bed railing and stared down at the bluish lids closed over unmoving eyes, the slack jaw, the gentle rising and falling of his chest as if he dreamed of islands and sand. *You can't die,* Ruth thought now, urgently, frantically. *We aren't finished yet.*

When Ruth turned to go Mrs Shapiro reached out and seized her hand. 'Where are you going? You can't go. You can't leave your father like this. You're a doctor, Ruth.'

'Mom, if both you and I stay how can the others come in and see him?'

'Then send in Judy. I want Judy right now.'

'The others have a right too, Mom, just in case.'

'Just in case! Just in case *what*, I'm asking!'

'Mom, lower your voice.'

'Some daughter my husband's got. Look at you, not a tear even.'

Ruth saw the nurse at the monitor bank look up with a disapproving frown. 'Mom, this is CCU. We have to keep quiet. I'll shed tears later.'

'Later! Later when? When he's dead, God forbid?'

'If you keep this up, Mother, I'll have you sedated.'

'Sure, sure, that's it. No heart you've got.' Mrs Shapiro buried her face in her handkerchief. 'You've always resented your father. Why, God only knows.'

'Mother –'

'You know how it broke his heart, Ruth, you going to medical school when you know how much he wanted you to get married. You broke your father's heart and now he's near death and your mother's heart is breaking. That's all you've ever done, Ruth, is break your parents' hearts.'

Ruth started down at the face of the slumbering stranger and thought: *All my life I've been breaking his heart? Well then, I've finally done it. It's broken.*

'I'll send in Judy.' And then on an impulse, Ruth turned

back to the bed, bent over the railing until her lips almost touched the warm, dry ear, and whispered, 'Wait . . .'

He had briefly considered taking a later ferry just to avoid seeing her, but that wouldn't have accomplished anything. What was he going to do? Get to work and back late for the rest of his life because he'd acted like a jackass in front of some girl he didn't even know. Best thing to do was pretend nothing had happened. Well, nothing *had* happened. *And maybe*, Arnie hoped as he descended the ramp for the return ferry trip, *maybe she didn't realise what a jerk I was being. I think I was pretty smooth, actually, confessing my ignorance and all. Women like that, don't they? When a man confesses a weakness?*

It was 6 p.m. and still daylight. The equinox was coming and a winter of long, cold nights. Only three months ago the sun rose at 4:30 a.m. and set at 10. The two edges of night were slowly squeezing the day so that soon Arnie would be setting off for work and coming home in night darkness. Right now he stood at the centre of a panorama that encircled him completely in wind, snow-draped mountains, slate water, and blue, blue sky. He'd ridden this ferry for thirteen years: why was he only just now, today, noticing the God-given world around him?

He wasn't going to look, he wasn't going to. But he did anyway and this time she didn't stare back. She was sitting in the smoking section again, at the nucleus of a cluster of Indians, all smoking; she was sketching something on an artist's pad on her lap. Arnie stared and stared, almost trying to *will* her to look up, but she didn't and he was disappointed.

So. He'd gone and blown it. By stumbling into her store and blurting his gringo ignorance of what was obviously very important to her. The love affair, as they say, was over.

Thirty agonising minutes later the ferry sounded its horn: one long, two short. From the speakers a voice blared: 'Attention! Now arriving Winslow, Bainbridge Island.' Arnie joined the rest of the tired and hungry Bainbridges in the stern and hurried up the ramp to the parking lot in hopes of getting a head start.

He was sitting behind the wheel, buckled in and ready to

go, when he caught sight of her again; and then he sat, helplessly, and watched her come through the crowd, walk over to her car, throw her purse inside, and get in behind the wheel. If she saw him she gave no indication.

Ah well, thought Arnie with the same sort of resignation as when he gave in to Ruth. It wouldn't have amounted to anything anyway. Time to get back to reality.

And then he saw that she was having trouble starting her car.

He watched her get out and lift the hood and stare down into the engine; then he decided, on an impulse, to act.

'Need some help?' he asked, walking to her car and instantly regretting his rash move. Arnie didn't know the first thing about automobiles.

She straightened, wiped her hands on an old towel, and smiled apologetically. 'I'm afraid this happens all the time.'

He gave the motor a masculine look-over, as if he knew what he was doing, and said, 'You know what the problem is?'

'I'm afraid so. And it means getting towed.'

'Ah,' he said as he stepped back while she slammed the hood down. 'Well, I imagine there's a phone in that bar over there.' He pointed to Hall Brothers, where many ferry regulars unwound on Friday afternoons.

Tossing her long black hair off her shoulders, she said, 'I'll have to call my brother but he won't be at the gas station for another two hours.' She frowned at the car. 'And it'll be dark then. I guess I can leave it here and come back with him tomorrow.' Then she raised her eyes, eyes which made Arnie think of tiger's-eye gemstones.

He almost missed his cue. 'Oh! Can I give you a lift?'

'If it's not out of your way.'

'Not at all,' he said effusively. 'Where do you live? Kitsap?'

A faint smile played on her lips. 'No, right here on Bainbridge Island.'

Arnie blushed until he could have died. 'Oh, of course. I didn't mean –'

She laughed and went around to the driver's side. 'It's all right. Most of us do live on the reservation.'

After she retrieved her purse and sweater and made sure the Volvo was locked, she followed Arnie back to his station wagon. Getting in, she said, 'Oh, you have children.'

He scowled at the profusion of toys in the back seat. Tell her this is a friend's car and that you're really a bachelor playboy. 'Yes, I have five kids.'

'I love large families,' she said, snapping the buckle of her safety belt. Arnie had to fight to keep his eyes straight ahead. The way the shoulder strap pressed down between her breasts . . .

'I come from a large family,' she said as the motor chugged to life. 'And some of them do still live on the reservation. My oldest brother owns his own gas station, and my two younger brothers are with the fishing fleet. My little sisters are at Kitsap High School.'

As Arnie manoeuvred the big station wagon out of the lot he cast about for something to say, something that sounded caring without being nosy, witty without being cloddish. Was it okay to ask an Indian what tribe she came from? 'What a surprise, running into you at the gallery,' he said lamely. 'Do you own it?'

'Oh no. It's a cooperative. All the artists contribute to its operation. Some of us work there full time.'

'Us? Are you an artist?'

'I'm more of an *artisan*. I created the pot you were looking at today.'

Arnie's mind launched into action. What *was* the name on the bottom of that pot? 'You're Angeline?'

'The *famous* Angeline.' she said with a laugh.

'It's a beautiful name.'

'I was named for Chief Seattle's daughter, Princess Angeline.'

The city of Seattle was named after an Indian? How could he have lived here for thirteen years and not known that? Arnie clamped his mouth shut and nodded knowingly. His ignorance, he just knew, would appal her.

They rode in silence a short distance, both staring out of the window. The foxglove was no longer blooming but the tall green stalks still lined the roads. In fact there weren't too many flowers out at all any more, just a tapestry of amazing greens that would soon turn miraculously overnight to reds and golds.

'I'm on High School Road,' Angeline said finally, and Arnie thought he detected a note of awkwardness in her voice. Or was he imagining it? Was he only wishing that she were as affected by him as he was by her?

High School Road. Arnie's heart sank. They would soon be there. Now what? Say something. Now that it's started, keep it going. Now that *what's* started? Keep *what* going?

'So, where do you make your pots?' That's suave, Arnie, really suave.

'In my apartment. Instead of a kitchen table I have a potter's wheel. It's messy but it's a convenient excuse for not entertaining! And there's a kiln at the back of the gallery that we all use.'

Arnie saw it all: the modest apartment sparsely decorated with Indian handicrafts, the clay-dusted kitchen, and Angeline at her wheel, a smock covering her small body, her swimming brown eyes intent on the creation rising up between her slender fingers. *An excuse for not entertaining.* He saw the lonely, solitary evenings...

'What do you do?' Angeline asked.

'I'm an accountant. And my name's Arnie, by the way.' He took one hand off the wheel and held it out. A cool, dove-gentle hand glided into it and rested there.

She said, 'Pleased to meet you, Arnie the Accountant,' and then a minute passed in which nothing was said but the hands remained joined. Finally, withdrawing from his clasp, Angeline said, 'Here's where I live.'

Arnie slowed the car and let it roll to a stop. Angeline lived in a large apartment complex that admitted only people with low incomes. They sat for a moment in unsettled silence – she seemed in no hurry to hop out – until Angeline said at last, 'Thank you for the ride.'

'It was my pleasure.' Trying to loosen up, he shifted slightly in his seat, but could go only as far as the restraining safety belt would allow (would it be too obvious if he unbuckled it?). 'I hope your brother can fix your car.'

'Oh, he will. You can practically set your calendar by that car's breakdowns.'

'It's a good make though, Volvo.'

'Yes, but that one has seen too many miles. Over a hundred and fifty thousand.'

'No kidding.' Arnie had never noticed before how intimate this station wagon was. With Angeline sitting just two feet from him along the bench seat, filling the small space with her dusky beauty and faint perfume, Arnie felt himself stir with long-dead, unaccustomed feelings. 'Well, then it's handy to have a brother in the car repair business, isn't it?'

'Yes it is.'

Another silent minute passed. Arnie grew anxious. She was going to get out, she would have to. 'I really did like that pot.'

'You did?'

'Yes, and I really would like to buy it except that...'

'It's too expensive.'

He reddened.

Angeline laughed. She did that a lot, Arnie noticed. 'Everything in that gallery is expensive! *I* wouldn't be able to shop there! But what price *can* you put on an artist's skill and labour and long hours?'

'Oh, it's not that I don't think it's worth it –'

'I know.' Angeline reached down and unsnapped her safety belt. 'But it *is* a lot of money.'

Foolishly, Arnie wanted this to go on for ever, sitting in front of this low-income apartment complex in his toy-cluttered station wagon talking with the beguiling Angeline. 'You said you had smaller pieces at the gallery?' Very cunning, Arnie Roth. An excuse to go back. And then maybe ask her to lunch...

She gazed at him with those incredible eyes for a second, then her cheeks dimpled in a deep smile. 'I'm afraid those are expensive, too. But I tell you what. We have to raise the prices on items in the gallery to cover our expenses and pay the rent and give the artists a profit, but I have some very nice pieces in my apartment that are a lot less expensive. You are welcome to take a look at them...'

Arnie sat dumbfounded. Had he heard right? Was she actually inviting him up to her apartment?

'I often sell my stuff out of my home,' Angeline continued.

'It's the only way I am able to move my work. If I'm lucky I sell four pieces a year at the gallery. It's what I sell out of my apartment that's my bread and butter.'

Arnie crashed back to earth. And to reality. *Middle-aged men can get into a lot of trouble misreading young ladies' signals.* Looking at his watch, he said, 'I'd like to see what you have, but I have to get home.'

Angeline fumbled inside her purse and withdrew a business card with cockled edges. 'Here. Keep this in case you ever find time.'

Arnie took it. *Angeline. Native American Art.* And a telephone number. Very professional, very businesslike.

Arnie sighed. There's no fool like a forty-eight-year-old fool. 'Actually, I need a present for tomorrow. The party's tomorrow night...' He did some rapid thinking. Tonight was Ruth's support group. She'd be gone all evening. And it *was* his last opportunity to buy her a gift. 'Will you be home later?' he asked, sliding the card into his wallet.

'I'm in all evening tonight. If you want to drop by, feel free. I'm in 30.'

'I might do that.'

She smiled again, but not so deeply this time, or confidently. Shyly, Arnie thought. As though she, too...

'Thanks for the ride, Arnie,' she said softly, reaching for the door handle.

'It's getting dark. I should walk you to your door.'

'That's not necessary. These people are my friends. Good night. See you later, maybe.'

It had been years since Arnie Roth had felt, well, so *damn dumb.* What did he think he was doing? Making a fool of himself in front of a girl he barely knew – *a girl who was young enough to be his daughter!* She was probably enjoying a good laugh right now at the short, balding Anglo getting all blushy and nervous over her. She was probably hoping to sucker him into buying ten pots, enough to pay a month's rent on her apartment, then share a good laugh with the other artists!

Arnie brought the car into his driveway, turned off the motor, and stared ahead through the windshield at the big tree with the tyre-swing dangling. No, Angeline wasn't like that at all. He was being unkind to her just to save himself, to stop himself from making the world's biggest blunder.

There was no way he was going there tonight.

He opened the front door and called out into the house. There was no response. Where was everyone?

Wearily removing his jacket and loosening his tie, Arnie flipped through the mail he had picked up off the floor.

Yes, he was being unfair to Angeline. She was a struggling artist hoping to sell her pottery, and living in an apartment where the only requirement to get in was that you be poor. It wasn't her fault his curiosity about her had blossomed into a full-fledged adolescent crush. Why should she lose a sale just because Arnie Roth was confused? Besides, he *did* have to get a present for Ruth.

He'd go later, after he'd fed the girls.

'Hey!' he called out, heading for the kitchen. 'Where is everyone?'

Maybe even take one of the girls with him. Rachel liked ceramics. She'd be interested. *I'll take her along to make sure I don't make a further mess of myself.*

He stopped in the cold, dark kitchen.

But then... What if Angeline had the same thing on her mind as he had on his and here he was dragging his thirteen-year-old daughter with him?

Arnie tried to discipline his thoughts. It was almost seven o'clock. He'd never before come home to an empty house at this hour. No lights on. No TV going. Where were the girls?

*Angeline. Maybe I'll go later, alone...*

He tried to think, to remember. Had Ruth told him the girls were going somewhere after school and he'd forgotten? But the pets were prowling the backyard making hunger noises. Ruth always made arrangements for them.

How late could he go to Angeline's?

Where *was* everyone?

When the phone rang Arnie thought for one crazy moment that it was Angeline. But that was impossible. She didn't know his number or his last name.

It was Ruth. 'Arnie, Dad just died. I'm at the hospital with Mom. No, don't come. No need for you to. Hannah has the girls over at her house. Mort collected them from school. They'll spend the night there.' Her voice broke. 'I have to stay here a little while and make arrangements. Then I'm bringing Mom home. She's hysterical, Arnie. Oh, God . . .'

After he hung up Arnie walked to the glass door that led to the back porch. He saw the image of a silly man in the glass, a man who was losing his hair and his shape and his senses. A man who had, a short while before, lived a brief Walter Mitty dream but who now saw that dream shatter into a thousand pieces, like a red-clay pot crashing to the floor.

# Chapter Thirty-two

With a USA retractor in one hand and the fibreoptic light in the other, Mickey lifted up the breast and inspected the chest wall underneath. 'I think it's dry,' she murmured to the scrub nurse standing across the operating table. 'Let's give it a rinse.'

Using a large bulb syringe, Mickey filled the newly created breast pocket with antibiotic solution, vacuumed it all out with the rubber suction tubing, then, using a damp gauze on the end of a long tonsil clamp, did a mop-up around the entire inside breast circumference. The sponge came out clean. 'Okay,' she said, laying her instruments down on the magnetic mat draped across the patient's abdomen. 'No bleeding. I'll take the prosthesis now.'

The prosthesis was a soft pad of silicone gel that looked like a large, transparent vitamin pill. Making sure one last time that this was the size she needed, and the same size as the implant already in the other breast, Mickey rinsed off the prosthesis in the bowl of bacitracin and began gently feeding it into the cavity beneath the breast. As the implant went in, filling out the chest space with a soft swell of bosom, Mickey said to the other nurse in the room, 'Check her blood pressure, Mildred. Is the Jobst bra ready?'

'Yes, Dr Long.'

Mickey was pleased. The operation was going well. Soon she would be off for the weekend with Harrison, the weekend they had planned for so long and which she was looking forward to. Christmas in Palm Springs!

After the subcutaneous stitch was in, Mickey threw a buried nylon suture along the two-inch incision, which was at the base of the breast and would scarcely be detectable, then washed the blood off the entire chest. 'Carolyn!' she said loudly, sharply. 'Carolyn, wake up! Surgery's over!'

The patient, a young woman who had been sleeping, rolled her head, fluttered her eyes and mumbled thickly. 'When're you gonna start, Doctor...?'

'It's over, Carolyn. We're all finished.'

'You mean...' Her chest rose and fell in deep sighs as she climbed to consciousness. 'You mean... I have *boobs*.'

Mickey laughed. 'Yes, Carolyn, you have boobs.'

'Nice work, Dr Long,' said the scrub nurse after the patient was wheeled into a private recovery room. 'She's going to be a knockout.'

Carolyn West was the last surgery for the day, now it was afternoon and there were patients to see. This was Mickey's office; she did most of her surgery here. Cases of grander proportion, such as breast or thigh reduction, or instances where the patient wasn't comfortable with the idea of office surgery, Mickey worked over at St John's Hospital, which was just down the street on Wilshire Boulevard.

She had been in this office for three years, ever since she and Harrison had moved from Hawaii to Southern California.

The move had represented new beginnings: for Harrison, the selling of Butler Pineapple and the decision to concentrate on his film investments; for Mickey, it was the start of a fresh career – in Santa Monica she would no longer be in competition with the doctors who had trained her. And for the two of them together, it was a laying to rest of a futile dream. After two more years of trying for a baby and failing, Harrison and Mickey had found the stately rooms and halls of Pukula Jau somehow cavernous and mocking. The move had been both a *from* and a *to*, and in the three years since, neither had looked back.

In the small bathroom off her office, Mickey stripped off her blue surgery clothes and slipped into slacks and sweater: she looked at her wristwatch. In three and a half hours she and Harrison would be off for their weekend in Palm Springs.

She paused to look at herself in the mirror. In the cold wash of glary light she examined her right cheek. Yes, there were the faint outlines, the slight discolouration, the ghost of

345

the demon skilfully exorcised by Chris Novack – how many years ago? *Sixteen years ago.*

'I was twenty-one years old...'

Mickey had run into Chris Novack three years ago, shortly after she and Harrison had moved to Southern California, at a plastic surgery seminar at the Beverly Wilshire Hotel. His hair had thinned and he'd put on a lot of weight; but even more dramatic than that had been the change in his eyes. The light had gone out of them. That had both stunned and saddened Mickey, to see Chris Novack looking and acting like a second-rate imitation of himself. Where had the spark gone? What had sapped him of his energy? After his pioneering work in port-wine stains, Chris had moved on to cleft palate repair but had, at some early stage, either dropped the ball or lost track of the score. Something had gone out of him; mediocrity and complaisance had invaded his veins, like an indomitable virus, so that today he had a nice, comfortable practice out in the Valley, fixing noses for the insurance money.

*Chris, what did it to you?*

A tap on the door announced the arrival of the first patients. 'I put Mr Randolph in One, Mickey,' came Dorothy's voice on the other side of the door. 'And Mrs Witherspoon is in Two.'

'Thanks, Dorothy, I'll be right there.'

Stopping first in her office for pen and prescription pad, she noticed the fresh pile of mail Dorothy had left on the desk; Mickey would go through it after she was all done with her patients.

This was it, what she needed, just what the doctor ordered; bullet-speeding along the Indio Freeway with the beams of the Mercedes devouring the blacktop ahead and the taillights leaving a scarlet wake behind. Times like this, Mickey wished they owned a convertible so she could pull her hair loose and throw her head back and challenge the stars overhead and really *feel* the sixty-five miles per hour. Instead, Mickey pushed a button that lowered her window to admit the perfumed desert night air, pushed a button to turn on the tape deck, pushed another button to fast-forward to the beginning of the movement, and lastly pushed a button to recline her seat slightly. As the melancholy arms of Beethoven reached out and embraced her, Mickey closed her eyes and gave up totally.

What exactly had the letter done to her? She wasn't sure. She should be happy right now, she had expected to be, had *planned* on being happy, so it was a bit of a disappointment to discover that, after all, she was not. Mickey and Harrison had planned this for months – a weekend in the desert, staying at the best room of the Erawan Gardens, dinner at Fideglio's, a romantic ride up to the San Jacinto summits by skyway, the big Christmas party at the Racquet Club. Away from patients and telephones. Alone with Harrison, who still, after seven years of marriage, made life so, so special. Mickey's excitement had mounted as she'd got through her afternoon patients, dictated orders, cleared the charts off her desk and left everything in the capable hands of Dr Tom Schreiber, her partner.

It was only at the last minute that she sifted quickly through the pile of mail on her desk – mostly thank-you notes from patients, invitations to parties, and medical updates – and came across the flimsy blue airmail envelope with Kenya stamps on it.

*Sondra,* she'd thought initially. *I haven't heard from her since, well, a card last Christmas and a letter some time in the year before that.*

But no, it wasn't from Sondra. The address hadn't been written in Sondra's hand and the return address was headed by the name of the Reverend Mr Sanders.

Mickey had stood holding the letter a long time, staring down at it, inexplicably fearful, almost feeling with her fingertips the unwanted message inside. She'd briefly considered leaving it until Monday but air letters are like jangling telephones – impossible to ignore. So Mickey had finally slit it open and brought out not one, but two letters.

The first was signed by the Reverend Mr Sanders and was a scant few lines:

'My dear Dr Long: As Mrs Farrar is unable to write for herself I took down the enclosed missive at her dictation. We are not on the telephone, so should you wish to reach us you can do so by calling Voi Hospital at Voi-7, who will then pass along your message to us by wireless.'

Then Mickey had opened the second letter, found it to be longer than the first, and taped at the bottom of it . . . a photograph . . .

'Honey?' came Harrison's voice. It was accompanied by the reassuringly familiar touch of his hand over hers. 'A million dollars for your thoughts.'

Mickey lifted her head and smiled at him. Southern California living had turned out to be good for Harrison; at sixty-eight he was handsomer, sturdier, and more virile than ever. It was a good decision they'd made to come here, even though Mickey had at first protested – the move had mainly been for her; but Mickey was now glad she'd given in. With new friends and new interests for Harrison, and a new medical practice for Mickey, there was no time, no need to dwell on that old subject any more. Wisely, they'd capitulated and left the unanswered dream of babies back on Lanai.

'Are you thinking good thoughts?' he asked gently, squeezing her hand.

'I was thinking about Sondra. I'm sorry, Harrison,' she said, laying her other hand over his. 'I know I promised to leave doctor work behind, but this is different.'

He nodded in understanding. Mickey had shown him the photograph. 'What have you decided to do?'

'I believe Sam Penrod is going to be at the Christmas party Sunday night. He's one of the best hand-men in the country. I'm going to ask him if he'll take her on.'

'You mean you're not going to do it yourself?'

'I don't think I should. Her injuries were extensive. They might be beyond what I can do.'

In her letter, Sondra had said: 'I'm asking *you*, Mickey, because I believe in you. But if for some reason you can't, then I shall go to Arizona. My parents don't know about this yet. I'm waiting until it's all over. Why add their nightmares to my son's?'

And then there was the photograph inside the letter. Two badly scarred and twisted claws that had once been hands, lying on a white background. Hideous hands, the kind one

348

does indeed see in nightmares. 'There is a thick contractile scar over the dorsum of the left hand, with loss of extensor tendons of the second and third fingers. The right hand has cicatricial contractures of all fingers. Prolonged immobilisation in hyperextension after initial grafting was done has caused shortening of the collateral ligaments. Both hands are completely useless.'

There had been a fire, Sondra had said in her letter, six months ago, from which she had suffered burns to her hands. After emergency treatment at Voi Hospital, she'd been taken to a major hospital in Nairobi where infection had been controlled and skin grafting attempted. According to the photograph, the operations had not succeeded as hoped.

Mickey turned away from Harrison and settled her eyes on the desert blackness swimming past the car: palm trees against star-washed ink, jagged mountains standing asteroid-like at the distant edge of flatness, and silence, silence. As the second movement reached its *allegretto* crescendo, Mickey closed her eyes again and returned to the letter.

'I have money enough for the airfare to California and back,' Sondra had said. 'The Reverend will see that I am boarded properly in Nairobi and that the stewardesses know what to do for me, but I shall need assistance at the other end – if I may ask this one imposition of you. Roddy will stay here in the care of the mission.'

A sparse letter that was little more than a catalogue of declarative sentences. It read probably as Sondra had dictated it – dully, bluntly, starkly. 'They did their best in Nairobi. I don't blame them. I wouldn't pursue this at all were it not for the fact that I am a burden on others. I cannot comb my own hair or hold a teacup or touch my son's face. They told me in Nairobi that it is hopeless, that my hands are beyond saving. So anything at all that can be done for me, Mickey, will be appreciated eternally.'

Sondra. How long had it been? The wedding, seven years ago, when Mickey had brought Ruth and Sondra to Lanai to stand up with her at the altar. What a happy, fleeting reunion that had been, dredging up the old memories, a brief uniting of the old threesome they had once been at Castillo. How they had pushed Mickey to letting Chris Novack experiment on her, secretly flushing her C –over down the toilet in the middle of the night! Where did it go, that special three-ness? How had time and events managed to insinuate themselves wedge-like between the three friends and slowly press them apart, causing the letters and phone calls, so frequent in the early years of separation, to slow, so that all that was left now was a precious memory?

*That's* what the letter had done to Mickey, it had lifted the lid off an old attic trunk and showed her the stale, neglected contents inside: her first real, conditional friendship with someone else; the beginning of the long road that brought her to this hour, in this car, with this man. The letter had reminded Mickey of things long forgotten, almost lost.

But not totally lost, she thought now as the Seventh Symphony switched to a lively *presto. I've been too busy, too all consumingly involved in my own life these past three years. I'd forgotten . . .*

'I'm going to write to her at once,' she said to Harrison as the Mercedes sailed down the Indian Wells off-ramp. 'I'm going to tell her she can come and stay with us until we get her situated somewhere. That's all right with you, isn't it, Harrison?'

'You know it is.'

'I think I'll write to Ruth as well. I haven't heard from her since I don't know when. Maybe she can take some time off and come down for a visit. It would do Sondra good, I'm sure.'

Mickey smiled, feeling better. Then, with a slight frown, she remembered Derry and realised Sondra hadn't mentioned him. Was he coming with her or staying at the mission?

It was one of those glamorous events where the stars in the crowd outnumbered the ones in the sky. Mickey enjoyed nodding acquaintance with quite a few, mainly through Harrison who, after selling Butler Pineapple to Dole, had turned his money and ingenuity to high-tech investing that brought him into a select, elite circle. But there were some luminaries with whom Mickey had become acquainted on her own, as their face-fixer and youth-conjurer. Like the

female rock singer who was currently the highest-paid
entertainer in Las Vegas: she owed her famous narrow waist
to Mickey's skilful removal of the lower ribs and a tricky
skin-tuck. Several tight faces above the Galanos gowns were
Mickey's doing; her signature could also be seen on the
chiselled nose of a US senator's wife.

It was a gala evening that would be written up the next day
in all the newspapers; a 'must' event that drew guests who
wanted to be seen, who needed to be seen, and who all could
profit from the positive publicity, simply because this was no
ordinary Christmas party but a charity benefit for the raising
of funds for Alzheimer's Disease, and the evening was
dedicated to Rita Hayworth, one of its tragic victims.

The catering was by Cloud, the music came from four
alternating bands, the entertainment was co-hosted by Jack
Lemmon and Gregory Peck, and the forty-foot Christmas
tree was drooping beneath the weight of hundreds of snow-
white donation envelopes. After a traditional dinner of roast
goose and plum pudding, during which comedians enter-
tained the guests, there was dancing under the Milky Way,
and mingling and socialising late into the night.

When Mickey sighted Sam Penrod on the other side of the
pool, casually chatting with one of the Gabors, Mickey left
Harrison with the state supreme court justice who had
shared their table during dinner and threaded her way
through the crowd. She heard snatches of conversation along
the way:

'I'm thinking of getting my bottom lifted.'

'Oh my dear, it's *torture*. You have to keep your whole
body straight as a board for two weeks. You can't sit down or
bend even the eensiest bit. I mean, *everything* has to be done
standing up!'

'– give us at least an edge with the five million. But I
warned him that not one penny over budget –'

'– has had the goddamned script for three goddamned
months and he isn't returning any of my calls. I swear, if that
bastard is thinking of pirating –'

'– all three wearing the same gown! You should have seen
it! Of course, *hers* was the tunic and pants version, but it was
the same white jewelled material by Fabric *and* –'

'Is it true that there are more plastic surgeons per capita in Palm Springs than anywhere else in the world?'

When Mickey reached Sam Penrod he was just turning away with an empty glass in his hand. 'Hello, Sam,' she said, laying a hand on his arm.

'Mickey!' Dr Samuel Penrod was an orthopaedic surgeon who specialised in the hands and feet of front-page people – sports stars, Olympic medal winners, politicians, actors and actresses, none of whom could risk sacrificing their careers to arthritis, tendonitis, tremors, or palsy. He operated a posh clinic in the desert that was one of the best in the country, and he had also twice, in the past three years, seriously propositioned Mickey. 'Looking gorgeous as ever!' he declared, claiming her hand and squeezing it significantly.

'How are you, Sam? Is business good?'

'Business couldn't be better. As long as ballplayers need to throw a straight ball and actresses have to look like they're gliding instead of walking, I'll always be in business. How about you? Still caught up in the youth-quake?'

She laughed. 'More than ever.'

'Did you get a chance to see the lady I sent to you last week? Mrs Palmer?'

Mickey discreetly extruded her hand from his. 'Yes, but she decided against surgery. I couldn't guarantee there would be no telltale scar afterwards.'

'She used to be very fat, you know. I've known her for years. I play golf with her husband every Wednesday. Anyway, she met a twenty-year-old towel attendant at the club and decided she wants to be a teenager again. I warned her about the rapid weight loss but she ignored me. Now she's got those arms.'

Mickey nodded. She often saw women with Mrs Palmer's problem, wings of loose, flabby skin hanging from the upper arms, due either to age or improper dieting. The problem was, the surgery for removal and tightening left disfiguring scars.

'But hell,' said Sam, taking her hand again. 'Let's not talk business. I suppose you're here with that watchdog of yours?'

'Harrison's here,' she said with a smile. 'Still the same old

Sam, I see. However, business is exactly what I want to talk about.'

Feigning disappointment, Sam Penrod theatrically returned her hand to her and struck a professional pose. From the stage came the strains of 'Around the World in Eighty Days' – tonight's musical theme being movie scores.

'What's the business, Mickey?'

Her silver satin purse hung from her bare shoulder on a long silver chain; she opened it now and brought out Sondra's letter. 'This will explain.'

'Jesus, you really mean it, you really do want to talk business.' With a dramatic sigh, he placed his hand on the small of her back and guided her to a vacant table. After they were seated, Sam read the letter by the flickering torchlight that ringed the area.

He studied the photograph for a while, frowning, then handed it back to Mickey, saying, 'Wow. That's bad luck. A lot of that could probably have been avoided with proper splinting in position of function and extension of the wrists. She doesn't give enough information – what about median nerve and ulnar nerve involvement; was the palmar fascia destroyed; is this contracture due to ischemia of fibrosis or spasms of the intrinsic system?'

'I imagine she thought that could wait till she got here. What do you say, Sam?'

'Why don't you do it, Mickey?'

She blinked at him. 'Me!'

'Sure, you do hands.'

Mickey folded letter and photograph back into her purse. 'Why not try it? You do beautiful work.'

She laughed and slung her purse back onto her shoulder. 'That's very sweet of you, Sam, but I know my limits.'

The band now lapsed into the *Godfather* theme. 'How about a dance?'

'Can I tell my friend you'll take her?'

'Only if you'll give me this dance.'

She stood up and shook her head. 'Still the same old Sam. Can I tell her you'll do it?'

'All right. For you, Mickey, the world. When is she coming?'

'I don't know, as soon as I tell her to, I guess. I'll collect her from the airport and bring her out. Maybe have her stay at my house for a few days first.'

Sam stood and started looking around the milling and dancing crowd with a wolfish eye. There were a few starlets for the picking. 'Just let me know and I'll reserve a room for her.'

'Thanks, Sam,' she said quietly, touching his arm. 'I knew I could count on you.'

'Yeah,' he said mock-sadly. 'That's me, good old Sam,' and he headed off in the direction of a backless sequined gown.

Mickey turned away. She was more relaxed now; she would write to Sondra first thing and tell her the good news. Mickey took a few steps in the direction of her husband and stopped short.

Standing between Mickey and Harrison, in conversation with a few people, was Jonathan Archer.

She stood marble-still, staring at him. This was definitely a day for time travel; first Sondra, now Jonathan.

He was standing with his profile to her, slender and fluid in his black tuxedo, speaking with the secure, insouciant gestures of a man totally in control and aware of his royalty. An older Jonathan – almost fourteen years older – a wiser, calmer, more mature Jonathan. He would be forty-three now and have standing behind him a string of *international* awards, a movie empire, and one of those larger-than-life images. And also, Mickey thought as she slowly walked towards him, three ex-wives.

It was one of the others in the small group, a Beverly Hills lawyer who did business with Harrison, who noticed Mickey's presence and who interrupted Jonathan's soliloquy with: 'Why, Mrs Butler, hello!'

When Jonathan turned to smile at her, Mickey was rocked with an unexpected tremor. 'Hi, Mickey,' he said. His voice seemed to come out of an old dream, an old memory, and she felt her anxiousness mount. *This is how he greets me, after all these years, after I stood him up?* 'Hello, Jonathan.'

'I saw you sitting over there with Sam Penrod. I decided not to intrude.'

What were his sea-blue eyes really saying? What was the unreadable message behind that still boyish smile, after all these years? Mickey relaxed at once. There was nothing there. No malice, no grudge, no regret. Just the easygoing Jonathan of her salad days, a little older, ruddier, a little travelled, and, like Alexander, lamenting the lack of new worlds to conquer.

The others in the small group, picking up obvious signals, murmured their excuses and drifted off, leaving Jonathan and Mickey to stand smiling at one another while the band played.

'How are you, Jonathan?' Mickey asked, marvelling at how easy this was.

'I can't complain. I got there, you know.'

'Yes, I know. I read *Time* magazine.'

'Ooh.' He winced. 'So you know all the sordid scandal.'

Mickey laughed. 'Three divorces don't exactly make you a Bluebeard.'

'And you? Who is Mr Butler?'

'I'm married to that man over there.' She nodded to Harrison, who stood not far away, vigorously agreeing with something Gerald Ford had just said.

'I thought his wife's name was Betty.'

'The other one.'

'Hm. Ask him if he'd like a part in my next picture. I like his looks.'

'So do I.'

'And you, Mickey, did you get there?'

'Yes.'

Their eyes never left one another's face for an instant. They stood close to each other, their voices low in the midst of the hubbub, oblivious to everyone around them.

'Are you ridding the world of deformities, like St Patrick?'

'I like to think I help people, Jonathan. Some of it might be vanity work, but some serious psychological problems can be cured through plastic surgery. I ought to know.'

'And are you happy?'

'Yes, Jonathan, I'm happy.'

His smile deepened. 'I'm going to be in LA for a while. Will you have lunch with me some time soon?'

She felt herself tighten. But that was silly; there was nothing to be afraid of. 'I'd love to. I'd like to hear what you've been up to all these years. Ever since –' She caught herself.

'Ever since the belltower?' Jonathan laughed softly. 'Yes, there's a lot to fill in. But more than that, Mickey, I have a present for you. Something very special, and I want to give it to you in private.'

# Chapter Thirty-three

She was a member of the Suquamish tribe, she liked seafood, her favourite season was autumn, and she'd never been south of the Washington-Oregon border.

Bit by bit, like collecting fallen leaves and pressing them in an album, Arnie was sedulously garnering the scraps and pieces of Angeline's life, little treasured facts that went into forming the precious whole, such as noticing the brand of cigarettes she smoked or that she sometimes carried a Farley Mowat book, or hearing, during one of their innocuous ferry ride conversations, that her little sister was going into nursing school. Things like that. The things that made Angeline.

Since that day last September when he'd *almost* gone to her apartment to buy a pot, Arnie had retreated with all the survival-sense of a turtle that knows instinctively when not to stick its neck out. How close he'd come! What on earth had got into him? 'Your planets must be lined up, Daddy,' all-knowing and sophisticated thirteen-year-old Rachel would say. 'It's either that or midlife crisis.' Rachel picked up talk like that from her mother; all five girls did. They sounded too wise and womanly for their years.

Arnie and Angeline had settled into a comfortable and safe routine, casually waving to one another on the ferry, sometimes sharing a two-minute exchange of vapid dialogue, but in five months their relationship had gone no further than that. He hadn't been able to screw up the courage to invite her somewhere for coffee, or to return to the gallery, or to insinuate himself among the Indians and sit next to her on the boat. And every afternoon, with maddening reliability, her Volvo started up and purred out of the parking lot.

Arnie hoped very much his feelings weren't pinned to his sleeves like badges, that he looked as cool and indifferent as he tried to put on, because she clearly didn't think of him beyond the occasional 'Good morning, Arnie,' or the 'Nice day, isn't it, Angeline?' And what was worse – or maybe better, he could never decide which – was that the staring game was over. Ever since he blundered into the gallery and stuttered about pots and gave her a ride home in a station wagon full of toys... well, clearly the mystique had vanished. Angeline now saw him for what he was and all curiosity had subsided.

So he should be glad. He had no business longing for something to happen between him and this girl, not now, now with these new troubles at home.

He hung back, pretending to be so absorbed in his evening paper that he wasn't aware the mob was descending into the ferry. Arnie didn't pull this every night because that would have been too obvious; once in a while he forced himself – and it really killed him to do it – to push on first with the other tired and hungry Bainbridgers, leaving her back there, because Angeline always got on the ferry last, morning and night, rain or shine. So it was on Arnie to manoeuvre their chance proximities *and* to do it so she wouldn't suspect it was on purpose.

With his nose buried in the *Clarion* Arnie was able to keep a lookout through the corner of his eye. This wasn't easy, it was a skill he'd worked on and perfected over the five months, once almost missing the ferry, another time slamming into the back of a stranger. And he was cold, freezing from the inside out, in this arctic February evening that was all mauves and purples and plums; he would like to deliver himself into the relative warmth of the cabin and exchange body heat with the fifteen hundred other commuters. But he couldn't. Angeline had not been on the ferry the past two days and Arnie had been so worried he'd barely been able to get any work done at the office; but then this morning she'd been there and he'd forgotten himself and had waved energetically at her and *she'd looked right through him* so now he had to reassure himself that their tiny relationship, such as it was, still stood and hadn't collapsed into nonexistence.

'Hello, Arnie. Aren't you going to get on board?'

He jerked his head up and said 'Huh?' before he could

catch himself, and then he felt a summer warmth invade his frosted bones because he was looking into her eyes and dimpled smile. 'Good lord!' He snapped the paper closed and thrust it under his arm. 'I wasn't paying attention!'

As the ferry blatted Arnie realised that he and Angeline were the last ones to board, that they'd almost missed it, and *if they had* what else could they have done but go back inside the terminal for some coffee until the next boat came forty minutes later? Now *that* was something to contemplate – how to finagle that into happening some chilly night.

Angeline went to her usual smoking section and Arnie drifted on, finding a whole row to himself so he could sit and sulk and mentally scold himself.

You're forty-eight years old with a wife and five kids, so get hold of yourself and grow up!

Determined to really read the paper and not think about her, he whipped open the *Clarion* to the page he had minutes ago used as a ruse, and discovered without missing the irony of it that it had been the page of Ruth's column. 'Ask Dr Ruth' was so popular that it was now a daily column instead of weekly, and it took up half the page.

Arnie didn't always read it – the main thrust was usually women's problems – but when he did he was always struck with the curious sense that, lately, this was the only way he and Ruth communicated.

'Dear Dr Ruth, What makes pregnancy test kits work and how reliable are they? Tumwater.'

'Dear Tumwater: The urine of a pregnant woman contains HCG (human chorionic gondaotropin). When a few drops of this urine are added to a test-tube which contains antibodies against HCG, a reaction takes place in the form of a brown ring at the bottom of the test tube. The test is 97 per cent reliable. However, a word of caution: it can also produce false negatives. That is, a negative reading in a woman who is in fact pregnant. The kits advise to start testing on the ninth day after a woman's period was supposed to have started, because that is when the HCG becomes present. At this early stage, however, there is a 25 per cent chance of a false negative. Since the HCG level rises as the pregnancy develops, the later the test is done, the more reliable the results. In all cases of suspected pregnancy, however, a woman should see a physician. The EPT is no substitute for proper medical care.'

Arnie figured Angeline was about twenty-five or twenty-six. Why wasn't she married? Why wasn't she producing babies? Wasn't that tribal tradition, early marriage and big families?

'Dear Dr Ruth, I took up jogging six months ago and have started spotting between periods, usually around the time of ovulation. Is there a connection and, if so, am I causing internal damage? Bremerton.'

'Dear Bremerton: With the increase of women in athletics, new problems have arisen which have heretofore come under little or no scrutiny. "Sports gynaecology" is a fairly new field of study and certain phenomena have been . . .'

Arnie's mind drifted again. What did Angeline do on the weekends? She didn't appear to be the jogging type; he couldn't picture her aerobicising or engaged in any other sweaty endeavour. Did she slave over her potter's wheel day and night? Or did she have a boyfriend to fill her Saturdays and Sundays?

He let the paper fall in his lap. It was no use; no matter what he did he couldn't get her out of his mind.

He settled his eyes on the picture of Ruth at the top of the column and stared at it for some time. *Dear Dr Ruth, Are you aware that your husband has become obsessed with an Indian girl? Bainbridge Island.*

What were they these days, Ruth and Arnie? Were they still husband and wife? It was hard to tell. They slept next to one another in the same big bed, their toothbrushes hung side by side in the bathroom, they shared children that looked a little like each of them, and they filed a joint tax return. But beyond that . . .

When had the sex stopped? Really stopped, not just the slapdash accidental once-in-a-blue-moon that they had lived with for a couple of years, but grinding-halt stopped. *When we finally had that big fight two years ago and I put my foot down and said absolutely no more babies.* Was that all sex was to Ruth, a means to an end? It was almost as if the sole satisfaction she derived from sex was not the act itself but the product that sprang from it.

He raised his head and looked out at the black bay strung with distant city lights. *Maybe snow tonight*. It was cold enough.

They lived in two separate worlds, Ruth and Arnie, he plodding Monday-Tuesday-Wednesday-Thursday-Friday to and from work while Ruth saved lives and delivered babies and wrote an advice column that was becoming the medical Bible of the Olympic Peninsula. And on weekends – Ruth busy writing her column or rushing to the hospital or getting crisis calls from the patients she privately counselled while Arnie sawed his precious logs and took the girls on outings and thought of Angeline.

It was an existence so mundane and routine as to be comfortable; its very predictability was pleasantly opiative, which was why Arnie didn't fight it, didn't want out. The idea of divorce had flown in and out of his head like a bird hurriedly going south. How could he leave his girls? Where would he go? He did still, in his way, love Ruth. And there was his fantasy life, keeping him going. It was an existence almost pleasant in its dullness. Except that, lately, the comfortable mediocrity had undergone a perilous upset and it worried Arnie.

Ruth was changing.

He craned his neck ever so slightly, as if looking back at the boat's wake and searched the cabin reflected in the glass. He couldn't see her.

What on earth was going on with Ruth? It hadn't happened all of a sudden, it had been a gradual, seeping thing, manifesting itself in abrupt gestures, circles under her eyes, ash trays full of half-smoked cigarettes, and finally, the corker, Ruth's announcement that she was going to start seeing a therapist.

That's where she would be tonight, at her weekly three-hour session with Dr Margaret Cummings, no doubt pacing the rug bare and smoking like Bette Davis and spilling it all out – whatever 'it' was. As near as Arnie could judge, it had started somewhere around the time of her father's death.

The letter from Mickey had also triggered something. They barely exchanged Christmas cards, ever since Mickey had been here five years ago, and then all of a sudden came that long letter from Mickey and it had made Ruth . . . *angry*. Now that was a bafflement. Arnie had read it; all she was asking was if Ruth could spare a few days and come down to LA to help give Sondra support, and Ruth had inexplicably gone into a snit, saying things like, 'What does she think I do with my time? Let *her* do the supporting, she's got it to give! Where were they when *I* needed support?' Arnie, not having the faintest idea what she was talking about or why she should be so angry, decided not to say anything and, as usual, clammed up.

*Dear Dr Ruth, Why don't you talk to your husband anymore? Bainbridge Island.*

'Arnie?'

He whipped around. Angeline. Standing there and smiling down at him.

'I hate to do this but you're the only person I know on this boat. I was wondering if I could ask a favour of you.'

What? Pluck the moon out of the sky and have it set in a tiara for you? No problem, I'll have it for you in a jiffy. 'Certainly. Anything.'

'It's my car again. Gosh, I feel so silly, but my brother came and took it today and towed it to his garage to work on it and it isn't ready. I was wondering if I could trouble you for a ride home again . . .'

It was absolutely incredible. Only that morning the imagined vision of Angeline had sat on this very seat in the station wagon and chatted up a storm with a debonair Arnie and now here she really was, and talking just the way she did in his fantasies, only Arnie was too tongue-tied to be debonair so he just concentrated on the driving while Angeline threw a few more crumbs his way to be added to that fact-collection.

'He keeps after me to get a new car, but I just can't afford it. The sales at the gallery aren't paying much so I have to make up for it on weekends. I take my pots to the Pike Street Market and sell to tourists.'

Arnie could hardly contain himself. He didn't know that! How many times did his girls beg him to take them to the Pike Street Market on Sundays?

'I'll have to look for you. I do still intend to buy one of your pots.'

362

Angeline was wearing a quilted down jacket of a pale lavender that was a nice contrast against her straight black hair. Her small hands were bundled in thick mittens and she wore blue jeans and hiking books. Like this, she looked like a teenager, almost as young as Rachel.

They drove in silence for a while, relishing the warmth of the car's interior. Finally, Angeline looked at him and said quietly, 'You know, you look just like Ben Kingsley, the actor.'

Arnie blushed and laughed.

'I'll bet everyone tells you that.'

'No, not a soul.' He took his eyes off the road long enough to look at her, significantly, in silent communication, then he returned to watching out of the windshield and said softly, 'You're the first, Angeline.'

The apartment complex loomed disappointingly soon and Arnie cursed the clock and short roads. Again, like the last time, she seemed in no hurry to get out but lingered a little, as if trying to create the perfect opportunity, and whether she was or not Arnie took one of the few mad plunges in his life. He said quietly, 'Well, I don't care what you say. It's dark out and I feel responsible for you so I'm going to walk you to your door.'

And Angeline said simply, 'All right.'

They stepped over tricycles and across a yard that was once grass but was now frozen dirt and up stairs decorated with ethnic graffiti. A family fight was going on on one side, a TV blasted on the other, and then Angeline's door came too soon and Arnie was once again cursing the swiftness with which the cherished moments passed.

He was about to say, 'Well, good night,' when Angeline, inserting the key in the lock, said, 'Would you like to come in and look at my pottery? I promise not to turn on the hard sell.'

And there he was, stepping into the very room where he had spent half his waking life these past five months. In a way it was just how he imagined it would be, but in another way, not at all.

A poster of sad-eyed Chief Joseph hung on one wall; on another, a framed batik of the familiar Thunderbird-Stealing-the-Sun. A few pieces of native pottery stood about, a feathered peace pipe, very old-looking, topped a doorway, but otherwise Angeline's apartment looked very un-Indian. Aside from the large Madonna statue on the TV set and, in the kitchen, a portrait of Jesus exposing his Sacred Heart, this might be the apartment of any young woman who didn't have a lot of money but who spent it well and wisely and who did clever things with colour and lighting.

After turning on all the lights and closing the front door, Angeline led Arnie into the dining area adjoining the kitchen, shedding as she did so her down jacket to reveal a bulky cable knit sweater and, around her neck, a delicate gold chain with a small crucifix at its end.

'This is where I work,' she said. And it was indeed the mess she'd warned him of: newspapers spread about on the floor, sealed bags of damp clay, unfired pots, straw packing spilling out of crates, the throwing wheel and etching tools strewn over the table.

Picking up a small round bowl incised with a geometrical pattern, Angeline gently placed it in Arnie's cold hands and said, 'This is the kind of thing I sell at the Pike Street Market.'

He turned it over and over in his hands, touching it where she had touched it, drawing her life-force out of it, this object she had created and with which she had once been intimately involved. *I'll buy it, Angeline*, he thought. *I'll buy one for each of my girls, and one for each year I've been married to Ruth, and one for every Shapiro in the state of Washington. I'll buy the whole goddamned lot, Angeline.*

'Would you like some coffee?'

He raised his head. Her look was shy, her voice had been uncertain. 'Yes,' he heard himself say. 'That would be very nice.'

And *then* his brain went into action. *What time is it? Where are the girls right now? Where is Ruth? Oh, that's right. She's going to her therapy session with Dr Cummings so Mrs Colodny will be at the house, like she always is on nights when Ruth doesn't come straight home from the office; Mrs Colodny will watch them and see that they're fed. Just in case, just in case . . .*

The kitchen was painfully small. After he had shed his coat and muffler and moved awkwardly to the edge of the linoleum while she pulled out a Mr Coffee filter and withdrew a can of Hills Brothers from the fridge, Arnie was poignantly aware of how closed-in they both were, the mere inches between them, the air they breathed in common.

He tried to think of something to say but all he could do was watch the movements of her slender hands, those gentle artist's hands, as she scooped out measures of coffee and paused every now and again to toss her silky black hair off her shoulders. It was all he could do to keep himself from reaching out and doing it for her. Running his fingers through that luxurious black hair . . .

'Oh, darn,' she said with a pretty frown. 'I've run out of coffee.' She was holding the Hills Brothers can and trying to jiggle out the last of the grains.

Arnie felt his stomach sink. No coffee, no reason to hang around. Now I put on my coat and lumber to the door –

But Angeline was reaching around the side of the fridge and dragging out a small folding step stool. 'I know I have another can up here somewhere . . .' she said as she opened it out and steadied it before the cupboards.

'Let me get it for you –'

But she was already stepping up.

Arnie filled his eyes with her slender body as she stretched herself up to the top shelf, holding on to the cupboard with one hand and reaching high up with the other. 'Careful –' he said, taking a step towards her.

'I do this all the time,' she said with a laugh. 'I'm very stable.' And then she slipped and she fell and he instinctively reached out and caught her and Angeline was suddenly in his arms and laughing and getting her balance on her own two feet.

But then she didn't move. They just stood there in the miniscule kitchen, Arnie with his arms still around her, Angeline with her head against his chest. An unseen clock ticked somewhere and the fridge hummed noisily and someone next door slammed out of his apartment and climbed down the stairs.

Then Arnie laid his cheek on Angeline's head and inhaled the sweet fragrance of her silky hair. He felt her hands creep up and go around his neck and then at last they were kissing.

It all happened so suddenly that Arnie didn't have time to wonder if it was real or if he was imagining it again.

The kissing was urgent right from the start, as though a cork had been pulled and a lot of bottled-up love and need and hunger had been released from both of them. Arnie was suddenly aware of the time – *there was so little of it* – and all he could think of was all the things he wanted to say to her and do with her and *there just wasn't enough time*.

Long pent-up thoughts and feelings broke from them as their mouths came away and came together, as their bodies found each other's contours and comfortable places and exciting places. 'I've dreamed about this, Arnie –' 'Oh, Angeline, I didn't think you even knew –' 'I was always so afraid I'd make a fool of myself with you, Arnie –' 'I can't believe this is happening –'

She was so small, so light, she came up into his arms like a doll. She clung to his neck and they kissed as he carried her across the living room to the sofa.

And at last Arnie Roth wasn't concerned with time any more, not at all.

# Chapter Thirty-four

Doctors don't cry. That's what the training is for, the hard-knocks school they go to, to have their tender hides tanned so that when they come face to face with the tragic and the pathetic, they don't break down like ordinary people do. However, on this drizzly April night as the antique clock on the mantel ticked away the last hours of the day, Mickey found herself coming perilously close to doing just that.

Aware of the effect she was having on her friend, Sondra kept her movements to a minimum so as not to spotlight the two big bulky lobster paws at the ends of her arms. She always wore bandages even though her hands were completely healed because, as she explained to Mickey at the airport, 'People accept bandages, no matter how extensive, but deformed flesh is repugnant.'

Everyone on the British Airways flight had been helpful, and going through customs at LA Airport, Sondra had been given special consideration. Immediately on the other side, Harrison and Mickey had been there to pick up her one suitcase and lead her swiftly through the exit to the limousine. Harrison had been wonderfully charming, embracing her and treating her like visiting royalty. He was now tactfully sequestered in his study while Mickey and Sondra were getting reacquainted in the living room.

This was Mickey's house, a half-timbered Tudor set back from Camden Drive in Beverly Hills, a large and beautiful house filled with antiques and pieces of oriental and Polynesian artwork that the Butlers had brought with them from Pukula Hau. Mickey and Sondra were drinking tea out of large coffee mugs instead of the usual delicate china teacups because Sondra had to use her clumsy hand-bundles like pincers.

'I can eat without help, but I don't like anyone to watch me – I make an awful mess,' Sondra said now, wedging the cup between the two bandaged lumps and bringing it to her lips. 'But I have the dickens of a time washing myself and dressing myself and going to the bathroom. I'm as helpless as a baby. That's why I decided to try for the surgery, to see if I can make myself less of a burden on people.' She replaced the mug on the coffee table. 'Actually, I should be thankful I have even limited ability. In Nairobi they wanted to amputate my hands but I wouldn't let them.'

Mickey was having a difficult time swallowing. Sondra's story was just too much to take in all at once – losing her husband and her unborn baby as well as her hands.

'I'm doing this for Roddy. The first time he saw my hands he screamed. I frighten him and he won't let me touch him. I think he feels responsible. You see, just before the crash Roddy had caused some trouble at the mission, in all innocence of course. He caused a little boy to get bitten by a rat, and so Derry had to go off at once to Nairobi for the rabies vaccine. Roddy senses that he is somehow the cause of all this.'

Mickey turned towards the heavy drapes covering the lead-paned windows and thought she could hear, over the crackle of the fire in the fireplace, the incipient fall of April rain in the garden outside.

'I wanted to die at first,' Sondra said quietly. 'I didn't speak for weeks. I don't recall much about that time. The plane burst into flames and I ran to it, thinking I could pull Derry out. An explosion flung me back. It was a miracle, they all said, that my face wasn't burned as well. My hands looked like two steaks that had been left too long on the grill. They were black and peeling with bits of pink flesh showing underneath.'

While she spoke, with the soft British accent she had picked up at the mission, Sondra kept her gaze down on the imperial yellow carpet. 'The infection was the worst of it. They did a wonderful job in Nairobi. They wouldn't let me die even though I begged them to. And then, when I started to come round and I thought of my little boy, that for Derry I must live for Roddy, and I no longer wanted to die, that was when the grafts were failing and they wanted to cut my hands off.'

Sondra leaned forward and started to reach for her mug, then, changing her mind, leaned back. Mickey had to resist the impulse to pick it up for her and raise it to Sondra's lips. She tried to think of something to say. It was all so tragic, so awkward. In one way, Sondra who had offered Mickey the loan of her clothes that first day in Tesoro Hall. But in another, perverse way, Sondra was a stranger, a frightening, intimidating stranger, and Mickey couldn't think of a thing to say to her. 'Sam Penrod is one of the best doctors in the country,' she said at last.

Sondra looked at her. 'But you'll be there, too?'

'Of course I will. I'll visit every day.'

'I mean during surgery.'

'Let me see what Sam says.'

Sondra nodded.

'He really is very good,' said Mickey quickly. 'I've seen some of his results.'

Sondra nodded again.

Mickey stared into those unblinking amber eyes and felt a small tremor of alarm. How stable *was* Sondra? On the surface she appeared calm, accepting, and it had been nine months since the tragedy, nine months to learn to cope with it. But was she coping? What if Sondra's surface were but a thin veneer and inside she was frail and on the brink of collapse? How much was Sondra expecting from Sam Penrod, what miracles was she imagining? *What if he fails?*

Now, for the first time, Mickey allowed herself to look directly at Sondra's hands. Like parcels containing bad luck they lay in Sondra's lap: wrapped from elbow down, widening layers of white gauze that looked like two big, unlit torches. Mickey felt her anxiety mount. What was underneath all that swath; what nightmare was Sondra hiding?

'What will you do?' Mickey asked suddenly. 'Afterwards. Will you go back to the mission?'

'Yes,' came the firm answer. 'My life is there. Roddy is there. And Derry is still there. That's why I haven't told my parents about this. They would insist we go to live with them

369

in Phoenix and I wouldn't be able to take that, being treated like an invalid. I want to continue my work. Mickey,' Sondra leaned forward and said earnestly, *I want to go back to practising medicine.'*

The patter of spring rain beyond the windows grew insistent; a pocket of heat in the fireplace popped and shot sparks up the chimney.

Sondra shifted to the edge of her chair. Her voice was passionate, her look, intense. 'Mickey,' she said. 'Derry was my life. He was all I wanted, all I lived for. I found in him the end of my wandering. With Derry I felt as if I had come home. There is no anodyne for my pain; my every fibre weeps for Derry. And I confess there were days, dark, terrible days when I wanted to leave this world and join Derry. But now I know what I have to do. I have to continue his work. I have to carry on what Derry started at the mission. His death must not have been in vain, Mickey. I have to live for Derry, and for our son.'

Sondra paused briefly, then she leaned forward, stretched out a bandaged hand, and rested it on Mickey's knee. 'Mickey,' she said. 'I want you to do the surgery. I want *you* to restore my hands to me.'

'I can't,' whispered Mickey.

'Why not? I remember that you did a lot of hand work back in Hawaii.'

'I've done very little since.' Mickey returned Sondra's hand to her and stood. Walking to the fireplace where a small portrait of Jason Butler stood in a pewter frame, she picked up the poker and stirred the glowing logs. Then she set the poker down and turned to face Sondra. 'It's been a long time since I've done anything like that, like reconstructing hands. I got away from it somehow. I do a lot of face work, and breasts. It wasn't intentional, Sondra, but my practice has become mainly cosmetic.'

Sondra regarded her friend with a long, considering look. Then she said, 'Yes, I understand. We've all changed, haven't we?' She sighed. 'All right, I'll let Sam Penrod do it. Now, will you look at them?' Sondra lifted up her bandaged hands.

Mickey crossed the room to a cherry wood drum table in

the corner. From out of its small drawer she withdrew a pair of blunt scissors; she came back, pulled up a petit point footstool, sat on it, and calmly took one of Sondra's claws into her hands. The scissors trembled as they snipped the gauze. Mickey didn't want to look, she didn't want to see. As a doctor who had spent the last thirteen years immersed in the complexities of stubborn human flesh and the grotesque aspects it can assume, as a plastic surgeon whose clinical eye had looked upon the worst and the best of the visible human condition, Mickey Long Butler knew that nothing, nothing she had beheld in the past was going to come close to this.

Sondra's hands.

'Are you familiar with the Barnacle?' Jonathan had asked over the phone.

Yes, Mickey was familiar with it. Ever since Venice had undergone a renovation, displacing the winos and warehouses with elegant condos, the affluent class had 'discovered' this stretch of beach and boardwalk between Santa Monica and Marina Del Rey. It had been converted into a playground of bike paths, pretzel vendors, roller skaters, and classy little sidewalk cafés that served tepid food at outrageous prices. The Barnacle was a block from the pier.

It had taken them four months to get together, not because of any reluctance on either side but simply due to conflicting schedules: when Jonathan was available Mickey wasn't, and vice versa. It was reminiscent of the old days, back when trying to synchronise schedules had been a big obstacle in their relationship. They had actually laughed about it over the phone.

Mickey hoped they would laugh today, that this was going to be nothing more than a pleasant lunch between two old friends, catching up on the years, dipping into the memories and bringing out only the good ones.

He was already there, sitting at one of the small round tables in the fenced area in front of the Barnacle. Whenever Mickey had been here before, she and Harrison had had to sit on a bench and wait for their name to be called, often waiting for up to an hour, while enjoying the people-watching. The Barnacle was always crowded on weekends, usually with

371

patrons who arrived in Porches and Ferraris; today it was as deserted as the beach and boardwalk, and Jonathan was sitting all alone.

'Hi, am I late?' she asked, coming around the wrought-iron railing.

He jumped to his feet. 'No, I was early.' Jonathan looked younger this morning than he had at the Christmas party. He was wearing jeans and a blue cambric work shirt, clothes which drew Mickey back fourteen years to St Catherine's when he'd hauled a camera around on his shoulder. He reached for her hand. 'Mickey,' he said softly.

As she sat down at the small table she saw a package lying on the checkered tablecloth, beautifully wrapped in gold foil and silver ribbon. He had said he had a present for her but she hadn't somehow thought he meant it in the material sense. But then, Mickey didn't know exactly *what* she had expected.

'I've ordered a carafe of Chablis,' he said, taking the seat opposite her. 'I hope that's all right.'

'No patients, if that's what you're wondering. Tuesdays are my hospital surgery days, no office patients.'

'So you're free,' he said quietly, his blue eyes studying her face.

Mickey was relieved when the wine came; it gave her something to do with her hands. 'Are you back in LA for good?'

'No, I go back to Paris next month, when my next film goes into production.'

She felt herself relax a little. Mickey had to admit that she had been apprehensive about this luncheon with Jonathan, and she had slept fitfully the night before, waking with misgivings. On the surface it seemed perfectly normal to see him – two old friends getting together after all these years. But below that surface churned unpleasant currents. She and Jonathan had been more than friends once, and they had not, after all, parted on the best of terms. She had found herself asking a thousand questions: *What does he want? After all these years, why now? And what is this gift he mentioned? Am I afraid to see him again? Am I afraid of him, or am I afraid of myself?*

'I thought of looking you up, over the years,' he said now, slowly turning his wineglass by the stem. 'I was even in Hawaii once, looking for a location for *Starhawks!* I came this close to marching into Great Victoria and saying hi.' He grinned and the skin at the corners of his blue eyes crinkled. 'And then I decided maybe it wasn't such a good idea.'

Mickey turned her face seaward. What would that have been like? What would have come of that? Because that was exactly during the time she had been pining for him, before Harrison Butler came along and rescued her.

'Are you happy now, Mickey?'

'Yes, I am. And you?'

He shrugged and smiled wistfully. 'What is happiness after all? I got where I wanted to go. I built the movie empire I dreamed of.'

Suddenly Jonathan made her feel sad. 'Do we have a waitress?' she asked lightly.

As if she had been eavesdropping, the waitress appeared, dropped two menus on the table, and disappeared. 'I'm curious about you, Mickey,' Jonathan said after giving a quick glance at the menu and laying it aside. 'Was it worth it? All the years at Great Victoria? All the sacrifices?'

She looked at him, searching for any bitterness in his eyes or in his tone. Was he referring to himself, to the life they could have had together but which she had sacrificed to her ambition? No, she saw no bitterness in him, no anger. Jonathan seemed oddly subdued, almost resigned.

'Why did you and your husband leave Hawaii?'

'Lots of reasons. After I completed my residency at Great Victoria I discovered that no matter where I set up practice I was in competition with the men who had trained me, and that didn't seem fair to them. Harrison thought it would be better for my career if I moved to new ground, so to speak. The plantation wasn't doing well anymore and he wanted to get out of it. And since most of his investments were here in Southern California this seemed the logical place to come to.'

'So now you have a ritzy medical practice,' he said, signalling to the waitress.

'Yes,' said Mickey, deciding on the seafood crêpe.

After the waitress had gone, Jonathan said, 'You seem

preoccupied. Does this bother you, us having lunch together?'

She shook her head and smiled. 'No, I was thinking about a friend of mine. Well, you knew her once, she was in medical school with me...' Mickey went on to tell him Sondra's tragic story and ended with, 'I'm taking her out to Palm Springs tomorrow. Sam Penrod is going to try to reconstruct her hands.'

'He's a good man,' said Jonathan. 'My leading starhawk was injured on location and the local experts pronounced he would never walk again. Sam reconstructed his foot and enabled him to go out and battle space villains once more.' Jonathan paused to look at Mickey. Then he said quietly, 'I'll bet you haven't seen any of my movies.'

Mickey laughed. 'I once slept with a Lobbly, does that count?'

'There was a time when you slept with its creator.'

Ah, here it was, the dangerous ground. Well, Jonathan had taken the first step, but Mickey wasn't going to follow. Not just yet.

He looked down at the wrapped box in the centre of the table, frowned at it, twiddled the silver bow for a minute, then looked at Mickey. 'Have you ever regretted it, Mickey? That we didn't stay together?'

She thought a moment. 'There were moments back at Great Victoria. I had some very lonely nights and thought about you a lot. Yes, there were times, long ago, when I wondered if we did the right thing.'

'But not anymore?'

'Not since meeting Harrison. And you, Jonathan? Have you ever regretted it?'

'Yes. Very much. Mickey...' He paused to search her face, weighing something, then he said, 'That's why I wanted to see you privately. I wanted to clear things up, settle the books, so to speak. I guess you've been pretty mad at me all these years, and I don't blame you. But I want to put it to rest.'

Mickey tilted her head to one side, not catching his meaning.

'I know it's late, but it's a sincere apology all the same.

Mickey, I'm sorry I stood you up at the belltower.'

She stared at him. 'What did you say?'

'I said I'm sorry I stood you up at the belltower. I really tried to make it. But the reporters arrived at my house and I couldn't get away. By the time I got to a phone it was nine o'clock and there was no answer at your apartment. I tried for hours to get you. You must have been pretty mad.'

Mickey stared at him dumbfounded as her mind backpedalled to that night. She saw herself sitting along in her apartment, counting off the strikes of the belltower clock, crying on the sofa, and imagining Jonathan pacing out there in the cold night, wondering why she hadn't come. And then afterwards, Mickey had run to Gilhooley's where Ruth and Sondra were celebrating with the other classmates who had got the internships they wanted. There had been a party afterward in Teroso Hall, which had lasted all night, and then they'd taken the phone off the hook so they could sleep it all off the next day. By the time Jonathan did get through to Mickey she didn't want to talk to him, didn't want to explain why she had stood him up, didn't want to go through it all again, wanted to have it just end so they could get on with their separate lives. She had carried that with her for fourteen years, the image of Jonathan standing at the foot of the belltower, alone, waiting.

Mickey had come to this luncheon armed with a whole arsenal of defences and ammunition in case he should ask her to come back to him, in case he pulled certain emotional strings. She had been braced for anything: Jonathan wanting to have an affair, Jonathan spilling out his old anger at her for leaving him, Jonathan boasting about how great his life had become since they'd parted. Mickey had been prepared, she thought, for everything. Except this. She hadn't been prepared for this.

'Are you mad at me, Mickey?' he said quietly. 'If so, I don't blame you. I was the one who pressed you, I was the one who insisted you come to the belltower. And then I was the one who changed the rules at the last minute. It all happened so fast. Getting the Oscar nomination, all the publicity. Suddenly offers were coming in from studios. And then *Medical Center* was going to be aired as a network special. And I also thought, well, everything was over between us.'

Mickey stared at him. *You gave me up that easily?*

'I'm sorry, Mickey, I really am.' He reached across the table and laid a hand on top of hers. And she let him. Then she stared at the foil-wrapped package. *What was this, then? A conscience salve?*

But as she looked down at the sunburned hand covering hers, suddenly the anger dissipated as quickly as it had come on. Jonathan, after all these years. *Should I tell him the truth? That I stood him up, too? That we had both decided to pursue another dream? No, let it lie, let it go.*

'It's all right, Jonathan,' she said softly, meaning it. There was no more anger, no more regret, no more wondering what it would have been like. What was done was done; they could each take new steps now, be the friends they should have been long ago. Mickey was filled with a sense of peace.

'This is for you,' he said at last, nudging the gold box her way.

Mickey picked it up and started to undo the bow. 'No,' he said, staying her hand. 'Open it when you're alone. Not when I'm around.'

'What is it?'

'It's something I owe you, Mickey. Something that belongs to you.' When she gave him a puzzled look, he said simply, 'When you see it you'll understand.'

And then their crêpes came and they ate lunch and talked like two old friends catching up on the years.

Sondra was upstairs, resting for the trip tomorrow to Sam Penrod's clinic. Harrison was up in San Francisco signing a real estate contract. And Mickey was sitting in the living room of the Camden Drive house, curled up on the sofa with a glass of white wine, staring at the gold box on the coffee table.

It had been hours since she had left Jonathan at the Barnacle, hours since they'd kissed each other's cheeks and said goodbye, most likely for the last time, although neither had said so. Once over the initial hurdles, they had discovered that they really were old friends and that nothing stood between them anymore. Nor did anything bind them together. The past was no longer what it used to be.

And now she was all alone with this enigmatic box that was going to 'explain everything.'

Like a child at Christmas, she had shaken it. It was light, rectangular, and rattled slightly. It had to be a necklace, that was just what it looked like, a jeweller's gift box. But what would a necklace explain? And why would he 'owe' her one? Finally, she picked up the box and delicately peeled off the foil. And stared inside.

It was a video tape.

She turned it over in her hands. There was no label, no note of explanation. Just a video tape cassette.

Puzzled, Mickey carried the cassette and her wineglass into the den where the TV set and a video machine were set in walnut cabinetry. *I'll bet you haven't seen any of my movies,* Jonathan had said at the Barnacle. Was that what this was? The latest in the *Invaders!* series? A print of the episode that was due to be released in theatres this summer? If so, it was a valuable gift indeed, because so far not one of Jonathan's famous films had made it to legal video cassettes, and probably wouldn't for some time to come.

Well, thought Mickey, her curiosity piqued. She refilled her glass, dropped in an ice cube, got settled on the den's comfortable sofa, dimmed the lights, and picked up the recorder's remote control.

She pushed a button and the machine went though a series of clicks and whirs. As Mickey stared at the snowy screen, there was a minute of grey blankness, and then all life and light exploded

A baby was plunging out of its mother in a rush of black blood against white sheets.

Mickey blinked.

The camera pulled back, showing the Emergency Room team at work, resuscitating an unconscious mother, her clothes cut away from her body. Then, trying to slap life into the baby, a chaos of white uniforms, a young policeman collapsing to the floor in a faint. All taking place in the unnatural vacuum of silence. No sound, to symbolise that first dramatic, terrifying emergence of life. And then a startling blast of noise – a cacophony of voices, sirens, running footsteps, at first all distinct and inseparable, gradually diffusing, drawing apart, a voiced command here, a sharply slammed door there; finally, a quieting down, a settling of that primal chaos, not unlike the opening Big Bang of *Invaders*! Then one lone voice saying wearily, 'They'll both live.'

And on the screen: *MEDICAL CENTER*

Mickey was held in a trance. There it all was, in all its clear familiarity – St Catherine's. Faces that had long ago gone fuzzy in her memory, now were sharp and alive again: Dr Mandell leading a bewildered group of SAPs down a corridor; a psychiatric team overpowering and subduing a frenzied patient; a little boy crying; a candy-striper sneezing into a bouquet of flowers; Dr Reems, the head of Cardiology, lighting his next cigarette with the butt of his last one; a scalpel slicing through clean skin; a group of interns tossing a football in the grass; a long shot of an empty hallway with one stretcher holding a sheet-covered body. St Catherine's telling its own story, from birth to death, with no narration, no script, filmed by one man and his assistant, and winner of three Emmy Awards.

Mickey's eyes misted over. There was Ruth in her obstetrical greens, looking angrily at the camera, a thinner Ruth moving with more energy, snappier movements, a woman in a hurry. And there was Sondra, beautiful, exotic, glancing frequently over her shoulder as if a phantom were chasing her. And Mickey, a younger, brasher Mickey, walking with a clipped gait, out to prove something to the world.

Mickey saw herself running down a corridor, her white jacket flying, her face tight with urgency, following a crash cart. In the next instant, an odd-angled shot of a nurse up on a patient's bed, straddling the moribund man, her white dress ridden up over her plump thighs and exposing the tops of nylons; and then a quick pan to Mickey, grim-faced and handing up a long needle.

*No script, no story, no actors,* Jonathan had said fourteen years ago. This was no actress, this was Mickey Long, the *real* Mickey Long, fourth-year medical student, young, obdurate, resolutely following a vision, indomitable champion of the afflicted. It was almost embarrassing, she looked so determined.

The tape let open the floodgates of other memories: twelve-year-old Mickey dragging her feet into yet another doctor's office, wanting to run away when he touched her face; Mickey near tears because she had to get to a ladies' room and cover up her face and she was already late for Moreno's lab, Mickey taking Great Victoria by storm, arguing with Gregg and locking horns with Mason; Mickey repairing the shattered face of young Jason Butler; Mickey taking on every challenge that crossed her path, letting nothing intimidate her.

She saw her entire life in a glance – the determination, the fighting spirit – and she thought: *When did I stop taking chances?*

Mickey dashed a tear off her cheek. Jonathan had indeed given her a great gift; he'd given her back to herself. And a chance to be that person again.

When the tape ended, Mickey turned up the lights and unfolded herself up from the sofa. She turned around to find Sondra standing in the doorway, her amber eyes wide and unblinking. 'I thought I heard something,' she said.

'How much did you see?'

'Enough.'

Mickey smiled. 'Have a seat. I'll run it again. And then later I'm going to call Sam Penrod. I'm afraid he's losing a patient.'

Sondra returned the smile.

# Chapter Thirty-five

*Dear Dr Ruth, I had bad headaches and went to my doctor who sent me to another doctor who had my head scanned in the hospital. The pictures showed that I have a 'pineal shift'. What does this mean and can I avoid surgery? Seattle.*

Ruth laid the letter aside and picked up another.

*Dear Dr Ruth, My husband and I have been married for six years and desperately want a baby, but my husband is sterile. We applied for adoption but there is a minimum four-year wait. Our doctor told us about artificial insemination from a donor bank but when we asked our priest about it he said that in the eyes of the Church artificial insemination is adultery. What can we do? Port Townsend.*

Ruth dropped that letter also and scowled at the large pile of envelopes covering her desk. They had been delivered that morning from the newspaper, making yesterday's pile twice as big, and it would still be here tomorrow to be added to and trebled. Lorna Smith wasn't going to be pleased.

Ruth had tried, had honestly tried to keep the column going, to keep it fresh and upbeat and interesting. But now it seemed tedious. She glowered at the stack of mail as if it were something that had just crawled up between the floorboards.

Pushing away from her desk, Ruth got up and strode to the window. September. The start of the dying season. It's not fair, why can't *we* shed our old layers and be born anew each spring? Aren't we more important than trees or snakes?

She hated herself this morning. In fact, she had been hating herself for the past few mornings, for the past hundred mornings, because she couldn't put a lid on her thoughts, she couldn't find the antivenin for the bitterness poisoning her blood.

Five years ago writing the column had been fun, even four years ago, three, two; *just two years ago I had still enjoyed doing it, dispensing my medical wisdom like pills, knowing that people out there relied on me for their quick cures. But who does Dr Ruth write to? Who has the instant solution for her?*

Ruth looked at her watch. She should be getting ready to leave for Seattle. Her therapist, Dr Margaret Cummings, had asked if Ruth minded coming in this afternoon instead of her usual evening appointment and Ruth had cleared her schedule for it: there were some things you just had to make room for.

Was Margaret Cummings helping her? Ruth wasn't sure. She'd been going to her once a week ever since February, seven months; you'd think something would have happened by now. Ruth knew she couldn't live without the therapy. She had come to rely on those evening sessions in Margaret's safe-harbour office, with Margaret's quiet accepting, uncritical presence. Ruth could pace the carpet and smoke a pack of cigarettes and air all the dirty linen she could think of. Maybe one of these days there would be a breakthrough and Ruth would be healed.

Turning away from the window, Ruth looked again at her desk. And that pot. That goddamned pot.

There might have been a breakthrough with Margaret Cummings, Ruth might have actually got down to the core of her present unhappiness, if it weren't for this whole new complication about Arnie. First there was that pot for Ruth's mother's birthday. And then another pot sent down to Tarzana for his parents' wedding anniversary. And then a pot for Rachel's fourteenth birthday. And finally, a pot to beautify Ruth's office. It wasn't enough that Ruth had the recurrent nightmare to contend with, the insomnia, this insufferable lack of self-control. Now she had Arnie to worry about. Arnie and his pots.

*I will not go to that gallery. I will not stoop so low.*

That had been Ruth's initial reaction – to go the gallery. She had become curious about the proliferation of Indian pottery around the house but had chalked it up to a phase Arnie was going through, like this night school class he was taking every Friday night at the local high school. That was fine, if it made him happy. But then there had been that evening when her support group had cancelled for various reasons and she'd come home early and taken a shortcut, and seen a car remarkably like their station wagon parked outside an apartment complex. And when she'd realised it *was* their car, she'd thought: *Isn't this Arnie's school night?* And then she'd seen it again, a few weeks later. That was when the suspicion had started to form.

She never would have connected the pots to the apartment house if Arnie hadn't left that business card in one of his shirts. Ruth had found it while doing the laundry. Cockle-edged and engraved: *Angeline. Native American Art*. When it occurred to Ruth to take a closer look at those pots, she wished belatedly she hadn't, because she found what she was looking for: they were all made by Angeline.

Still, was there a connection? She couldn't be sure. One of the pots had come in a box with the name of an art gallery on the lid. Ruth's first impulse had been to check out the gallery; pride had stopped her. Dr Ruth Shapiro did not stoop to snoopery, she did not let herself get bogged down in a morass of unfounded suspicions. Arnie having an affair? Not likely. All she had to do was ask him, straightforwardly, who lived in that apartment building and she'd find out it was something innocuous, like some of the class members getting together afterwards to hash out the evening's lectures. What *was* it Arnie had said the class was about? Ruth couldn't remember.

It wasn't fair of him, to complicate her life like this, now, at this crucial point; she needed to work out her problems, to sort through and analyse all the elements of her life, and see what to keep, what to toss out, like reorganising a closet that hasn't been touched in years. With Margaret Cummings' help she might be able to do it, but not if Arnie was going to let her down.

Ruth's eye fell on a letter not addressed to 'Ask Dr Ruth.' It was from Mickey. Another report on her progress with Sondra. 'Defects of the extensor tendons were bridged by transplanting a tendon graft from the fourth toe to second finger. I also reconstructed the junctura tendinum between third and fourth fingers by tendon graft from proximal tendon stump of third finger. I'll immobilise the hand in extensions for three weeks, at which time the splints will come off and, God willing, most function will have been restored.'

Although her current bitterness extended to all things – her children, her husband, her old friends, even the birds in the air – Ruth admitted that Mickey was doing a brave thing. And what Sondra was enduring was impressive, too: the numerous surgical operations. The sewing of her hands to her abdomen for the skin grafting, being immobilised for weeks in a half-body plaster cast, the countless stitches and injections and cutting and sewing. The wondering and praying.

In a way, Ruth envied them. Mickey and Sondra had clearly defined their work, their goals were solid, recognisable; and they worked together, joined, like Sondra's hands sewn to her stomach, holding each other up in an intimate sharing that Ruth had not experienced since – when?

*Since we took turns washing the dishes in that apartment on Avenida Oriente.*

You know you're turning forty when you start wishing you were back in college. Ruth wished Mickey hadn't written, wished she didn't have to envy them and compare her life with theirs, because she could never win.

Well, soon it would be over for them. This letter had been written two weeks ago; Sondra's splints were coming off in a few days and Mickey and Sondra would have their answers; their lives and their futures would be decided.

As for Ruth, it was time to be getting over to Seattle to Margaret Cummings.

'But that's just *it*,' Ruth said, getting up from the chair and pacing the floor again. 'I don't *know* what I'm angry about. Or *who* I'm angry with. That's what's so frustrating. It's with me all the time, like it's sunk its tentacles into me, clinging to my back and I can't shake it off. There's never a minute of let up. I wake up angry, I fall asleep angry. And I have nothing to direct it at.'

Dr Margaret Cummings watched her patient march a repetitive track around the office, suck on a cigarette, then mash it, half smoked, in the big glass ashtray on the credenza. Then back to the chair, pick up her purse, pull out a fresh cigarette, light it, and start the circuit again. All the while talking, in clipped sentences, her short, compact body a mass of nerves. When Ruth had first come to her seven months ago, Margaret Cummings had seen a woman bottled up with undirected fury. The same woman now thrashed a path across the broadloom, just as mystified about the forces inside herself today as she had been back in February. And no closer to the solution that both were certain was buried inside her.

'And it's making me lose control,' Ruth continued, pausing before the Dali lithograph on the wall and glowering darkly at it. 'There are two kinds of fury, you know, Margaret. There's the kind that injects you with power and helps you get things done, like getting through medical school. And then there's the kind that leaves you miserably impotent. Imagine that, Ruth Shapiro impotent!'

Swinging away from the Dali, Ruth strode to the credenza, killed another cigarette, and came back to her chair.

Margaret's office was nice, conducive to talk; it looked like a den in anybody's house, with comfortable furniture, a wall of books, a few plants. There wasn't a desk. You could believe your aunt Mattie had invited you over for tea and you figure this is a good time to get things off your chest because she's a good listener and you know she'll keep your secrets.

Ruth sank into the chair and regarded her friend on the sofa. An aunt Mattie indeed: Margaret Cummings was as unpretentious as her office, with grey hair, plain skirt and sweater, low-heeled pumps, and a Timex watch with a large face. Margaret Cummings' appearance belied her reputation as one of the best, most sought after psychologists in the city.

'I don't know what to do, Margaret.'

The therapist shifted on the sofa. 'Let's talk about your husband. How do you feel about him right now?'

'Arnie? That shadow I live with?'

'Are you angry at *him*?'

'I should be. I think he's having an affair.'

'So you *are* angry at him then?'

Ruth averted her eyes. 'I'm not sure. I can't tell. That's the trouble with my life right now – there are no clear definitions. My life feels like a sentence without a verb. I know how I

384

*should* feel, but in reality I think I'm more angry at his letting me find out than at his actually *doing* it.'

There was a trim of piping on the end of the chair's arm; Ruth now traced it back and forth with her fingertips. 'I feel as if I'm losing control of everything. I can't make my deadlines at the newspaper, I have more patients than I can handle, even my kids seem to have gotten away from me. I look at them, and they're five little strangers. Rachel turned fourteen this month. She came home from school the other day with a safety pin in her ear. I was stunned. Wasn't she a baby only yesterday? And wasn't it only last week I sat down with a calendar and calculated when she would be conceived?'

Ruth rubbed her forehead. 'My life is telescoping, Margaret. I'm losing my grasp of time. I've started thinking a lot about the past, medical school. God, those were the days!' She looked at Dr Cummings and smiled. 'There was a lot of good, free sex in those days.'

'What is sex like now, with your husband?'

'Non-existent. He's very unimaginative. The woman he's seeing must be very hard up.'

'Do you suppose he might be open to suggestions, to experimentation?'

Ruth shrugged. 'What for? To what purpose?'

'Have you confronted him on this affair?'

'Not yet. I don't know what I'm going to do about it. I have so much on my mind. There are so many things to juggle. Some days, I feel like the walls are closing in on me.'

'Are they now?'

Ruth looked around the office. 'Yes.' Then she bowed her head again and studied the piping of the crushed velour as if it were the only important thing right now. Ruth knew what she was doing: she knew she was talking in circles, that she was feinting as in sword play, tossing out heartfelt declarations to Margaret Cummings because that was what was expected. But Ruth knew she could not keep up the avoidance for long because Margaret would see through it. So she finally said, softly, 'It's come back. The dream has come back.'

'The one you had as a teenager?'

385

'It started when I was ten years old. I ran a race and my father laughed at me. It was a nightmare I had all through my adolescence, when I was fat and my father was always after me to diet. Whenever he criticised me, I would have the dream.' Ruth rolled the piping under her fingertips, then plucked at it. 'It went away when I was in medical school and then came back when I had the amniocentesis, nine years ago. It started again last week, on the night of my birthday. My fortieth birthday, as a matter of fact.'

'Wasn't that also the anniversary of your father's death?'

Ruth looked up at her. 'Yes, it was. On the night that marked one year since his death, the dream came back and it's just like it was before, it's exactly the same, it hasn't changed at all, in the tiniest detail.' Ruth rested her head on the back of the chair and gazed up at the ceiling. 'It's a short dream and nothing really happens in it, but in my sleep, while I'm experiencing it, I feel real terror. And when I wake up, my heart is racing.

'A big, black space engulfs me. I don't know if it's a room or a cave or an ocean. I can't see a thing. I'm blind. And I believe it each time. You'd think with a recurrent dream I would catch on and at some point say, "Wait a minute, I've been here before. This is only that dumb dream." But I don't. Each time I'm duped. Each time, I *feel* the terror of the Void. I am bodiless, fleshless. I am a floating entity in a terrifying, hostile oblivion. I start to panic. I start to wonder who I am. I can't think. I can't reason. I am not developed. I am either the beginning or the end of something, I don't know which, and this makes my terror worse. Fear of what is to come, what I shall evolve into, or fear that it is all behind me and *this is it for eternity*.'

Ruth's hands curled over the arms of the chair, her fingers dug into the fabric. 'You cannot imagine the horror of the space surrounding me, the horror of knowing that I *am* and yet I am *not*, of being but *not* being. The pure, frozen terror.'

She raised her head and looked at Dr Cummings. 'That's all there is to it. The dream ends there.'

Margaret studied her with calm hazel eyes. 'What do you think it means?'

'I don't know. Wait, yes I do. It must mean that I think of

386

myself as unformed. Either not yet born, or dead. I don't know which. All I know is it has started making me afraid to go to sleep at night, because I know I'll find myself floating in that awful terribleness.'

They sat in silence for some minutes, Ruth studying the arm of her chair, Margaret waiting for Ruth to say something more. Finally, as a signal that the hour was drawing to its close, Dr Cummings moved to the edge of the sofa and said, 'Ruth, I want you to keep a journal of those dreams. Each time you have one, I want you to write it down while it's still fresh in your mind. Don't leave out a thing. Even if you think you're just saying the same thing over and over. Describe every little sensation, every emotion, and then write how you felt about it when you woke up.'

'Isn't it going to be very repetitive?'

Margaret smiled. 'If there is the slightest variation, if there is one new detail, no matter how small, it could tell us something.'

Ruth looked at her watch. It was still early afternoon. No patients to see in the office, no one in the hospital. Of course, there was that odious stack of Dr Ruth mail, but that could wait. She turned to the window and narrowed her eyes at the mote-infested sunbeams which pierced the panes and flooded the carpet. It might be a nice day for a walk.

When she stood with Margaret and they started for the door, Ruth said, 'I won't be coming next week, Margaret. I've been invited to spend a few days down in Los Angeles with friends. Maybe if I get away for a while, into new surroundings, get together with old friends, my perspective will shift back.'

'Sounds like a good idea.'

Ruth smiled wryly. 'I'll let you know if I have any lightning flashes of Freudian insight.'

It had been a long time since Ruth had been to the Pike Street Market, and never alone. Always the girls tagged along, demanding ice cream cones while Arnie dropped dollar bills into the open guitar cases of the street musicians. She had never been here on her own before, and it felt strangely exhilarating, curiously liberating.

And then her footsteps brought her face to face with the gallery.

Ruth stood for a long time staring through the plate glass window; passersby would assume she was examining the items on display – the tall totems, the eagle-feathered lances, the large oil painting of teepees by a placid river. But in reality she was trying to peer into the dark interior without having actually to go inside. Was *she* in there right now? The Angeline who turned out pots with such speed and skill? How did Arnie come to be here? Which came first, the girl or the gallery?

The sun was at the wrong angle; all Ruth could see in the glass was her own sad reflection, a short, dark-haired woman who looked every single day of forty, indecision distorting her face.

*Why should I go in there? For what possible reason?*

*For the same reason that any wife wants to look at the 'other' woman: to see what she's got that I haven't got.*

Even as she was walking through the door, Ruth was blaming Arnie. It was *his* fault that she had stooped so low. This was a lie, coming in here and pretending to be a customer. And she knew she would feel awful afterwards, and childish, and that would be his fault, too.

The displayed pieces were beautiful; there were several, in fact, that Ruth wouldn't have minded owning. That rust and tan batik, for instance, in the round frame, some sort of Indian demon with big eyes, jagged teeth, and eagle feathers descending from the bottom of the hoop. It was very striking; it would look stunning over the fireplace. Why couldn't Arnie have bought her this instead of those pots? *Because Angeline makes the pots.*

*You really don't know that for sure, Ruth. You could be imagining the whole thing.*

She stopped before an engraving of an Indian squaw with a fat-faced papoose on her back.

He's been going to someone's apartment after school, probably to study together, or maybe it's someone who likes sports and they drink beer and argue. And those pots, it could just be a coincidence they're all made by the same woman; maybe he just likes that particular style.

Turn around and walk out right now, Ruth, before you make a fool of yourself.

'May I help you?'

Ruth turned to a young woman, very pretty and smiling. 'Yes,' she said quickly. 'I'm looking for something for my husband. A gift. He's mentioned this gallery before. We have a few of your items in our house. So I thought...'

'Certainly. Did you have anything specific in mind?'

'Pottery. Large pots. With mythological motifs around them.'

'We have several very nice examples.' The young woman turned and crossed to the other side of the gallery. She stopped next to a large pot standing on a tall pedestal. 'This is a very lovely item. The pottery itself is in the Pueblo style, but the decoration in Northwest Coast.'

Ruth walked slowly up to it, not believing her eyes. She had the baby offspring of this same pot in her living room. 'He, ah, is particularly fond of an artist named Angeline.'

The young woman brought up a slender brown hand and laid it delicately on the pot. 'This was made by Angeline.'

Ruth moved her eyes slowly over the pot, grudgingly admitting that it was beautiful, that Angeline, whoever she was, had real talent.

'I'm curious,' she said as offhandedly as she could. 'Would you happen to know Angeline? Does she live in this area?'

The girl's smile deepened and was accompanied by a faint blush. 'I am Angeline,' she said softly.

Ruth could have been hit by a lightning bolt, she stood and stared so dumbly. *This* was Angeline? An *Indian?* Ruth was amazed to hear herself speak, to discover that she could *maintain*. 'Well, then, maybe you know my husband. I am,' the pause was so fleeting that it wasn't perceptible as Ruth, for the first time in her married life, said, 'Mrs Roth. Arnie Roth is my husband.'

The smile vanished and the copper complexion lightened a shade.

'Do you know my husband?' asked Ruth, seeing the answer exposed on Angeline's beautiful face.

'Yes, I know Arnie,' she said with dignity. 'He comes in here sometimes.'

Arnie! *Arnie!* She calls him Arnie! She doesn't even have the decency to put up a front and call him Mr Roth!

'My husband has become quite an expert on Indian things in the last few months,' Ruth said, hating the sound of herself and at the same time wondering what it felt like to claw eyes out. 'In fact, he takes a class every Friday night, studying Indian things.'

Angeline said nothing. She regarded Ruth with large, unreadable eyes.

Then Ruth saw it, something Angeline did not, could not, because it came not from outside but from *behind* Ruth's eyes, a gathering darkness inside the gallery, as though the lights were failing, as though a black fog were rolling in through the heating vents. It blanked out the sun that was streaming through the plate glass window, it obscured the overhead track lighting; it was a growing, billowing penumbra, the penumbra of death, perhaps, of isolation, of loneliness, *of being cast loose in the terrifying Void.* And Ruth knew what it was. She knew what it was.

It was the sun of her life. It was the spectre of failure.

She looked in the direction of the spot, where she thought it was because she couldn't see it through the engulfing blackness, and she heard herself manage to say, 'No, I don't think that's what I want after all.' And she felt herself move, fly, escape to the door and out into the darkening sun.

# Chapter Thirty-six

'And then what did you do?' asked Mickey.

'I ran out of the gallery and made it to a bench outside just in time to get my head on my knees. I very nearly fainted.'

They were sitting on the beach and watching the breakers roll in, Mickey in a wide-brimmed straw hat, Ruth letting the sea breeze ruffle her short hair. A little way down the beach a solitary figure walked. She paused every so often to look out over the ocean and tilt her head as if to catch an answer on the wind.

Ruth looked over at Sondra and then returned to Mickey. 'I walked for hours,' she continued. 'I must have looked like a zombie. I vaguely recall people staring at me and I remember thinking: So this is what it's like to have a nervous breakdown.' Ruth narrowed her eyes and squinted out over the white-capped waves. 'I found my way to the ferry and got in around eleven o'clock. The girls were in bed, but Arnie was still up, watching the news. He didn't say anything to me when I came in, he didn't even look up, and then I realised that that's how it's been with us for a long time. I had just never noticed before.'

The September day was uncommonly sharp and clear. All colours seemed to stand out: the undulating blue of the Pacific, the bone-yellow sand, the trees up on the cliff protecting the medical school. Ruth dug her fingers into the warm sand, scooped some up, and let it sift away in the breeze. She felt hollow inside, all carved-out and empty, as if she had been cored. She looked down the beach again, at the slender figure inclining herself into the breeze. Coming to Castillo had been Sondra's idea. Now she walked barefoot along the teasing edge of the surf, her long black hair flowing free, her large eyes searching the distant horizon.

At forty, Sondra looked younger and more beautiful than

ever, or so Ruth thought; the hardships of missionary life seemed not to have brushed her. She was still slender, still naturally graceful. Even with those splints, which were not much of a handicap.

Sondra's arms were encased in sleeves of metal and foam rubber, her fingers were fixed into position by wires and elastic bands. 'Active splinting,' Mickey had called it. While Sondra's grafts were growing and adjusting, her fingers were kept at a mild stretch with tension applied – somewhat on the principle of isometric exercise. Although Sondra's fingers appeared to be frozen, they were continually working against the elastic bands; her muscles and new tendons were being exercised even though it didn't appear so.

When Ruth had arrived at Mickey's house yesterday morning she had been shocked to see the extent of Sondra's injury. The letters had not shown the complete, horrifying picture. Ruth had not been prepared to see such monstrous damage; such massive repair – the patches of pale skin lifted from abdomen and thighs, the minute tracks of stitches, hundreds of them, the astonishingly thin arms, like bird bones and the fingers flexed into claws. Ruth knew what Mickey had done these past five months, knew what Sondra had been through.

The first thing Mickey had done, back in April, was take photographs of Sondra's hands. She had studied them like a jeweller commissioned to cut a raw diamond, contemplating every angle and line, filling sketch pads with the various possible approaches, and straining her eyes over books late at night to reacquaint herself with the intricate structure of the human hand. The goal had been to free up the frozen tendons and muscles in Sondra's hands, and remove all badly scarred skin, replacing it with grafts taken from elsewhere on Sondra's body.

When she was ready to begin treatment, Mickey had set up a schedule. The operations would be performed at St John's Hospital, where Sondra would remain for the initial post-operative recoveries, after which she would come home and stay with Mickey and Harrison under the care of a private nurse. In all that time, five months, Sondra would have no use of her arms and hands.

The first operation, at the end of April, had not involved the hands: this had been the raising of the abdominal flap.

Sondra's left hand had suffered trauma too deep for a simple skin graft. The underlying tissue, the subcutaneous, had also to be replaced, and this called for the removal of an entire thickness of skin and subcutaneous tissue from an area where she could spare it. As this 'flap' had to remain attached to its original site while it was regenerating at the new site on the hand, the abdomen was the donor area of choice.

The first step was to raise this flap, which Mickey did under local anaesthesia: two parellel incisions were drawn along Sondra's abdomen, the skin and subcutaneous tissue delicately lifted up from the underlying fascia, like a little footbridge rising up from the abdomen, and then it was sewn back into place. The purpose of this was to ensure blood supply through the strip of flap and it was watched closely for three weeks to make certain the feed-up skin layers were healthy and thriving.

When Mickey determined the flap was viable and had good circulation, she next began the process of removing it from the abdomen, which called for freeing up one end while leaving the other end still attached to the abdomen. These two places where the raised skin met the abdomen were the pedicles: Mickey narrowed the first pedicle with two small incisions so that the whole flap took on the shape of a fence picket, then she attached a laboratory clamp to the small portion that still joined the abdomen. There followed a series of days during which, on each day, Mickey tightened the laboratory clamp a little more, cutting off the blood supply to this pedicle without causing trauma to the tissue. For the pain this crushing of the tissue caused, she repeatedly injected the area with procaine. Finally, when the crushing was completed and Mickey determined that the flap was still healthy, pink, and had no swelling, it was time to transfer it to Sondra's hand.

In June the dorsum scar of Sondra's left hand was cautiously and painstakingly removed. With Sondra under general anaesthesia, Mickey excised the rubbery contracted tissue, cleaned the roughly pancake-shaped area, made sure all bleeding and oozing had stopped, and then brought the hand up and sewed the abdominal flap over the raw, open wound. With the flap still attached to the abdomen at its other pedicle, the skin and tissue received a good blood supply as it began the miraculous process of regrowing on its new site. Sondra was then fixed into a figure-eight plaster cast which went across her chest, over her right shoulder, and down the length of her left arm.

One week later Mickey applied a laboratory clamp to the remaining pedicle of the flap and repeated the process of the daily bit-by-bit tightening. As the clamp slowly crushed the junction of flap to abdomen, she studied the graft for complications – this was the crucial stage when success or failure are determined.

But the graft thrived. Sondra's hand was removed from her abdomen, the donor site on the abdomen was closed up, and her hand was left to heal on its own.

For her right hand, a different process was used. In this instance, while her left hand had been mercilessly stretched back, as though her knuckles were trying to touch the back of her arm, Sondra's right hand was curled in like a snail. This called for a series of operations in which Mickey gradually cut away the contractile scar tissues and freed up the traumatised nerves and tendons. Simple skin grafts were lifted from Sondra's thighs, using an instrument very much like a carpenter's wood-shaver, and transplanted over areas of ugly, thickish skin. Perpetual splinting kept the hand in a natural position to prevent recurrence of contraction.

When the grafting on the left hand was completely healed, Mickey then launched into the final, decisive phase of the reconstruction – the tendon transplant: the removal of tendons from Sondra's toes and replacement in her fingers. This was done near the end of August, and thereafter her hands were again immobilised for three weeks. The splints were coming off this afternoon.

'Does Arnie know?' Mickey asked now, breaking Ruth's line of thought.

'About my going to the gallery? I don't know. I would think *she* would tell him, but he didn't give any indication of knowing about it when he drove me to the airport.'

'How did he react when you told him you were coming down here?'

Ruth shrugged. 'He didn't react at all. He just said that he'd look after the girls and that I wasn't to worry.'

'He didn't think it odd? All of a sudden, out of the clear blue sky you announce you're leaving the next day for Los Angeles?'

'If he did he didn't show it.'

'How long did you tell him you would be here?'

'I didn't. I just said "a visit". And he didn't ask.'

Mickey looked away from Ruth and out over the rolling ocean. Overhead, gulls rode the air currents and filled the beach silence with their cries. Mickey felt sad. Yesterday morning, when Ruth had ridden up to the house in the taxi, the reunion of the three friends had been wonderful – with laughter and tears and reminiscences. They had talked at the same time and brought up old things and new things and commented on appearance, how they hadn't changed at all, how much they had changed. The last time Mickey had seen Ruth was six years ago, when Mickey had gone up to Seattle for fertility treatment; Ruth and Sondra had last seen one another two years before that, at Mickey's wedding. And before that the three had last seen one another at Castillo College, fourteen years ago, when they had received their medical diplomas.

Those first few hours yesterday had been sublime, a sweet nostalgia; and then, after a while, Mickey had started to realise that things were not right with Ruth. The signs were all too familiar: the jerky movements, the pinched mouth, the slight strain in the voice. They had reminded Mickey of the way Ruth used to act when she was studying for a final, or waiting for the grades to be posted. Ruth was hiding something; she was play-acting. It was almost as if she had sent her body down here but had herself stayed up in Seattle.

And then, last night, Mickey, in the next bedroom, had heard Ruth cry out in her sleep and had found her friend this morning looking as if she hadn't slept at all, her face drawn, her eyes smudged.

Now, just a short while after coming to sit on the sand and after Mickey asked her friend if there was anything wrong, Ruth was telling it all: her father's death, the nightmare, Arnie's affair with Angeline. 'Remember when I wanted to have one last baby, Mickey?' Ruth murmured, her face

395

turned toward the sea. 'And Arnie said no and threatened to get a vasectomy? It's a good thing I didn't have another one. She'd be five years old now and too much for me to handle. The children I have now are getting away from me. My girls are strangers. I don't know them any more, they've become so independent. Rachel has a boyfriend who's a punk rocker. She comes home at all hours of the morning. And the twins have been bringing notes from their teachers – there's an attitude problem or something. Their grades are dropping. Leah is positively unmanageable. She's a discipline problem in school.

'Mickey, I'm losing control. My life is falling apart. The newspaper column was the first to go; it started to fall behind and before I knew it I was buried under it. And then all of a sudden my patient load was more than I could handle. I started to panic. I had lost my ability to *make* time. Where did I find enough hours to do everything in? I look back and I'm amazed at myself. These days, it's a struggle just to get dressed in the morning and get to my office on time. And when I do get there, I see all the work waiting for me and I think: *I can't do it.*'

Ruth felt as if a cold metal spring lay coiled in the pit of her stomach, and it was tightening with each wave that crashed on the shore. What was she doing here, in this place where she no longer belonged? This beach, the medical school up on the cliff, even the crying gulls seemed to be mocking her, reminding her of what she could have been, of the failure she had become. This morning, when Sondra had suggested they visit the old campus, Ruth had thought it a good idea. But now she wished she'd stayed away. Even here, at the ocean's edge, she felt penned in, trapped.

'God, Mickey,' she said now, wrapping her arms around her legs and hugging her knees tightly to her chest, 'what am I going to do?'

Sondra had strolled back down the beach and now came up just as Ruth was saying, 'I've always been good at spotting vital signs. Remember in SAPs when we were learning to use the stethoscope and I detected a heart murmur in Stan Katz? Remember Mandell's reaction? He *swore* I'd had years of practice. It seems I can spot the vital signs of an illness, but I completely missed the ones that indicated the disease that had invaded my life – a failed marriage, an unhappy husband, daughters who are turning wild. And *I don't know what to do.*'

The Pacific wind picked up, carrying on its moist breath the promising whisper of surf, the scent of distance and untouched space. Sondra, not knowing what it was like to *not know what to do*, looked away from Ruth's bleak expression and turned her face into the wind. She closed her eyes and saw a shore on the other side of this large body of water. A shore of lime-green water and sun-baked buildings and people brown as mahogany. *Her* shore, the shore that beckoned now as it had years ago, before Kenya, before medical school, before the discovery of adoption papers – a strange, almost mystical beckoning that had tugged at the heart of a little girl who, even then, had sensed that she was being called, that she needed to go. Sondra had always known what she must do.

And she knew it now. It had been six months since she had held her son in her arms, six months since she had talked quietly to the gentle mound of earth and flowers in the mission graveyard. It was time to go home.

But not yet, not yet. There was something unfinished here, something that had to be completed. Now, today, because Sondra knew they would never pass this way again. She looked down at Ruth, whose hands were opening and closing over empty air, as if to grasp something that wasn't there, and she said, 'Let's go for a walk through the school.'

They had to help Sondra back up the cliff because the trail was steep and rocky and in places required the use of hands as well as feet. 'Wow,' puffed Ruth when they reached the top. 'Am I ever out of shape!'

Mickey laughed as she brushed dirt off her hands. 'You never were an athlete, Ruth!'

'No,' said Ruth. Then, more quietly, 'No, I never was, was I?'

They followed familiar flagstone paths, passed gardens remembered, were amazed that so much was still the same. But the apartment house was gone and Avenida Oriente was now a cluster of luxury condominiums with security gates. St

Catherine's had grown: there were more buildings and parking structures, and a whole new breed of young men and women in white jackets hurrying in and out of its doors. Gilhooley's was gone, and gone, too, was the Magic Lantern, where Ruth had dated a fourth-year student whose name she could no longer recall. But Encinitas Hall was there, where Mickey had met Chris Novack. And they walked past Tesoro Hall where a few early students were moving in with suitcases; past Mariposa Hall where the anatomy lab was (and they wondered if Moreno was still teaching there); until at last they came to Manzanitas Hall where they stopped in silence.

This was where it had all begun, eighteen years ago.

The building was unlocked. It was cool inside, and quiet. The footsteps echoed on the polished floor as they walked slowly down the hall, marvelling at how unchanged it was, as if they'd left it only yesterday. Ruth felt the coil tighten inside herself. She found herself hating this place, feeling in it a hidden threat; the walls seemed to lean in close as if to bar her passage.

They came finally to the amphitheatre. 'Try the door,' Sondra said. 'Let's go inside.'

Indirect lighting bathed the amphitheatre in a soft glow. Eight rows of seats rose up in carved tiers, all facing a deserted stage below. And on that stage, a solitary lectern.

'Orientation and Welcome is next week,' Mickey said. 'I saw the notice posted outside. This time next week, a whole new batch of terrified and hopeful medical students will sit in these seats. Just as we once did.' She walked slowly along the top tier, wondering why the amphitheatre seemed smaller than it had been in her memory, and came to stand behind the exact seat she had taken on that first day eighteen years ago. 'If I had known then what I know now...'

Ruth came to stand next to her. 'Would you do things differently?'

'I wouldn't alter a single second of the past eighteen years,' Mickey said quietly, and Ruth felt a stab of envy.

Sondra walked to a side aisle. 'Look,' she said, raising a splintered arm. 'This is something new.' Arranged along the wall, descending with each tier, were photographs of

Castillo's graduating classes. 'I'll bet we're in here somewhere,' she said, and started walking slowly down the steps, studying each picture.

Ruth and Mickey were silent for a moment, then Ruth said, 'Remember Dean Hoskins' opening speech? How it made us want to run out and heal the world?' She let out a short, bitter laugh that echoed in the large auditorium. 'I was seeing a patient in the hospital last week and her TV set was tuned to a game show. One of the questions was, "Can you name the four gods mentioned in the Hippocratic Oath?" The contestant was stumped. So my patient looked up at me and said, "Well, *you* know the answer, don't you, Doctor?" And do you know something, Mickey? I couldn't remember!'

Mickey frowned slightly. 'Isn't one of them Apollo?'

Ruth looked down at the lectern and pictured Dean Hoskins standing there. It was a good memory, one to hang on to: it eased the tension that gripped her stomach. 'Those were the days, weren't they? Remember that stunt Mandell pulled on us at the end of our SAPs course?'

'What stunt?' Mickey kept a careful eye on Sondra, who was moving down the side aisle, inspecting the graduation pictures.

'Don't tell me you don't remember!' Ruth's voice was too loud and it rang high up in the dome of the amphitheatre. 'The test with the ophthalmoscope? You have to remember, Mickey, you were so nervous that your hand shook badly enough to almost knock the patient's eye out!'

Mickey shook her head. She remembered those days very well but she preferred not to call them back. The days when her face had been a curse and any close contact with a patient, such as the ophthalmoscope called for, terrified her. And how sarcastic Mandell had been, suggesting she wear her hair in a less 'obstacular' style.

Ruth continued in a forced voice, as if to drown out other sounds: 'He gathered us around that old man's bed and told us the patient had papilloedema and each of us had to examine his right eye with our ophthalmoscopes. I remember it so well because I was the last one and everybody ahead of me had taken a look and they all said they saw the papilloedema at the back of the man's eyeball very clearly. But when my turn came I looked and looked and couldn't see a thing! I remember my fear, my terror. I couldn't fail the SAPs course, it would have knocked me down in class standing. So I stood up and declared like everyone else that I had seen it. And then Mandell chewed us all out because we'd been looking into a glass eye!'

Mickey turned and looked at Ruth. The familiar signs were growing more pronounced: the involuntary snapping of her head, the clipped words, the fluttering hands. Mickey was worried. The rising tension in her friend was as palpable as if it were a living, tangible thing. Which it was for Ruth – a ball of anger and confusion growing within her with every passing minute.

'Wonderful days,' said Ruth. '*Better* days. Simple and uncomplicated. When all we had to worry about was grades. And they went by so fast. I remember when I first sat here listening to Dean Hoskins' speech and thinking, My God, four years! But now, it seems as if they passed in the wink of an eye. Where did they go?' She turned bewildered eyes to Mickey. '*Where did they go?*'

'Hey!' called Sondra down at the third level. 'Here *we* are!' She turned abruptly to look up at her friends, at the same time reflexively flinging up a splintered arm to point to their graduation photo, and lost her balance, going over backward on to the steps.

Mickey took off like a shot. Ruth immediately behind her. When they reached Sondra she was struggling to her knees, cursing her own stupidity, and wincing.

Mickey and Ruth helped her into the seat at the end of the row. 'I forget sometimes,' Sondra said as her face twisted in pain. 'I forget about these arms of mine and I try to use them as if they were normal. I haven't fallen downstairs since I was a kid!'

While Mickey went down on her knees to examine Sondra's arms, Ruth stood back, staring down at her friends with an unreadable expression.

'Where does it hurt?' asked Mickey.

'Ouch! Here. The splint is digging into my flesh.'

Mickey tried to manipulate the arm and Sondra cried out.

'It must have banged against a chair when you fell. It's bent and out of place.'

Sondra cried out again and followed it, to Ruth's surprise, with a laugh. 'Trust *me* to wait till the last day to pull a stunt like this. Let's take it off, Mickey, it really hurts.'

'Okay. It was coming off this afternoon anyway.'

As Mickey worked gently and carefully to release Sondra's arm from its metal prison, inspecting the place where the splint had dug into the tender flesh and where a bruise was starting to form, Ruth remained standing stiffly behind them, her body rigid, her lips pressed into a thin line.

The cool air on Sondra's bare skin felt good; she felt strangely light all over.

'How is it?' asked Mickey.

'Like I've been let out of solitary confinement. These things were making me claustrophobic!'

Mickey looked down at the slender hand lying lifeless in Sondra's lap, palm up, fingers delicately curled. A beautiful hand, she thought, despite the fine scar lines and pools of pale, grafted skin. A hand Mickey was intimately acquainted with, a hand she had re-created, made pleasing to the eye again. The crowning result of not only five months' work, but of eighteen years of medical study. Mickey was suddenly filled with a glowing sense of pride and accomplishment; *this* was her purpose in life. Now, if only . . .

'How does it feel?' she asked. 'Do you want to try moving it?'

Sondra looked down at the motionless hand that had once been charred like an overdone steak, a hand some doctors had once wanted to amputate, and she felt a strange new fear go through her like a thrill. She had known for five months that this moment must come. But now that it was here she was inexplicably afraid.

'Can you move any of the fingers?' Mickey asked softly.

'I don't know. It's been so long since I've moved my fingers I don't know if I remember how.' Sondra laughed tremulously. 'In any case, they'll always make a nice pair of book ends!'

'What the *hell* is the matter with you!'

Sondra and Mickey, startled, looked up at Ruth. Her face

401

was shockingly pale, her eyes wide and dark. Her arms, held stiffly at her sides, ended in two trembling fists. 'How can you laugh!' she cried. 'How can you joke about this! My God, you treat this as if it were nothing! I don't understand you, Sondra. How can you be so accepting of the ghastly thing that's happened to you?'

'Ruth,' whispered Mickey, stunned.

Tears rose in eyes full of pain and bewilderment. Her voice shook. 'You lost your husband, Sondra! Don't you *know* that? You lost him and he's gone for ever and you'll never get him back! How can you sit there and joke about the travesty your life has become?' Ruth brought her hands up to her face and sobbed into them.

Mickey, who had never known Ruth cry, stared up at her for a split second, then rose to her feet and reached out to lay a hand on Ruth's shoulder. But Ruth fell back a step, her tear-streaked face twisted in fury. 'And you're as insane as *she* is! How can you be so accepting of things? You never got what you wanted, the baby you so desperately tried to have. How can you be so damned accepting of it all? It's perverse!'

When Ruth turned to run back up the steps, Mickey seized her arm and held her fast. For a moment, their eyes locked in a silent contest, then everything inside Ruth seemed to give way: her body started to collapse, her face shed its anger and folded into weeping. Then she was in Mickey's arms and crying on her shoulder.

They stood for some moments while Ruth let it all out at last, the poison, the anger and bitterness and depression that had been building up behind a door, building and building until the weight of it pushed the door open and it all spilled out. 'I don't want to lose him,' she cried into Mickey's embrace. 'I love Arnie and I don't know how to keep him.'

Mickey eased Ruth down to sit on the carpeted stair and sat next to her, her arm still around her shoulders. 'Talk to him, Ruth. You haven't lost him yet. Arnie's a good man. He'll listen.'

Fumbling in her purse for a handkerchief and blowing her nose, Ruth shook her head. 'I'm so scared. I've never felt such fear in all my life. It feels as if the earth suddenly dropped away from under my feet and I'm floating in space.'

Her voice grew quiet; the tension was melting away. 'I'm sorry about the outburst,' she said softly. 'I didn't mean those words. I'm just so confused.'

'It's all right,' said Mickey.

'I don't know how you do it, Sondra. Where do you find the courage to face what you have to face?' Ruth raised her swollen eyes. 'What if your hands never work? What if it was all for nothing?'

Sondra stared at her for a moment, then frowned down at the sleeping hand. 'Oh, it will work all right.'

'But how do you *know*?'

'Because... because there's life in it. I can *feel* it.'

'Life? What kind of life could there be in that hand? A clumsy, uncoordinated life. Good for nothing more than basic function. What kind of a doctor can you be with those fingers? How will you be able to suture, how will you be able to find a pulse?'

Sondra regarded Ruth with steady, unblinking eyes. 'I'll do it by learning all over again, if I have to.'

'All over again? After all these years, you're willing to start *all over again?*' Ruth struggled to her feet. She looked around for a moment, indecisive even about taking one step, then leaned against the wall, not knowing she stood beneath a picture of herself from years ago – fresh, smiling, hopeful. 'Where on earth do you find the courage for that kind of commitment? How are you able to face each new day, not knowing if you're going to be crippled all your life, dependent on other people from now on? Tell me, Sondra, how you're able to live with what happened to you, watching your husband die so horribly, losing the child you were carrying, and now to have those, those...' Ruth's voice caught; she waved her hand toward Sondra's lap.

'I've made peace with my dead, Ruth,' Sondra said quietly. 'Yes, I mourned for Derry. And I still do. And in the beginning, I wanted to die; I had no courage to face each new day. But now I know I have to live, for our son, for the work Derry and I had together. If I give up now, then his life and his death will have been for nothing.'

The tears returned to Ruth's eyes. She looked away and focused on the lectern where Dean Hoskins had once filled her with a sense of purpose. 'I wish I could make peace with *my* dead,' she said in a tight voice, her chin quivering. 'My whole life was built upon him, you know. The measure of me was only as against my father; without him I had no meaning. I only lived for him, to please him, to curry his approval. When he died, the main reason for my life died with him. That's what the nightmare means. Without my father, I have no definition.' She turned back to Sondra and Mickey. 'I knew, all along *I knew* that I could never please him, but I also knew I would never be able to stop myself from always trying. And that's what kept me going. It's what drove me, *I'm* the one who is perverse. My whole life with Arnie has been a front; I never really gave it any thought. But now –' She brought a hand up to her mouth. 'I don't want to lose him!'

Mickey was on her feet and guiding Ruth to a chair. As she wept anew into her handkerchief, Ruth said, 'I wish I could stop this crying!'

'Don't try to,' said Mickey. 'Let it come as it will. Get the infection out so you can start the healing process.'

Ruth cried a while longer, then she wiped her eyes and said quietly, 'I haven't the faintest idea how to go about salvaging my life. I don't even know if I have the strength to try.' She dried her face one last time, then squared her shoulders and drew in a deep breath. 'There's so much ground to cover, so much to rebuild. I would have to go back to the starting line and redefine the rules of the race.'

Ruth paused to look at Sondra, who was staring intently down at the new hand lying in her lap, her expression one of deep concentration. Where does she find the courage? Ruth wondered. How does she face the gamble that those hands will never come back to life, that she's wasting her time?

Now Mickey, suddenly aware of the silence filling the auditorium, also turned to look at Sondra. The unblinking amber eyes seemed to be trying to send a telepathic message to the collection of muscles and nerves and skin that looked like the work of a master sculptor. Sondra appeared to be trying to raise it, as if she were a magician.

Mickey started to say something, then decided against it. The moment was too delicate to disturb with a voice.

Somehow, she knew, this was going to be it – the turning point. And Ruth, also captivated by the intense concentration that held Sondra's body so still and rigid, kept her silence and stared down at the hand.

It started with the barest movement, just a ripple, like sea ferns stirring in an ocean current. Then, astonishingly, as if fingers had never before moved, the little finger jerked forward and bowed down to touch the palm. Next, the ring finger curled forward, followed by the middle and index fingers, and finally the thumb, all closing over themselves like the petals of a flower closing up for the night. And then one by one, spasmodically, they opened up, away from the palm and spreading out like a sunrise. Sondra looked up at her friends with a smile.

Mickey sat speechless for one thunderstruck moment, then she cried out and reached for the miraculous hand. 'It works!' she said, her eyes misty. 'Sondra, your hand works!'

Sondra started to laugh, and Mickey with her, while Ruth stared in amazement. Sondra performed her feat a second time, painstakingly opening and closing her fragile fist, and her laughter grew, mingling with Mickey's high up in the amphitheatre's dome.

Then she flexed them again, and again, and she laughed so hard tears tumbled down her cheeks and splashed onto the baby-new hand. All of a sudden visions flashed before Sondra's eyes: the rustic compound of the Uhuru Mission, the little hut she had shared with Derry, the round smiling face of her son, and, from far away, the face of a boy named Ouko, a man now, who had walked proudly into the mission last year carrying his spear of manhood. Africa was waiting; she must go, she must go.

Mickey was seeing other visions. In Sondra's clumsy fingers she saw the countless fingers of future patients, victims of accident and illness and birth defects coming to her with no hope and departing restored, made whole again. If Mickey could never give life out of her own body, then she would give life through her hands, and her skill.

Ruth, having risen out of her seat, walked a few paces away from her friends and stood watching them, envying them. This was *their* moment, it was their victory. She was not part of it. Two stout hearts and two determinations had wrought this miracle; she envied them their unity.

And then, strangely, Ruth started to feel herself become curiously heady, as though an enormous weight were dissolving and dropping away from her. And as it fell, she found something new start to emerge, spouting up like a sturdy little winter crocus, something that was old and familiar and dizzyingly sweet in its familiarity.

She had thought it had died inside her, thought it had died with her father, because she had always thought it had been generated by her father: her old sense of fight and resolution and pugnacity. Ruth had always believed her strength had come from without, that there never had been anything so strong inside Ruth Shapiro herself, a courage that was truly her own. And yet here it was, surfacing with each flection of Sondra's fingers, filling Ruth like a blinding new sun, causing her to reach for the wall for support. And she thought suddenly: I'm going to fight for him. I'm going to keep Arnie if I have to go all the way back to the beginning and start with the first step. I have fourteen years to make up to him, to my girls, to myself.

And then Ruth no longer saw Sondra and Mickey as two who were sharing a private victory – she was suddenly part of them, this moment belonged to the three.

There was haste now – haste to get started on revitalising the hands, to get started on a new future in medicine, to return to a country and a people who were in desperate need, to get back up to a family in Washington that could still, with luck and fortitude, be made whole again.

When they reached the glass doors of Manzanitas Hall, before going outside Mickey swung her purse off her shoulder and said to Sondra, 'Before we go, I have something for you.'

She took out a small white box, and inside was the turquoise stone Ruth had given her six years ago, bright blue and full of promise. 'It's for luck,' she said, placing the stone in Sondra's hand and curling the fragile fingers around it. 'It's from both of us. Neither of us used the luck that was in it, so you're getting a double dose.'

On the other side of the glass doors a sunny September day

shined. Ruth pushed open one of the doors and in rushed a breeze that was scented with flowers and fresh grass and the salty sea. 'You know,' said Sondra, hesitating before taking the final step. 'The Kikuyu have a saying: *Gutiri muthenya ukeaga ta ungi.* Which means, no day dawns like another. I have a feeling this is going to be a special day for all of us.'

And Ruth thought: *When we three first met we were just starting out. Soon we will be parting again, possibly for ever, and yet it feels as if we're just starting out again.*

Out loud, she said, 'After you,' and held the door for Mickey and Sondra as they walked out into the sunshine.

# A selection of bestsellers from SPHERE

## FICTION

| | | |
|---|---|---|
| NOCTURNE FOR THE GENERAL | John Trenhaile | £2.50 ☐ |
| THE BEAR'S TEARS | Craig Thomas | £2.95 ☐ |
| HOTEL DE LUXE | Caroline Gray | £2.95 ☐ |
| FUR | Jeremy Lucas | £1.95 ☐ |

## FILM & TV TIE-INS

| | | |
|---|---|---|
| AUF WIEDERSEHEN PET 2 | Fred Taylor | £2.75 ☐ |
| LADY JANE | Anthony Smith | £1.95 ☐ |

## NON-FICTION

| | | |
|---|---|---|
| HOW TO SHAPE UP YOUR MAN | Catherine and Neil Mackwood | £2.95 ☐ |
| THE DUNGEON MASTER | William Dear | £2.95 ☐ |
| 1939: THE WORLD WE LEFT BEHIND | Robert Kee | £4.95 ☐ |
| NO BELLS ON SUNDAY: THE JOURNALS OF RACHEL ROBERTS | Alexander Walker | £2.95 ☐ |

*All Sphere books are available at your local bookshop or newsagent, or can be ordered direct from the publisher. Just tick the titles you want and fill in the form below.*

Name _____

Address _____

_____

Write to Sphere Books, Cash Sales Department, P.O. Box 11, Falmouth, Cornwall TR10 9EN

Please enclose a cheque or postal order to the value of the cover price plus:

UK: 55p for the first book, 22p for the second book and 14p for each additional book ordered to a maximum charge of £1.75.

OVERSEAS: £1.00 for the first book plus 25p per copy for each additional book.

BFPO & EIRE: 55p for the first book, 22p for the second book plus 14p per copy for the next 7 books, thereafter 8p per book.

*Sphere Books reserve the right to show new retail prices on covers which may differ from those previously advertised in the text or elsewhere, and to increase postal rates in accordance with the PO.*